Little Bit of Faith

SAVERIO MONACHINO

Dedication

There are so many I need to thank for actions I have no recollection of but, without whom I would not be writing these words today. Several of these unknowns helped pull a damaged body out from what remained of his car. Others include the EMTs who rendezvoused with the chopper and, of course, the pilot who delivered a comatose body to the trauma center. Then there were the doctors, nurses, and staff at Robert Wood Johnson whose attention to detail gave me a chance, along with an all-inclusive stay in their ICU.

Only snippets of memory seeped in and stayed with me during the time spent at the Johnson Rehabilitation Institute. And, while these memories include visits by family and friends, the most endearing was that of a nurse who brought me a small bowl of ice cream when she found me sitting alone in the hallway, in the wee small hours of Christmas.

I also need to dedicate this book to my neighbors, all of whom helped my family during our hour of need. And, to a group attending mass weekly in Parrsboro Nova Scotia who, thanks to a whisper down the lane from a friend in Texas, added my name to their prayer book. And, of course, to all those who helped in my recovery at the Kessler Institute for Outpatient Rehabilitation.

Little Bit of Faith is also dedicated to everyone in my family, both near and far, especially near. My son and daughter had to adapt to the changes the accident brought to all our lives. And they did, in a positive, loving fashion.

But most of all I need to dedicate this effort to my wife whose love is the brightest of all beacons. Without her I would not have found my way back home.

Acknowledgements

No matter how hard one tries to be 'original' in one's work, it is always likely someone else has put pencil to paper with very similar ideas. This is why it is best to acknowledge any 'borrowing' which might occur in the writing process. For instance, in this book the author uses names of many real people who have populated chapters in his own life or who have appeared from time to time in documents, whether fiction or non-fiction, he has read. These names were 'borrowed' because they either fit the mood or helped bring clarity to the story line.

Within the text itself, snippets of John Lennon's *Across the Universe* become part of a karaoke scene in one chapter and, in another, the author borrows bits of Chauser's *The Miller's Tale*. To cover all bases, writing styles (structure) from *The High History of the Holy Graal* (thanks go out to Project Gutenberg) and Geoffrey of Monmouth's *History of the Kings of Britian* were also used.

Two more very important acknowledgements: Jeanne Balsam for the drawings used in the development of the book cover and Norma Lorre Goodrich's book *King Arthur* which became a physical prop in several chapters. In addition, the findings described in her book were of paramount importance to the lead character in *Little Bit of Faith* while at the same time her book taught this author the value of philology.

Chapter 1
Who Am I?

Emily Selwood's Journal
Greystone Park Psychiatric Hospital

Who am I? Now, now, I wish I knew. Who was I? That one I know, Emily, Emily Selwood. What am I? This question, like the first, is difficult. A practitioner in the art of clinical neuropsychology or possibly, a quack. Documents exist, piles of them, paper and electronic, all alluding to the first. My current state of being leans more toward the second.

How did I get here, with here being my physical surroundings, not my mental state of being? This I know. I'm working on the other. Both need some explanation.

Where do I start?

I've been asking myself that since self-enrolling at Greystone. Okay, okay, why Greystone? I was in a hurry, so to speak, and options for someone in my condition were few and far between. I thought I knew the place, knew what I was getting into. A hiding place is what I needed. A safe place offering a quiet environment where I could (with some help from the staff) focus on understanding what I had been exposed to. I needed a second opinion. Had I let my imagination run amok? This would easily explain everything, or would it?

Unfortunately, being here has not helped. Perhaps I should have sought refuge in a convent. Maybe if I had been a churchgoer, I would have thought of that. But now, now as I sit in my room staring at the walls, I find myself praying for an answer. Everything seems to have changed both by season and state of mind. I cannot logically conceptualize what I experienced, simple as that. Perhaps Greystone is my purgatory because, like purgatory, there are only two doors. One in and one out, or up and down, in the end, it's all the same. And like purgatory, it depends on a person's ability to choose the door. One thing I do know, if I don't choose either, I stay and tread water where I am. Perhaps I do need a confessor, not a shrink. Perhaps I should calm down and let the sedatives kick in. Perhaps I should go for a walk or just keep...

Okay, two doses and fresh coffee, I think that has done the trick. For now.

On a generalized platform, at this moment, I'm taking a hiatus, of sorts. Really, more an escape than a hiatus. I needed a safe space where I could think things through and, hopefully, become more aware, more understanding of what I had been exposed to. Put the pieces together so to speak and, more importantly, put my head back in sync with the world at large, the world I know, or is that "thought I knew"? It seems my ability to conceptualize reality has hit a roadblock. "Why?" you ask. Because someone had thrown that ever mysterious fourth dimension, time, into the equation and...and having not even a toe hold on the concept of a space-time equilibrium—oh shit, I had to take physics pass-fail as an undergrad and still barely got a pass. Let me cut to the chase. What does all this have to do with my current situation? I don't really know. Basically, I don't know what happened, but I do know this. It's all his fault. He was my patient, and since I'm now at Greystone, I must wonder if he will be my last.

Working at Kessler often led to interactions with the staff at Greystone, and now I am one of Dr. Tey's patients. Tey is the head of the department, so on paper, I am being taken seriously. I am sure with her taking my case, in future, a bevy of reports will appear in various medical journals. I might even become the poster child for whatever they can figure out is ailing me. But heaven forbid she begins to dig down too far; we might become bunk mates.

I am afraid I am no longer good with temporal spacing. I need to backfill my meandering or take a nap, one of the two.

Nap is over. Now I will try a little backfilling.

I'm now the one sitting on the proverbial couch. Tey's couch. Let's call me doctor number 1 and Tey; Tey is doctor number 2. The reason I'm on the couch and not in the analyst's chair all has to do with doctor number 3. Doctor number 3 is Arthur, Arthur McAiden. He was a patient of mine, and what this doctor brought to the table is why I'm now on the couch.

McAiden's grouping is amongst those who don't practice medicine. His degree is in philosophy, as in the philosophy of science. He was, is, still is, I don't know which, a scientist in the field of biomedical research. PhDs call themselves the thinking group. I have no doubt about this claim to fame, and I believe Dr. McAiden would have done just as well in any of a plethora of other fields of study whether professionally or just as an intellectual hobby. Perhaps my old patient could add fabulist to his skill set as well. T o be honest, he is now a TBI survivor; so only time will tell how much, if any, of his old skill sets will return. He became my charge when he began his outpatient therapy at the Kessler Institute. Before Kessler, he had spent roughly two weeks in the ICU trauma center at Robert Wood in New Brunswick and a few more at the Johnson Rehab over in Edison, and I was to learn later, several more weeks may have passed between his leaving Johnston and arriving for treatment at Kessler.

While in the ICU, there were so many meds dripping into his system it would take me half a page to itemize. When he was discharged from Johnson, his medications were just a set of the usuals, Dilantin, Ibuprofen, Keppra (seizures were still a worry), Protonix, and Trazodone. Physically, he was stable and in repair mode. Mentally, he had scored extremely low on all metrics. The reports coming our way from Johnson revealed receptive and expressive language deficits, diminished performance at all levels of verbal memory, with perseveration and disinhibition consistent with frontal and temporal lobe dysfunction due to his TBI. Simple verbal attention, working memory, visual memory, and basic conceptual reasoning were found to be intact, but none of these were what one might call up to par. Cognitive rehabilitation was recommended at that time. Basically, we at Kessler had a lot of work to do.

Let me cut to the chase. Two minutes into my first session with the patient, it was obvious he was having difficulty engaging in simple conversation. Especially if I quickly changed topics. Nothing more or less than what I was expecting. So I asked him to write down whatever he could remember of his experiences. Not right away, not all at once, just as a mini homework assignment. In the future, we would be meeting three times a week, and so I hoped at each visit he would present me with some of his work. If the patient can write things down, then the problem isn't in cognitive processing per se, but more along the lines of speech management. Knowing which would allow me to better tailor our sessions and monitor his progress, or lack thereof.

The field of neuropsychology, like all areas of medicine, constantly evolves, and it is the responsibility of those working in this arena to keep up with the changes, all of them. Cross my heart, I've done my best in this regard. At least I thought I had a pretty good handle on the advances in anatomy, physiology, and genetics relating to brain functions. I was also up to date on the medicines, those in play and those showing up on the horizon. I will be humble for a moment. I was an expert in the areas relating to cognitive functions and the damage done to these processes by TBIs or I thought I was.

Now I must confess, even from the start, I had trouble interpreting what he wrote. So I ignored the content and concentrated on the quality of the work. I just wanted to assess thought processing versus speech management. Of course, the quality was beyond expectations, and as such, it became impossible to categorize the problem. Thinking back, I must wonder if his ailment was infectious.

Again, I'm babbling, not filling in the gaps. Maybe I overcaffeinated. Maybe under, who knows. I do know this: I'm having trouble getting this out chronologically—that is for sure.

Okay, all research data needs to be written down, verified, repeated once, twice, three times while holding all variables but one as controls and then, only then, conduct an analysis of said observations. Dr. Arthur McAiden ended up as an outpatient at Kessler because he was involved in a multi car pile-up on Baden Hill Road (which is over in the western part of the state) and airlifted to the regional trauma center, Robert Wood, in coma, at least he was labeled as such upon his arrival at the ICU. That was all the data available to me in which the variables were accounted for.

Badon Hill residents will never really know, whether they spoke with one of the on-scene policemen or not, exactly what happened. Nor do I, but to the best of my abilities, I extrapolated data provided by the police, some local mechanics who got their hands on the damaged cars, the on-scene EMTs, some of the residents, and on and on. Marie was the main source, her now ex-husband (Roger) also verified some of the details as did a retired lobsterman from Maine. How he ended up in Jersey I could never figure out. After speaking with all these individuals over the telephone, I could visualize both specific characters and events that showed up in the opening pages of Arthur's story.

Now, when I asked Arthur to write I was hoping to get a few lines, first-person limited, conveying simple thoughts, how he felt, was he depressed, short-term memory problems, type of work he felt comfortable with, basically anything that was close to events in his current situation. What he presented to me was different. It was more third-person omniscient, like a fly on the wall, or perhaps a magpie watching from above, waiting to swoop down and pick up a shiny tidbit or two. Citing names, backgrounds, personal information of friends and other acquaintances, he must have known are one thing, but those he did not know I could only attribute to a "creative" mind in action. Or as I read somewhere a long time ago, "A quintessential provocation of the human spirit searching for enlightenment of the spiritual kind." Basically, he was having fun at my expense.

Forget I just wrote that down. It was just my own self meandering within the cesspool called intellectualism. Back to earth, what he wrote was a good read but still, to me, just fiction, especially after he upped the ante and threw in a bit of time travel.

Perhaps it is best if I just present what Arthur wrote, all the pages, in the order given to me at various times during our six-month interaction at Kessler. Then I will try to explain how his imagination turned my life upside down. As they say, seeing is believing!

Chapter 2
Bellum Badonis

Those who wrote of the clash of arms on Badon Hill got it all wrong. A little skirmish for sure, and yes, many eventually joined the fray but there were no winners, only losers. Where is Guinevere? As I now search *pour la bête en quête*, I miss her dearly. Who else is there to keep me warm as I search for a world I once knew?

Why did Selwood ask her patient to translate his thoughts into words? And when he sees no fixed rules within the space around him (and only an extremely limited functional vocabulary), how does one even phrase that narrative? To convey thoughts to words is no easy task, especially if he has no real grip on that task itself.

I wonder if Dr. Selwood is related to Alfred's wife, part of the family tree so to speak. Genetically, of course. I am a fan of his Arthurian work. *Idylls* was a bit idealized for sure, but still, not bad. His Guinevere, like mine, like all those found in every legend ever imagined is pretty much spot on, always looking for another dinner table. Emily was Alfred's muse, he told me such. No, wait a minute, this, I only think he did.

I have already given my doctor an oral synopsis: something bad happened. End of story. For some reason, don't ask me why, she told me to write more of it down or, to be more precise, try to write it down. Maybe it was more a suggestion, but nuances in meaning have always been difficult for me. Either way, now I will give it a try. But by moving in this direction, another problem appears from amongst the traffic jam within my head. Which threshold of consciousness did the doctor want me to draw from? And with that said, which timeline is she interested in? I should have been paying closer attention.

I will start with recent events and hopefully manage the reconstruction of those, though they were happening in the wee small hours, and me, I only stayed for the first act. Then again, why? The doctor knows many of my neuronal pathways are either no longer connected or if, so linked via alternate routes. So any effort to connect memories formed within the conscious state, in daylight or on a wet street in the middle of the night, will be hard to segregate from the shadows floating about in the unconscious realm. And what about embellishments, what's a story without some of those?

Badon Hill Road winds its way through a small housing project on Badon Hill proper. It is not much of a hill, more a hillock. Most of the houses dotting the landscape alongside the road are relatively new, as is the vegetation planted amongst them. The builder did leave a line of ancient oaks along both sides of the roadway, though. These mighty trees spread their wings out across the narrow street as one sees in a picture postcard, quite a sight but it did have drawbacks. The trees blocked the long-range view of anyone driving up, or down, the hill. Coupled with a lack of streetlamps, anytime the pavement was wet the perpendicular intersection at the bottom of the hill, River Road, was downright challenging, especially in the early morning hours. This night, the pavement was wet.

No one living along the Badon Hill Road eye-witnessed the accident but *ex post facto* a good number of them stood around watching the police sort out the mess that had ensued. What trigger mechanism brought them out? Each sound emanating from the successive collisions at the bottom of the hill had reached a crescendo. It was the first of these that woke Marie. Since she hadn't been sleeping well, it didn't take much to rouse her. A moment later, she was sitting up jabbing her husband's side as she not so quietly told him what to do.

"Wake up!"

Her husband had never fallen asleep, but still, he answered his wife by mumbling something incoherent while acting the part of a petrified log. It seems he had implemented this strategy to avoid rolling over to face his wife. That, he believed, would have been a tactical mistake. Many hours earlier he had ingested one of those little blue pills men take to please their woman. Now the problem he faced was this; he had taken the damn pill at least six hours earlier to please his woman, not his wife. The telltale effect of said pharmaceutical enhancement was difficult to hide, and given it had been a while since he last presented himself thus to Marie, he thought it best to avoid any pointed interchange. Marie had a good idea of his indiscretions, hence, her trouble sleeping; but at that moment, she wasn't concerned with activities between the sheets. She only wanted to know what was going on outside the house.

"Roger, get your ass up. I think there's been an accident!"

Roger closed his eyes tighter, trying to fight back the pangs of guilt while nervously searching his memory for prescription label content, four to six or six to eight had never been a problem before.

Not eliciting a response from her husband, Marie slowly sunk back down onto her pillow with one eye closed. Part of her tried to relax while another part was listening for further anomalies amidst the ambient sounds outside. She remained, thus, wondering what she had heard or if she had heard anything at all.

People tend to hear things when stressed. This she told herself. She obviously had a lot on her mind, all of which centered on the lump of humanity pretending to be asleep. *Could he get any farther away and not be on the floor? I could put him down there with one little…* She needed to have a talk with her husband but now was not the time for a heart-to-heart, so she just lay still, thinking and listening. Within seconds, a quick succession of obscenity-laced yelling, a squealing of tires and a resounding crunch, which, she would soon discover, was a second collision, invaded the quiet.

"I wasn't dreaming!"

Before she could jump to her feet a third clash of automobile parts finally roused her husband who quickly moved into the bathroom searching for his slippers and a robe.

"Stay here," he commanded—more to buy recovery time than for her protection. And like a matador hiding his sword from the questioning bull, he held his bathrobe in front of him as he shuffled down the stairs and out the front door.

Marie waited as instructed, sitting upright on the edge of her side of the bed, staring at the window, trying to sort out the sounds seeping in. When she heard the far-off wail of sirens, she could resist no longer slowing only to zip up her jeans and wiggle into a sweatshirt before taking the front steps on the fly and didn't slow down until she reached the bottom of the hill.

Accidents happen on Badon Hill Road, and statistically speaking, they happen a bit more often at the bottom of the hill than at the top. The downhill run ends at a "T" where River Road follows the contours of a winding stream on the far side. Drivers hugging the rivulet as they approached Badon Hill Road from either direction don't have much time to assess the situation. At three in the morning, it can be harder, and if a damaged car was waiting there, for a lack of a better phrase, "dead in its tracks," it would be harder still. But no matter how one counted the numbers, a multi-vehicle pileup in the wee hours of the morning is out of the ordinary.

Marie was thankful the rain had stopped as she raced along trying to avoid puddles. By the time she reached the accident scene, she found a good number of her neighbors already assembled beneath overhanding branches of oak. Like Marie, none of the current onlookers had left their houses at the first toll of the bell—some had even debated the point when they heard the second. But by the time the quick succession of follow-ons had pierced through the stillness of the night, everyone moved. Now they were clustering together behind a makeshift barricade the police were hastily throwing together, everyone but her husband, that is. She spied Roger on the far side of River Road peering into a dense growth of bushes. *Perhaps he is relieving himself,* she thought, but rather than dwell on this possibility, her attention was drawn elsewhere.

The onlookers watched a young, tired-looking officer try to make sure no one got too close. He was a member of the town's police force, not the township's, but his car was nearby when the call came in and thus was first on scene. The neighbors didn't mind the police officer's efforts. The harm had already been done and they were only there to watch. Now, in surreal fashion, the horrific traffic accident was evolving into macabre theater. And like an audience at a play, the neighborhood collective sucked in its breath and watched for signs of human damage. If a body was found, those in attendance would pray for the injured soul, what else could they do? But at the same time, those praying would also guiltily thank the same God it was not them.

The first residents to make their way toward the sound of hissing radiators, like Roger, had thrown whatever was nearby over their pajamas. Most kept their hands buried deep in pockets and were stomping feet against the damp chill. Under normal circumstances most residents of Badon Hill would not have engaged in conversation with each other at three in the morning. But this was not normal.

"This ain't the first time." The man who spoke lived alone near the bottom of the hill and had been the first to arrive. The newer arrivals had trouble understanding him, but they always did. It wasn't because he sounded like a lobsterman from Maine, though many years ago, that was his calling. No, the problem with his speech had more to do with the man's tongue. It was always busy moving a well-worn cigar butt from one side of his mouth to the other.

"Looks to be worse than usual, though, don't cha think?" Condensation formed around the respondent's face, making it difficult for Marie, or anyone else, to see who it was.

Highlighting the obvious, the first man spoke again, "Fog gets thick down here."

"Something to do with the water," a third neighbor replied, meaning the stream winding its way through the pastureland beyond River Road.

"It sure is chilly tonight," the first man spoke again just to give himself something to do before he, and everyone else, went quiet and watched as an unconscious body was eased out of the car closest to them. They listened as a nearby policeman yelled updates into his radio begging an EMS team to hurry as his deputy placed a rolled-up coat under the head of a lifeless man.

A moment later, Marie shifted her attention to the far side of the intersection. Four young men were standing beside their wrecked vehicle. Each was trying to remain still and, if possible, avoid stares from the onlookers. All but one, that is who, of course, drew all eyes in his direction. Everyone watching saw this figure removing empty beer bottles from the damaged car and, once he had an armful, nonchalantly stroll over to the far side of the road and begin tossing them down into the creek below.

His efforts went for naught. One of his companions had decided to comment, in a stage whisper, "One would think people had better things to do than shuffle around outside in the middle of the fuckin' night." This outburst drew the attention of the nearest police officer.

"Something's not right here," Marie murmured while watching all the comings and goings. She tried, in her head, to arrange the incoming data, but no matter how she arranged it, it was not adding up. Then another problem came to the fore as she looked down at her house slippers, torn between a desire to stay and the need to pee.

Chapter 3
A Hero and a Goat

While Marie grappled with her need for a bathroom break, another township police car, with an ambulance following close behind, arrived on the scene; and those watching were pushed farther back. At three in the morning, it can be hard to find a pleasant demeanor. It can also be hard to find someone in charge as two jurisdictions and three different functional groups were now on scene, each trying to get their assigned tasks taken care of. The young officer now on crowd control encouraged the growing throng of onlookers to move, it was all he had on his assignment list, and so with members of a better paid jurisdiction watching, he continued to tackle it with a polite gusto.

"Just a few feet back, please, just a bit up the hill. We've got at least one more ambulance coming and we'll…"

In compliance, those watching retreated up the hill moving from beneath one tree's bough to another's and were soon joined by the late arriving neighbor who also happened to be the head of the local homeowner's association.

"Do you know what happened?"

As the question passed amongst the crowd, everyone began to sidle up close to one another like herd animals trying to keep warm. It did help in that regard and served to increase the available pool of commentators. Soon, there seemed to be as many theories as there were people available to spew them out. Everyone tried to untangle the order of events, everyone but Roger that is. He may have been trying too, but he was still standing a good way off from the herd, continuing to keep his back to them.

"I count four cars," someone deep within the neighborhood crowd uttered this just loud enough for all to hear.

The cigar chewing ex-lobsterman worked the possibilities through his caffeine deprived synapses before responding, "Yeah, me too, but I haven't figured it all out yet."

Marie was too tired to work out the math, all she could come up with was *Something's not adding up*. This she kept to herself.

"Did anyone ask the police officers?" This came from the newest arrival who, it seemed, hit the nail on the head. It was quite simple: If you want information, it might be best to ask someone who had a better understanding of what was going on. The only problem being those who might have known didn't.

The ex-lobsterman took center stage for a moment. "I sleep with the windows open. Now, I was returning from the loo, one of my many trips each night mind-ja', when I hear a man cursing out on the street. 'Thank God the brakes still work. Nothing else in this f'-in ol' piece of shit does.'"

What came next the ex-lobsterman didn't quite understand; the man in the car had delved into a streak of blue derived from literature he never had a desire to read. "Why is Dante always drawing his rings of hell around my life? I need a horse, my whole bloody kingdom for a horse, or better yet, a car that f'-in works! Oh hell, why didn't I go straight home? Merde! Merde, et plus de merde! Why me, Lord, why me?"

During the moments preceding the accident, a problem with the car's alternator may have caused its lights to flicker and then die along with the rest of the motor. If this is true, he said, it explains what happened next. The first car did stop at the bottom of the hill in front of the stop sign in a perfectly legal position, distance-wise.

"I did look out tha winda' but with no lights on the damn road I couldna really see what was going on." He did hear the man, and even from his distance, he felt the anger, as the car door was kicked, followed by a series of stomps, putting the late-night visitor in a position dead in front of the vehicle. What happened next, the lobsterman had no clue. He did not see or hear the man open the hood, but he figured he did. He also did not see the man planting his hands firmly on hips to better enable an angry stare at the engine. After all, this is what most men not skilled in the art do, right? The driver stood thus for a good ten seconds before admitting defeat.

"I have no clue what the hell is…" Continuing to lament, the man reached for his phone and his reading glasses; both were eventually found in the mess that ensued.

"I do hope Lucan won't be pissed off, but I…"

While he was in mid-dial, a second car, American-made and, without doubt, a bit aged, came rolling down the hill—headlights off. The driver of this car was busy studying a map with a small booklight trying to figure out exactly where he was. This second driver did not see the stalled vehicle or the man standing in front of it. But he, like the driver of the first vehicle, was cursing with gusto. His dialectic had a more proletarian take on things than the driver of the car stalled in front of him. The lobsterman might have understood most of this man's oration except for the fact it was delivered in Darija, an Arabic dialect and flavored, for good measure, with copious helpings of *sales jurons français*.

This was the Moroccan. His diatribe must have included a bit of self-flagellation, too, as he had dozed off when he should have been listening in. "This device, top of the line, it says, 'Records fifty meters, through brick' and all that yada, yada. I paid top dollar for this, this merde. It had better have worked. Now where the hell did my mark go?"

He looked up from his map and noticed something he was not expecting, a stop sign. This he saw, the car stopped in front of the stop sign he did not see. When it did register in his line of sight, it was too late. The tires on his car screeched, but it didn't matter. He still rammed into the vehicle in front of him. This is what first woke Marie and most everyone else in the vicinity. The transfer of kinetic energy from the moving automobile to the stationary one and then on to the man standing in front of them both was almost instantaneous and forceful enough to hurl the last object in the chain a good, long way. As the body catapulted across the intersection it passed over a metal railing on the far side of the road before hitting solid ground. With energy not quite spent, the body continued down an embankment, stopping only when it reached the water below.

A moment later, the next actor, a sporty-looking Shelby-inspired Ford Mustang traveling at a speed well beyond the posted limit, took the stage. This car, following the rivulet, had just swung around the last curve in the road before the intersection. As it approached, the driver quickly swerved to avoid hitting a dead deer just coming into his line of sight. As he did so, the car's headlights briefly illuminated a figure, it may have been a large boy or a small man, he couldn't tell, running away from the intersection. Whether the figure he saw running was holding his ear or talking on a phone wasn't clear to the driver, and he didn't have time to think about it. All he could do was report in. "Did ya' see that?"

No one answered. The body in the passenger seat was much too drunk to notice anything, and the two riders in back hadn't a clue what he was referring to. The driver forgot about the man running and turned his attention to choreographing a change in the radio station, this with his right hand, and with his left, a controlled steering of the wheels directing the car back over to the proper side of the road. To help in this regard, he pressed down a bit harder with his right foot.

The fourth and final act in the tragedy, a late-model dark sedan, traveling down the hill behind the first two, now out-of-commission, vehicles began. Its driver was watching in shock as the Mustang slammed into the first now abandoned car sitting in the middle of the intersection. As he watched the accident in progress, he began to slow down, but being focused on the scene playing out a distance to the fore, he completely missed seeing the darkened second car. But he did not miss it. This he slammed right into. His car became the last to add its image to the horror unfolding on Badon Hill. The impact jolted the car he hit, which was now empty, back into motion, causing it to once again ram into the backside of the first vehicle and become part of the crescendo that had brought everyone running.

Those assembled watched as the unconscious driver who had been removed from the fourth car was placed on a stretcher and lifted into a now waiting ambulance. The onboard med-tech began checking vitals and removing objects that might get in the way, like the man's wallet. A moment later, he yelled over to the nearest law enforcement officer, "I've found his ID. Wanna have a look?"

The officer only nodded his head as another police car arrived bringing the total to five. A few tow-trucks were followed along as was another ambulance. Now the many sets of flashing lights ripped through the fog, making it almost impossible to see in any direction or for the poor police officers to think clearly.

"Looks like everyone's here." This came from one of Marie's neighbors.

"I don't see any more bodies. Why'd they call another ambulance?"

Whoever uttered that statement, or the responses to it, Marie did not remember, but it helped her connect the pieces that led to her jumping out of her slippers with excitement.

"That's it!"

"What's it?" those standing nearby chorused back.

Funny how something can seem so obvious once you are told the answer. Marie didn't bother to stop and explain. This was too important. She ran past the crowd control officer and literally into the next policeman. What was said between the two, and the officers being motioned to join them, could not be heard by Marie's neighbors, but they did watch intently and noticed the policemen, like Marie, becoming animated.

The senior member of each jurisdiction started pointing fingers at their counterparts until the young man who had been assigned crowd control raised his voice and began barking instructions to everyone who could hear. Soon, whistles were blowing and those watching were being recruited for an impromptu manhunt, though these new recruits were all wondering if "man" was a euphemism for "body."

The residents had barely started looking when, from the far side of the road, Marie's husband called out. Roger was glancing back over his shoulder, yelling for all he was worth and pointing at the creek beyond. The two closest officers hurried over and were down in the ditch in a flash with a third coming to retrieve Roger and guide him away from where the EMTs would be setting up their gurney.

Roger resisted as best as he could, but the officer insisted so he slowly turned and began to walk toward the gathered crowd, giving everyone an opportunity to get a clear view of exactly what pharmaceutical help could do for a man even eight hours post ingestion. Luckily, the attention of everyone was fixed on the bottom of the ditch. Everyone except one that is. Marie looked, then she began flipping through her internal rolodex in search of listings for divorce lawyers.

Chapter 4
Stepping Out for a While

It took a while for the medics to maneuver the body out of the ditch. Not really knowing the condition of the man they were dealing with, those engaged took things slow and easy. His appearance was, simply put, not pretty, and as the broken figure was gently lifted and placed upon a gurney, those watching stared in silence, each praying in their own way for the man, whoever he was. Residents and emergency respondents alike were now wiping back tears. Some spread the love and prayed for his family too.

The gurney was soon aboard one of the waiting ambulances, and when the doors closed, the driver adjusted the flashing lights and eased the vehicle back onto the road. As soon as he cleared the line of police cars and arriving tow trucks, he pushed it into overdrive. The destination he plugged in was the county's medical center, which sat a good twenty minutes away, if he followed the posted speed, that is. This he didn't plan to do and told those waiting in the emergency room the ETA, "Ten minutes max!"

The EMT in the back was busy too. First, she strapped the prone body down then hooked up an IV, all the while punching in vitals to transmit to the ER. When the acceleration kicked in, she was pulled back, though; being well practiced in the art, she caught the safety bar in time. Regaining her balance, she began another quick check of the vitals but became distracted by the sounds of squealing tires as the driver negotiated a turn at warp speed. She didn't notice the patient twitching till the vehicle was back on the straightaway. Twitching was not a good sign, and from that point on, things began to accelerate, or slow down, depending upon one's view of, or position in, the situation.

"He's beginin' to shake," the paramedic called out.

"Oh shit! Seizures!" This came from the driver as he and the woman tending to the body moved into well-practiced emergency procedures. The county hospital was no longer in the cards. The EMT loosened a nearby leather strap and tried to slip it between clenching teeth as the ambulance sped around another bend. "Slow down a sec. I've got to get this in his mouth. If I can't, he might…oh, hell, he's got a…"

Not knowing exactly what the EMT wanted to tell him, the driver did understand the significance. He eased up on the gas. He had to. He was now busy scoping out the local map while simultaneously punching in numbers for both the closest state trauma center and its medevac.

"Damn, damn, DAMN… I thought so!"

"What?"

"It's a big one." By "big," the EMT meant the hemorrhage. "We're a basic. We don't have the advanced gear!"

"Look," the driver responded. "I've got the emergency team at Robert Wood patched in. I'm putting 'em on speaker."

She relayed the position of the wound to the medical team and, in doing so, pushed the level of emergency to extreme, "left temporal lobe, large epidural hematoma and…oh shit, I do mean *big*! Didn't see it till he started shakin'. I grabbed his head to get the mouthpiece in and that's when the hair moved. I got a good look. Blood loss ongoing and probably a pneumothorax. Intubation underway, now do ya' want me to admin some benzos?"

"Okay," the driver chimed in. "I've got a nearby field on my GPS and the chopper pilot says ten tops before he gets there." *Or I'll crash into the fuckin' hillside* were the pilot's last words on the subject, but these, the ambulance driver kept to himself.

As the paramedic redirected the readouts to the trauma center and verbally reported everything, she could to the assembling team in New Brunswick, the man strapped in was having a long-distance conversation of his own. With whom he was communicating, he was not sure, at least not at first. He only felt warmth next to him, covering him really, like a blanket. Or perhaps, a cloud, wafting up and over.

Am I in a dream? This he addressed into the ethereal void around him. He wasn't crying out for help, just information. The information needed had nothing to do with the massive buildup of blood on the exterior of his blood-brain barrier, even though if it did leak through, it would destroy any gray matter it touched. Physiologic events in the space he now inhabited did not register high up on the importance scale. Apparently, he had a new place of residence. It was a few paces off the colloquial beaten path, also known as his normal center of gravity. He had no sensory input referencing his time and event schedule, so his memory was taking over like *cinéma vérité* and what it was playing was snippets of his life. All he could do was sit back and watch.

No external monitors can really define the level of pain needed before a damaged brain begins to shut down. But what is known is this: fear, playing off the pain, brings the biological defense mechanisms into action hastening the closure of neuronal processes. Effects of trauma inside a body can, and has, been studied. First and foremost, it reduces the flow of chemical signals traveling from the brainstem. When this happens, the reticular activating system begins shutting down nests of neuron bundles (nodes), which, when connected, are the interface with the world around the individual. When shutting down the concept of three dimensions, four, if one includes the space time continuum, things begin to break apart leading to an altering in one's state of consciousness. One does, eventually, become comatose or, perhaps, something worse.

What do you see? A response to this query. It was a voice, a soft essence of being coming to him from a place above the thoughts streaming in and out of his head like ghosts passing through a fence.

Mother? Recollections of times past moved front and center and information stored amidst one tangled relay of neuronal tissue somehow communicated with the surrounding connections. A ray of light had entered the dark fog in which he lay.

What do you see? Was repeated—this time, from within.

He paused and looked about his memory portal. He was sitting on a porch overlooking a garden. A voice was there too, a woman's voice, like a soft, peaceful melody; and somehow, it brought warmth. Whoever it was, she held a tray out before him, and he accepted the gift. He looked again and saw his mother and sitting next to her was a boy too sick to go to school. Together they sat and talked about so many things as the morning passed, none of them important but all meaning so much to both. They spoke of school and his father, and what they should have for lunch. *Will you toast the bread in the oven with all the, the…?*

His mother smiled. *When I drizzle it with oil and add a bit of salt and pepper?*

They were in the kitchen now, peeking in the oven, watching the top of the bread brown to perfection. When it was ready, they sat down, and the boy listened to stories as he chewed the manna offered to him by the same angel who had, years before, brought him into the world. She told him of the time he was stuck in the tree. His recollection told him he was far away from home. He had cried out for help; no one came except one, his mother.

I will always be here for you, she whispered into his ear.

Thank you for making me lunch. I'll be better tomorrow. He said this almost sadly. He loved being with his mother, just the two of them, sitting and talking. The descriptor of heaven is different for each of us. To the young man sitting and eating lunch, being with his mother was his version. He was then honest with the angel sitting across the table. He told her he didn't want to go back. He was happy where he was.

Are you sure you are finished?

He thought for a moment but didn't answer. The voice within moved in a different direction.

When I planned to visit the professor, I saw something, something bad.

Go on.

I don't know from where it comes. It was just a vision, or a dream. A message perhaps. Problem being, I was a little late on the uptake.

And the message?

Don't drive on Badon Hill.

Have you had this vision before?

He stopped and gave that some thought. *How long have I been alive?*

The boy took the last bite of his lunch, and as the taste of this memory left, he was no longer sitting with his mother.

I am wet, he thought. It was dark, but he could feel shapes nearby. There was noise too, an incessant rhythmic pounding he could not place. He tried, but vision was refusing to engage. Other senses tried to pick up the slack and report in. He heard the sounds and smelled…something. *What is this ungodly odor?* The smell, like the noise, was impossible for him to define. It was crap, and blood, and vomit and every other biological odor not associated with the living all rolled into one. It was decay.

Focusing on the smell did not extinguish the noise. Now he heard a *click, click, click* of tires over oft repaired surfaces, almost rhythmic, almost a heartbeat. Listening closely, he could hear (or feel) vibrations that had also found their way in, all helping form a symphonic outpouring. The emitted peeps and buzzing from the defibrillator found harmony with the ventilator the paramedic had struggled to attach. The nebulizer mist played softly overhead and counterposed with the slowing spasms of the man tied to the ambulance bed. Then the volume increased. A crescendo seemed to be nearing.

Think, think, think came in time with a thumping sound overhead.

Think he did. *Why did I go to the professor's house? There was a reason, but I cannot remember what it was.*

Think.

I needed something.

Think.

I needed to know if it was time.

The voice in his head stopped for a moment before asking. *Time to move on?*

No. Time to find Percy.

Percy had come out of a neural linkage tied to memories percolating within the head of the man as he lay crumpled in the ditch. These memories were replayed at a speed none could imagine, or understand, as physical torque was applied by the ambulance racing through the curves. The memories had been sparked by a book, a book that was, in a way, the reason he was where he was on Badon Hill Road at three in the morning. Unfortunately for the man, the shutdown process was underway, making it extremely difficult to find anyone, let alone Percy. Thoughts no longer flowed in a linear fashion leaving him to overlay similar subject matter pulled from distant experiences:

"Sir," saith King Fisherman, "Can you tell me tidings of my sister's son, the son of Alain li Gros of the Valleys of Camelot, whom they call Perceval?"

This passage squeezing along an ever-narrowing stream of axon transmission lanes was unable to tell the fading soul where Perceval could be found, though the quest for the man wove together with the quest for purpose, and as often happens, the purpose lay in the genealogy:

"This high history witnesseth us," saith King Fisherman, "and you have heard tell how Perceval was of my lineage, the lineage of Joseph of Abarimacie."

The search for the questing beast, and for Percival, too, were in the works as an Agusta AW-139 sat on the grass, waiting. The Robert Wood Johnson trauma center was a good forty-five minutes away from this spot by car even at three in the morning, but only a short ten-minute hop by helicopter.

In the ambulance, the paramedics watched as the flashing lights rose and moved off into the darkness of night. Neither said a word about the man on the gurney. What could they say? They had given him an IV to replace fluid, some meds to hold back the clots, and a bunch of painkillers. There was a slight pulse when his body was placed in the chopper, but the breathing was slowing, and as far as they could tell, there was no brain activity. From the looks of it, there wasn't much anyone could do, except perhaps, the man with the knife. It all depended on the helicopter ride, the neurosurgeon, and a bevy of other well-trained people, all ready to go to work when the chopper landed. All they could do now was wave farewell as they prayed in silence for the man they didn't know.

Neither those in the ambulance nor those flying the helicopter knew the injured man had one more thought tracing its way along his neuronal network: *Where is Guinevere?* Then, like the images of an age he was reconstructing in his head, everything went dark.

Conscious life is only an island floating upon a much vaster universe, so if lost, it may be difficult to find a way back. A retrospective analysis might define how love from many, passing through the interstitial space within our physical reality, combined to help the comatose body choose the correct path. But now, those who watched the events unfold, residents of Badon Hill and emergency respondents alike each, in turn, slowly began to exit the comatose man's story line.

Chapter 5
A Cappella in a Car

The emergency responders and all attending residents of Badon Hill had jumped to quarters. The search was on for a lost soul. In retrospect, it was in the nick of time and, as the ambulance carried the damaged body off to rendezvous with a helicopter everyone, in their own way, said a prayer. Then the locals slowly began to drift off to their respective homes while those left at the bottom of the hill moved into the cleanup phase of operations. But Arthur's wasn't the only lost soul and this time it took a blaspheming survivor to put the night shift back into action.

"Where the hell is that motherfucker?" This came from the first body the EMTs had placed on a gurney. It was believed he had been concussed; and so tranquilizers, and a few preventative pain meds, had been administered before he was hoisted into the first on-scene ambulance. No one was expecting him to wake up, but he did.

The EMT adjusting the straps on this body and the nearby police officer responded in unison, "Who?"

"That short shit of a goddamn Arab! I've been tailing that shit head all night!" This he mumbled as he tried to get up. The tranquilizers held him back.

The medic leaned over to speak with the policeman. "The man we just pulled out of the water wasn't really um…short, was he?"

This question brought up the possibility they were, literally, a body short.

The injured man collapsed back into a prone position and was soon being treated to a drug-induced slumber. The nearest senior police officer now walked over, pulled the sleeping man's wallet off the ambulance floor, found the identification cards, and spat, "Son of a bitch, he's FBI."

These words were not whispered which, in turn, drove the expression on to all those in the listening audience. Having an FBI agent in an ambulance placed the multiple on-scene police units in a quandary. "Now what do we do?" was passed around until a consensus was reached; no one was certain of the proper protocol.

"Do we contact his local office, or do we pass the buck upstairs?"

"Is there a local office?"

"If he was on assignment, it is our duty to call this in, right?"

"What if he wasn't?"

"Who was he following? "

These questions led to copious amounts of head scratching, and when no answers were forthcoming, they tried groupthink.

"Were all those kids in the same car?"

"I wish that lady was still here, or her husband. Boy, could he spot 'em."

Ten minutes later, with no other body found and still in a predicament, the senior officer on scene decided, given the circumstances, to be on the safe side.

"I think we should call in the feds."

The local FBI outlet in Newark was called shortly after their on-scene agent went for an ambulance ride. Newark then pushed the information upstairs to the regional office in New York City, which nudged the on-duty to marshal troops for action. Marshalling became difficult as she ran down her list of available assets and only one name showed up, Special Agent Michael MacLean. This name was well off on the top of her list, but it was the only one available.

MacLean was not on assignment that evening; he did live in the area and an agent on the ground was needed ASAP. He got the call. After five minutes of shaking his head and grunting "What?" he hung up the phone, grudgingly got out of bed and began to dress.

Unfortunately for Special Agent MacLean, his wife wasn't going to make things easy. "Don't you remember your promise?"

Mike had met Donna when they were both seasoned officers, an FBI euphemism for being in their forties. They were both assigned to the organized crime task force, international division. Mike was fluent in Russian and never one to back down or miss an interesting assignment he became a consistent point man for collaborative duties with the spin-out groups of the former KGB.

Donna was an extraordinary addition to the FBI surveillance team. She was fluent in French and spent a great deal of her time finding ways to listen in, whether with wire taps, directional microphones, or just sitting close and being inconspicuous. Both had posted overseas as legates for the Bureau many times, and after they married, Donna quickly tired of spending time anywhere but home, so she opted for early retirement. This was when she began pestering her new husband. Now Donna made it her life's work to keep her husband out of danger until he, too, took an early retirement package.

"Yes, of course I remember. I've already begun the paperwork. In six months, I'll be out of that rathole too. But until said time, I still have a job to do."

"If they know you're on the way out, why would they call you? Why now?"

"Because everyone else is busy!" Given the situation, his response came out a little more bitter than proper. The simple truth of the matter, he was the Bureau's last choice; there literally was no one else around. But in the middle of the night, Mike didn't want to explain his position in the pecking order and didn't have to, Donna understood.

"Tailing some punks at night? Aren't you too old for this sort of thing? I mean really now, after all you've done for the Bureau?" Even though she was trying to belittle the assignment verbally, on the inside, she had a feeling he wasn't being called to work on a case related to any ol' punk.

"You know, and I know, everything changed after 9/11. Now it's all about terrorism. When you and I were reassigned to that task force, our seniority vanished, and we had to get back in line. Besides, this might be…"

Noting the look in her eyes, Mike realized he was doing nothing to allay her concerns. "This is more of a pinch-hitter role, seems our guy in the field had some trouble with his car." He left out the bits that involved the accident and the ambulance as he gave his wife the two-minute version of the five-minute briefing he had just received.

"Well, how in the world are you going to find this missing person?" was the first question out of her mouth.

"Apparently…he phoned someone."

"Who?"

"The Sheik."

"Not the…"

"Yep, that one, and we were able to triangulate on his cell."

Donna was still a line back in the conversation. "What? He placed a call to the Sheik!"

Though she was not happy being woken in the middle of the night, it didn't stop butterflies from making an appearance. She was no longer in the office, and her husband wasn't one to bring too much of his work home but anyone who spent time with the task force knew about the Sheik. This man was the Bureau's newest, John Gotti. He was the biggest fish in the tristate area, and like with Gotti, the Bureau was building a case against him one painstaking brick at a time. Until this very evening, no one on the task force had "officially" gotten a recording of the Sheik on the telephone. Without a FISA, no official recordings were allowed.

Now fully dressed and holstering his firearm, her husband chimed in. "We can finally start to tie the bastard to operations. It's the beginning of the end for him."

"I bet the Sheik wasn't happy about that," his wife continued the conversation as she got out of bed and looked about for her slippers.

"Happy about what?"

"About getting the call."

"Who's happy with being woken up in the middle of the night?" Irony hit them both, and they shared a dry laugh all the way down the stairs and into the kitchen. It wasn't until the coffee was brewing that Mike could get serious again. "Maybe he wasn't happy, but whatever the mark told him, he sure got off his ass lickety-split. The guys downtown think he may be coming in person to pick up this operative."

This little tidbit of information made his wife jump. "Oh no! If he is coming, this could be dangerous, very, very dangerous."

She moved between her husband and the coffee pot, planted both feet, looked him straight in the eyes, and let loose. "I forbid you to go." Then, just for good measure, she put her hands on her hips and stamped her right foot down on the cold tile floor.

Mike stared back for a moment before pirouetting around her to get closer to the coffee. Donna swiveled to stay in front, and seizing the opportunity, Mike bent down low and kissed her on the top of the head. This gentle act did little to slow her down.

The five-foot-three, 120-pound woman wrapped her arms around the girth of her 220 pounds of still mostly muscle, former West Point intramural boxing champion and held on tight.

"Sweetie, this is just surveillance. I'm not going to get anywhere near them, that is, if I can actually find the mark, triangulation or no triangulation."

"I'm still not letting you go unless you have major backup." She knew this was a losing battle, but she had to try. Then...a miracle occurred.

"Then get dressed."

"What?"

"There's no one else. Everyone is on vacation, or on assignment, or who knows where and no one expected the Sheik to move. They said double pay would be authorized for your, um, consulting efforts tonight. Come on, what do you say, it'll be like old times."

"Yeah, right, two middle-aged lugs like us riding around the backcountry in the middle of the night."

Despite her not quite jocular response, she couldn't have been happier. Christmas had come early. She hated all the bureaucracy but, like her husband, had always loved the field work.

Knowing he had successfully lassoed in his help for the night, Mike moved down his list of things to do. "Honey, do you remember where I put the bullets?" The wife didn't hear him; she had already bounded off to get dressed.

⟫◆◆◆⟪

It didn't take long for team MacLean to begin their search. They moved first to the scene of the accident and, from this point, began to slowly canvas outward, hoping telephone contact between the Sheik and the man they were looking for would be reestablished. It was and, as husband and wife, drove somewhere along the winding roads north and east of Clinton, New Jersey, another car had already zeroed in, found the target, and hoisted him aboard.

"New Jersey! Samir, are you crazy? What made you think to even call?" This was articulated in a rather loud voice by the man in the passenger seat. Samir, in the back, didn't answer. He knew better. As the Sheik continued berating, Samir just lowered his gaze and tried to act humble.

"You don't ever, ever ask me to drive to New Jersey again. And in the middle of the night no less!" The man speaking clarified his first invective. "You are crazy!" before adding, "Praise Allah we have the GPS."

"Praise Allah," the refrain came from the muscle in the back between whom Samir was sandwiched. The driver, Abdul, said nothing. He was too busy trying to negotiate his way along unfamiliar ground.

Of those in the car, the least happy was the man in the passenger seat. Physically, he was only slightly larger than Samir, sported a beard and, like many religious elders, a *kalansuwa*, turban and all. Dressed thus, it was hard in the dark of the car to make out his features, except the eyes. These burned with purpose and seemed to add fuel to his diatribe as he threw every derogatory name in the book at Samir using a delivery pace bound to make both the sender and the receiver sweat. As he spoke, he tugged at the frayed ends of his scraggly, salt-and-pepper beard, trying to somehow tie it into knots.

The Sheik was a seasoned veteran, having served with the tall one in Afghanistan for years before the infidels attacked Tora Bora. He was also a friend of the Egyptian. In fact, it was the Egyptian who arranged his matriculation at the prestigious Ivy League school in New York City. When he attended class, he often wondered how Americans had managed a dominant role in the world when a person such as himself was able to walk into whatever university he wanted, providing he had money to pay for his studies. He had taken only one class there before the department head asked if he would be open to teaching a seminar series on international relations. The Sheik had assimilated into the eclectic mixing bowl of the city that became the target of his dreams, and awaited instructions.

"Never! Never! Never call that number direct! Now we have to change everything! You are an idiot!" After telling Samir what not to do and what he was, and where to shove it, the eldest man in the car got to the crux of the matter. "Do you know it took us forty-five minutes just to get out of the city? The tunnel traffic was—"

"We should have taken the bridge," the bodyguard sitting to Samir's right mumbled this.

"And we find you miles off the big road, out here in the middle of, of…" The elder caught his breath midrant and looked out the window, trying to establish just where, in fact, he was "Antelope country."

It was pitch-black on the patch of road Samir had blindly migrated to. Long, intertwined tree branches overhung the narrow lane, blocking any shafts of moonlight trying to seep through. Those coming from New York had been hesitant to turn onto this road, their global positioning system showed it as a path but could not offer up a name. The only reason they continued was Samir. Scared but resourceful, he used his cell phone in walkie-talkie mode to guide them along. When the Sheik's car slowed and flashed its lights, Samir crept out from behind a thick growth of shrubs and stood there shivering, more from fear than the damp chill of the early morning air. Now, as they struggled to find a way back to a road, any road, their GPS system could identify with a name, the gray light of dawn began to creep up over the horizon.

"They're deer, not antelope." The driver cut this line across to the group's leader. These were the first words out of Abdul's mouth since the car emerged from the tunnel on the Jersey side of the Hudson. This may or may not have been the right thing to say to the seething man sitting next to him, but nevertheless, he continued, "I've a cousin who once drove in this forsaken land [New Jersey], and he tells me they're everywhere. He should know—he hit one. They have no natural predators and, look…" Here, he accentuated his point by slowing the car down so everyone could see what he was talking about. On their left, a field ran down into the valley below and in it were deer. Everyone counted and then compared notes. It was agreed there were, give or take, fifteen animals grazing in the fenced pasture.

"Do they raise them like cattle here?" As ridiculous as it sounded, that was exactly what it looked like.

Past the deer-infested region, the road split, and Abdul stopped the car, looking forlornly at his navigator. The Sheik clenched his teeth and rubbed his hand through his beard once again before making it clear a fork in the road was not anticipated. "Merde!"

Even though the GPS system did not register a fork in the road, there it was. One branch continued east; the other moved off more southerly. The GPS could only direct them southward. Two minutes later, this road hit a dead end.

Abdul had come to the US a few years back and had never been a Boy Scout, but he did like to be prepared for contingencies. He stepped on the brakes and took out an old map, the kind printed on paper. The lettering was small, and even with a reading lamp held close to the map, he had to squint. *Oh no...* He thought. *The map doesn't show a road here either!*

Everyone in the car voiced their opinion, except Samir. He was just happy to be back among his network of comrades. It had been approximately six months since he hesitantly accepted a cover assignment, an assignment that had left him penniless and stranded in Jersey. He knew he had screwed up badly in Montréal. Up there he was a scientist, and he had an opinion, but his lab mates didn't seem to buy his point of view, or his methods. In fact, they more than politely asked him to leave the company. He also knew it was the contacts from his network that landed him in the cushy position with the provincial police, *la Sûreté de Québec.* That job he screwed up too, even more badly, so bad in fact he had to leave Canada—on the fly. His network helped him resettled in Jersey, but now he was living in constant fear. Fear he would be found. Fear he would be deported and, worse yet, fear the tolerance he had been shown by his network would run out and he would be considered a liability; this is why, in the early morning hours, in a car in the wilds of Jersey, he rested, taking comfort in the plan he was hatching. *The information I carry*, he thought, *is bound to please. Then I can branch out and do what I want. I will be needed. I will be important.*

Meanwhile, the GPS system insisted the road straight ahead was workable, corn field or no corn field. This opinion served to fuel a multi-partied discourse focusing on navigation devices in general and at Abdul's in particular, until a rather discordant crescendo was reached.

Unfortunately for those in the car, a consensus eluded them leading to an eerie silence broken only by an occasional lowing of a distant heifer.

When the Sheik had calmed enough, he suggested the driver turn the car around and drive out the way they came in. He also casually mentioned how inept the Americans were. "They cannot even provide us with a functioning GPS system. This is all President Bush's fault."

"Yes, yes," the others agreed, and reminiscent of a troupe of fraternity brothers on a road trip singing ribald shanties (while drinking beer), the men in the car began to chant, "Down with Bush!" (sans bière). The fraternity bros passed only one car as they searched for the road to take them home. This car was occupied by a middle-aged couple who appeared to be, like those in the Sheik's car just minutes before, arguing over a map. As they passed this vehicle, their chanting had become outright singing, which, though not harmonic, was a salve helping wash the tension out of Samir's system.

The middle-aged couple were also smiling as they listened to the chorus drive by.

"That was him."

"Agreed," Donna shot back at her husband. They gave each other mini-high-fives and then, as Mike slowly turned the car around to follow, Donna prepared to call in her report.

"Stupid idiot, he left his phone on the whole time."

Confidence in one's ability can be fleeting. They did not see the Sheik order Samir to surrender his phone, and the car they were now preparing to follow had already moved past a bend in the road when the phone's chip was removed and thrown out the window. All they knew was the signal went dead and the trail cold.

For the Sheik, the return trip gave him time to think. From what he could understand of Samir's late-night phone call, as garbled as it was, the information the Moroccan now carried may, just may, need to be transmitted up the ladder. *The best way to do this*, he surmised, *might involve sending the idiot himself.* For a moment, a very brief moment, a smile developed across the Sheik's usually rigid face. *This pain will no longer be in my ass.*

Chapter 6
A Stakeout

The first operation on Arthur McAiden was a left temporal craniotomy and removal of the epidural hematoma. Here, the surgeons retracted the scalp, found the fractures, began the craniotomy, and therein found the hematoma. After removing this, fragments of the fractured temporal bone were put back together using a microplate system, all of which was then reattached. The final words from the neurosurgeon that night scribbled onto the report's margin read, "I hope we got to him in time."

When he was all sewn up, the plastic surgeons came in for the second operation, the reattachment of his left ear. After completion of this procedure, he was moved to the ICU, still in a coma and listed as such on his chart.

It was two days post-accident when Special Agent MacLean visited. MacLean was joined there by an assignment officer from the New York City office. If this man had been out of school more than two years, MacLean would have guessed wrong. The two didn't say much as they navigated their way through the busy corridors, and once they reached the ICU, what could they say? Silently, both reconnoitered for a moment and then, not knowing what to do, they approached the bustle of activity around the nurses' station. From there, it was the charge nurse who led them to the patient they had come to see. The damage was as expected. Arthur did not look pretty.

"Can we speak with the surgeon who operated on him?" This the assignment officer mumbled, looking down at who knew what.

It turned out the surgeon(s), nurses, med techs, and everyone else involved with Arthur's emergency procedures were penciled in as the night shift for the month. Lucky for those employed by the FBI, the charge nurse filled in without hesitation. Unlucky for the two men, she used technical jargon beyond their comprehension.

"Post-surgery, the patient needed 'round-the-clock' so he was stationed here, the command center," the nurse began. "This area is laid out like a wheel with the cluster of beds positioned close to the central monitoring hub. In this configuration, all patients are within eyesight of operations staff and within seconds of the on-call rapid response team. He's in a coma, the blood clots are controlled, and the meds are helping prevent more seizures."

Then she ran down a list of broken bones, the filters inserted into the veins. "He had subarachnoid hemorrhaging and craniotomy so we had to stop the anti-co-ags and insert the filter"; the titanium plates and other attachments placed over portions of the skull "using the Midas Rex"; and last but not least, repairs to the left ear, "we had to reconstitute the cartilage with monocryl sutures, nothin' but the best for our patients, and later, the stellate lacerations were closed up with V and Y type advancements." She finished up with comments relating to the collapsed lung and the shattered T3, "That's why we had to tie him down so tight. Can't have him movin' around now, can we? Oh, in a few days, we'll insert a feeding tube if"—she left that sentence dangling as she handed over all of Arthur's personal belongings—"we were told not to give it to his family until you had a looksee. Maybe you can pass at least some of this stuff along to his wife. You'll find her in the waiting room."

The nurse moved away, mumbling something derogatory about everybody needing a surgeon. The FBI assignment officer proceeded to ensconced himself on one side of the comatose patient's bed and, as soon as the nurse was out of earshot, launched into his first question. "What's a T3?"

MacLean, standing now on the other side of Arthur's bed, wasn't sure, and since neither man wished to ask for help in this regard, the assignment officer moved on.

"Very little to go on," he started. Then pointing in Arthur's direction, he continued, "We know who this guy is, and we think our Moroccan was tailing him, but we're not one hundred on that. All we really know is everyone was in the same pile up. It would be helpful if you could talk to the wife. Not sure you'll get much out of her till she calms down, but then…"

MacLean knew what to do. He had more years of operational experience than the young man trying to give him instructions, many more. It made him want to laugh or, perhaps, throw a punch. But he did neither, he just continued nodding along.

"We've been following him off and on ever since he showed up over at that bio-tech place in Newark. We thought he was connected to the Sheik but weren't sure…"

"Until the phone call?" MacLean added.

"Yeah, until the phone call."

The discussion moved in and out of possible reasons why McAiden was on Badon Hill, though none were in any way verified by facts, and each possibility was adding tasks to MacLean's growing list of things to do on the Jersey side of the river. When the possibilities ran out, the assignment officer figuratively handed over the relevant documents to the case by performing a bureaucratic blessing, he wrote down the password to the case file. Just like that, MacLean had access to all available information.

"How big a group will I be handling?" This, MacLean needed to know.

With the answer came the lay of the land, there was no real support.

"Oh, the Canadians might send someone on horseback riding your way, but we cannot count on Dudley yet."

Thinking he was the butt of a joke, those in the New York office were, after all, encouraging him to retire, and having no real need for an accident-prone Dudley Do-Right, he tried haggling with the man standing on the opposite side of Arthur's bed. "At least let me keep my wife on the team. She speaks French and…"

⟩⟨⟩⟩◆⟨⟨⟩⟨

MacLean wasn't sure if it should be called a stakeout, he was just waiting for the proprietor to return. He wasn't happy, that was a given. He was stuck in Bayonne while the FBI's A team was trying to infiltrate the Sheik's organization in Manhattan. Everything west of the Hudson and east of the Delaware, which was, basically, New Jersey, had been left to MacLean and his not-yet-existent B team.

So there he was, stuck, trying to back-fill information on his one and only lead, by himself (the paperwork for his wife had not yet been finalized), watching heat trails rise up off the asphalt around his parked car, waiting for someone to open the door of the Second Storey Detective agency. With nothing to do, he sat and wondered if "storey" was a misspelling. It helped pass the time.

For MacLean, it was all about the car. Rather, it was all about the missing driver of one of the wrecked cars. It would have been just a run-of-the-mill accident, bad accident for sure; the man was, after all, hooked up to so much life support it could turn tragic at any time. But at that moment, it was still just an accident. With that said, one of those involved was now hiding out in Manhattan. They did not know his name. He had just recently appeared in Jersey. He was on the watchlist now, but as with others living in Jersey, he was down near the bottom of said list. But when the Sheik answered his call, he had moved up the list, way up. Now they just needed to find out who he really was. This is why Special Agent MacLean was sitting in his car, in the late afternoon, in Bayonne.

The fingerprints found in the abandoned car had given them something to go on, but if there was no database match, it wouldn't really help. The car itself was the prime source of information, and it was the only thing MacLean had at his disposal.

The car was a rental. The rental agency in question was not one advertising a number 1 ranking nor was it a company claiming to work harder, for less. In fact, unless someone dug deep in the yellow pages covering south Newark—way down, in unassuming small print—he or she would miss this outfit altogether because the rental agency catered to the locals; people who needed a car for a few hours here or there, possibly a weekend getaway to nearby exotic Garden State hotspots. There weren't any late-model cars in their entire fleet, just your solid workday types bought as castoffs from those who longed for newer editions. Most sported dents.

MacLean's adventure had started in the morning as he went in search of the rental agency. He was wearing a dark summer weight suit, a light-blue one-ply oxford cloth shirt (neck buttoned down) and a red tie. He also had use of one of the Bureau's newer cars, a dark, midsize sedan built for safety, bullet-proof glass, and sides included.

The rental company was buried in a neighborhood in the southern reaches of Newark, which was definitely an eye opener. The locale could have been prefaced with a qualifier like "little" as in "Little Italy" or provided with its own unique identifier, an identifier that turned the enclave into a municipality, such as Chinatown. Basically, it was one of those ethnic enclaves of homogeneity found scattered within the more heterogeneous backdrop of North America.

When MacLean pulled off the east-west highway, a road he had many monikers for, all of which included references to hell, and headed north into South Newark, he was met by something totally unexpected. Apparently, the address MacLean was looking for was pretty much right below the approach pattern for Newark International. At this location, every forty seconds or so, another jumbo jet would pop into view just meters above, and the concomitant roar of the engine would drown out all background noise. When the vibrations receded, along with the noise, the smell of the jet exhaust would waft down upon the surroundings like soot downwind from smokestacks.

To get away from the overhead air traffic, he hunched behind the dashboard of what now looked to be a Plymouth DeLuxe, only surveying the local environs once he felt safe to raise his head. When he did look, he came to the realization that his area of cultural expertise was limited. His knowledge of organized crime and fluency in Russian combined with passable French, and German, had always worked for him in times past but South Newark was different. As he moved deeper into the neighborhood, the scene unfolding could have been taken from any *suk* found from Marrakesh to Kabul. Women covered from head to toe in drab *burkhas* stood side by side with fashionistas showing everything the burkha clad women couldn't. All were busy arguing over the price of flat breads and vegetables in front of any one of a dozen kiosks.

Bearded men in robes, some wearing turbans, some not, were exchanging animated bantering with those clean shaven in blue jeans. All, young and old, were watching the men standing over deep-fry pans, cooking falafel and kebabs. When the planes weren't passing overhead, music, like the smell of the fried foods, filled the air. To make matters worse for the FBI agent, each street sign was painted over, in Arabic. From the get-go, it seemed as if nothing was going to be easy this day.

It took a while to find the building he was looking for, and when he did, the second of the three Gorgons raised its head. Everyone in the room was male ranging in age from "probably not having a license" to "shouldn't any longer." They all seemed to be locals, as one would expect, the rental agency catered to them and most depressing, no one in the room appeared to be in a hurry. The next labor of this almost ready to retire Hercules involved dusting off an old skill, the "waiting patiently" skill. This was never his forte, and from his position at the back of the line, he had become stuck not so patiently waiting for movement, any movement.

A good ten minutes passed and being his "waiting patiently" endurance limit MacLean now introduced himself by raising his voice and displaying his badge. "I'm Special Agent MacLean, FBI." Then he strode to the front of the line with a badge held high. When he stepped up to the counter, things got worse. The man across from him, the manager, stood rock still, staring at the FBI agent without blinking. This problem persisted until MacLean pulled out pictures of the car, dents and all, for the attendant to peruse. Before he could pass the serial number of the damaged vehicle across the counter, the manager spoke in a tone someone earmarked as royalty might use.

"I am Tariq. I am in charge here."

Tariq then toned it down a notch, and in a voice often used by high-end salesmen, he proceeded to tell MacLean how he couldn't be sure if the car in the picture was one of his. "You see, sir, I specialize in very new…um, how does one say…upscale cars?"

MacLean was momentarily confused and took a notebook from his pocket, looking for the serial number, but before he could speak, Tariq continued (apparently, he had just gotten a good look at the picture and now there was a bit of animation in his delivery). "The late-model car I rented out was in perfect condition when it left the lot!"

The car MacLean was interested in was not a late model and would have been classified as totaled by any insurer's definition. He didn't need an appraiser to tell him that. What he wanted was the name of the man who rented the piece of shit, pronto. The manager wasn't ready yet; he needed to bargain, so he cross-referenced the car and the customer as he formulated his opening gambit. When ready, he gagged and then, matter-of-factly, told MacLean, "I do not think I can tell you."

MacLean rolled his eyes heavenward. "I don't have time for this shit. What are you playing at?" The federal agent then took out his mobile phone, pushed a button, and began talking fast using a tech-savvy mode of speech to an imaginary respondent, all covering immigration issues and potential tax fraud.

The monologue went on for three or four sentences before he paused and pretended to listen. Then he answered the phantom on the other end of his connection.

"I'll ask."

Turning to the proprietor, he did ask, "He wants to know your full name—both of them—American and…"

What the federal agent mistook for defiant belligerence was nothing more than a cultural demarcation. When he asked Tariq a question, he wanted Tariq to supply an answer. But in Tariq's world, haggling was the norm. Eventually, Tariq won out. MacLean was forced to negotiate with the man. The small nuggets of data given over were scanned onto MacLean's mobile device and uploaded to the FBI office for analysis. Then, shaking his head and still fussing, he left the shop. Once outside, MacLean stopped, tilted his head to one side, and began to wonder if he really needed to make good on a promise to come back and rent a car next time he was in town.

That was South Newark; now MacLean was in Bayonne waiting for someone to show up at the detective agency, the only business address listed by whomever had rented the car in South Newark. The Second Storey Detective Agency was close to the water, a few blocks south of the bridge. There was a good view of Newark Bay and the busy piers on the western side of the river. Beyond the piers lay the airport. To MacLean, the view from this spot would have been infinitely preferable to watching the underbelly of jumbo jets passing over South Newark, but all in all, beyond the rundown buildings near his car, the boats across the bay and airplanes at a distance, there was nothing much to watch. The entire vicinity appeared to be devoid of human inhabitants.

When he first climbed the rickety steps up to the detective agency's second-floor office, he had wondered why a Newark-based car rental agency was used by a low budget affair in Bayonne.

"How can this company even afford to rent cars?"

This question was directed internally as he stood in the musty corridor long enough for his mold allergy to kick in. At once, he moved right back down the steps into, comparatively speaking, the fresher air found outdoors in Bayonne. Once outside, his thoughts remained internal as he watched the cityscape slowly change. The feeling in the air was more Southern now, more like New Orleans than Bayonne. Across the water, the boats, too, seemed different. They had a post-WWII look about them, and below his feet, streetcar tracks were running along the center of the road. He was sweating, too, profusely. He took off his jacket before climbing back into the DeLuxe and with windows rolled down, he slouched back and listened to the crawdads before slowly drifting off to sleep.

When he woke, a slight drizzle was helping to cool the neighborhood, and multiple activities were coming back online. First, streaming onto his smartphone in rapid fire were replies to his earlier queries. The name given for the man who rented the car, Arshad Siddiqui, was basically John Smith. There were several with this name in both Jersey and Canada. The actual number on the driver's license, when crossed-checked, belonged to a woman who, according to records, had left the state more than a few years back. These dead ends were not unexpected but did close investigative avenues. Fortunately, the detective agency was legitimate, at least it was on paper.

The agency's registration was filed appropriately with the state and incorporated in Nevada. There was nothing exceptionally unusual there including how, for a number of years, they had not filed taxes. Again, nothing unusual, and from what he read, the Second Storey Detective Agency was a serious, albeit nonprofitable, corporation.

Other activities, non-telephone-based, were also in play. The shifts had changed at the docks, bringing the small taverns and other shops catering to the union crowd to life. The men moving along the now-damp streets had a look and feel of longshoremen, stevedores, and teamsters. Possibly a few other trades were in the mix too, but it became hard for the FBI agent to discern any distinctions. "Union crowd" also served as a euphemism for burly men who sported tattoos and drank beer. These characters were now populating the fronts of the tavern and other doorways up and down the street, some holding pool cues. From inside his car, MacLean kept one eye on the assortment of bodies now milling about and the other on the second-floor windows over the bar. When the lights were finally turned on up there, he moved, but not knowing exactly how long he would be in the building he reached into his side pocket and pulled out the little bottle of pills needed to combat allergen rich environs. He took two. Next, he called the city police for backup. The neighborhood didn't seem as safe as it had midday.

Ten minutes later, two uniformed officers arrived, and after making sure they understood where he was going and why he might need backup, MacLean swallowed hard, wrapped his trench coat tight, and pulled his fedora down as he climbed out of the car. Now the scene changed once again. Noise was coming from various windows, sounding like hundreds of sewing machines answering the call to duty, the garment district in its prime. Warehouses, packed to the gills, were venting exhaust in all directions as trucks lined up for loading. Boats, too, joined the party as they approached wharves, which only now could be seen abutting the streets on the Bayonne side of the river. MacLean raised the brim of his hat for a moment to take it all in before he opened the door and began to, once again, climb the stairs.

As he moved up, a steady stream of longshoremen passed him going down. Where other men may have been unnerved by the sight of so much muscle with five o'clock shadows, MacLean wasn't. In fact, he didn't notice. He was still lost in his own thoughts. It was those coming down the steps who were unnerved by the non-union specter on its way up. Each moved as far as possible to one side and tried to avoid eye contact with MacLean.

"I'm getting too old for this shit," he spat out halfway up the stairs. Then he stopped for a moment, wondering which went first, memory or field craft. The last few days were beginning to take a toll on him.

Once he reached the top, he paused to catch his breath and survey the situation. What he saw was a long line at the far end of the corridor waiting to enter the detective agency. This line continued to grow as men ambled up the stairs on the far side of the building. Apparently, the detective agency doubled as a sports betting emporium. Once bets had been placed, each left the building using MacLean's route, which was, he learned, the back stairs.

For the second time in one day, MacLean was stuck in a slow-moving line. This time, though, there was no attempt to be patient; he pulled out his ID and before saying a word the line in front dissolved into thin air, allowing for immediate access to the betting counter. An agreeable receptionist with an air of Blanche DuBois (in her younger days) now stood in front of him, wearing a low-cut tank top. She was the bookie, and as such, she patiently waited for MacLean to present her with his picks. Apparently, Special Agent MacLean wasn't the first FBI employee to place their bets at Second Storey.

For a moment, impasse existed. It seemed to the woman on the far side of the counter that MacLean was having trouble deciding, so she directed his attention away from her chest and over to the daily numbers. Instead of placing bets, MacLean slammed his badge on the counter and began pulling out his cell phone, hoping to reenact his earlier scam over in South Newark. It didn't work. The woman got mad and told the FBI agent to piss or get off the pot. "If you don't," she threatened, "I'll call the manager." A second later, he was alone in the room.

When Blanche returned, she was followed by a short man wearing a muscle shirt, standing as tall as he was round. The short man took a quick look at the FBI agent and roared in recognition. "Well, well, look who we a got-ta here. I haven't seen ya since…" The owner of the detective agency paused as he counted the years on his stubby fingers. When he ran out of fingers, he gave up. "How long has it been?"

In days past, the two men had been both part-time antagonists, part-time collaborators. They spent a few moments playing catch-up, exchanging awkward pleasantries and inquiring about one another's families. The entire time they skirted their current situation until a police officer came up to see if MacLean needed help. Then it was down to business.

"Look, Guido," MacLean started, "I'm not here to run you in today." The round man smiled politely as the FBI agent continued, "I just came for some information."

"Like-a ol' times?"

"Sort of, but perhaps it's more serious this time."

Guido responded with a weak, humorless laugh. In the old days, he had been MacLean's stool pigeon. Even back then, he tipped the scales, and so the moniker "pigeon" didn't seem apropos. Pigeon or not, the last time MacLean had seen Guido he was on his way up the river for a "minor" offense. Fortunately, the time allotted was far less than it would have been if he hadn't been MacLean's informant.

Finding Guido in Bayonne, a few towns away from his old stomping grounds, had surprised the FBI agent, and being inquisitive, he had to ask. "You got balls or what? I mean, why not witness protection?"

"It's got nothing to do with my cojones." Here, Guido had to grab his crotch to make sure the meaning was understood. "It's not like the ol' days." Then he lowered his voice, looked around, and continued in a whisper, "No one was ever sure it was me back then. So now I keep a low profile, stay out of big stuff, run a few numbers, and manage this," he finished, indicating the office with a wide, sweeping gesture.

After a quick glance around the now-empty room, MacLean asked one simple question, "Guido, with all the legal lotteries and gaming houses, why would anyone come by here and risk placing a bet with you?"

"Odds are better."

"Oh." MacLean couldn't think of anything else to say on that topic, so he moved on, "Listen, I have to ask some questions about one of your employees."

It turned out the Detective Agency really did, from time to time, engage in bona-fide private investigations. The "old" guys, MacLean was told, worked in the detective agency when they needed a few extra bucks. "They track down a delinquent alimony check, a cheating wife. You know, everyday stuff, very dull, private dick stuff."

MacLean understood; he also knew Guido, being a bad thief, but a good businessman, was working with what he had available. Apparently, after conducting some research, his old stool pigeon figured running numbers in the area was a better business model than tracking down adulterous longshoremen. It was just that the Second Storey guys were all his old friends, his *gumbas*. He couldn't lay them off, so he kept them around and kept the detective agency afloat, even if it wasn't profitable.

"So this is a front for running the numbers." MacLean stated the obvious.

Guido didn't answer. Instead, he brought the conversation around to what MacLean really wanted to know. The FBI man passed rental car receipts one way, and Guido passed information back. The man known to Guido as Siddiqui had shown up a few months back. "He needa work, he bring a high-priced surveillance stuff with him. So I figured, why not? They all geta paid by the job. He say he get his own cases, just need to be official, know what I mean?"

"Background check?" the special agent asked.

Guido laughed.

"What can you tell me about him?"

Not much, it turned out, so the FBI man started at the beginning.

"Height?"

"I'd say maybe five-six, five-seven."

"Weight?"

"A hun-red forty, give or take…if he was wet." Guido then disappeared into the back room and reemerged a minute later with a few manila folders—just a few.

"Like I said, he was only here a short time."

MacLean reached for the files. Guido hesitated. "Now wait just a sec. I show them, you no take them." Guido scratched his head for a second before continuing, "Can you?"

"Well, my old friend, here's the thing. This is a Homeland Security issue. It'll save me a lot of time if you let me have them." As he spoke, MacLean leaned over the counter, separating the two men, and gave the shorter man a very, very official look. "If I come back with a warrant, I'll have to close you down."

"Say, what kind-a trouble is this guy in?"

Giving no response, MacLean thanked his old informant for the folders, promising to take good care of them, and "In no way will this compromise the trust your clients place in the special services you offer." As MacLean walked back down the stairs, a smile began spreading across his face.

By the time he was back in his office, the fingerprint analysis was in.

"We got a hit," the technician had relayed over the phone.

The man known as Arshad Siddiqui at the Second Storey Detective Agency had another name: Samir Mounir.

Chapter 7
Visiting Hours

Herodotus of Halicarnassus wrote many things. *The Histories* was one, and within it can be found the following: "Here, I present the results of my investigation into adventures experienced during my life in both the here and now and, in ages dark." *This pretty much explains what I am up to. Is it memory that elevates man above beasts. Is this what designs the contours of one's soul? Did the accident remove them from me? And if they are erased, who am I? What if, by reaching back I only pull up memories from long ago, who will I be then? I suppose I should thank my psychologist for pushing me to write. Or perhaps I should hate her for this.*

When the two FBI agents visited the ICU, the man in the bed was listed as comatose. Blood seepage into his brain had been plugged in time, thanks to the speedy helicopter ride, the talented team of surgeons who met him at the door and, basically, everyone else. But in the first days following his arrival, no one knew if the efforts had been in time. It became a waiting game.

The left side of his head was completely shaved, making the horseshoe scar easy for all to see. It began on the temple above his left eye, wound its way toward the back of his head and then curved around ending up behind the repaired ear. This scar was inflamed with no intention of returning to a less agitated state. The repaired ear was caked in blood caused by a constant leaking from both the perforated eardrum and the exterior scars where it had been reattached. The reattachment of the ear itself may have been just for show as no one yet knew if he would ever be able to make use of that ear again.

The visible scars were eye-catching as were the tubes entering his body through various openings. One delivered oxygen to the right lung, the left had been crushed and was still not functioning. The other, a feeding tube inserted just after the FBI visit had ended, wound its way down his esophagus. Other lines attached to veins were helping administer saline and various medications while monitors of all shapes and sizes were glued on or taped to various body parts. There were a lot of vitals in need of tracking.

Besides the head wounds, five of the ribs on the left side were broken, the left hip and shoulder were both in bad shape, and the T3 had been shattered into a thousand pieces. If he was not strapped firmly into a motionless position the probability of the bone fragments finding the right alignment in his body was close to zero.

As word got out of Arthur's accident, many people wished to show their support for both the man and his family by visiting. Unfortunately, ICUs have a limited space for nonessential personnel. In this hospital, one visitor at a time was allowed into the command center (the FBI agents had skirted this rule), and only two visitors per patient could occupy space in the ICUs waiting area at night. During daylight hours, the number was upped to three. The problem for all those wishing to visit was this: his wife, Jennifer, and his sister, Anna, were there night and day, leaving room for only one more visitor at any given time. Many straws had been drawn that first week.

Anna had flown over from England on the first available flight after hearing the bad news. This put her on scene a full two days after the accident. Arriving late didn't make her happy and not being able to really do anything productive sent her anxiety level through the roof. Of course, Anna's state of being did very little to support Jennifer, who, besides the patient, was most in need of attention.

The wife and sister spent a lot of time playing tag-team for entry into the ICU. Neither slept much; it's not the thing to do when holding vigil, and when not allowed in the ICU proper, they sat side by each in the waiting area with Anna distributing update information to whomever would answer their phone and Jennifer, well, Jennifer rocked back and forth, in silence, when not crying. On multiple occasions, the two women teared up in stereo.

The fourth night after Anna's arrival, the attending physician had come to the waiting room to give an update. He motioned the two women to follow him to a nearby conference room, and once there, before anyone sat down, he began, "His condition has stabilized. There is nothing else we can do for him here. Soon we will move him to a room out of our central hub until you"—here, the physician meant Jennifer—"decide what you want to do."

It was the physician's attempt at consoling. Neither woman, he noted, had left the patient's side, or the waiting room, day or night; and he sincerely thought his words would give them a little comfort. He also hoped one, or both, would go home for a while to get some sleep and, perhaps, a shower.

"God knows they could use one." This he had mentioned more than once to each member of the ICU staff over the last few days.

The problem for Jennifer and Anna was this: The doctor wasn't trained in the subtleties of delivering patient updates to stressed relatives. "The patient," he continued, "was already comatose when the helicopter landed. He stayed this way during the CT and, of course, surgery. He had a few more seizures since arriving, but all the meds have, like I said, stabilized him. Just a while ago, we noted his eyes opening."

Both women gasped with excitement when he said this, but the doctor wasn't smiling. "It was just for a bit but...but...um...there was no movement." Before either woman could interject, he continued, "This is unusual but not unheard of for those in coma. Their eyes open but the vitals don't change."

"What is usual?" both women asked.

He gave them a short rundown on behavior of those regaining consciousness just before the killer question he was hoping to avoid was launched in his direction.

"What is unusual about this?"

He told them and then quietly backed out of the room.

Neither Jennifer nor Anna moved. They were too busy dissecting what they had just been told. The doctor may have been a very gifted professional in the diagnostic arena but wouldn't even qualify as a minor leaguer when it came to relaying information to grieving relatives. He said, "At the moment, Arthur is like a vegetable." He didn't mean "vegetative state," though this is what they thought had come out of his mouth. He had left out all positive possibilities, first and foremost, the likelihood of Arthur regaining consciousness. When he said "vegetable," they both internally machinated on the right-to-life debate, and as the MD left the room, Jennifer did her best to ease herself into a nearby chair while Anna skipped that altogether and just fell to the ground.

Chapter 8
The Command Center

Shortly after Anna's fainting performance, brother and sister were sharing a room just a short hop from the ICU command center. This room was just outside the ICU area of control, which allowed for more relaxed ruling on the number of guests allowed in per unit time. This accommodation was a gift of sorts from the hospital. As the doctor had mentioned they had planned to move Arthur to a room out of the central hub and with Anna refusing placement for her recovery, if it wasn't within spitting distance of her brother, a cot was added to his room, et voilà, they shared accommodations. Arthur lay quiet (as a comatose patient might), trying to stay out of the way as his sister spent her time tossing and turning and spouting expletives at whomever was nearby. Most of those in the line of fire would beat a hasty retreat. Everyone who could, that is. Unfortunately for Arthur, he was physically unable to do so.

Physicality didn't really matter to the man on the bed. His neuronal network was still pretty much shut down—out of mind, out of body, so to speak. There was no physical world for him to relate to. At least not according to modern medical (or physical) measurements. He was stable, so it was written in the medical reports, but with nowhere to go, the man was just biding his time, waiting to see where his corporeal chips might fall. If they fell in one direction, the door would open for him to climb back in and turn the proverbial lights back on, all the lights. If they fell in a different pattern, well his current placement would make it easy for him to move in whatever direction that might be.

Wherever he was at that moment in time, none of those who were now in his room seemed to care. They were more worried about where the body occupying one of the two beds in the room might end up. His wife had, without consultation, decided this. "It's settled," a choked-up voice announced, "we'll transfer him to *Our Lady of the Still Lake*."

It had been difficult for Jennifer. That was obvious; she had made her pronouncement with tears helping deliver the message. Then she straightened up and quickly skedaddled. Stress affects people in different ways, and as the door was closing behind Jennifer, her sister-in-law let a few invectives fly while flinging the one and only physical object she could get her hands on, a book. Whether she was aiming for the back of Jennifer's head no one can say for sure. It started off in that direction but halfway across the room, it sliced left, making for the in-suite bathroom instead of the hallway door. Now, all those standing in the room were possible targets, and as such, everyone jumped for cover. Arthur, of course, could not jump, but as he heard the projectile arcing over his bed, he, too, retreated by moving into the only space available to him.

Once there, he began altering some of what he was hearing in the space around him into phrases he understood better. First, "Our" to "The," and once ensconced within Scott's *The Lady of the Lake*, he began scanning the Cantos for the proper geographic locale. The political feuds between lowland and highland clans held the message but the time frame was wrong. Looking further he switched from Scott's poem to Lowell's *Vision of Sir Launfal*. This was closer to the *Sangreal* for which so many had searched and helped tie together his need to find Percy. But still, the cast of characters wasn't exactly right, so he continued perusing the indexed files stored deep within his memory banks.

Snippets of Tennyson's *The Lady of Shalott* came into view. This brought out *L'ancelo*, but this was not the man he was looking for. *Idylls of the King* did bring glimpses of *Sir Percivale*, who had become a monk and died after giving his account to Ambrosius, a fellow monk. This discourse only brought confusion. A different source, a source that the bed-bound patient just couldn't put his hands on, had once told him Ambrosius was the senior and Percival the junior and Galahad, *Dindrane's* "knight of heaven" was a figment of Malory's imagination and there was no *Morte D'Arthur* because Arthur was on the bed in front of everyone, yet everyone spoke as if he could not hear and this made him want to run and hide but he had to find *Percivale*. Again, not Tennyson's Galahad because a lifetime ago, he had finished lunch with his mother and began searching for Percy until realization hit. He had to find his way back first.

When the book was no longer in flight, those unscathed stood up straight and stared anywhere other than at Anna and the only voice heard was being broadcast in via Anna's phone. It was Yglais, and not being physically present, she had not been directly affected by the flying object. Madam li Gros was in Lothian, sitting in her family's home, gazing out the window, saddened by the events and trying hard to follow the conversation. She wanted to join her half-sister and brother, but it was difficult for someone wheelchair-bound to simply jump up and run. All she could do was pray as she stared out across the manicured lawn rolling down to the lake and dream of days past. It may have been the sound of her voice that pushed the imagination of the man on the bed into the realm of romance lit or, perhaps, kept it there.

Everyone else crammed into the room was also listening to the exchange between the half-sisters with on muttering invectives for all to hear while the other stroked the agitated woman's hand from afar. "Anna, please try to stay calm, you cannot help Arthur, or anyone else for that matter. Not from bed anyway, and well, it is you who must rest too." All those listening, besides the two bed-bound occupants, inched closer to the telephone, nodding in affirmation.

When Anna calmed, the discussion based on alternatives began. Apparently, everyone wanted to bring Arthur home; that was a given. But the wife had just ruled this out by virtue of her unilateral decision. He was headed to a hospice, a local hospice, so there was very little those standing in the room could do, except kvetch.

"He'll be in a nice place, and he'll be safe," Yglais stated this, though deep down, she, too, wished they could whisk Arthur back to his ancestral home. "I'm sure," Yglais added, "he'll get round the clock care and…" It wasn't enough.

"But he won't be home, it's not where we"—Anna cried harder with each word—"need to take him."

Some in the room were related by blood, a few were not, but all had the utmost respect for Arthur McAiden and his family. Another reason all those crammed into the hospital room had to do with a problem at work. This, too, had a family theme running through it. Unfortunately, Jennifer's decree was not expected, and Anna's distraction with the book made it hard to get the group to move off the first issue and on to the second.

The largest in the room by either height or width was Angus, who while hiding behind the mass of reddish-brown hair, also known as a beard, was now using a hushed voice to add solemnity, and his opinion of the unexpected problem "I hate to say it, but Jennifer may be making the right move here, at least to get him someplace more comfortable." When no one spoke, he tried to turn attention away from Arthur's health. "Wayne, look what I found." He smiled and held up the book, which, moments before, had been sailing across the room. Given the fact no one could see his lips through the beard the smile wasn't readily detectable. "Anna," he continued, "I didn't know you were a *King Arthur* fan. I've never heard of this author before, Norma Lorre…"

"Goodrich," Wayne finished. Wayne was Anna's son, Arthur's nephew, "It was near his body when they found him in the ditch."

It was obvious Anna didn't care about the book or any modern interpretations related to this ancient storyline. This was Arthur's hobby.

She was more concerned with the here and now. "Angus, do you really think it right for his wife to move him to a hospice! They pulled him out of a ditch so he wouldn't die there and now she wants to put him in another ditch. The kind where you go to…"

Talk of the book nudged Arthur's focus. Goodrich's methodology centered on the structure and development of language, and taking his cue from the noted author, Arthur converted Angus back into an ancient Latin equivalent, Anguselus, and then modernize it to Old French and, via techniques only someone versed in philology could do, transformed the name into l'Anseló. Angus was Lancelot, and now, within this hospital room Arthur Pendragon's Gosgordd was beginning to marshal. It was time to take roll.

Angus and Wayne were both present. It would be hard to imagine a pair of warriors so dissimilar in appearance and talent. Angus was a bit over two meters, broad of shoulder and had forearms one could not miss even beneath his long sleeves. He dressed as casual as an event would allow and often had trouble with color coordination, but no one ever seemed to take him to task on this issue. His red hair was inching back on his forehead but flowing in full down from his chin. He was a gifted orator, his delivery very similar to those who trained for the stage. When he was happy, his voice sang out, melodic and fair; but when angered, he snorted like a horse, and the exhaled breath sometimes seemed tinged with red. He spoke fiercely at these times, like a trumpet playing at the gates of hell. When mad, he also tended to shatter anything and everything he had in his hands, but he was working on this little problem.

Wayne headed up the acquisitions team for the company. He was outgoing, and on most occasions, he was in the vanguard as the company made inroads with intellectual property filings and technology platform developments. He was not tall, a bit shy of two meters and slender by comparison to Angus, but he was, without doubt, in shape. His body tone was a blend between an investment banker ready to make a killing and a Special Operations trooper also ready to kill. He always looked to be relaxed but was like Dagan (who was standing nearby) when focused.

The problem being, he only focused-in during the heat of battle. And as casual as his uncle dressed, Wayne was the opposite. His dark hair was always perfectly trimmed and combed, and the fit and the style of clothes worn spoke of either an interest in the fashion industry, or paid help.

Howl, too, was in the room. He was an elderly man with rounded shoulders and tended to stoop. His head, like his shoulders, was curved; and he sported a rather large, elaborate mustache. Howl's physique was not at all like that of the man he stood next to. That was Tristan. Tristan was different. He was younger, he was in very good shape, and...he was handsome, handsome to a point where women would prefix "handsome" with "Oh my, yes, yes he is," while men, when asked, would add the suffix "as a motherfucker" to their descriptor.

Another of those in attendance was Lucan. He, like Wayne was impeccably dressed, precise in his manner, and always well informed. Lucan was the butler. A thousand years ago, butlers moved in rarified strata. Whatever he was in the past, during this meeting, Lucan stood near the door, quietly holding a computer tablet on which he wrote down notes.

Dagan, too, stood quietly by the door. Dagan handled the security operations for the company. Dagan was similar in height to Wayne, was tanned brown, obviously fit, with strands of muscle showing in any exposed skin. His eyes were small, dark, and all-encompassing, like the lens of a surveillance camera. His intense, slow movements reminded any observer of nothing else but a jaguar...when it was hunting. His voice, when he did speak, was soft. But when Dagan was quiet, he commanded the most attention. Anyone with any experience in the field knows, when there is no noise around you, the jaguar was about to pounce.

As far-off times were coalescing in one train of thought, conversation carried along by those around the beds percolated in the present. If Arthur awoke from his coma, he would need rehabilitation, lots of it. If his condition worsened, became increasingly "vegetative," then the argument became "to be or not to be," and this no one wanted to talk about. But not knowing which direction left Anna, and everyone else, nothing to do but argue, when not praying. What made the situation worse; arguing didn't help. Legally, only Jennifer's opinion really mattered; everyone else was just betting on the horses.

The discussion slowly lapsed away into nothingness. Those in the room stood quietly shuffling their feet or gazing about, so when Angus's phone rang it startled the lot of them. His time on the phone was brief, and when he hung up an impromptu, lively tête-à-tête between himself and Wayne began. Everyone knew what was coming, they could hear the discussion, but it didn't stop Angus from calling each of them out as he passed along instructions.

The meeting now being held was not impromptu per se. It had been planned, and what they were going to discuss could not have waited. The phone call, though, was indeed unexpected. Now Angus stood near Arthur as Wayne took up position just a short step away from his mother. One was the chief of staff, the strategist who, smooth as silk, plotted indirect stratagems that could cut an enemy like a stiletto. The other was the tactician, sometimes just a no-holds-barred battering ram. Which was which?

"Be wary of what a man does, not what he says or looks like" was one of the lessons a mentor named Dubric had imparted to Arthur. "Those who do not pay attention will, without doubt, soon be defeated."

Angus was the strategists, the chief of staff; and Wayne, well, for Wayne, Mr. Tzu's idiom always came to Arthur's mind: "Let your plans be dark and impenetrable as night and, when you move, fall like a thunderbolt." Wayne was the well-dressed man about town who doubled as one hell of a tactical thunderbolt. The reason Wayne was always in the vanguard was simple: "Set Wayne loose on an opponent and the result would, well it would not look pretty for whoever got in his way."

When Angus began to speak, the problem that touched all, including the patients on their beds, came into view. He quickly reached the point he needed to make, "Malcolm has called for a vote! Without Arthur to vote company shares, he may get enough to really change things. We know Percy has the right to vote these holdings if Arthur is not present, but Malcom doesn't know this. We must find Percy." And just like that, Arthur and his whole team were on the same quest.

Angus gave everyone a moment to take in the magnitude of the problem they faced. Malcolm, those in the room knew, was on the governing board. Representatives of each of the major investing firms were. Malcolm was not a proponent of either the short- or long-range plans the management team had recently laid out. Malcolm, it seemed, was hoping to make changes in senior management or, possibly, just sell the company to the highest bidder.

Yglais spoke first. "This is what we thought would happen, but he moves sooner than expected." Her tone was serious but not alarmed; in fact, at that moment in time, she was the personification of intellectual detachment. "I do wish we knew where Percy was. Without him, everything will have to be packed up and moved off site, and I think it would be best if all of Arthur's personal memorabilia could also be collected and taken somewhere safe."

Angus then barked out assignments to what was, apparently, a plan that had been put together long before Arthur's accident. A knock at the door interrupted everyone's train of thought. It also brought the meeting to a close.

Chapter 9
Medical Jargon

When business teams are treading water, searching for answers to difficult issues, an interruption, like a knock at the door, is often welcome. Not today. Today, that knock only served to supersede the problems in front of them. Trepidation ensued, casting a state of pallor over everyone.

Cai entered first. He shook hands all around and even bent down to kiss Anna. All the while Arthur's son stood in the doorway, staring off into the space within his head. No one knew what to expect or in which direction Lute might fly. Quietly, each nodded welcome in his direction or softly mumbled his name.

Getting him to the hospital had not been easy.

"He has to come now, in case Arthur doesn't..." was Jennifer's plea from day 1. Everyone agreed. But as Arthur's condition stabilized, they were thankful for the reprieve. Until, that is, guilt set in; and it became a matter of honor to bring Lute to his father's bedside.

Cai had drawn the short straw. His assigned task was to visit the boarding school and make contact. Information had to be conveyed but not too much, only enough to entice the boy to travel. Too much, they feared, would launch him into one of his fits. Even so, it had taken a while before Lute understood what he was being asked to do and then it had taken a lot of surreptitious administration of sedatives to get him on board the plane. Much, much more medication was needed throughout the flight over the Atlantic.

Autistic was the medical term. Savant was thrown in from time to time, depending upon which expert was giving their assessment. Lute was autistic. He had a developmental disability (or two), but he was also quite gifted in many areas, including several of the usual ones found in savants, like the ability to solve complex calculations at a speed bordering on that found in supercomputers. And when not solving tidbits of high math, he could overlay the proper day of the week for any calendar date either years in the future or centuries past. These are the usual strong points for those classified as such. It is also the reason, though young, he had been placed in an assisted living arrangement as he attended class at UCL.

The fact his mother had left the room a few minutes earlier made the coming situation difficult. One could say the problem was Lute's. His condition made it difficult for him to communicate with people. This was a simple explanation. Or possibly, an explanation for simpletons. People had trouble communicating with Lute. Why the problem? Simple. Lute inhabited a different world, a world where cognitive processing would be, at the least, dissonant with patterns formulated by most neurotypical humans. The exchange of normal, civil discourse was difficult for him. He wasn't good at understanding facial expressions, eye contact, or physical gestures, especially those that came anywhere close to his body. The reverse was also true. Lute had trouble expressing his needs in a language others understood. His mother had developed a skill in this regard. She was often able to decipher his meanings and pass that information down the line. Unfortunately, Jennifer was not in the room, and Arthur's sister was now swallowing hard. Just a few minutes earlier, she had aimed a diatribe (with a book for punctuation) in Jennifer's direction. Now all she could do was pray Jennifer would get her ass back ASAP. She wasn't the only one wishing for Jennifer's return.

"Where is Jennifer?" Cai asked after carefully nudging Lute into the room. Cai had a nonthreatening, almost comic look about him. He had a small head, which was almost perfectly round under its close-cut crop of white hair. His ears were small and plastered to the side of his head. His nose, too, was small and barely helped carry along the curve of his face from his bony forehead to his small chin (which hid behind a tuft of white hair). His eyes were round, blue, small, and watery. Basically, he looked a bit like Mr. Potato Head. He would scare no one, and this was the reason he was given the task of retrieving Lute. The job placed on Cai's shoulders was nearing completion, and all he wished for now was to pass the torch along. "It would be better if she was um…around."

As Cai spoke, Lute stepped forward. He acknowledged no one but the man on the bed. He did this by touching the tips of his fingers to the extended but limp digits on Arthur's right hand. Then he traced the line of the surgical scar on the shaven side of his father's head. After sniffing his fingers and tilting his head to one side to get a better view of the malformed ear, he seemed to lose interest and moved off to examine the various pieces of medical equipment attached to Arthur's body.

All those in the room who could, claiming a need to begin their assigned tasks, began to slowly drift away. While passing through the threshold, each wished Lucan the best of luck and prayed Jennifer would return before, "well, before all hell breaks loose. If she isn't around and he goes off…Lord, have mercy." Lucan stood in the hall, acknowledging their concern as he, for the tenth time, wished Jennifer would pick up her phone.

In the room, only Anna and a nurse who had just arrived, remained with Arthur and his son until, that is, the attending arrived. The physician offered a cursory hello and, with case report in hand, began to quickly examine the prone body before proceeding to give instructions to the nurse.

"So you're moving him out soon." The man spoke more to give himself something to do than to engage in conversation.

"Yes, yes, I suppose we are." Anna responded to his query, but her heart wasn't in it.

Only Lute seemed to take any real notice of the doctor. He followed the man around the room, looking over his shoulder as they shifted from one monitor to the next. The doctor didn't notice; he and the nurse were too busy checking items off their to-do list.

"Seems like everything's in order. Right now, he's on Dilantin and Keppra. Had seizures pre-op, and his legs started twitching again once or twice post so we put him on both just to reduce the risk. Please note, in a week or two, he can be taken off the Dilantin, the Keppra…probably the rest of his life if he tolerates it." Anna didn't know if she or the nurse should be taking notes, so she reached down the side of her bed to find her tote bag, pulled out a few loose sheets of paper, begged a pencil from the nurse, inched her way up a bit in the bed, and then she, too, became engaged, scribbling down whatever came out of the doctor's mouth.

The doctor didn't really care what either was doing; he was too busy. A list of the other medications being administered came next: "Nexium, metoprolol, and a high dose of acetaminophen. Change that to ibuprofen. It'll supply some muscle relaxant as we move him off the sleep inducers. If he wakes up, he'll need to use his jaw again. The protonix he'll need for a while. He had a lot of acid damage in the esophagus."

As he moved down the list of medications, he ignored the Trazodone. The man on the bed listening in wasn't sure why the doctor didn't mention it. Possibly because he wasn't exactly sure how to explain what it did. If anyone asked, he might say "sedative," this the doctor knew. The fact it was also an antidepressant and good for chronic pain made for other applications. He could address all of this, but the potential for side effects he just didn't want to talk about. The relationship of Trazodone to mind-altering psychedelics hadn't been proven yet, so both the doctor and the seemingly comatose patient wanted to ignore that conversation altogether.

"We will probably start disconnecting an hour or so before he's moved. We've got the feeding tube in so he'll—"

"Why is this?"

The doctor took a quick look over toward Lute and saw that he had followed the nurse to the far side of Arthur's bed. She was now busy checking various monitors, and to do this, she had pulled back Arthur's gown. As he spoke, Lute was pointing to one of the many incision scars on his father's torso.

"That's a scar," the doctor responded, totally missing Lute's question.

"Why here!" Lute had stopped the doctor in his tracks, and Anna quickly filled in.

"I think he wants to know what procedure left that scar."

"Oh." The doctor stared directly at Lute and continued, "Why didn't you just ask?" Then he scrolled through his hand-held computer pad to pull up the proper report. "Ahh, here we go. The patient came in with a fractured skull, including subarachnoid hemorrhaging, and underwent the craniotomy. Therefore, we couldn't give anticoagulants. Let's see, it says he had deep venous thrombosis through the popliteal and common femoral veins. Some floating thrombosis was found as well in the common femoral vein on the right side. So it seems we put in an inferior vena cava filter. It says retrievable but I doubt it will ever be removed, too risky. Does that answer your question?" The physician spoke as if lecturing and, as such, didn't care if he was understood or not. He wanted one-upmanship and thought he had obtained that position. Problem for him, he didn't know Lute, and when he finished talking, he couldn't find the boy. Fortunately, Lute's next query told him where to look.

"What does this measure?" Lute had moved to the wall behind the physician.

The doctor, not used to being interrupted, looked around to make sure the question was directed at him. "I beg your pardon?"

Almost monotone, Lute repeated, this time motioning to the EEG machine, "What does this measure?"

"Don't you see the scar on his head?" The doctor decided to take his response down to the middle-school level. "It was hit or miss with him. Head injuries usually are, but we managed to pull him through." This announcement he delivered with a big smile on his face while forgetting to mention what the probabilities of total recovery were.

"What does this measure?" Lute said, one more time pushing his right index finger out until it touched the machine in question.

"Oh, that," the doctor acknowledged, slightly put off. "That measures activity in the brain." Feeling himself in his customary role of omnipotent purveyor of information, he misread his predicament as he moved back to the EEG readout that was slowly scrolling along. "You see," he began to explain, "we have it set to measure the alpha waves. Earlier we monitored the beta and delta too, but given his condition at this point, it is only necessary to look at the alpha. The delta waves check dreaming activity, but again, given his condition…"

"What is it measuring?" Lute wanted to know, his voice almost shaking as he pointed at the display monitor. Anna tried to sit up further to see what Lute was pointing at, but the nurse was checking her pulse at the time and thus held her fast.

"I just told you we are measuring the alpha waves. Alpha waves measure basal or resting activity in the brain, and…"

"You don't understand what you are measuring."

This statement confused the poor doctor and was a bit too much of an affront to his position to be glossed over, so he dropped all pretense of the polite but superior lecturer and reverted instead to his impolite "I'm too busy to be bothered mode," which he delivered in a very, very condescending tone. "What are you getting at? I've repeated myself twice. If you don't understand what is going on here, I suggest you read…"

Lute now took the stage, and as those with advanced, advanced degrees know, when the lecturer is at the podium, it is time to sit back, shut up, and listen. "Waves travel in three dimensions. When the wave orientation of a particle, such as a photon, is measured, its entangled partner would have a correlated orientation—such as an opposite, vertical orientation—at the same instant, which implies entangled particles don't exist in a particular state until they are measured, and that, once measured, the particles communicate their state to each other at a rate faster than the speed of light that, of course, appears to violate Einstein's theory of relativity. This machine is only plotting two, what happens in the third dimension?"

While articulating his question, Lute reached up and traced the two-dimensional plots as it moved across the monitor and added, "And no gamma. How do you measure cognition?"

Caught with his proverbial pants down, and not having a memorized line of explanation handy, the doctor felt he had spent more than enough time in Arthur's room and made to leave but not before trying to reassert a modicum of authority. "Please don't touch the equipment," he muttered as he reached up to grab Lute's guilty finger.

In a fit of near panic, Anna tried to convey a message to the doctor without causing any undo alarm; the only problem was, she was too alarmed. "DON'T!" she blurted out. Anna had a pretty good idea what would happen next if the man touched Lute. She tried for all she was worth to get between the two while still prone on her bed. "Lute, look at this book. It's your father's. It's all about King Arthur and..." As she turned slightly to pull the book off the bedside table, the doctor did the wrong thing. He tried to pull Lute's finger off the monitor to which it was still pinned.

Anna's voice became lost in the three-alarm claxon that was Lute. His screaming was so intense, it drew a code blue team. Who knew when Lute would stop? The doctors who raced into the room didn't, nor did the poor nurse who was there from the beginning. Anna, too, was helpless, but lucky for them all, Lucan walked in with Jennifer in tow. Lute stopped yelling and smiled at his mother. The instigating physician was nowhere to be found when explanations were being handed out.

Chapter 10
Conversations in a Car

No one in the room cared if waves propagated in more than two dimensions. If the EEG machine had been set to watch all transmissions, it might have captured a transient gamma pulse even if only checking in two dimensions. But the machine was not set thus. The medical report at the end of the day (and signed off on) was this: No immediate change in patient McAiden's condition.

Whether noticed or not, whatever happened to Arthur before, during, or after the commotion was a step in the right direction. It may have been elicited by a feeling transmitted between fingertips. Or possibly, it was the sweet sound of the young man's voice calling out for help. It could also have been the tolerance buildup within his system to the Trazodone, but whatever the cause, the man on the bed somehow knew his son was in the room. It was a start.

Those who managed to slip out of the ICU missed the fireworks. Some were on their way to Teterboro to catch flights back to England. Others were off to Bethlehem. No overt religious connotation here, just the regional office, the US footprint so to speak. This was where Angus and Wayne were heading. Both were still based in Wales, and neither had yet visited the facility and neither really had to go; there was so much else on their plate. But it was a show of strength for the company and for all those not yet able to visit the man in the ICU.

Starting from the hospital parking lot the chauffeur had carefully negotiated a path through the busy streets of New Brunswick and then the stop and go on the congested northbound highway. When they merged onto the interstate heading west, they picked up speed, the number of accompanying vehicles slowly thinned out as well as signs of human habitation. Further west, a line of darkness kissed the horizon. All those in the car knew the rain would come, but for a few minutes, none cared as they relaxed and silently watched the rolling green countryside pass by.

A good half hour passed before the river was in sight. The sky had darkened as did the passengers' mood, and as the car passed over the Delaware, Wayne bit his lip and said, "Do we need our passports to get into Pennsylvania? I think I left mine at the hotel." The driver shook his head in the negative, and with relief, Wayne moved on to other topics.

"Why Bethlehem?" He thought he knew, but he asked anyway just to keep his mind busy.

"Price per square foot for starters: relatively speaking, it was cheap." Angus's answer was rote, and as he continued, his voice remained monotone. "Privacy too. Right?"

"Right."

"Had to keep everything secret. Not exactly off the beaten track, but provincial, know what I mean? Keeps us out of the limelight until…"

Leaping ahead, Wayne automatically finished, "Until all possible variables are nailed down and patents filed."

With the preamble out of the way, Angus moved on with a more emotional delivery, "Aye, but the VCs over here are like sharks. Any inkling of product being good, they'd smell it."

Interestingly, being found by the VCs is what they needed and feared. The company was in its infant phase, and like infants, it had difficulty sharing its toys because eventually the toys no longer belong to you. But without alternative investments, they might lose control. Both passengers ruminated on this dialectic giving the driver no one to listen too.

Finally admitting the real problem, Wayne delved in: "What will happen if we cannot find Perce?"

"Malcolm will win, and he'll get his hands on the company, simple as that."

"How did we get to this state?"

Wayne's query is metaphorical and, as such, difficult to answer. To help in this regard, what he was referring to needed clarification. Was "this" an adjective held before a nonexistent noun or an adverb without its adjective? It was also possible, in the grand scheme of things, he was trying to impose the perpetual mess known as humankind as in "we the people," but that referral was too American to cover the big picture, so to speak. Now, without a succinct point of reference, all three in the car moved their analyses in different directions.

The driver first rolled his thoughts around the here and now, trying to figure out what he missed. *Didn't I get them to this state? I mean, we're in Pennsylvania now, right?* Then he moved the temporal process as he navigated the vehicle up and over the many hills in Eastern PA. *Me, with a linguistics degree from Carleton and a minor in English lit, now a glorified taxi-man. What the hell, Goodrich had the same degree and she taught at Carleton. She became famous and I... How did I get into this mess of a state?*

Angus had thought the question through before trying his hand, "I blame Dubric!"

Wayne, off in his own musings, woke up. "What?"

"He never should have let Arthur stay in Cardiff."

"Why?"

"Why! Because, by staying, Arthur was undergrad and grad at the same place."

"So?" This, the driver asked before Wayne, ignoring the driver, jumped in. "So?"

Angus refused for a moment to explain the obvious to his listening audience, "And Dubric was his mentor."

Again, both driver and Wayne responded alike, "So!"

Not quite finished with his train of thought Angus barreled along, "Under the tutelage of Dubric or not, it is against most known rules of etiquette."

"What rules?" Was chorused back at him.

"To stay put for post-graduate endeavors at the same place you do undergrad. You don't do this."

"Why?" the accompanying duet hit their cue.

"Why!" Angus didn't hold back. "Arthur STAYED, right? BUT if he didn't, we wouldn't be where we are now! That's why."

"Huh," mumbled the driver.

"Hindsight," Wayne added.

The car moved off the interstate and began winding its way up along the eastern edge of a hill, angling its way to the top. The dark clouds were now hanging just overhead seemingly nesting on the hilltop. For a moment, a very brief moment, there was calm inside the car. What came next could have echoed through the lower vales if the windows had been open.

"It's f'-in hindsight but I'm tryin'. I'm tryin' to get all the damn ducks in a row, and this is the best I can come up with. The company hasn't patented anything yet, except for the flu shit, right? The plan was to keep it all quiet. We tried. I mean the research group, aye. Nothin's been published anywhere. Has it? Why the hell did Arthur give that damn lecture? Now what? Now what? NOW WHAT?"

The car, mid-ascent had steam venting out its windows. Point of origin being the space between Angus's ears. The volcanic eruption paused and when it resumed the decibel level was more tolerable. "Sorry, not mad at ya', just, ya' know." Both the driver and Wayne kept their fists clenched. Angus continued, "I'm workin' on this little um, problem of mine. Really, I am."

He took a deep breath, exhaled, and continued in a more civil tone, "Can we really pack up and take our research with us? If so, we'll have to start over again from scratch. But then again, if we lose the IP will we ever get new investors? And…um…what about, oh hell, you know, all that other crap?"

Relaxing just a bit, Wayne tried to move the conversation in a different direction. "Remember that party where he got so drunk, he…" It was "the party" Wayne was referring to, and as the two men in the back seat rehashed memories, the driver multitasked. He listened in while keeping their destination in focus.

It was a celebration to say the least. Dubric was moving to the emeritus state of being and so had endorsed his prized student to fill his shoes. The young Arthur was only too happy to oblige, and when the votes were cast in his favor, he moved up to the tenure track position. A happy celebration ensued, complete with free alcohol for all and toasts all around. Therein lay the rub. One of the senior faculty members, as a way to complement one and all in his intellectual stratum, spoke of hardcore scientists as nerds being driven, no matter which particular branch they swung from, to satisfy their lustful craving to find the holy grail. In other words, they sought fame whether for fame alone or, possibly, to save the world from pollution, or global warming or eternal damnation. Whatever. Arthur was two sheets to the wind (squared) at that moment and his answer, which became his axiom whenever he found himself in that same state of inebriation, was blurted out for all to hear, "I don't need to search for no bloody *Graal*. I already know where it is!"

"Good thing he got his drinkin' under control."

"Cheers" was all Wayne could add.

"Percy was already Arthur's student when the company was started."

"Student, yes, but Arthur always said it was Percy's idea."

"Dubric helped too."

"Right, don't forget Dubric. Has anyone gotten in touch with him yet?"

"Can't find him. Not sure if he's off with the Botanical Gardens crew looking for new shit or trying to set up another homeless shelter."

"The man stays busy. And Perce?"

"Not sure where he is either. Sometimes he tags along with Dubric on those wildflower hunting trips."

Wayne tilted his head to one side, trying to peer through the darkening cloud cover, took a deep breath, and then responded, "Don't think he helps much on those. He tends to internalize searches, more likely searching for the meaning of life in general, not narrowing the search on any specific species. Perhaps being in the wild helps him get to the heart of things."

The linguistics major (English lit minor) in the front seat couldn't hold back. "Are you paraphrasing Conrad by any chance?"

"Which Conrad?" Angus's interest was piqued.

"He was the guy who wrote *Heart of…*"

Before the driver could finish his response Angus interrupted. "Was he Welsh?"

"No, Polish."

"Nah, never heard of him."

"But he lived in England when he…"

Wayne wasn't bothering with the literary side bar between Angus and the driver, the need to find Percy was front and center. For reasons he could not quite grasp, it was Percival who had been assigned voting rights to Arthur's shares in the company, if needed.

When the car finally stopped, it was just a few feet in front of the Technology Incubator. Both passengers quietly extracted themselves, but instead of heading inside, they walked to a nearby overlook. The miles of abandoned steel mills hugging the river below were, like everything else, blanketed by the engulfing cloud. They could not see the large sections of buildings rusting into obscurity or the small enclaves here and there, which had been claimed by various entities, slowly bringing the riverbank back to life. From where they stood, they could only detect a few spires of the university buildings dotting the hillside below while quietly staring out into silent nothingness. When either of the two exhaled, a condensed vapor became visible for a moment before it drifted off to join the fog enveloping them.

"Do you think Arthur will make it?"

"We can only hope and pray for his return."

With nothing else to say, they turned their heads to face north. What happened next was something neither liked to do in public and luckily a damp drizzle had begun helping to camouflage the tears streaming down their cheeks.

Chapter 11
Dudley-do-right

Now I am stuck. Selwood didn't specify. Write "anything that was close to events in my current situation" is what she asked me to do. It's like telling an artist to just paint anything they want, and what exactly is my current situation? How does one silo that concept? Okay, needing a place to start, why not the accident? Done with that. Now what? Everything after that point of reference is linked, oui? So where does the current situation end? Or perhaps I should ask, in this timeline, when did I awaken? I blame Selwood for this problem.

All this time, I have felt as if I am on a platform trying to catch a train. Unfortunately, I am not sure which one. There is a crush of people all around, all talking at once, all bumping elbows, hustling to and fro while all I can do is stand motionless and watch. Snippets I catch but too few. I am unable to build upon my current platform to properly reconstruct the events I have seen. I have been searching for words with enough meaning to allow for any conveyance of thought. They are few and far between. Sometimes I wish I could just turn around and go back to my safe space. When perched up high, I could analyze without the physical discomfort now imbuing my every waking hour. Solitude is what I need, and painkillers and my muse. Once again, in my hour of need, she is naught to be found. Once again, as I write, I will dream of Guinevere and wish she was by my side.

I don't believe I ever met the man, this *inspecteur* from Canada, formally. You will see that we did, in fact, run into each other but not until much later. So why am I introducing him here? I am not sure. But I do know in the overall sequence of related events, this was his first appearance on stage. How do I know what he and the FBI agent said? This I cannot explain, but when I began to jot it down on paper, the story just flowed.

⤖◆⤐

> Never anger your boss, you might get sent to Jersey.
> (Post-scriptum personnalisé du rapport de cas
> Inspecteur Gervais, *Sûreté du Québec*)

Catholics do not have a monopoly on guilt; neither do Canadians, but both are good at directing it their way. Some, like Christian Gervais, are both. Inspecteur Gervais was not Dudley-do-right; he was a member of *la Sûreté du Québec,* and he was a good Catholic who had practiced this art form all of his life and now, now standing outside the office of the FBI's Special Agent MacLean, he felt guilty, very guilty. The last place he wanted to be was where he now stood. He feared taking this posting would require explanations which, like confessions, were not always easy. He had seriously thought about getting down on his knees and begging his superior not to send him. But he didn't; he got on the plane as ordered. Hence, he was not in a good mood.

Not so long ago, Inspecteur Gervais had confessed to his *capitaine* one of his little dalliances with rules and in so doing found common ground with his erstwhile antagonist. But while the confession had helped forge a working relationship with his boss, his actions had instigated quite a bit of blood-letting both within *la Sûreté* and the Mayor's office. What had he done to cause such a stir? Simple, he had revealed who was leaking information to the press. This is what he had confessed. Why had this caused such a problem? Most everyone, both in *la Sûreté* and the Mayor's office, had been leaking confidential information to the press. Now a lot of people in Montréal were mad at him. Both he and his captain knew this, and so when the opportunity arose, Capitaine Dionne was quick to shuffle him out of town.

"The FBI needs a little help with a suspect of theirs and I need to keep you out of sight for a few days. Pack for a week, or two, just in case, okay?" Capitaine Dionne didn't bother telling his subordinate the mayor himself had suggested it.

What Christian knew about Samir Mounir was another reason he had been selected to go. It was also the reason why he hesitated before knocking on MacLean's door. He and Mounir had spent time together at *la Sûreté*; this was a fact. The Moroccan had been an *ad hoc* member of his Special Operations unit on one case and one case only. Of course, it was the results of that case that had Christian wondering if he would be damned for life. Why the Moroccan had fled the country Christian had no clue, only a few ideas; ideas he pieced together after the fact. Now he stood in front of MacLean's office seemingly in a stupor, trying desperately to find a formula to make his appointment more palatable. All the while a security camera hidden high up in the corner of the hall watched.

Special Agent MacLean had been alerted as soon as the Canadian had checked in, and knowing it was a long walk up to his office, he had plenty of time to finish up a few last-minute items while, courtesy of his computer's tie-in with the security system, out of the corner of his eye, he followed the Canadian's progress. When Inspector Gervais took a wrong turn coming off the elevator, MacLean smiled, but only for a moment then returned to the task at hand. He took one more look at the two identical dossiers on his desk before placing them on the small table in the corner of his office. With the table, his desk, and a credenza the room was rather cozy, so cozy, in fact, breathing became difficult when two humans occupied the space at the same time.

Nothing bothered the FBI agent as much as being middle management. He could do nothing on his own but nod his head and follow instructions. The dossiers he placed on the table contained information he had been allowed to share. Standard operating procedure they called it. His direct supervisor even called him out on this, "Unless the situation becomes necessary," he was told, "keep all the info on photos, and the Sheik himself, a secret."

When he was satisfied no omissions or additions had been made, he managed the two steps needed to return to his desk and took one last look at the dossier he was instructed not to share. *I hate this shit*, he reminded himself. *We bring in international help, and we want to give him no more than what we share with the local police.*

When Inspector Gervais hit the home stretch, he slowed down and started reading name tags on the wall. Watching on the monitor as the visitor approached MacLean moved to his side of the office door to await the knock. After a half minute or so of standing and staring at the back of his door, he began to wonder if there was a problem. The international duet stood thus, just feet apart, one man wondering at the vagaries of fate, the other wondering why no one was knocking. After what was, to MacLean, a polite passage of time he returned to his desk and checked his monitor. *I wonder if he overshot.*

Inspector Gervais had not overshot but what was going through the man's head as he stood in the hall MacLean could only guess. When the knock finally came, it seemed to awaken the FBI agent.

Things went a little better after that. "More normal" is how MacLean related the interview to his wife. "We exchanged cards, talked about his trip, accommodations, the weather, you know, the usual crap."

When the retired MacLean first found out an agent from Montréal was being assigned to her husband's crew as a liaison, she had gotten excited. "We'll be speaking French again, oui?" Then, with a smile, she began to give her husband a crash course in French pleasantries.

"They like it so much when we make an effort. Of course, if he's from Québec, it's not really French now, is it?"

"What makes you think he speaks French or any variation thereof?" Mike was trying to dissuade his wife from her self-appointed mission because, while Slavic tones came surprisingly natural to him, he had a much harder time wrapping his brain around those with a Latin base.

Donna ignored her husband as she took command of the room, "Sit still while we conjugate some verbs."

During the evening debrief, Donna's mind centered on the issue of language, as in, "Did you use any of the French I taught you?"

"He was taller than me and thin. He had nice manners, was very polite."

"And?" his wife persisted.

"I tried…once. He politely told me to stick with English."

"Oh." Donna was slightly let down.

"But like I said, he was very polite about it, and of course, his English is far better than mine. But then, isn't everyone's?"

The Canadian was not really taller than the American, but he was thinner. Thus, from a distance, he would appear so. Up close in the confines of MacLean's office, one very important attribute was noticed: They were both big men. The cramped expressions on their faces gave that away. What was more tell-tale than his height and weight was Gervais's thin, hawklike nose and penetrating eyes, which gave his whole expression an air of alertness. The high forehead with creases near the hair line added a semblance one usually found on those with a penchant for decision-making.

The two professionals quickly moved beyond pleasantries. They sat at the small table fingering through the file folders MacLean had placed there. A minute later, Inspector Gervais reciprocated the gift by pulling a dossier out of his briefcase and pushing it across to his host.

MacLean found interesting passages within and began his inquisition, "So, Inspector, it says here this Mounir fellow, first name Samir, reported to you."

"Non. That is not what it says. He did work for *la Sûreté*, but he did not work directly with Special Investigations."

Evasion wasn't what the FBI agent was expecting right out of the box, and in his frustration, he overlooked the possibility it was clarification the Inspector was striving for.

"It says right here, his last known assignment," MacLean read, "Special Operations... Lead investigator Christian Gervais, that's you right? Multiple murders under investigation."

He skipped a few lines until he found what he was looking for. "On the night of...blah, blah, blah... A surveillance team consisting of François Bélanger." The names of the two women with Inspector Bélanger were beyond his ability to pronounce so he muddled through on a first-name basis, "Sophie and Julie caught up with him at...no, no. Here it is... Bélanger was at the St. Joseph's Observatory."

"Oratory."

"Excuse me?"

"Oratory. Not observatory."

Later that evening, when he was setting the table for dinner, Mike gave his wife a sentence-by-sentence replay. That wasn't hard to do, he had recorded the whole conversation. As he relayed the information, he eased out a few of his impressions. "Everyone's so territorial."

"A stickler for details," Donna chimed in. "But really, dear, you should have known that." She handed Mike more dishes and continued her thought, "If you had tried a little harder with the French, he might have been a little more forgiving."

MacLean shrugged off his wife's critique in the same casual way he did during his morning session with the inspector. "Oh yes, excuse me," he exhaled, gracefully acknowledging Christian's corrections, then reinserted himself into the missive exactly where he had left off, "joined at the, um, oratory by this fellow whose name is Samir Mounir."

Then he set his notes down and looked across the table at the Inspector. "Now, I know there may be somewhat of a language issue here, but it does seem to me that Mr. Mounir was working surveillance for Special Operations, and let me get this right, for a case you were not only involved with but in charge of. There aren't two Inspector Gervais in your department now, are there?"

Before answering, Christian stole a quick glance at his wristwatch. *Fifteen minutes, that's all, fifteen minutes, and I'm already into my first revelation.* He tried to make it short and sweet. "There are many Gervaises in Canada, mais, de rien. I was trying, though obviously unsuccessful, to be clear with you, to avoid potential problems. It would not do to start this way. Surveillance is an independent unit in *la Sûreté*, which assigns people upon request. M. Mounir worked surveillance, not Special Ops. Further, while I knew who he was, I did not know him personally. I don't believe anyone did. What we do know of M. Mounir is not much and we've shared that information with Interpol and now, with you." For emphasis, Christian tapped the file folder he had passed over.

"Yes, yes, let me see. We know he came to Canada on a student visa and…" MacLean began paraphrasing as he ran his middle finger down the page.

"Pardonez-moi," Inspector Gervais interrupted. He was running his finger down his copy of the same page. "He was a post-doctoral fellow. The visas are similar but not identical."

"So he has a PhD? Does this make him some sort of smart guy?"

"I presume," Christian responded as a fleeting reminiscence of Samir at St. Joseph's meandered about in his head. "But I'm not sure."

"Let's see, umm, he went to work at…" Having trouble again with pronunciation, he faltered, and as before, the Canadian came to his rescue.

"L'Institute Armand-Frappier, which is in Laval."

MacLean looked up from his sheet and smiled. Returning to his list, he continued, "Left the institute and took a job at BioPharma, which is also in Lay-val Quebec. That is some sort of drug company, right?" Before

Christian could answer, he was hit with another pressing question, "Say, Inspector, where exactly is Lay-val?"

Christian corrected MacLean's pronunciation then gave him a quick geography lesson before leaning back in his chair to better absorb the incoming wave.

"Then this Samir guy abruptly disappears from sight, right under your nose." MacLean was barreling along now, trying to quickly dump the small amount of information he was officially allowed to share. "His fingerprints are found here in Jersey. We matched them via Interpol. Then you were sent down to give us a hand, and well that's the end of my list. Pity that's all we have to go on." MacLean had nothing left to tell, so he invited the Canadian to contribute. "Now, do you have any information to add, Inspector?"

"Non." Christian called his bluff and, in so doing, raised him.

The two men sat for a minute with MacLean trying to figure out what to do. If information wasn't to be shared, how much help could Inspector Gervais be? MacLean did need feet on the ground, a whole team would have helped. This is what had been promised. A team of Canadians wasn't his first choice, but if they had familiarity with the person of interest, it was better than no help. Problem was, no Mountie arrived, only a provincial.

It was Christian who moved first. Solving puzzles seemed to elevate his endorphins and he had been feeling more than a bit parched wading through office politics. He never admitted as much to anyone, though perhaps his boss had an inkling of his need. Christian was, like Donna and Mike, addicted to the chase. Now the scent was in the air. He knew the FBI man either had more information but was not sharing, or he didn't even know what he had. This happens when one's calculus is rusty or perhaps, the man across the table was not good at math to begin with.

"I know why I am here." Christian almost whispered this. "People in Montréal are, how you would say…not happy with me." He smiled. A big smile and all MacLean could do was smile back. Then he laid it on. "But, Agent MacLean, I need to know why you really need a member of *la Sûreté*. I feel your organization is working on a bit more than an illegal alien in a traffic accident." That was obvious. So, too, became Gervais's interrogation talent. MacLean was soon telling him much more than he had been instructed to do.

"Your former employee was trailing a man who is now lying near death. It might be Mounir's bad driving that put the man in the hospital. We only know of the accident because we were trailing him, Mounir, not the accident victim. So hold on a minute…I've got a bit more I wasn't supposed to share with you."

MacLean pulled one pic after another out of a second folder while Gervais was doing the same on his side of the table. Just like that, two sets of photos emerged, all having originated in a camera being held at one point in time by Samir Mounir.

That evening, MacLean told his wife his version of how the exchange of classified information came about and how both he and Inspector Gervais broke a few rules. "It appears as if this Mounir guy had been takin' photos north of the border too. Christian"—they seemed to now be on a first-name basis—"had pictures of several different locations in Montreal where explosive devices could wreak a lot of damage."

Of all the photos they discussed, the most interesting was also one of the more recent: "This is one we found in the back seat of Mounir's damaged car. If you look closely, the signage in this photo tells us all we need to know. The subject matter clearly visible in the photo is a high-level biocontainment research facility in Newark, part of the university. I'm told they keep some really nasty stuff in there."

Chapter 12
Our Lady of the Lake

Oh my. Oh my. Oh, f'-in my! I don't know where any of this came from. But here it is. Please don't show any of this to my wife. Please.

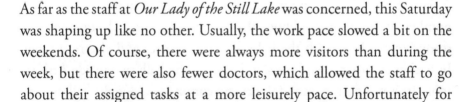

As far as the staff at *Our Lady of the Still Lake* was concerned, this Saturday was shaping up like no other. Usually, the work pace slowed a bit on the weekends. Of course, there were always more visitors than during the week, but there were also fewer doctors, which allowed the staff to go about their assigned tasks at a more leisurely pace. Unfortunately for those manning the controls this day, the influx of visitors would have made a major league sports complex turn green with envy.

Starting early in the morning, a steady stream of old acquaintances, coworkers, neighbors, and relatives stopped by to pay their respects. But there were more, lots more, who somehow had come to know this man without his immediate family having an inkling of who they were. The sheer number of people asking directions to his room took everyone by surprise.

Arthur appreciated the turn out for various reasons. One being the more people traipsing through his room meant the longer the respite from the constant barrage of prodding needles, thermometers, and other biometric devices shoved into most of his veins and all of his orifices. He was, at that moment, enjoying the quiet brought on by the influx of visitors. Another reason he delighted in the number of people streaming through was obvious, he had made a lot of friends over the years. It was good to see so many familiar faces slowly pass through some section of his static field of vision.

Unfortunately, the nurses weren't trained in crowd control. Neither was the short-staffed building detail. The grounds crew wouldn't have been of much help either, but they didn't work the weekends anyway. One of the young men who ran trays up from the kitchen remembered seeing large reels of electrical tape, "And some sawhorses somewhere in the basement, I think." No one cared why this boy had been in the basement in the first place, they just gave him their blessing and off he ran. A few minutes later, he returned bearing gifts. The problem now was this: No one knew what to do with them.

The number of visitors continued to increase, and when it seemed a deluge might burst upon the hospice, the local police were called in. A few officers showed up for crowd control, and though stunned at the number of people assembling, they were able to slowly organize the throng into a line (with the help of the sawhorses and electrical tape). In backward order, the procession began in the hallway outside Arthur's room (this was on the second floor) and continued along the hall, wound through double-doors and past the nurses' station, around the back hall, then down the stairs where it eventually merged with the center hallway. From here, the line continued till it reached the entrance lobby where it congealed into a not-too-quiet, but respectful, mass. This was as good as the police could manage on such short notice, and because the weather outside was threatening, they couldn't ask those clotted up in the lobby to extend out the door. Equilibrium was eventually reached as the places of those leaving were taken up by new arrivals queueing up just inside the front doors.

But things did get worse. The news teams began to arrive.

This is not what Jennifer had expected when she signed the transfer papers. She just wanted her husband out of the ICU, out of the hospital itself if there wasn't anything they could really do for him. She also wanted a quieter environment as she fumbled her way through the pros and cons of her next big decision, the one that might be, without doubt, a matter of life or death.

"We only moved him yesterday. How the hell did everyone get the message?" This was part of a discussion she had with Arthur's sister. She didn't know whether to blame an individual or whether it was just a case of social media running amuck. Either way, there was now a crowd of people standing in a line waiting for a chance to see her husband, which served to drive her anxiety level up one or two notches.

"It's like they came out of the woodwork," Jennifer whispered loud enough for all in the room to hear as she eased out with two of her friends in tow, Margaux Gorlois and Elaine Guildford. The three ladies left under the pretense of searching for tea or coffee or anything that would get them away from the crowd.

"Who are all these people?" Margaux muttered.

Under certain lighting conditions, Margaux and Jennifer might have passed for sisters. Both were derived from Welsh stock, were slender (having fine bone structure), displayed symmetrical facial features, and copious amounts of wavy hair held sway at the top. The only differences here being the coloring; Jennifer's auburn hair lay somewhere between reddish and golden brown while Margaux's drifted more toward a darker pitch. Freckles were prevalent on both, and if one counted, it would be hard to tell which had more. Elaine was totally different. Whereas Jennifer and Margaux had petite, slender figures and hair color untouched by chemical enhancements, Elaine was unnaturally blond, a bit more curvaceous and, most likely, artificially endowed.

Jennifer had made new friends when she accompanied Arthur, and his business enterprise, to the US. All, like Jennifer, had recently moved to Jersey and they all belonged to the same country club, so being strangers in a strange land, they bonded. Her friends had not been able to see her when Arthur was in the ICU but were first on her call list when he had been moved to the hospice. Apparently, they had a lot to talk about.

Talk they did, only to pause here and there to allow Jennifer time to nod a silent thank-you to those she knew standing in the line. Some worked with Arthur at the facility over in Bethlehem. Other members of the company, along with old friends, had flown in from Great Britain. But where in the world all the rest had come from, she had no idea.

She may have picked up on an expansive network of friends, or admirers, if the flowers had continued to arrive. When the news of Arthur's condition was first released, floral arrangements showed up at her Tewksbury address by the truckload. So many deliveries, in fact the butler had to ask the mail services to redirect new arrivals to local charities.

"To use as they see fit" were Lucan's words to each of the delivery services.

There was mail too, lots of it. This Lucan placed in large duffle bags hoping to give the entire stash to the intended recipient, if he ever recovered. Lucan told Jennifer what he was doing, but he placed these deliveries in the carriage house, so she had no idea of the volume.

Jennifer tried hard to smile and thank those moving in the opposite direction while Elaine and Margaux physically pushed her onward. The pushing didn't help when they closed in on the nurses' station. It was here that an elderly man holding a ruffled-up plaid fedora took a half step out of the line to grab Jennifer's attention. He bowed his head as she approached, but by the time he had raised his eyes and opened his mouth, the ladies had already passed by.

If Jennifer heard the man's salutation, she did not let on. She just kept walking, caught up in her own thoughts and the pull of her two friends.

Of the three companions, it was Elaine who had noticed the man. "Who was that old guy?" This she asked after they turned the next corner.

"Which old guy?" Margaux wanted to know. "There's a whole herd of them in the hall."

"The one with the hat." Before either could answer, they approached a flight of stairs.

On the ground level, the threesome passed through swinging doors and stopped dead in their tracks. They had run smack into another section of the elongating, serpentine line. Several heads turned, but no one spoke. Instead, those recognizing Jennifer would reach out and, as if in slow motion, touch her in some sad, sharing way. Jennifer tried to keep smiling as she walked along but it quickly became a losing effort.

I barely knew him. She was right about this, no matter how much time you live with someone, it is hard to know what is really inside their head. She acknowledged the crowd for what it was, evidence of a rich, full life. *Seems he had so much going on, besides me, his faculty position, his company, and that stinkin' bimbo!*

Much of Jennifer's sadness came from her feeling of involvement, causal involvement, that is. Her contribution to the events now playing out in front of her came down to communication or, in a sense, miscommunication. The communication issue involved Morgan Tuath, one of her newfound friends. Morgan's family line may have originated in England, like those of Jennifer, Margaux and Elaine but, where the other three were of Welsh decent Morgan was hard to place, and she grew up in Texas, deep in the heart of. How she got to Jersey and obtained membership in the same country club was never quite elucidated, but through mutual friends and her nasty tennis stroke, she had become part of Jennifer's close support club too.

When Vivienne Gwynedd (Malcolm's wife) had a chance to swing by on her visit to the States, Morgan became her best friend too. Morgan did not have a job per se. She lived off some inheritance from an uncle or, possibly, an aunt; but she wasn't sure which. It was enough to keep her solvent, but it wasn't enough to satisfy all her needs, so she partnered up from time to time with a married man, or two. This is how extra income came her way, under the pretense of gifts. The gifts helped her get the things she needed, like cars. She did like her cars. When the dating scene was between conquests, she looked for odd jobs. This is why her relationship with Vivienne had flourished. Vivienne was very accommodating in this regard. She needed "boots on the ground" to supply real-time intel.

Well, before Arthur's accident pushed their agenda into a fast-forward mode, attempts to secure a majority voting bloc was a constant theme of Team Gwynedd's breakfast time discussions. "Leodegrance is the swing vote, has been since the start. Malcolm Gwynedd cannot get to be chairman without his votes." M. Gwynedd spoke in the third person when he was upset. He also tended to play fast and loose with facts, all to better convey his points of interest. Leodegrance's holdings were no more the swing vote than half a dozen other investors. But due to an incredibly old family feud, no one in the house Gwynedd took a liking to anyone of Leodegrance lineage and whenever an opportunity arose to place a Leodegrance in a negative light, Malcolm would take it. "None of those bastards knows how to make money. They just dole it out and sit back and hope for success. Now, how the hell is Malcolm going to push McAiden out of the way if he ever stands up again?"

As her husband lamented, Mrs. Gwynedd led him on, "You will need a bit more information, inside information."

"Yes, yes, but how is Malcolm going to get this information?"

Enter Morgan Tuath. No matter how much money Vivienne was paying Morgan for any personal information she could get her hands on, what came next was simply out of the blue. This can happen when the best laid plans are superseded by chance occurrences like the possibility of infidelity and the hiring of a private dick.

Luck, of sorts, came Morgan's way when a small man from Morocco came into her life. Samir was parked near Arthur's home in Tewksbury waiting for a chance to speak with the wife, privately. He was in surveillance mode. Morgan was not. She was just visiting Jennifer.

When Morgan left the house, Samir, having no idea what Arthur's wife looked like, followed. He found the woman he was tailing seated at her country club's bar, sipping her afternoon allotment. This is when the short, slender young man approached. Mistaking him for the hired help, Morgan motioned for a refill. Samir didn't move. Before she asked a second time, he introduced himself. "I am Arshad, Arshad Siddiqui," and immediately presented his business lure. "I have seen your husband at the home of a professor, a Princeton professor."

Morgan tried her hand at putting two and two together and got it all wrong. "Which one of my ex-husbands was that?" When the problems were sorted out, she promised to pass the information along to Jennifer. She called Vivienne first, though. Together, the two women on opposite sides of the Atlantic discussed how best to proceed. Morgan was instructed to approach Jennifer. So she did, after Vivienne told her what to say of course.

Morgan, conniving in her own way, played the middleman for both the Moroccan and the Gwynedds. "Oh, you'll like him," she told Jennifer. "He's a skinny little guy with a dark complexion, very sweet. I'm sure he'll be able to deliver the goods. Oh yes, I almost forgot. He's foreign and talks with a cute little accent." She built the case up as if it was just a game, never mentioning exactly how much money the detective was asking for. This, of course, allowed her to skim a little off the top. By adding this to the amount coming her way from Vivienne, Morgan was confident a new car would soon be in her parking spot.

Morgan convinced Jennifer, and this was how the man named Arshad was hired, sight unseen. No one gave a thought to how or why he had come by the information he was disseminating. In the end, he did speak directly with Jennifer one time, by phone. "Your husband," he told her. "Will fly home tonight," he continued. This she knew, what she did not know followed, "Scheduled a meeting with the professor of history. Name is Caldwell, Élan Caldwell. M. McAiden meets with Professeur Caldwell many a time after return from his travel. I bring you pictures."

The day after she received this call was the day of the accident. No one in Jennifer's field of interest had seen or heard from the detective since.

At the time of the call, Jennifer had only one question. "Professor Caldwell?"

"Oui, c'est ça. Professeur Élan Caldwell, History…Princeton."

She ignored the man's accent and mingled language word usage; she was too busy fuming as she extrapolated her own conclusions and tried to pat down the hairs on the back of her neck. *A history teacher, he's fucking a fuckin' history teacher! I'll kill him.*

Now, as she walked the halls of the hospice, Jennifer thought about killing her husband. This time, though, it was not to alleviate her suffering but rather to lessen his. She blamed herself for everything. She didn't know who had rammed into Arthur's car, but she was starting to put the pieces together. Jennifer had no clue the man she had hoped would disappear had, basically, already done just that.

Chapter 13
Horns of a Dilemma

The Gala was moving along nicely, then that woman
showed up. So much for dress codes. She looked as if
she had just got off the stage at La Moulin Rouge. No
one could stop staring. Makes for good press though.

—Society Page Editor, *The Star Ledger*

Three women paused for a moment, trying to figure out how to open
the sliding doors. What lay beyond was more of a resting place for old
vending machines than a coffee shop. Once they managed the doors, all
three ambled across the floor to the far side of the room. Here, beyond
another set of doors was a small, covered porch. Beyond that, a gray,
dreary sky descending onto the weed strewn garden abutting the porch.
Further on, the hospice lawn sloped down and away with portions of a
walking path crisscrossing it. If any one of the three stood upon their
toes, they might have been able to see a small man-made pond. None of

them bothered to do this and so missed what the hospice advertised as a lake.

"Our Lady of the Still Lake" was the official, though somewhat ambiguous, name of the hospice. The marketing department had come up with it, hoping to make everything on the grounds (and in the building) evoke images of peace and tranquility. Promoting serenity, it was believed, was the salve that somehow helped the transition for those who would soon be moving on. The problem for the grounds-crew was this: There was no lake on the property. Rectifying the problem wasn't easy given their assigned budget. In the end, they managed to paste a small, shallow pool of water onto a section of the green lawn, threw in a few koi and a sprinkler in lieu of a fountain, *et voila*, the marketing department could now justify the naming.

Vending machines lined the entire interior wall of the room. None dispensed tea, only coffee, ersatz coffee. Others were home to a host of calorie-filled sweets or salty chips. The women settled for coffee, and by the time each had cup in hand, thick black clouds were rapidly moving in so low they seemed to touch the nearby trees. The swaying branches made it easy to see how hard the wind was blowing and this caused each, in their own way, to be thankful they were inside looking out.

As a group, they found a table clean enough to almost pass for sanitary and then Elaine's phone rang. "Vivienne wants to know why you told everyone." Elaine paused, listened for a moment then held the phone away from her ear before passing along the rest of the query, "If you didn't want them to come."

"I didn't tell anyone," Jennifer responded after they each had wiggled onto a chair. The women stirred their coffees in silence; and Vivienne, too, for a moment stopped talking. Each was lost in thought. Jennifer was the first to speak, "It's all my fault, isn't it?"

Margaux tried to move Jennifer off her topic of choice. "A lot of people up there."

"I didn't know he had so many friends," Jennifer whispered back, more to herself than to the others.

"And with this weather," Margaux added. To accentuate her meteorological assessment a flash of lightning streaked across the darkened sky. In short succession, it was followed by a massive thunderclap.

Everyone flinched and then Elaine spoke for all of them, "Gawd, I hate it when it does that. Poor Morgan, she's stuck in this." Jennifer wasn't listening; she had become busy counting the seconds between each lightning flash and the concomitant booming of thunder. The table went silent again but only until Elaine became a connecting link for two incoming calls. "Morgan's texting. Says she'll be here in a few."

They didn't have to wait long before Morgan made her entrance, and without doubt, It was dramatic, or as dramatic as an entrance can be in the coffee oasis of an elder hospice. Strutting like a choreographed supermodel, Morgan came to a stop beside the table, and as if on cue, the heavens opened. Rain covered the windowpanes to a point where it was impossible to see five feet beyond. Yet as the deluge began those around the table didn't notice, Morgan had just thrown back her dark, ankle-length trench coat revealing an outfit which, in turn, revealed quite a bit of Morgan.

Three women sat with mouths agape for several seconds before Margaux was able to voice what each thought. "Morgan dear, this is a hospice. Why in the world are you wearing a bustier here? And I must say, that does look uncomfortably hard."

"It's not a bustier, it's a breastplate!"

Bustier or breastplate didn't really answer the question, so Margaux pushed on. "Okay, it's a breastplate, but what are you—"

Morgan interrupted the flow with a question of her own. "Do you like it? I just had to show ya'll. I'm fixin' to wear this little ol' thang to the charity ball tonight."

Jennifer gave the outfit a quick once-over and couldn't help but notice the large crystals protruding from each pinnacle of sculpted breast, not to mention Morgan's own barely covered features. "Are those real?"

Taken aback by the bluntness of the question, and not quite sure which feature she was being asked to authenticate, Morgan did her best. "Yes, of course they're real," she responded, lying to either query.

"And look, it comes with a chain that I attach right here." She said this, indicating a small loop around the navel. "He'll be able to hold onto it like a leash and lead me around all night, and girls, I do mean *all* night. Isn't this the…"

Margaux didn't mince words. "How clever, you little harlot. That socialite reporter from the *Star Ledger* will be there and tomorrow you will be the talk of three states."

Morgan was clever when it came to attention getting and yes, she had the looks, scoring high on the fashion model runway scale, but if anyone asked her if she ever thought about pursuing this route to personal fortune, she demurred, "I don't want to be just eye candy." With that lie out of the way there was another, overarching, reason why she had not pursued this career path. It involved work. She managed well enough on her own career path. Being eye candy helped a great deal in this line of work too, and yes, she did appear on the front page of the society section the very next day.

Morgan had stolen the spotlight, and the mood around the table seemed about to lighten up until one more flash of lightning brought them back to the business at hand.

"What the hell am I going to do?" Jennifer had been asking herself this, with tears, quite a lot recently. "Of all the stupid, stupid stunts, hiring someone to follow him!" The guilt she felt for hiring the private dick was real, but it wasn't really her current dilemma. To pull or not to pull was. Ever since the attending physician told her Arthur was like a vegetable, being the one legally charged with deciding life and death caused her to internalize to a point where catatonia was on the horizon.

Morgan responded to the guilt made public. "I can't get in touch with the guy"—meaning, the private dick—"tried calling the number he left to ask if he had the pics. Got no response. I have no idea where the hell he is!"

There was a mist settling around Jennifer, making it difficult for her to grab hold of a stabilizing influence. The private detective she had never met appeared with tidings she interpreted as infidelity. "If he ever wakes up I'll throttle him," Jennifer spat this out along with her latest sip of coffee.

Those around the table added their take on infidelity and marriage until Elaine changed the subject, asking what was, for varying reasons, on everyone's mind. "Do you think he will wake up?"

The room was silent for almost a minute. Then after a long-distance prod from Vivienne, Morgan jumped in. "What will happen to the company? I mean, now that your husband is not able to run it? Do you think any of those others are up to the task?"

"If he doesn't wake up what happens to his share of the company?" Vivienne chimed, taking the direct approach. "Does it go to you? Will you become the major shareholder?"

What came next surprised everyone, most of all Vivienne.

"Some shares will come to me and a stipend of sorts but not enough to really count in any fashion. Most of his ownership goes to whomever is marked to succeed him."

Across the ocean, Vivienne bit her lip, tried to calm herself down, counted to ten and then asked, "And who might that be, my dear?"

"That would be his nephew, Percy."

————◦◦◦◦————

His first day at the hospice hadn't been a viewing per se, but this was the common descriptor used by those who stood in line. Each had waited patiently as individuals, or in groups, for their turn to enter his room. Once inside, all they could really do was stare at the man on the bed. Tears were shed, of course, and encouragements whispered or, like the man holding the fedora, snippets of Chaucer were recited, as they passed.

At some point in the late afternoon, Jennifer returned sans friends. Soon after that, the house staff began encouraging those still in line to return on the morrow as visiting hours were nearing an end. Lucan came to help herd all family members into waiting limos; and for the first time since being airlifted into the ICU, Arthur was, literally, alone.

Chapter 14
The Local

Since the early morning rescue in the wilds of Jersey, the irritable one had blamed Samir for every ill known to man. Samir concluded the Sheik did not like him and his attempt to get on the man's good side only strained the relationship, such as it was, and just when he thought it couldn't get any worse, it did. Someone in the compound told the irritable one it was Samir who broke the television minutes before the big football match between Saudi Arabia and Malaysia was to air.

Not long after, Samir had his marching orders. He was headed back to Montréal. In fact, as visitors first began to arrive at the hospice to pay homage to Arthur, Samir was standing in New York's Penn Station. He was traveling alone, and he wasn't Samir anymore. Years ago, when he was first recruited, his handlers had mentioned, in passing, how, in future, he might, just might, need to make some changes. The changes came complete with a new name, work history included, and forged documents to match. What he had pulled off on his own to get a detective posting in Jersey was amateur in comparison.

"Samir is no longer Samir. He is Hicham." The Sheik had basically declared this.

There were so many questions Samir wanted to ask, most centered on or around the word "why," but the Uber-Sheik had made it quite clear he would tolerate no more of Samir (or Hicham). From that moment onward, those standing nearby knew him only as Hicham Marjoun El Maroc. "As if anyone would believe I was from the southern tribes" was Samir's personal take on the developing situation. All he could do now was stand on the platform perfectly still and accept his instructions without uttering a word. Then with dread as his only companion he boarded the train, found a seat, and made himself as comfortable as anyone in his situation could all the while wondering if Hicham would ever again be allowed to visit Samir's mother. Having no answer to that, he began counting halfway toward infinity the bundles of trash strewn about the tracks as the train wound its way through the Manhattan tunnel system. The Moroccan couldn't help but wonder how Americans landed a man on the moon. *It must have been staged. Trains are so much cleaner in France*, he paused for a moment before adding, *Et la pièce de résistance, they are faster too*. Then he wondered why, with all the things wrong with the train line, he and so many others wanted to live here.

The lament of the forlorn came next. *How did it come to this? When I was a student in France, everything looked better, at least on paper*. Together with his classmates, he had planned and schemed the days away. He was young then. He was idealistic, and he happened upon the university scene ten years after communism had gone out of vogue. *Making money, your own money, was no longer a sin*.

Other young, unemployed men of similar backgrounds (also known as college students), channeled their exuberance in many directions), some just happened to be reengineering the caliphate system. It was no longer enough to take down the imperialist societies of the west with a socialist system that redistributed wealth to a select few. Imagine instead a world where women were no longer evolving into competitors; instead, they remained barefoot and in the kitchen. In other words, the good ol' days.

"Paradise lost." He mumbled in rhythm with the train as it left Yonkers and began to accelerate. No other business models put forth by the infidels would be tolerated. Feudalism will do just fine, thank you. Jobs were to be portioned out by those in charge of assigning jobs, and individualism was a four-letter word in the caliphate of fanatics he had been lassoed into. Every action in his adult life now had him walking a tightrope. When he wasn't dreaming of himself in a position of importance in the western world's industrial complex, he imagined a more equitable distribution of that which he did not have, *if you cannot join them, overthrow them, and…redistribute their wealth*. Hicham exhaled and audibly recited the lament of the have-nots. "Where have all the good socialists gone?

While sinking deeper into the funk that was now his life, he absentmindedly watched the panoramic view of the Hudson valley open before him, a conspicuous reminder of other people's wealth. While chewing the cud, he paid no attention to those boarding or where they sat. Every single bit of spy craft he had been taught was left behind at Pen Station proper, keeping company, no doubt, with his original identity. Apparently, being mostly nonexistent until this point in time, Hicham thought himself immune from procedural protocol. When he finally surveyed the car, he ran down a list of things he should have been checking off. The cabin in which he was seated was laid out in clusters of four chairs, two facing forward and two back. No one sat near across from him or in the section on the far side of the aisle. *Nothing to be worried about…nothing.*

Two overweight middle-aged women several clusters back were incessantly conversing away for all they were worth, oblivious to everything outside their immediate verbal exchange. *Nothing.* Several young mothers traveling with their broods half a car length forward were, like him, gazing out at the old estate homes lining the riverbank. If these women were listening to anything at all it was, again, like him, the rhythmic clatter and swoosh of the train as it sped alongside the mighty Hudson.

Hicham took a second to thank Allah for portable music players with earphones as he watched a group of young heads bobbing up and down to various, individual beats.

They wouldn't hear me if I shouted.

Several old men were scattered about, some sleeping away their morning. One of these sat several rows up in a rear facing seat with his head tilting out into the aisle. A pair of crutches were also visible. These the man kept close, laying them out across his ample midsection. They too, like the man's head, protruded out into the aisle.

Why is everyone in this country so overweight?

Where any of these passengers had boarded he didn't know and didn't care. No one looked to be a threat. Feeling somewhat secure, he nestled down lower in his chair, trying, through extrapolation, to pinpoint the defining moment in his life, which culminated with him on a junk bucket heading for Poughkeepsie. To Samir, or Hicham, the answer, like the question, was more complex than it seemed. To find a workable answer, he leaned back, closed his eyes, and tried to take inventory.

Early childhood, to the best of his recollection, was carefree. He was never lacking. His family lived in Al Khémissat, a small town to the west of Meknes and a bit to the east of Rabat. His home was a compound with a central building where he lived with his father, mother, and five siblings. Two smaller wings were perpendicular to the central core of the house. In these both sets of grandparents, and some less well-off uncles, lived. On the odd weekend when his parents weren't working the olive trees, they traveled, usually to the beach. Samir liked the family trips, but if it was solely up to him, he would have preferred to be left to run free with his friends in the nearby fields. He had sustenance and materials to transform into whatever play toy he needed on any given day. Life was easy.

Samir wasn't interested in pan-Arab nationalism or any nationalism for that matter. He and his playmates were just pretending, envisioning themselves to be warriors from the past, riding, slashing their enemies with the sword of righteousness. They didn't realize the historic characters they were emulating on any given day had sat on opposite sides of the political (or religious) spectrum of earlier times. In their imagination, the characters were just wild horsemen slaughtering any foe who stood in their path. Samir and his friends didn't distinguish titles such as "ruler of the faithful" from anything more secular like "Genghis Khan." Basically, they thought nothing of it. Unfortunately, as they grew older, several of the boys continued to miss the nuance of this distinction. A supreme ruler was a supreme ruler whether military, religious, secular, or in the case of Ali, a neighborhood bully.

They called Ali "the boy who walks strange." It only took one look to know why, he wobbled a bit, and he couldn't run fast; but if he caught you, watch out, you were as good as dead, or worse, he was apt to humiliate you.

As Samir and his friends entered their early teen years, they adventured away from the well-tended olive groves. The foothills to the south became their new stomping grounds where the vales opened suddenly in undulating fields. It was these rifts that drew their attention for here, tucked away and hidden from view of those down slope, was the real agricultural heartland of the region. This was where cannabis was grown. Samir's mother would harangue his father mercilessly about this side of the family business, but at the end of the day, she did know where their buttered *khobz* came from—though she didn't accept the status quo without proving one overriding house rule.

"I will not have that in the house. Our children will grow up to be doctors and lawyers and take care of me in my old age while you rot away in prison. You had better say your prayers, religiously, if you hope to be saved. You know what the Iman says about these sins."

Samir would be at university before he caught on to what the farmers, his father included, meant by the phrase "olives for show, cannabis for dough." The production of hashish was the money industry in their part of the country. No amount of government rules, regulations, or initiatives was going to change this. Once again, the good ol' days came to mind as the man now known as Hicham tossed and turned in his seat.

The political upheaval when Morocco was struggling to regain its independence from France now entered the fray. It was over well before Samir was born, and he only really learned of its ramifications when once, just once, he tagged along with his father to the village bazaar. This is where old men, his father included, sat around a communal hookah, smoking whatever was burning and opinionating *ad nauseam*.

Those sitting thus waited for the oldest to exhale and begin. Usually, his opening remarks centered on the community at large by pointing to those sitting around the hookah with his free hand, and it's (their) disgust for the status quo in a variety of ways.

"A constitutional monarchy," his father would add, "is all we ended up with and thirty years of a *de facto* police state." Continuing, he berated both the Europeans and Americans. "Finally, those sons of donkeys forced some changes, but it took too damn long."

Everyone sitting would spit, make faces, scratch themselves, or pass gas to indicate their particular feelings. This is when Samir learned how to read between the lines, whether following western- or eastern-based news reports. Apparently, the monarchy was not good for the village, constitutional or otherwise.

"Diplomats," one of those in the group spouted out, "talk while people die. And now, now that we have begun to see change, what happens?"

"I'll tell you what will happen," another chimed in, not realizing exactly how prophetic it would be. "These mullahs will come in, and it will be nothing but more trouble."

Several exhaled in unison before offering a different opinion, "If the mullahs come to power our daughters will be safe at home."

"But…" a voice to the left of his father cut in, "if the mullahs come to power, they will not let us sell hashish."

"Yes, they will, if we sell to the infidels."

"But they are bombing Christians and Jews, driving them out of the country. If there are no infidels left, to whom am I going to sell my crop?" After beating this goat for a while longer, they switched topics. This was also about when Samir figured out what was burning in the hookah.

Chapter 15
An Interrogation
Waiting to Happen

Special Agent MacLean's team now consisted of three people, Inspector Gervais, on loan from *la Sûreté*; a former agent brought back as a consultant (his wife); and himself. They knew where Samir had been hiding, a mosque in Manhattan's lower west side. This was out of bounds for the NJ crew. The top players in the NY office had everything under control, complete with very sophisticated listening devices. The tasks assigned to team MacLean were simple, follow up on leads from the accident and twiddle thumbs. If the Moroccan or any others holed up in NYC slipped back over the river into Jersey, they might be reassigned to surveillance, depending on available head count in the NY office of course. Basically, they were the support group for the A team.

There was one problem with the A team. Poor management of all three paradigms of successful business operations, personnel, time, and budget. When their top-notch on-site surveillance team were finally able to translate some trash talk amongst lower echelon members of the Sheik's congregation, they learned Samir would be heading north, in the morning, on the Adirondack. With no one in the city available to cover Samir's out of city jaunt, the case mangers once again had to call the MacLean house, and like before, the occupants were sleeping. This time, though, they asked to speak with the consultant.

"Apparently, French-speaking women are in demand." Mike tried to deadpan. Dry or wet, Donna ignored his assessment of the situation. She was too busy surveying a map and train schedule, trying to calculate time and distance.

With the Adirondack leaving Penn Station early in the morning, no matter how fast she drove, it was unlikely she could reach it in time, too much rush-hour traffic. In fact, it was unlikely she would catch it anywhere south of Saratoga. Even that would be tough if she didn't leave soon, very soon.

"Mike, call what's-his-name. I know he's retired, but see if you can push him for a one off. I think he still lives up near Rhinecliff, he could board there." Ten minutes later, they were kissing each other goodbye through the car window with Donna anxious to get started and Mike passing along a reminder: "Drive safe, for cryin' out loud."

This she did not hear, she had already stepped on the gas, pinged the tach, and popped the clutch. She did have a train to catch; the only problem being, the station was two hundred miles away.

When Donna left, Mike's mini task force dwindled down to two. He feared it would be less than that if he told Inspector Gervais the Moroccan was on his way to Montreal, so he didn't. Their activity for the day had already been planned out before the early morning wakeup call. He and the inspector were to meet someone at the International Center for Public Health on the campus of the University of Medicine and Dentistry, Newark campus. It had only taken MacLean ten phone calls to sort out the relationship between the Biodefense Center, the Center for Public Health, and the university. When the sorting out was done, it led him to Dr. Nancy Connell the only director of the Biodefense Center who lived, or worked, in New Jersey. "Might as well start with the local" was MacLean's rationale. Gervais would be filled in on the ride over.

"Today we're headed for UMDNJ."

"Où?"

"The med school, the biodefense center is there. It's a consortium. Lots of research space, investigators from different institutions share it."

It didn't take the men long to reach Newark. Parking was another issue. They pulled up to the entrance for a multilevel lot, servicing their destination and waited as the security officer checked his lists. This took a while. The Biodefense Center was not easy to enter, for good reason, and this is why the guard on duty had to run a mini background check, including several calls just to confirm the legality of MacLean's FBI badge. There was nothing the attendant could do with Inspector Gervais's ID, though he tried. As the minutes passed, Gervais took note of the twitching of his partner's ears possibly being caused by the pressure buildup between them. Fortunately, no gasket was blown before approval was obtained. MacLean didn't smile; he just grabbed the wheel tight and drove into the lot proper where both men were quick to note something extremely interesting. Very few cars.

The Canadian had to ask, "This is a day of work, oui?"

Building upon the unexpected lack of cars in the parking lot, it was quiet inside the main building, eerily so. Considering the size of the atrium and the time of day, they had expected a bit more foot traffic, more bustle. The only occupant they could find was a rather young-looking man with dark skin, wearing a turban. He stood behind the information kiosk, waiting to hand over their already-prepared day passes. Then he led the way to an elevator bank. Obviously nervous, after a few insincere attempts at polite conversation, he gave up.

Once off the elevator, all three turned down one corridor, walked a bit, turned again, then again. All hallways, like the atrium below, were virtually empty. In silence, they marched on. When the turbaned man finally stopped, he hustled the two quests into a small room that served as an antechamber of sorts. All three now stood silently, two of them taking in the lay of the land, shelves stacked with scientific journals, while the guide just looked at the floor.

After about two minutes of standing motionless, the turbaned one received a call. When that was over, he lifted his eyes and gave instructions: "You are to stay here. The director will be along shortly." Then he left the room with an audible sigh of relief.

The investigators waited, one patiently, the other not so, both browsing at back copies of *Antiviral Research* or *Journal of Virology* and at least ten similar publications. Both exhausted their quota of both patience and interest in scientific literature well before the inner door opened. When it did, they were summoned into the inner sanctum. Dr. Connell was not small, but when she stood beside either of the two men, an aura of petiteness descended upon her personage. She was casually dressed and only the loose yellow scarf hanging about her neck gave any semblance of fashion. Her hair was black with encroaching strands of gray and looked as if it hadn't seen a brush in a good, long time. Her smoldering eyes pulled the ensemble together.

Dr. Connell introduced herself as she, in turn, assessed the data in front of her. *Not that one, too big, but that other one, dressed so European, oh, what I wouldn't give.* She sighed, thinking of the unused treadmill in her basement. Subconsciously, she moved closer to the thicker man as they shook hands. Of the two, MacLean, was most taken in by the casual dress, considering her position at the Institute. From his experience, when the need arose, even academicians could dress up. Apparently, being interviewed by an FBI agent was not one of those times.

Later that evening, she confided most of her introductory thoughts to her husband.

"Bill, it all started so well. I kept them waiting a good long while as I finished my Sudoku, and some in my lab needed time to finish up before skedaddling. I had that FBI agent in my sights from the get-go. I was ready to give him a piece of my mind." In her data dump, she failed to mention how handsome the Canadian was and how his accent initially sent shivers of delight down her spine.

The good doctor began a reader's digest introduction to the center as she steered her supposed guests into her office and toward the only available seating, two chairs in the room barely visible beneath what had found parking space upon them, several old books, stacks of manila folders, reams of used scratch paper and what was left of yesterday's lunch. While continuing her opening remarks, she cleared space by refiling the inanimate objects from the chairs to the floor behind her desk. Then she sat and beckoned her visitors to do likewise.

The disheveled look Dr. Connell displayed on her body fit remarkably well with the organized chaos in her office. The usual objects, a desk, a computer, piles of scientific journals, a manuscript or two were here, there, and everywhere, sharing space with a garden supply catalog, all muscling for room on the shelves were pictures of family, work comrades, horses all mixed with empty candy bar wrappers hidden amongst, well, everything. Wall space was covered with posters, advertising this or that symposium, between which hung one interesting piece having the feel of a Warhol print using multiple slightly offset overlays of row upon row of inversed yellow, green, or red dots to make its point, whatever that point was.

The Canadian wasn't sure if he was proud or saddened. He understood, in a generic sense, what was conceptualized on the print. A caricature, or simply, an expanded presentation of scientific data, either way, it was open to interpretation. And yet, if he tilted his head just so and stood back a few meters he wondered if there was another image buried within, perhaps a Seurat.

As the men took inventory, Dr. Connell had begun delivering qualifiers. "The facility is very new, and well, there had been some kinks. This always happens in new construction, right? The pressure differential in the BL4 was…" She stopped for a second to pull back a few wayward strands of hair noting the FBI agent was sporting a vacant stare, which complimented his benign, vacuous smile, and for some reason, he continued nodding his head even though she had stopped talking. Inspector Gervais, on the other hand, had been listening, and when she paused, he used the time to request clarification. "Pardon, madame, qu'est que c'est le 'Bay-el-quatre.'"

The head of the bioterror institute found herself daydreaming of possibilities for a moment, *I do love those little bits of French,* before responding, "Oh, I am sorry. I hope I'm not rambling. BL4 stands for bio-containment level 4. This is the highest safety level there is. And we have one of the nicest facilities, not only in the country, but I must humbly admit, the world."

The two men smiled politely. *Neanderthals,* she thought. "This is where we work with the most dangerous pathogens known to man." The two men still didn't appear appropriately impressed, so she added, in a slightly higher, pleading pitch, "There are only a few such facilities in the country—no, in the world." Then she started naming names, using her fingers. "The oldest is at Fort Dietrich, then of course there's the CDC lab. If I haven't already told you, ours is the newest"—before circling back to list the amenities at the Northeast Biodefense Center like the proud parent she was—"the cleanest, the largest." Still her visitors didn't appear impressed, so she broke out the big guns.

"One second, gentlemen." "Gentlemen" is what she substituted for a less kind signifier. She swiveled in her chair and pulled a three-ring binder off a nearby shelf. Along its spine, the word *Demo* was written. She placed it on the desk in front of her, opened it up, and quickly flipped the pages until she found what she was looking for. Then she rotated "Demo" so the men, if they edged a bit closer, could do just that.

"Here," she said, accentuating her point by jabbing a finger onto the photo she was now viewing upside down, "is a picture of an individual suffering from Marburg. He died three days after the photo was taken. Total time from first presentation to time of death was about eight days. There are no vaccines available for this family of viruses."

"Huit jours?"

"Eight days?"

"That's about average."

"Mon dieu!"

Dr. Connell continued, her voice now very clinical and very cold. She turned the page, more patients, more ghastly sights of reality, and for emphasis, she began to explain. "The exploding red blood cells cause oxygen starvation in the organs. Roughly speaking, I'd say about, um, a 90 percent mortality rate." Now any worry she had about their attention span had gone out the window.

"Something like this would make quite a weapon." MacLean whispered this out of the side of his mouth. Gervais, with eyebrow raised, added, "In the wrong hands of course, quite the terrorist weapon."

Dr. Connell had a different take on the situation. "Yes, I suppose it could be used as such, but perhaps another would work better in this regard."

"Work better?" MacLean asked, trying hard to keep incredulity out of his voice.

Now, taking the podium like a scientist not caring one iota about the education level of those before her, she delved right in. "I think it depends on how one defines the terms *terror* and *weapon* both of which are distinctly deadly but deadly itself does not imply terror or weapon, right?" Her voice had lost all signs of friendliness and her pitch became dry, like most scientific seminars the world over. "For instance, let's start with infections like these"—she pointed generally to the pictures in the binder—"which are caused by one of the five *Filoviridae* family variants, Ebola constitutes four with Marburg being the fifth, but the *Filoviridae* are part of a larger consortium called Viral hemorrhagic fevers (VHFs). This grouping includes four distinct virus families—*Arenaviridae, Bunyaviridae, Flaviviridae, and the Filoviridae,* all of which cause severe systemic febrile illnesses. Hemorrhagic fever for short. If you have read your history, you'd know yellow fever, and from time to time, *Hanta* makes itself known here in the States. If you perchance follow WHO reports Lassa, Rift Valley, and dengue would have gotten your attention from time to time.

"While all are extremely dangerous, they are difficult to spread on a mass scale. It is spread via person to person contact and while yes it is contagious, you end up with foci of infection, which can be quarantined, if you have the resources. Of course, those infected"—here, she paused—"well, those usually die off. Basically, the disease will burn itself out. This scenario can be quite frightening, especially in the context of a terrorist act, but it would not really be felt by the country at large. So as a weapon system, it would scare some people and thus terrorize them, but I ask you, why go to all the trouble just to kill a few dozen people?"

The two men stared at her, mouths slightly open, but she wasn't finished.

"If you want to terrorize a given population, you should use a different virus family."

"Such as?" Both men coaxed.

A smile spread across her face much as one might see on a card shark about reveal their hand. "Have you heard of the Spanish flu?" Before either could answer, she barreled ahead. "It hit the world toward the end of World War I and went by several different names like *La Grippé* or *La Pesadilla*. You do know it caused a pandemic that killed more people than the war itself. Estimates in the range of twenty to forty million have been bandied about. No matter the name, it may have killed more than that, much more."

Goaded on, they both had to ask, "How much?"

"Eighty." After a short pause to let the numbers sink in, she continued, "If I were a bioterrorist—um, no let me rephrase that. If I were a bioterrorist radicalized to the nth degree, I would use a genetically modified version of H1N1, the meanest strain of flu we know of. You'd kill millions. Now tell me, which would you fear more?" Before either man could answer, she returned to an earlier topic.

"The only way for us to study agents that cause diseases like these"—accentuating her position by pointing to a picture of a dying patient—"is to work in a facility such as we have here."

Both of those listening responded as everyone did when understanding sinks in, they squirmed uncomfortably in their chairs, and in a subliminal effort to guard themselves from whatever infectious agent might be under study in the high containment labs located several floors beneath them, they slowed down their breathing.

With her presentation finished, she decided it was time to get down to business. Perhaps she could speed them out the door and call all her employees back to the lab. "I circulated your request. No one responded," she said.

MacLean woke from fear of terror agents on the premises and instead wondered what planet he was on. "For cryin' out loud, all I wanted to do was ask some questions."

Like he saw when waiting to park the car, Inspector Gervais noted MacLean's ears begin to twitch. He also noted MacLean's voice edging upward, again in concert with his blood pressure. "That was definitely not what FBI agents hope to hear, at least not right out of the gate." Dr. Connell turned to look him straight in the eyes, but before she could answer, he continued, "Let me get this straight, everyone is too busy to give us a few minutes of time?"

Inspector Gervais imperceptibly shook his head, though hoping his partner would notice. One of the few things everyone at *la Sûreté* could agree on; Christian Gervais had a gift for interrogation. Even those who were not particularly fond of him admitted as much. Now all he could do was sit tight and will, with all his psychic energy, his American partner to tone it down and try to engage the woman in conversation, not argument.

"No, it is not because people are too busy, it is more likely no one wishes to speak with the FBI." To her credit, Dr. Connell managed to pitch her voice to let the two men know they were in her house, while keeping a disarming *savoir faire*. Then she, like MacLean before her, upped the ante with a few disparaging remarks about the Republican president that would have made a longshoreman blush. And still, she smiled.

Both investigators did a quick double take, exchanged a glance and then, with feathers ruffled, and before the Canadian could gain control of the situation, MacLean responded. "Dr. Connell, we're not the bad guys here. We just—"

Before he could finish Dr. Connell quickly placed several old magazines beneath her bottom, swiveled in her chair, and poked her finger in MacLean's general direction, "Let me explain something to you…"

Still at the podium, she effortlessly moved from scientific dogma to political recidivism by attributing all the evil in the world, and then some, to the conservative administration in Washington. After she finished her assessment of the sitting president, she took a breath before continuing. "Most of the research staff is here on work visas. Do you know what it was like for them post-9/11? Everyone working here be they Pakistani, Indian, Middle Eastern, or hell, even my Moroccan post-doc lived in fear of deportation. Now, every time they attend a conference outside the States, we have to pull teeth with Immigration to get them back to work. I'm sorry they're all gun shy of Federal investigators. It's not a question of everyone being too busy to speak with you. Everyone called in sick, and if you come back tomorrow unannounced, we'll have one of those episodes you see on TV when ICE officials raid a restaurant full of illegals."

"Oh" was all MacLean said.

Chapter 16
With Stops in Saratoga Springs

Schrödinger and his cat got it started; now quantum entanglement is all the rage. Proponents say entanglement occurs when pairs (or groups) of particles interact in ways such that the quantum state of each cannot be described independently of the other, even when the particles are, distance wise, far apart. If they are far apart, then whichever "state" they are in is no longer individualized but rather the "state" must be described for the system as a whole, and so the argument goes, no matter the distance, there is an interaction. The particles are somehow connected.

For example, at the same time the international policing duo was interviewing the head of the Biodefense Center in Newark New Jersey, the Adirondack had just wound its way past Rhinecliff as it continued its slow crawl north. Soon thereafter, the passenger named Hicham heard the conductor call out the next stop, but with English being his third language, it was hard for him to phonetically equate Schenectady with what was written on the route map he was holding. Giving up on that, he peered about for a moment or two, but nothing captured his attention, so he returned to memories of his father and the hookah. This time, he partook.

Their conversations would, over time, move off politics and onto more important topics, like business. This is how he first learned of his father's plans for him, or more precisely, lack thereof. "You see, son, if you aren't in the mining business…" He had to mention this to cover his bases since mining of phosphates was one of Morocco's largest legal industries. "Or if you aren't growing olives…" Here, he gave Samir a wink. "There isn't much else to do. Your older brothers will get the farm. Your sisters, well, they will get their marriages—some are already arranged, but it is you, my diminutive one, who I am most concerned about. For you, I just don't know."

At first not knowing what the future would hold allowed Samir time to invent himself in any way he wanted, but as those around him grew and moved from fantasy reenactments to football, things changed. Being small is not a handicap in playing what is known in the west as soccer, if you have talent. Samir didn't, so when the choosing began, he was most often left on the sidelines. While his football talent was small his ego was inversely proportional. It hurt when the other kids turned their attention to sports. But it did give him time to sit around the hookah and listen to the old men in the bazaar. It also gave him time to make friends with the bully, Ali. In fact, Ali soon became Samir's only friend. It seemed no one wanted to play with the largest kid on the block, or the smallest. They made an odd couple of kindred spirits walking through the old neighborhoods. Ali with his peculiar gait looking down at Samir with his arm draped around the smaller boy's shoulders and Samir looking up at Ali, knees barely managing the strain of the extra weight.

Having time on his hands also provided Samir with ample opportunities to read. Often his father would return home from the fields and find him huddled in the cool shade of the family's high-walled garden. Alongside a bag of dates there was usually a stack of books, both within arm's reach of the boy. But as the years passed, the question of what to do with the youngest became dinner table discussion. Everyone always agreed he was a good student. "He likes to read," his oldest sister would start the communal assessment. From there, it was easy for them to reach a consensus.

"He should attend university."

Sending Samir to university was always the easy part. Figuring out where to send him was not. Arguing the point became their weekly dinnertime activity, and so no one was in a great hurry to reach any sort of consensus. Everyone stuck to their differing positions, and though present for most of these discussions, no one bothered to ask Samir his take on things. As he drew near to finishing his secondary education without a clear direction in sight, his parents began contemplating the merits of technical schools.

"To buy time," they explained, "until the right path is revealed."

Samir could not envision himself as a mechanic or carpenter or even a telephone-based technician in a call center resolving stupid computer operation errors for households in France. In fact, the simple suggestion of entering trade school panicked him. This is why, in a state of desperation, he did something he had never done before. He offered his opinion.

"May I interrupt please?" When silence reigned, and all eyes were on him, he continued, "I've been doing some thinking. I would like to study in a faraway place."

"Is Fez far enough? I like it in their old town."

"How about Rabat? It's near the ocean."

"So is Casablanca."

"Marrakesh is a bit further."

Each possibility was answered with a negative shake of the head causing his father to worry a bit. "Oh, please, not Algiers!"

"No, not Algiers."

"Thank Allah."

"So where then?" came from a chorus of voices.

"Italy."

It was a week later before his mother agreed. "Fine," she said, "but only if you study literature." She had it in mind to keep her youngest son away from the family side business, and she meant it.

At each stop north, passengers disembarking would change places with those boarding. All the while Hicham stayed reclined in his chair, head leaning against the window, none of his thoughts centered on the comings and goings of those around him; instead, he focused on the mysteries of life, specifically his life. If he had been more awake it would have been hard to miss the Saratoga stop complete with man on crutches getting ready to disembark. This passenger had sidled along the aisle, crutches unevenly splayed out, appearing ready to topple over with every hesitant step. If Hicham had noticed, he may have gotten up to help the poor man. It would have been the proper thing to do. If he had done this and gotten close, he may have noticed the man wasn't really an invalid. He would have also noticed the man was powerfully built. But Hicham's radar was turned off when the train stopped at Saratoga Springs, so he missed these two data points.

As the passenger inched his way closer, the size differential became obvious to anyone who may have been watching; and when he finally reached Hicham's row, he teetered precariously on one crutch, swiveled his body, and leaned in toward the Moroccan. Anyone who looked up from a relaxed, sitting position and saw a behemoth falling toward them would most likely have launched into a panic response. But Hicham didn't; his eyes were still focused outside the window and deep within his memory banks. The man quietly righted himself; collected the briefcase, which had landed in the seat next to Hicham; took a few last photos; and continued moving to the exit.

Hicham did see the man on crutches greet a woman on the platform and saw her hand him a set of keys. But he didn't hear her thank her old friend profusely for hopping on the train farther south. "Sorry, I had

Mike call you at such an ungodly hour. And how was your ride up from Rhinecliff?" He also missed her trying to discuss consulting fees. He did, though, see the man shake his head in the negative but didn't hear the response, "I haven't had a chance to ride the train in a long time, too busy writing. This was fun, like ol' times."

"I feel the same. It's been a while since I've been in the field, and don't tell Mike, I'm lovin' it." Then the FBI consultant did a few quick calculations in her head before asking, "If you don't want any money… are you going to turn this into another one of your spy thrillers?"

Donna's accomplice just smiled.

The conductor started calling, which brought Hicham's attention front and center. He watched new passengers seat themselves while out on the platform he missed Donna firing off one more question, "Why are you on crutches?"

The man turned, smiled, picked up both, did a quick two step, and then put them back under his arms.

"Always big on props, 'eh?"

When the train lurched, Hicham noted the station name, and as they picked up speed, he checked his schedule to see which little mote in the vastness of railroad lines he was leaving and the lineup of those still to come. The next station would be Fort Edward, followed by Whitehall, and then Ticonderoga (another unpronounceable location)—all parts in a long list of meaningless, inconsequential places that, *hopefully*, he prayed, *I will never see again.*

As the voyage continued, vestiges of human habitation became less. And as the train kept moving northward, the panorama broadened. The tracks once again were straddling the river which, in turn, was straddling two States and two mountain ranges. The gentle climb upward brought the highlands of the Adirondacks into view on his left while looking to his right the Hudson Valley was clearly visible. Trees now populated the landscape. It wasn't just trees. It was the expanse of trees that captured the Moroccan's attention. They carpeted the landscape. For several minutes, all he did was stare off with mouth open and tongue out. Further east, the Green Mountains gave name to the state they helped shape. Glancing forward, the hills were bedecked in ornamental buttresses with designs and hues unique to their individual mold from *phylum* to species. Everywhere trees stood at attention for all to see; monuments sculpted with patience by the Maker of all things, in art classes spanning creation and, thus, measured on an evolutionary scale. Individuality hit not only between families but even within the same. If one scrolled down the taxonomic rank, differences were obvious between *genera* as well. In fact, every tree within a species was different. Like snowflakes, each was original, each leaf unique in small, sometimes imperceptible ways, but different nonetheless.

"In the fall, they will all slowly change. It will become a patchwork quilt billowing in the wind. The whole is so much greater when there is individuality in the parts." Samir surprised himself with his sudden poetic waxing. *Perhaps*, he thought, *it is Hicham's influence?*

"Into each life a little suffering will fall," he continued, whispering this to the empty seat in front of him.

The train did not care for the young man's philosophy, it just moved on, dragging itself toward Ticonderoga. No one in the sparsely populated coach seemed to care either except a woman sitting nearby did appeared to be looking his way until he met her gaze. Then she went back to reading her magazine.

Chapter 17
On a Mission

Like quantum entanglement on a string, as the Adirondack was trundling into Ticonderoga events linked to it back at the Biodefense Center were approaching their next port o' call.

"Pardon," Inspector Gervais interrupted. "We can understand the sensitivities involved mais, à ce moment, we only need a confirmation." His voice was perfectly pitched, and the change in tone and tempo continued to deescalate the mood. As he spoke, he changed the topic and began inquiring about different objects in her office, pointing specifically at the Warhol-like wall hanging with his left hand while gently pushing a photo across the desktop with his right.

The doctor didn't follow either hand motion; she just counted to ten and then replied, "Why, thank you for asking Inspector. What you see on the wall is what a nasty strain of flu looks like in an RNA microarray. But I have to say this: Diagnosing the strain isn't really our biggest concern."

Now, less like an astute lecturer and more like a proud peacock, the doctor told her audience everything they never wanted to know and then some about how the constituents of the yearly flu vaccine are decided upon, assembled, produced, and distributed.

"Every year, it's a gamble. Pharma companies are still trying to move away from producing large vaccine quantities in eggs. Unfortunately, not all strains grow well in culture vats. And of course, some years the vaccine strain isn't even a close match to what is in circulation, but you never hear that in the news do ya'? I suppose I should also say this: A vaccine against the more virulent strains, like Spanish flu, don't exist. Therefore, protection isn't always what it is purported to be. If we ever get an outbreak with a strain like the killer flu of 1918 then gentlemen, I'm afraid we are all SOL."

At first, the importance of what she had just conveyed did not exactly hit the nerve she was hoping because the American, while staring at her open-mouthed, was stuck trying to understand the bit having to do with eggs, while the Canadian struggled with the English acronym, *I know what SOB means, but what is SOL?* Dr. Connell delivered more snippets of information and slowly the info began to sink in. The bottom line being each, in their own way, swore to never again bother with the yearly vaccine.

"Are you with me so far?" Knowing they weren't, she took a moment to peek at the picture Inspector Gervais had slid her way. After giving it a quick glance, she raised her left eyebrow, paused a second, and then began to address the content of the photo in a slow, deliberate fashion. As she spoke the photo itself was passed back across her desk.

"If you would have told me who you were interested in, I could have saved you the trip. This is Dr. Mounir. Nice chap, works for a biotech up in Canada, was in town visiting a friend here at the Institute. He gave us an impromptu, a very informal sort of thing. I think he was hoping to spark some interest, you know, looking for a job. After his talk, he was taken on a little tour of the place, routine stuff, all our guests get one. That was a few weeks back."

"Do you, by any chance, remember the exact day he was here?"

Dr. Connell shrugged her shoulders hoping she would soon be rid of the police investigators, swiveled in her chair, and began searching on her computer. "I've a daily planner in here somewhere. I should know this stuff. It was a few days after Arthur gave his talk. Now that was a seminar, he had us floored and…"

"Qui? Who?" Both investigators asked in their language of choice.

"I'm sorry, should have said Dr. McAiden, he heads up a small…"

"You know," she complained to her husband over dinner that night, "I had that big guy back on his heels, giving him both barrels, letting him know what I thought of that clown in the White House. They never said who they were after. I thought they were coming for one or more of my H-1s. Then, sitting there right in front of me is a picture of that Moroccan. Well, the long and short of it is…I panicked."

The download from wife to husband had not been organized, it was more a free flow of information in need of curating.

"Did I tell you that McAiden is in hospital? An accident put him there, a really bad one it seems."

"Not you didn't tell me this" was her husband's response. "Who is he again?"

"Mounir was the one who…oh my, every one of us at the center thought the Moroccan was just visiting his friend, but with this, this…do you think they will string me up for some sort of aiding and abetting?"

"Did what? Who did what?"

Dr. Connell ignored his requests and continued to vent for a good five minutes. When she finally paused, her husband had a chance to trail back, "Aiding and abetting what?"

"Hindsight is so damn good, but I had no idea where the Moroccan procured his data. I thought it was his, but…oh shit, you know we never checked to see if he still worked for Biopharma. I swear I didn't know he had left the industry. The Canadian told me this. Then, it got worse.

Both men really weren't interested in what Mounir talked about, they wanted to know what McAiden presented."

"And what was that?"

"That, oh husband of mine, was the DOD grant stuff, the work we're collaborating on. I couldn't just tell the FBI agent that!"

"Oh? Why not?"

"It's secret! That's why, you moron. I just gave them some generalities, explained the type of grant it was, and just like that, we were back to the bio-terror scenario."

"What happened next?" Having moved off intellectual curiosity, her husband's voice now conveyed a degree of discomposure. For the first time all evening, husband and wife were occupying the same emotional space.

"I told you. I panicked!"

"Panicked?"

"Yes, panicked. I didn't know what the hell to tell my interrogators. Can you pass the potatoes. Don't know why I'm so hungry tonight. Thanks. These are really good. I'll hire you full-time. Anyway, where was I?"

"I think you were going to…"

"Oh yes, I remember. I tried stalling them. I said I wasn't at liberty to discuss any aspects of that program. But they pressed. When I tried to bring the discussion back to the Moroccan, it didn't help matters. The Canadian asked if I've been in contact with him, which I haven't. Not since he finished his talk. I left the seminar room, that's the God's honest truth! I told them this and hoped the interview would end. Unfortunately, it didn't. The hole I was digging just got deeper. So what did I do?"

"I don't know. Perhaps you can tell me."

"I kept digging!"

"Huh?"

"I know I shouldn't, but I think I'll get the ice cream now, want any?"

Her husband didn't answer, he was too busy wondering if it was time to grab a valium or stay and listen to more of her recap.

She brought two bowls, so he stayed and quietly ate his allotment while watching her, spoon in hand, continue her play by play.

"I thought I had answered their questions, so to get out from under their, um"—she paused, thought for a moment, shoved more ice cream into her mouth and then jumped back in—"yes, it was an interrogation, and back on dry land I tried asking a few questions. Simple stuff like why the hell were they so interested in this guy. Of course, they weren't sure if I meant Mounir or McAiden and that gave me a few seconds of relief. Eventually, the Canadian spoke up telling me he had some pictures of the exterior of the Institute taken from Mounir's camera. So what? It's a famous place if you know what they're looking at. I didn't say that. Shit, I would take a pic or two of it if I didn't already have a bunch of them. I didn't say that either."

Dr. Connell slowed to a crawl, rubbed her stomach, and burped. "Shouldn't have had the ice cream. Anyway, things went further south. I had asked them point blank how come they had Mounir's camera.

"Apparently, everything revolves around the accident." Here, Dr. Connell burped again and had to stop for a moment, debating with herself whether to throw up or not.

Her husband watched her wince in pain and began to get out of his chair. She tried to stop him with a wave of the arm but when the tears came, he didn't follow her instructions. Instead, he moved to her side of the table, helped her rise, and then escorted her to the couch where they sat side by each with his arms holding her close, and gently petting the back of her head. Slowly the crying ran its course. When she regained her breath, she moved him back just a bit to give herself more room to turn and look his way. When she again began to speak, her voice had a low, sorrowful tone.

"I, I need to get this out. I need you to listen." She paused and belched one more time before continuing, "It was the accident. It did me in. McAiden was hurt bad, and it was Mounir's car that hit him."

Events beget by incursions to the status quo are like ripples on a lake. They move in all directions and touch the lives of everyone who is in their path. What Dr. Connell had assimilated earlier in the day had been processed through her internal analysis systems and no matter how many times she reworked the data the same result was reached. It had a little to do with feeling sorry for the man but most to do with worry. As in, her potential involvement with something akin to terrorist sedition.

"I couldn't get much more info except McAiden had been airlifted to the trauma center over in New Brunswick. They were more interested in showing me the pics Mounir took of the building, the fuckin' inside," she whined, "my goddamn lab, even the freezers." The tears returned for a moment, and she had to resist her husband trying to tighten his grip. This time in not more than a whisper. "I did attend his seminar, met with him briefly, but I didn't take him on the tour of the facility. Brian did that."

Her husband, like the two investigators, needed to know who Brian was so with voice regaining some of its spunk she filled him in. "After 9/11, everyone raced to assimilate. For a while, they all took English-sounding names. We called him Brian, but his name is Mohamed. He's one of my senior post-docs. Of course, the American was trying to take down some notes while the Canadian just kept his eyes glued on me. Both asked the same question."

"Which was?"

"Brian's last name, and well, by now, I was in a bottomless pit."

Dr. Connell's husband, knowing little to nothing with respect to virology or molecular genetics, was trying his best to get to the bottom of the issues troubling his wife and feeling the great reveal was soon to come, he kept quiet.

"I know what it is, but I stammered giving it to them, which made it look like I was reluctant or…" when the next belch was finished, she continued, "His name is Mohamed Labib, that's it, his name is Mohamed…oh, dear, I'm repeating myself and he's Egyptian. All they asked after that was if he spelled his name with one internal *m* or two?"

"What does that have to do with anything?"

"That's exactly what I asked. All I got from the Canadian was some more French, *une minute s'il vous plais,* and I tell you what, it no longer had that *je ne sais quoi* about it. Then he pulled out a pad laced with info, quite a lot of info. Did you know Mohamed can be spelt with one M or two?" Her husband's head stayed neutral, so she continued, "Apparently, they needed to confirm if Labib was Mounir's friend from his school days back in Paris. If he was, their paths overlapped quite a bit. When Labib did his post-doc at McGill, he also, for a short while was with Mounir at *Armand-Frappier*. When Mounir moved on to a pharma company in Montreal, Labib was here in Jersey working for me.

"Next, they wanted a quick word with Brian. Can you imagine?"

"Did you let them?

"Let them, let them." The vigor had returned to her voice followed by another eruption from her stomach followed by a very audible passing of air and for good measure, another burp. Then she calmed down, apologized, and with her voice softening to the limits of audio recognition, she continued, "Haven't you been listening? Yes, it would have been apropos for them to speak with Brian. It might have allowed me to get out of their line of fire, unfortunately he, like everyone in my lab and all the others, was not in the building. For Christ's sake, everyone knew the Feds were on their way. Only in Brian's case, I found out later in the day, he had returned to Egypt several days ago for a, a, you know what, I don't know why he left the States. Maybe he was just visiting family. I don't know! Oh hell. Apparently, I have no idea what's going on in my own f'-in lab.

"Of course, they wanted me to be more specific about the day Brian left the country. I told them I would have the lab manager supply that information and then turned my gaze everywhere and anywhere that was not in my office. When they didn't move, I wondered if they had missed all the clues."

"The clues?"

"To leave. They didn't understand. I wanted them gone and they didn't move. They wanted to speak, ASAP, with my lab manager."

"And?"

"All I could do was laugh. I thought I just told you. Sophie is the lab manager, and she's a green card wannabe too!"

"So those guys thought the Moroccan was after something in your lab? And your man Brian had shown him around, didn't he? Wow!"

Unfortunately for the husband, the wife had just run out of gas. Without her adrenalin keeping her hyper-link open, she sank deep into the couch and closed her eyes.

"Yes," she whispered.

"Do those Feds think this was Industrial espionage?"

"Oh no, something much worse."

"Worse?"

"Terrorism!" she responded, and though muffled in transmission, it made the point loud and clear.

"Oh my gawd! Did he get any of your um…" While talking, her husband rose from the couch, ambled into the bathroom, rummaged through the medicine chest until he found the diazepam, and quickly popped three tablets into his mouth, washing them down with handfuls of tap water. Then he turned back to his wife and called out, "How much you want?"

"Five" was her only response.

Thus endeth this noble but not quite joyous story of Dr. Connell and her troupe of workers card-green. Unknowingly, each had a part to play in the dolorous atrocity linked to the hill known as Badon. And now, as they exit stage left, Arthur's quest for Peredur and the *Sangreal* of consciousness will enter places only known to a select few.

Chapter 18
To Paris and Points West

Donna MacLean, now on board the Adirondack and situated in the exact seat her old FBI acquaintance had just vacated, was conducting her assignment with the least bit of effort. It's not hard to survey if the target wasn't doing much. Sophisticated devices she had, if needed, but even these could not help her figure out what was going on inside the man's head. If she could, she would see his thoughts zeroing in on higher education. And like the Adirondack heading north, the route Samir took to earn his advanced degree had a few stops along the way.

The first such stop was Milan. When all was said and done, he had to admit his year in Italy could only be classified as a complete disaster. He was homesick from day one and was in culture shock the moment he walked off the jet at Malpensa.

Try as he would, some things he just couldn't get a handle on, like the intro class his mother had suggested he take on Alighieri. This author's product was just too allegorical, Samir craved things in a more literal tone, like hard science. For a while, things got better. He began to find subjects that truly interested him and a group of acquaintances who cared little about a person's size and more about their ability to not hold their liquor. As part of the club, Samir allowed everyone else to move up a notch in bragging rights. The club consisted of a mixture of foreign exchange students, like himself, and a few misfit nationals.

One morning mid–first semester Samir attended a seminar filled with topics that tweaked his interests, all having to do with advances in biological sciences and related technologies. So when he met up with his friends later in the day for their espresso fix, he had a lot he wanted to talk about. The first problem, though, was how to get his point across. The only common language was English. Samir would have preferred French or Arabic, he was fluent in both, but that day it was all in English.

"Every day we hear of, of…many advances," he began. "The Americans they send man to moon what, thirty ago year? Now we have space station." He paused noting the others had begun side conversations, so he tried another tack. "The processor in my phone is better than computer I had at old school. And," he continued, saving the best for last, "they've cloned sheep in Scotty-land!"

One of those sitting amongst the group cut in. "Yes, yes that is all true, but Italy has a good chance this year for the world cup."

Apparently, this man wasn't as interested in the science end of things as Samir. For that matter, neither were any of the others. This was clear when a local girl proposed a day trip to Rapallo, "It will take our mind off stressful things. My aunt has an apartment there, and I'm sure she'll let us…"

"Take our minds off things?" Samir asked. "What things? What about class?"

"What about class? That is the problem with you, Samir, I can see it in you already. You are just too…too serious. You need to learn to relax. You have your whole life to study, but only today to go to the beach."

Five people, including four exchange students (two Moroccans, one Algerian, and an Egyptian) and the Milanese girl who was, for lack of a better descriptor, their tour guide, squeezed into what in the United States would have been called a very small car. Three Italians piled into an even smaller Fiat and together both groups drove like demons to Rapallo, a small town hugging the coast just south of Portofino. Stepping out of the sardine can at their destination, Samir took only a moment before he realized something was missing. The women on the beach wore no tops!

For the rest of his stay in Italy, Samir tried hard to become more comfortable with the cultural differences. He also tried to get all thoughts of what he had seen in Rapallo out of his head. The problem was, he couldn't, and any chance he had to return to the shore, he accepted. This became a bragging right of sorts when he spoke with Ali.

Ali had opted to study in Paris while Samir was in Milan. They stayed in touch over the internet. "But science," Samir wrote, "true science, not this sociology crap, now that is as straightforward as it gets, right? And guess what? We went to Portofino yesterday. Nice town, very pretty but they had no beach. Luckily, we took the water taxi back to Rapallo where we had access to the sand, and just like last time, every single one of them was topless."

Ali read every word Samir sent, sometimes twice, agreed with him on all counts relating more or less to science, and then, he one upped him. "I went to Cannes."

Through their email conversations, Ali somehow recruited Samir to join him in Paris. He started by pointing out how much better the opportunities were, especially for someone with Samir's interest. "Besides," he had written, trying to seduce his old friend, "there is such a wonderful supportive expatriate community here. You'll love it."

Next on Samir's agenda was to convince his parents a shift in locale was for the common good. "Look at it like this. One day I'll engineer the perfect olive tree so your groves will produce oil as good as anything they have in Spain." How he came up with this proposition he wasn't sure, but he attended a seminar once relating to the genetics of plant selection.

His father, skeptical about engineering anything beyond trains, naturally hesitated. But Samir persisted and, in the end, became demanding. "Send me to Paris. I want to go to France. I want to study science at le Institute Pasteur."

Then, softening his delivery, he continued, "Have faith." Samir didn't tell his father about the women in Cannes. France, it seemed, was the best of both worlds.

The train stopped at Ticonderoga, Port Henry, Westport, and then Port Kent at its slow, methodical pace. Hicham, having slept on and off for most of the trip was awake now, hungry, and with only a few stops left before reaching the Canadian border, his anxiety level was making sitting still most difficult. He would have loved to walk around, just stroll up and down the aisles, maybe visit the dining car, but lax spy-craft or not, he knew it best not to draw any attention to his frail frame. So he didn't get up. Instead, he reached into his pocket to feel if he still had the pills. They were a little present he had been given before he boarded the train.

"For your nerves," the man had told him. "Take them an hour or so before you need to show your passport. We cannot have you looking anxious, not in these times."

Samir, pretending to be Hicham, had looked the man in the eyes as he reached out and took the canister. Inside it held several small, white pills. With apprehension, he had turned to look at the Uber-Sheik standing a few meters away. The Sheik returned his gaze; and Samir noticed, barely visible through the thick tuft of the man's beard, his enigmatic smile.

Now Hicham consulted his train schedule one more time, trying to calculate how much longer until they crossed into Canada. *I wonder if they check passports at the border or if they wait until Montréal.* Then, remembering the look on the Sheik's face, he had another thought. *What if they are not for anxiety?* This idea did nothing to help his blood pressure, but it assured him of one thing. "I will face *ces agents en douane* without the help of these pills." This he proclaimed to the nonexistent occupant in the chair across from him.

Having no success making conversation with the empty seat, he got out of his seat for a quick trip to the loo. When he returned, he articulated his disgust with sanitary conditions on the train in three languages not caring if anyone heard. He wiped his hands repeatedly on a well-worn alcohol swab (he always kept a packet of these with him for emergencies).

Then, saying for the benefit of no one, "The hell with this," he rose again and gingerly made his way down the aisle and headed for anywhere but his current seat. A few minutes later, he was in the dining car sipping ersatz coffee and, not knowing when his next meal would be, working on a second package of cookies. The cookies were his only caloric intake since leaving Gotham. The coffee would not help in any way if he somehow managed to close his eyes for a moment.

He sat, eyes wide open, holding his coffee cup between both hands, staring out the windows while he sipped away. A never-ending growth of evergreens had slowly taken over from the deciduous forest in the lower altitudes. He had to admit to himself that there was something to be said for the uniformity of the green veil surrounding the train. Everything was orderly, standing above the chaos of color and design found lower down the slopes. "It is like a well-planned village with all the houses of the same design and, mostly, the same color, though differing somewhat in shade, and each with those beautiful, tiled roofs."

Looking again at the sea of green, this time with a more critical eye, he noted it wasn't quite as uniform as he thought. There was no one for all, and all for one. This region, too, was filled with diversity like the hardwoods down the slope. You just needed an objective eye to see the truth. It wasn't obvious, like picking a red-leafed maple from a yellow birch, but it was there. The evergreens were similar in name only, with the red juniper staking out its territory in steep glades between slopes while other varieties tried to outmuscle each other for position on the western faces. Then there was the tamarack, which gave up the slopes for the moist soil following the different streams emptying into the lakes, which, in turn, fed the Hudson. Of course, there were those that said the heck with segregation and grew and blossomed wherever their seed placed them.

Samir eventually finished his internal treatise on the distribution of trees and noticed the woman seated just a table away. *She is the one sitting near me in the… She's following me! Non, non, non, ce ne peut pas être.* To avoid eye contact with the stranger, who could not possibly be spying on him, he cast his gaze back out the window. Seated, thus, he watched as the sun slid behind the peaks to the west and shadows charged down the mountains turning everything shades darker by degrees.

Well along the way to dying from panic, he did notice the train begin its long descent into the lowlands. The journey he knew would eventually segue out of the Lake Champlain basin and slide into the St. Lawrence River valley. But right now, no amount of natural beauty could help calm his nerves.

Perhaps just one of the pills… was a thought that crossed his mind, but the vision of the Uber-Sheik smirking on the platform was enough to make him question again what they might be capable of. Looking for a safe space, he returned to his past life, picking up where he left off, his first exposure to life in Paris.

Starting fresh had apparently done Ali some good. He had not been fettered in his newly adopted county by past stereotyping, he was free to be himself and he had made friends, lots of them. He was also immeasurably helpful getting Samir set up in his new hometown. He showed him where to buy his carte l'orange and helped him register for classes. He introduced Samir to the ex-pat community, the Imam at his favorite Mosque and the tag along guy named Labib who had recently arrived from Egypt. He even let Samir stay with him; his old roommate had just graduated.

Ali also recommended Samir for a part-time night-clerk job alongside him at a nearby hotel. It was a small accommodation, more like an auberge than a hotel, and it catered to traveling Muslims. For the two young men in need of help with their expenses, it was a perfect fit. From that moment on, between hard study, Samir more than Ali, and work at the hotel, Ali more than Samir, the two had no social life outside the occasional outing. Some of these were arranged by their Imam and usually revolved around a day trip to Poitiers.

"Why do we always have to go there? Why can't we go to Cannes?" Unfortunately, this complaint was delivered in a voice loud enough for the Imam to overhear.

"Lest we ever forget," the imam intoned in his gravelly voice.

"Forget what?" Samir asked, wondering why Ali was walking away from him.

"Our destiny!"

Working the graveyard shift gave the two friends many long hours with little to do but talk, when Samir had finished his studies that is. One recurring topic was wealth; more precisely, how to obtain it and less on how to use it. Ali was of the opinion existing wealth of the world should be redistributed, "To make it more equitable. The problem is," he confided "the socialist movement here in France is either dead or corrupt."

"The socialist movement is passé" was Samir's take on the subject.

"No, not passé," Ali countered, his voice rising nearly an octave as it usually did when the debate picked up. "Look around you. France, Sweden, Norway and even Germany are moving in this direction."

Samir didn't like the socialist agenda one bit but when Ali asked for an alternative, he didn't really know what to say. "Work for it" is what he eventually added to the conversation. It seems Samir was already thinking of starting his own company and how to make a lot of money. At the time, he didn't have all the details worked out, so he didn't bring up this topic.

In between attending his undergraduate classes, Samir investigated graduate opportunities at *l'Institut Pasteur*. He also wanted to know the success rate faculty members had in placing their students at post-doctoral positions in the US, and most importantly, a faculty member with research money to spend, on him.

Samir would finish his university studies in three years, get his PhD in molecular genetics in just three more and then he accepted a post-doctoral position in Canada. This was not exactly where he wanted to be, but it was close, very close.

"You gave this some thought," Ali said as he watched Samir pack. "I'm very happy for you. I will miss you. Me, I studied sociology. How will I ever get to America?" Ali had a hint of a smile when he said this. He may have been thinking of his own new line of work, though, like Samir, he kept these cards close to his vest.

What one strives for individually often does not play along with what others are planning. This was the problem for these two friends. Without really understanding what was happening around them, men they had met with every Friday, after the Jum'ah and subsequent khutbah, of course, were channeling a hatred of all things Western. The positioning of others to do one's bidding is built one brick at a time; brainwashing doesn't happen overnight. Ali had been used to get to Samir because, well, because they were incredibly happy with Samir's career choice. In this regard, Samir had what he always wanted, attention. When those at the Mosque found he was interested in genetics, they encouraged molecular genetics. When Samir explained bacterial viruses as model systems for the study of genetic drift, they discussed the world of human pathogens and mentioned how one could study this drift and rid the world of dreaded diseases at the same time. This idea didn't take long to become part of Samir's own train of thought.

Ali bought the anti-western rhetoric they expounded, hook, line, and sinker; but Samir only paid lip service to it. He did see the plight of the poor immigrants in France. He did feel a sense of animosity to French policies, but Samir was becoming a capitalist at heart. The only reason he kept nodding his head in response to their teachings was simple; they told him of their connections who could get work for him in America. Unfortunately for Samir, when he heard America, he had one place in mind. When those who would become his handlers said

America, they meant more of a nebulous zone on the other side of the Ocean.

Samir had been recruited in France for a special post-graduate assignment in America, as in North America, specifically, Canada. His handlers had arranged for him to become part of the community around Montréal in a low-key, unassuming manner. This was the usual operating procedure when someone was being groomed for future endeavors. Why else invest all the time and money? What they had in mind for him Samir didn't know. Given his area of expertise he could imagine what it might be. He had been steered into a technical position at an institute that supplied the Canadian influenza vaccine each year. One thing he realized right away was this; his handlers did not have vaccine on their minds. Why else he wondered did they send both me and Labib to this same place?

Unfortunately for the handlers, while Labib acted content but a low-level position was not enough for Samir. He wanted a more lucrative posting, like a biotech start-up studying a topic of his choosing with a side order of stock options. This, he felt, would help him become established within the international scientific community, hopefully famous, but if not that, at least rich. This is what he wanted, and the more he wanted it, the more he developed a dislike for those who had sent him to Canada. This dislike increased a bit when the handlers sent Labib on to the US after only a short stint in the northern climes.

When Samir had to flee Canada, he believed all he had worked on, and hoped for, had gone up in smoke. Then, as the boredom of working for the Second Storey agency set in, he had an idea. He went to visit his old friend who was now ensconced at a research institute in Jersey, and without much effort, convinced Labib to hand over some samples of interest. Now he had something he was sure he could make use of. The problem being what he was transporting was not exactly what his European handlers would want to make use of. What Labib had passed over was a functioning sample of a new technology in the form of a potential vaccine. Oh, he had tried to get the intact virus, his handlers would most likely have liked that, but even Labib wasn't allowed in that section of the building. Mohammed told him the technology base itself, the Holy Grail so to speak, had originated in the laboratory of Dr. Arthur McAiden, so Samir undertook plan two, track him down and borrow his patents. That didn't work quite as he had hoped.

On the night of the accident, Samir didn't take any pictures of Dr. McAiden engaged in a romantic tryst. But he did manage to record parts of a telephone conversation the man had as he was leaving the history professor's home. The topic of this phone call was totally unexpected and very interesting. Samir replayed the exchange several times as he followed McAiden's car down Badon Hill Road. What he heard had made him rethink the action plan he had been formulating throughout his time in Jersey. The accident, well, this added a layer of complexity to everything. Hence, he was struggling with the proper sales pitch for what he did have, and those struggles led to his constitutional entanglements.

Samir woke with a start, "Merde! I must get back to my chair." Then he took a quick look around. Only one other person was in the dining car with him. It was the same woman he had noted before. She was sitting in the same place sipping a cup of coffee and talking on her phone. *Where did I put those pills?* he kept asking himself as he eased his way along the aisle back to his seat.

Chapter 19
A King amongst Men

"Hello there, my name's Flo. That's short for Flora. Flora Chirikjian. Now I know it isn't your wife's name, so you can't go pinching me and saying you were confused, got it? What's that? You want to know how to spell it. Oh, you are being too cute. I won't spell it for you, but I'll give you a hint. You spell it like it sounds and...oh, forget that, just call me Flo, and if it is okay, I'll call you Arthur? It just seems so formal in here and seeing how I'll be changing your sheets and washing your...well, let's just say, someone must do it for the foreseeable future and that someone is me, so we should be on a first-name basis. Don't you think?"

This is how the new nurse introduced herself. She wasn't part of the hospice staff. She had been hired by Jennifer. When she hired the nurse, she did not know it was the private dick who ran into her husband's car. She also didn't know Samir had left town, for good. No, Jennifer was two steps back in this regard. She was still worried about the Moroccan dropping by to collect his payment, but perhaps, that was just subconscious guilt gnawing away and to make her predicament worse, like with the private dick; Jennifer had not physically met the nurse. She had brought someone onto her payroll without the slightest inkling of their ability, or motive, just like the detective Flo had been recruited word of mouth via Morgan who somehow had gotten the name from Vivienne.

Where Morgan had dug up Nurse Flo, Jennifer never asked. Apparently, Morgan was fine with this. She didn't care any longer. Her association with Vivienne was going to end soon. Neither Morgan, nor Jennifer, had any idea who Kevorkian was and hence had never been privy to his teachings. Since Jennifer had no concept of this, no queries along these lines came up when she first spoke with the woman. But as the saying goes, "Make sure you kick the tires." Jennifer didn't.

When this nurse first arrived on the scene, Arthur's eyes were open but only stared straight ahead. The only way he could possibly get a glimpse of the nurse or anything for that matter was if it came within the proper field; that is, in front of his face. Slowly but steadily enough of her did indeed do just that. What Arthur saw was a woman a bit disheveled, her strawberry-blond hair slightly out of place, her dress just a bit wrinkled and her lipstick not quite between the lines. She looked plain, as a sixties love child might after spending too much time on the commune. She also seemed to be in a bit of a hurry. Amphetamines can do that to a person, and now, with her preamble out of the way, she walked right into the middle of the room and made herself at home all the while keeping up an incessant, one-sided banter. Arthur wouldn't have had a chance to respond even if he had been able.

"I see they've got you all hooked up. I am so sorry about the feeding tube. Don't worry, you'll get used to it." Flo continued speaking in a perky sing-song voice that would have, in many circumstances, invited engagement. She was very good at keeping up her side of the conversation until she was sure no more visitors were lurking around. Then she changed her tone, becoming much more businesslike.

"I'm here to help you transition. I'm sorry, but people like you don't get better. They come here for one reason only. It's my job to see you're comfortable till that time, you got that? It was a friend of your wife who hired me. I think she was a friend, but that is how these things run. This Morgan woman brought me the papers, which your wife signed, there is always a middleman, or in this case a middle woman and then she told me about this foreign gal who wanted information, information I can get from those visiting. She was going to pay me big time for that, but as I said, in reality, I am here for another reason."

While switching demeanor she also began a thorough reconnoitering of every piece of equipment attached in some way shape or form to the body lying in front of her and then she peeked under the blankets to see if he had left her any presents.

"Thank you for small favors, and in future, please try to hold your BMs until the morning shift, both of us will be happier that way. I guarantee it. Now, it's too soon to be rolling you, but I also guarantee it will be extremely uncomfortable once those bed sores start up, so a word to the wise"—here, she bent low to whisper in his ear—"pass on before they kick in, once you get 'em, you never get rid of 'em. And while someone in your condition isn't going to care, its sheer hell for someone my size to be rolling someone your size twice a shift, so again, the sooner the better, got that? Of course, if you decide to take your time, I'm here to help move things along."

Flo then made a quick check of the monitors not accessible from the nurse's hub down the hall and jotted a few notes onto her clipboard. When that task was complete, she paused for a moment and a mischievous grin spread over her face.

"Go ahead. Do it," she said as if daring herself. And to prove that she was no chicken she leaned over Arthur placing her chest close to his face, and after peering around once again to double check they were alone, she wiggled her ample bosom. There was no noticeable reaction.

"Kind of like my last boyfriend," she observed. "You keep up the conversation like him too." She took out her penlight and flashed it in each of Arthur's eyes. There was no noticeable reaction beyond the contraction of the irises.

"Why do they insist on these stupid tests? Arthur, you could be here a day, a year, or twenty years, and you ain't gonna respond, not if they say vegetable on your chart."

The nurse continued rambling in a light-hearted fashion more for something to do than for conversation, the night shift is, after all, a lonely time. "Now, it doesn't say vegetable, that's my literal translation. Perhaps you can explain to me the difference between vegetative, persistent vegetative and permanent vegetative?"

She paused to allow time for her patient to answer but soon gave up. "I thought not. It all boils down to time. Me, I'm just waiting for word from on high. I'll know it when I feel it, or the lady overseas lets it be known."

She jotted another note down and read it to the room at large: "Involuntary contraction," along with her analysis, "Something's working in there," and commentary, "Just not enough."

What we know collectively, as humans, and what we believe we think we know, should be measured on two entirely different scales. One might envision the extent of human understanding filling to the brim one very small sewing thimble, and the rest of the infinite universe the extent of our ignorance. This philosophical tangent was not a non-sequitur. It was also far from both the nurse's conscious and unconscious beings. She had no time for it, she was busy getting up off Arthur and moving to the foot of the bed. Once situated, she pulled the sheet up far enough to expose the toes and then, without thinking twice, plunged a twenty-two-gauge butterfly into the main vein on the big toe. Or at least she tried. It took several attempts before a nice crimson flow was achieved.

"Sorry about that." She apologized from her end of the bed then chuckled as she started to clean up the mess. "You do know I'm going to have to draw blood once a day for a week and you don't want your arms all bruised up now do you? Hell, when your loved ones come calling you want to look your best, right? Once all these tests are done, the doctors think they will be able to give a better assessment of your chances. But you and I know Mr. McAiden, they're just covering their butts, and…"

Flo stopped talking and listened to footsteps in the hallway. This is when she reverted to the perky-voiced flight attendant who had originally entered the room. She also began to massage Arthur's feet, cooing like a worried mother comforting an ill child. When the steps faded down the corridor, the massaging stopped and miss perky went back into hiding.

"Don't expect that too often. Now, during the night, I'll try to make myself scarce so you can get your beauty rest. But if any of your family happens to come by trying to pull an all-night vigil, and all things considered, I hope that doesn't happen too often, I'll be around because that is what I am paid to do. I'm also going to let you in on a little secret. They're already debating the feeding tube. You do know once that kind of talk starts up your days really are numbered. Shame, if they go that route, it leaves me nothing to do. If I were in her shoes, your wife's that is, I'd decide fast. If word of your condition gets out to the press, hell, you'll have all sorts of fanatics up here trying to save your life. They will come up to your room with cameras and start taking pictures and all you've got to show 'em is that stupid grin on your face. Next thing you know everyone will be talking about vegetables and you get your picture on T-shirts, what a mess. Take it from me, don't fight it, just pass because each person hooked up to the tube stays hooked up, and after a while, well, you just run out of things to do."

Flo had heard about Lute's visit to the ICU. It seems Arthur's transport crew had relayed the story to the hospice staff who passed the info along to, basically, everyone. "And make sure you get out of the way if the boy comes around the hospice. One more thing, that sister of his is a bitch."

Like everyone else in the gossip chain, Flo had no idea what Lute had been up to before he was touched by the attending physician. The fact he had been on the right track, like many scientific theorems, went unnoticed or worse, undocumented. Lute did not know the amount of activity going on inside his father's head. He only knew the attached instruments were not configured properly here. Internal reconstruction of glial cells with attached neurons is never easy and it takes time. Without proper equipment, or know-how, the efforts going on inside his father's head would pretty much go unnoticed, even on a good day.

"Now, you remember my name, right? It's Flo." Ms. Perky reappeared as she began to finish up. "I think the two of us will be getting along just fine, if you keep up your end of the conversation. When all is said and done, isn't conversation what is really needed in a relationship, especially when the sex is no longer there."

The nurse then moved to the side of the bed she had not yet examined. When she lifted the sheets with both hands, there was a surprise, but it wasn't a BM. Not realizing at first what was slipping off the edge of the bed she gasped and quickly moved her feet apart to get them out of harm's way. "Jesus H. Christ!" she almost yelled and simultaneously bent into a crouch bringing her arms slamming down onto the limp torso on the bed. One hand punched Arthur in the solar plexus while the second landed a wee bit further south. Both hands clutching in an involuntary manner whatever they could find.

The simultaneous body blows caused two new and most unanticipated reactions. First, striking the solar plexus caused Arthur to jackknife upward while the tactile stimulation in his groin area caused something else to jackknife up.

Flo was thirty-eight years old and had been practicing her craft in one capacity or another for almost ten years. As a nurse she had seen and heard a great deal, but nothing that, from her past experiences, could prepare her for what was happening under the pressure of her hands. Cringed over at the side of the bed she watched in fascination the rising body part in her right hand as she gently pushed his bent torso down with her left.

"Well, I'll be." She whispered this, reluctant to unclench her hand. "You, Arthur, are truly a king amongst men."

Beyond the bounds of medical measurement, Arthur's brain had been slowly rewiring itself. Under duress from the head trauma his subconscious had moved out to hover over what some might define as his physical entity. And as he lingered in this state of being, trying to decide which direction to take, the destruction in the neural network became worse, making it harder for him to find any reentry path. Basically, he couldn't get back in if he wanted to, at least not all the way. Even as the nurse paid him a compliment, too much of his information processing circuitry was still out of order or not properly rewired and without all cylinders firing reality became whatever he could make of it.

Flo, while still holding tightly with her right hand, stretched up onto her toes and leaned over his face once again. "I've got plans for you, dear boy," she whispered. "When I come back for my next visit, I'll be prepared. Don't worry, no one will catch us, we will steal a march up on that bed of yours and I definitely won't tell your *Genevieve*."

What the nurse said and what filtered through Arthur's head were not entirely incompatible, nor were they exactly in sync.

"Genevieve are you here" is what Arthur projected into the cavernous emptiness within his head.

"Now, I'm here to help you, but now I'm thinking maybe you can help me a bit in return."

Where am I?

At that moment in real time, Arthur was struggling, struggling to see, struggling to move, and like with his first recollections, he was struggling to find someone. This time it was not Percy he was looking for, it was *Genevieve*.

"Oh, I've got plans for us. Let's say 'round midnight. Will that work for you?"

Arthur had no clue what was going on within the nurse's head, at that moment, all he heard was a white noise in the background.

Where am I?

This he repeated to himself, and all others who might be inhabiting space within his thoughts, many times but each query was stuck in a waiting pattern. The question begged for information at a faster pace than his damaged network could provide until a disruption ensued, and just like that, he went limp both inside his head and inside her grip.

Disappointed the nurse let go. "Seems I'll have to work fast, eh?" Then her eyes drifted to the floor where lay the item that had fallen off the bed. It was a book. A smile unseen by Arthur appeared as she bent down to pick it up.

"Arthur, I can't believe it. Are you a fan too? I just love this stuff. I bet I've memorized the entire table-round. I love them all, especially Tristan. But I've never heard of this author."

She flipped the pages, stopped at a random page and began to read.

> In his major article, "Arthur and His Battles," Crawford concluded that King Arthur, in fact, died at the Battle of Camlan. Crawford pointed out that there is no place called "Camlan," despite a possible Old Celtic derivation from camb(o) = curved, and Landa = enclosure. The word was probably not Celtic but Latin. If it was Latin, then it would originally have been spelled "Camboglanna." There is such a place, and it is a prominent one at that—a visible antiquity.

"Oh, Arthur, this is really, really dry, like a textbook or something. The only King Arthur worth reading is in the Romance Lit. After all, without romance, what have we got? What you have here," she continued, holding the book up in front of his face, "is just trash. Oh, oh…I have a good idea! You know what I am going to do?" She stopped and stared at Arthur who, in turn, stared at the ceiling. Nurse Flo didn't need to go into details, but her plans had taken a new direction and this she was just dying to share. But there was a problem and she knew it. So her excitement waned a bit and she changed her delivery.

"You know what the problem with men is?"

Her patient elected not to answer.

"I'll tell you what." She didn't, every woman knew the answer. Men don't listen, especially after they get what they want, physically speaking.

Instead of lamenting this point she perked back up and began to relay her plans for the coming evenings. "I'll read to you some of my old books and I'll teach you everything I know about King Arthur. Then I'll climb on top of you and let you plant your..."

Chapter 20
History of the Kings of Britain

Local investigators had spoken with Mrs. McAiden a few days post-accident. The info they obtained had been passed along to the FBI before there was any connection of the dots. The man who had ended up in the ICU was just an inconsequential victim of bad driving conditions. What he had been doing out and about in the early morning hours neither the police nor the FBI had any idea and didn't bother to ask, they were all focused on the man who had run. As the American agent, Donna, followed the Moroccan, Hicham (or Samir), to Canada, and the Canadian component of the team stayed in Jersey, things began to change. Now MacLean's group was busy trying to backfill any information they could find on the bio-tech company and what it was the Moroccan was interested in.

The day after Special Agent MacLean and Inspecteur Gervais had paid a visit to the Bio Defense Center the two men climbed into MacLean's car post morning rush hour and headed for Tewksbury. It was a nice day for a ride but the Canadian couldn't really enjoy it. He was receiving an earful before MacLean had even pulled off the interstate. In

MacLean's view, Tewksbury was where the swell folks lived. The swell folks who lived in swell houses, which sat in swell little towns. The homes found in these "swell" locales he wouldn't be able to afford in his wildest dreams. But like dreamers the world over, he often took his wife for drives through the rolling countryside just to admire that which they could not have.

When not talking, MacLean was wondering how much longer before his three-man unit became reduced by a third. The reason Inspecteur Gervais had come to the States in the first place, Samir, was now back to his old haunts north of the border with one peg of his team, his wife, following close behind. He assumed the Moroccan was targeting biological agents being developed by McAiden's firm; it was Dr. Connell's take on weapons of mass destruction, which steered him in this direction, and so he thought it likely Inspecteur Gervais would soon be leading a team back on his home turf. But since the orders had not yet indicated this relocation, MacLean hoped to make good use of the man until it did.

Today's plan started at the top, Arthur's wife, and from there he hoped to work his way down the list of all employees still in country. Why not? At that moment, he had nothing else to do and Arthur himself was not available. It was Inspector Gervais who brought up another possibility during their ride.

"In Montréal, Samir had earned extra money moonlighting for my superior, Capitainne Dionne. Dionne believed his wife was playing the field and needed someone with surveillance skills to investigate for him. If I were to tip my hat to Samir for anything it would be his talent in this regard. Small people are particularly good at hiding. Peut-être he was following Dr. McAiden, for a little extra money."

The special agent gave this about ten seconds of thought before turning once again along the winding country lane and, with this change in direction, came a view of the McAiden home. It was set back off the road and before entering the driveway they had to stop at what in the olden days must have been called a carriage house. When cleared by electronic surveillance, and the security gates raised, they drove along a tree lined trail until arriving in front of a building that was easily beyond affordable. The carriage house at the base of the drive probably cost more than either of the homes the investigators lived in and neither bothered trying a comparative calculation on the main building. They parked to the side of a garage that had room for five and both men made efforts not to covet what was seen within. It didn't work. Five minutes passed before they stopped ogling the cars they would never own.

The walk to the main house took them past members of a crew who tended the grounds, none of whom appeared to be working. Whether this was because the head groundskeeper was off site, or they were on a break, the investigators didn't know and didn't care. In fact, they pretty much ignored the hired help as they marched up to the front door, one dressed in a light-weight sport coat and slacks with a classic Euro-French look, while the other wore blue jeans and a windbreaker with the letters FBI stenciled on the back. Neither paid attention as those they had just passed quietly stole away.

The man who answered the door was wearing a coat with tails, a bow tie, and very shiny black leather shoes. His face made a favorable impression on the two investigators. His smile was friendly and winning, his eyes, set deep under his forehead and overshadowed by his eyebrows seemed to sparkle with information to come. There was nothing of a con artist in his appearance, nothing theatrical or artificial. He was there to help.

He introduced himself as Lucan, leaving the two investigators to wonder if Lucan was the given or sur and motioned them into a small sitting room before quietly explaining the situation, "I am sure you are aware Mr. McAiden is now in hospice. I also must tell you Mrs. McAiden is utterly broken, so please be careful in your phrasing."

Then, after assuring the two men the lady of the manor would join them shortly, he added, "Please sit. Tea will be served" before bowing out of the room.

Both visitors remained standing since neither could bring himself to sit on chairs, which appeared to be antiques. A few minutes passed, and then a few more without any interruption, and as they continued to wait, the Canadian spent his time gazing out the window while the American took deep breaths trying to keep his agitation in check. A woman finally did appear, but it was not the lady of the house. This one carried a silver tray bearing refreshments, tea, and scones. Like the butler, she bowed her way out as the two men stared, open mouthed. They barely had time to register their own place in the world before Jennifer McAiden made her entrance.

She was in her late thirties or early forties for sure, though if she had raised the edges of her lips upward into more of a smile, she might have looked even a few years younger. Her hair was either reddish or golden depending upon the light and her face had a symmetry to it they both noted but couldn't quite explain. She was a looker alright, but not as one would see on the cover of a fashion magazine; she was more along the lines a modern photographer's efforts to find the soul within the composition. Her first words, though, were out of place with their descriptive classification.

"My lawyer will be a little late, there's a traffic tie up on Route 78."

The two men assured her there would be no need to wait, and she assured them they would, indeed, wait—though she was very polite in doing so. So they waited, Jennifer sitting, the investigators standing. No one spoke.

Jennifer tried to force herself to stay glued to her seat until, that is, she felt an episode of retching nearing the surface. To complete the task without making a mess on the situation before her she had to leave the room. Before she made haste for the privy an idea hit: "I think I will have to leave you gentlemen for a short time. I am sorry, but while I'm gone, Lucan will see you to, to…the library." Passing the butler exactly where she knew he would be, she gave him quick instructions and then double timed it to where she needed to be.

Jennifer's stomach problems stemmed from many things, front and center being her involvement in the chain of events, which put her husband in a coma and now brought two more investigators to her home. Trying to tie these events in the grand scheme she called life into an understandable roadmap was not easy. The private detective was the real cause of this malady. She had lain in her bed many nights wondering if the man she had hired had somehow been the one responsible for the accident. She feared this above everything else, and like icing on the cake, there was the letter, the one and only letter she had received from the man. After two months on the job, he had only produced one short report in the form of a two-line message, and one quick phone call. Both of which she had received on the night Arthur had flown back from Wales. Then they disappeared; Arthur into his coma and the detective into who knew where. The letter was all she had to remember him by. On it was written a name and that name, Ellen Caldwell, belonged to her husband's lover. This is where he was that night, it had to be.

Her stomachs continued to bubble as she raced along to the loo. She didn't look back and, for a moment, didn't care about the men she left behind. She was too busy getting ready to vomit. She also didn't hear Lucan apologize. "I didn't know she had called in a lawyer. I was not consulted, and I am extremely sorry." The two investigators didn't know whether Lucan was sorry the lawyer was called or that he was not consulted.

"Library" might have been a misnomer. The room did contain books, a lot of them and they were all old, very old. As old as the books were, other artifacts filling various display cabinets, plinths and shelves could have been older still. "Mon dieu, c'est un musée."

The Canadian was spot on. It was a museum, the contents of which were way beyond the ability of most people to really appreciate. The origins of several of the displayed items even Arthur had trouble dating, though the collection had been in his family for a very long time.

Lucan apologized again, and as he backed his way out of the room, he had one more thing to say, "Please, gentlemen…"

"Don't touch." The chorus came back to him.

Without smiling, he closed the doors.

Left alone, the investigators began their survey by splitting up. Gervais started on one side of the door where what he believed to be artifacts from some ancient Mediterranean civilization were on display, a short sword, a helmet, and a breast plate. The adjacent legends didn't mention replica or copy or imitation or any other phrasing that would suggest the items on display were anything but original. It just simply told what each was and who all of them had belonged to; the emperor Constantine when he was the provincial military commander, here coalesced into the word *Imperateur*, in Britain.

Fourteen hundred years separated Constantine's display from the one in front of the FBI agent. On his side of the door a rather colorful uniform belonging to one Lieutenant-Colonel Sir Henry Walton-Ellis, commander, the 1st Battalion, 23rd Regiment of Foot (Royal Welch Fuziliers) 1815, was found.

"The year 1815, 1815, now I know something happened in 1815, what was it again?" MacLean spoke to himself while pressing his face up close to the glass counter and patting his top shirt pocket. "Damn, where did I put those glasses?"

On the other side of the room the Canadian, believing his companion to be making a jest, turned and stole a glance at the Napoleonic era uniform. "Waterloo," he spat this out in a barely audible whisper. MacLean heard the reference but didn't care, he had moved on.

The men circled the room in reverse chronologic order. In both directions were found gilded copies of books spanning the centuries and covering topics from history to religion, all of which sat alongside legal documentations relating to property sales, incorporations, various ledgers and what appeared to be travel logs. The first books in front of the Canadian were treatises of Aristotle and Plato and histories attributed to Herodotus and Quintus Fabius Pictor, all in Greek and all looking to be exquisitely reworked, handwritten copies. As he advanced into the Latin section, he saw editions of Roman works and memoirs like *De*

Bello Gallico written by Caesar himself. On the other side of the room the FBI man passed T. H. White's book on King Arthur, Eliot's poem *The Waste Land,* Tennyson's *Idylls of the King* and without any understanding, worked his way through the entire Vulgate cycle ending with Chrétien de Troyes's work *Perceval, the Story of the Grail.*

The Canadian was not much better off with respect to understanding. He passed written versions of the Welsh Triads, the sixth-century work, *Y Gododdin*, and works of Taliesin. The language on these tomes was totally unpronounceable but fortunately there were handwritten notes below each giving him an idea of the content. This is how *Marwnat vthyr Pen* became *The Elegy of Uther Pendragon.*

At roughly the same time, both reached the middle of the far wall. Standing in front of them now was a display case within which sat a single book, obviously the focal point of the entire collection. The case was made of ash and on top was a very sturdy glass plate. In the case to the right of the book was a framed legend with circa 1136 written across the top. The book itself was closed, but from what they could see of the cover, it was a beautiful piece of craftsmanship. Hardened leather covers with gilded edged pages spoke loudly of the quality of the work within. But why this book was singularly displayed they did not know. The room was full of old books, all with pristine bindings.

Historia Regum Britanniae was written in gold lettering on the front cover and translated in several languages on the legend. An informative text followed, written like a data dump on a work sheet. The only problem here for the investigators was this; it was not clearly descriptive for those not familiar with this field of study. From what they could make out, the book was written by one Gruffudd ap Arthur who may or may not have also been related to Sieffre o Fynwy. The title told them the display case contained the *History of the Kings of Britain,* this they got, but neither had ever heard of Gruffudd or Sieffre. It wasn't until the end of the printout way down at the bottom of the page, before the mystery was revealed: Gruffudd ap Arthur was Geoffrey, surnamed, of Monmouth, who lived in the twelfth century and is celebrated in English literature as the author, or possibly the translator, of *Historia Britonum*, a work from which many writers have drawn material. In the year 1152, he was raised to the bishopric of St. Asaph. But neither of the investigators had bothered to read that far.

"Look at this," MacLean whispered. He was pointing at a small bank of controls on the back of the display cabinet. "Climate controlled, and I think, it's under vacuum too."

Inspector Gervais did look and then did a slow scan of the room at large, this time noting the construction of the room itself, not the displayed artifacts. "I think the whole room is hermetically sealed. Regarder!" He moved back to the door and pointed to its framing. "This door does not pass the air."

"The whole room is airtight. I wonder why he went to the expense." MacLean mused more to himself, but his companion had an answer ready, though it was a little hard to swallow.

"Perhaps some of this is, how do you say…the real deal?"

It was almost twenty minutes before Lucan returned and ushered the two men back to the sitting room. They found Mrs. McAiden waiting, a lawyer at her side. She looked pale but composed. The interview began without further preamble. MacLean led the way.

"Please tell us anything you know about this Moroccan. We got him down as Mounir, but you might know him under a different name."

Jennifer turned and looked at her lawyer. The lawyer nodded his head and Jennifer turned back to look at the Agents.

What came next was unexpected and made the agents scratch their heads.

"I was the one who hired him."

"But my client is not at liberty to discuss her relationship with…"

The strategy might have worked if either of the investigators paid the least bit of attention to the lawyer. They didn't. They only wanted to know two things. Why had Mrs. McAiden engaged the private detective, and "Can you identify him?"

The lawyer continued obfuscating when not threatening. By the time he got around to asking the men if they had a warrant the FBI agent's ears had turned a deep shade of red. MacLean seriously contemplated bringing them both in for questioning. Since the case had taken on a terrorist angle, he probably would have no trouble justifying it, and *Wouldn't that feel good to have this asshole wasting the rest of his day in a holding tank back at the office.* Of course, not having a holding tank back at the office didn't slow him down, something else did.

"For cryin' out loud…" he had begun, but an almost imperceptibly light touch on his arm caused him to pause. The Canadian then physically interposed between MacLean and the lawyer before turning his attention to Jennifer.

How the Canadian did what he did his American counterpart couldn't understand. They both asked the same questions in, more, or less, the same order, but whatever magic Inspector Gervais was weaving, it worked. Jennifer was now looking him in the eye and soon would be answering his questions over the objections of her legal representative.

It was a relief. Originally, they had come over to confirm information they already had and to see if she could indeed identify the Moroccan. Now with Gervais smoothly opening the door information transfer was underway.

A few minutes later, Jennifer again admitted to hiring a man named Siddiqui to spy on her husband, but she could not identify him directly.

"Pour quoi?"

"I never actually met him. I was in a moment of weakness. He told a friend of mine that my husband was seeing a history teacher, and well, I lost it."

Then she passed to Christian, over more muted protests from her lawyer, the short, handwritten note she had received from her hired man. "It's the only message he ever sent me. Apparently, Arthur had been to this woman's house several times." She paused and let a few tears slip before continuing. "The woman's name is Ellen—Ellen Caldwell. Siddiqui didn't mail it, he hand delivered it to my friend."

Morgan's name then found its way into the confession. "As Morgan and I arranged. I'm still waiting for the full report. Though I guess it really doesn't matter anymore."

Inspector Gervais pocketed the paper and then begged her leave, hoping to pull MacLean along with him but before the investigators left the room the lawyer chimed in one more time, "What does a woman's action regarding her husband's infidelity have to do with your efforts?"

Unfortunately for the Canadian, he had not yet gotten MacLean out of earshot. "Nothing. Absolutely nothing. We think the dick wanted an excuse to hold McAiden under surveillance."

"Why?"

"He was interested in other things."

"Such as?"

Christian was now physically pulling his American comrade out of the room, but it only made Mike talk louder as the distance increased, "McAiden's company you idiot!"

When she heard this, her stomach clenched up tight. Then the other shoe dropped.

"We think it was the Moroccan's car that started the chain reaction."

Once outside the sitting room, Lucan pushed the two investigators toward the front door but before they reached the great outdoors everyone heard what Lucan knew would be coming. It must have been very loud inside the sitting room. Even after the butler closed the door behind them, Jennifer's wailing and intermittent screams could still be heard.

"I never ever wanted anything like this to happen."

Anger at herself quickly transposed upon a seeming liaison. "That stupid slut, a history teacher, can you believe it!" Finally, a crescendo brought Lucan and the maid running. "He was seeing a history TEACHER!" Then she crumbled to the floor. "The accident was not my fault!"

The lawyer stood watching the scene tabulating his billable hours as he picked dirt from beneath his fingernails.

"That went rather well now, eh?" Inspector Gervais deadpanned this when they reached the car.

Chapter 21
Clandestine

"We're going in undercover, that's why!" This Morgan explained for the umpteenth time, all the while wondering if what was said about blonds was true. "Look, I was asked to meet the new nurse and drop off some papers for her and..."

"This color is hideous. It's so, so. I don't know, it's just hospital garb! Who wears green scrubs out on a Saturday night? And then you told me to wear sneakers." Elaine looked across the seat with sad, imploring eyes. "Morgan," she continued, "couldn't you just call this one in? Why can't Jennifer do this in the morning?"

The chauffer wondered the same thing even though he had no idea who Jennifer was. His whole take on the situation was like Elaine's *Why me, why here, why now?*

Morgan didn't mention it wasn't Jennifer who had given her the assignment and Elaine was only in the car because Morgan needed a companion. Walking into an elder hospice in the middle of the night can be downright creepy. Morgen didn't say this, she just closed her eyes and counted to ten. When they reopened, she got her first glimpse at

Elaine's pink socks, which made her bite her lip. "How are we going to be inconspicuous when you're virtually screaming for attention?" Now Morgan, caring a bit less about the need for companionship wondered if she should just throw Elaine out of the car…while it was moving.

"Couldn't we have gone to a…" Elaine's complaining continued, trying to get Morgan to understand reason, specifically, her reason. Morgan just stared out the window and Elaine droned on.

When the car pulled into the long, winding drive the repetitive whining was no longer registering with Morgan; she was too busy taking in the unexpected. First and foremost, there appeared to be a vast armada of news trucks with representatives of every local and national outlet present, all jamming the road up to the main building. The larger trucks were being herded around to the back of the building or to an adjacent road as the hospice managers prayed local law enforcement would take over shepherding duties. Smaller vehicles were directed along to the side entrance leaving the main parking lot free for those who really needed to be there. Along with the reporters and technicians setting up lights and stages with makeshift podiums, a stream of civilians was wandering about the grounds, some with backpacks others farther out on the lawn setting up tents. It had only been a few days since Arthur's admittance and all Morgan could do was shake her head.

Vivienne had relayed instructions earlier in the day. "It's very straightforward dear, and legal. You just walk into the room, introduce yourself and get a sense of the nurse's real interest. We aren't asking her to do much, just pass bits of information and don't forget, get her signature next to Jennifer's name. This is simply for our protection and please keep me posted if you see any activities going on when you are visiting." Vivienne hadn't mentioned what those activities might be but now it became obvious to Morgan, Vivienne had a hand in current events on the ground.

Morgan hoped dressing like nurses would be a layer of camouflage. This she got right, providing they didn't wear high heels. She also had assumed, wrongly this time, hiring a driver to drop them off close to the front door would keep them out of the limelight. Given what they now saw on the hospice grounds, the chauffeured car made them even more conspicuous which, in turn, attracted all the idle news cameras. When the car stopped, the two women impersonating nurses emerged, and holding whatever was available up near their faces, like celebrities do when trying to attract even more attention to themselves, they dashed toward the entrance.

"Good thing we wore sneakers" was all Morgan could think to say.

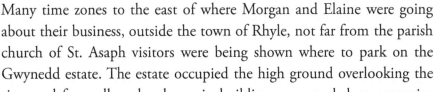

Many time zones to the east of where Morgan and Elaine were going about their business, outside the town of Rhyle, not far from the parish church of St. Asaph visitors were being shown where to park on the Gwynedd estate. The estate occupied the high ground overlooking the river and from all angles the main building commanded an expansive view. The visitors where there for a reason. It had become official, a special meeting of the board of directors would take place. The date had been set and it was looking like Malcolm's favorite getaway up near Dumbarton would host this event. Before Dumbarton, Malcolm needed to confirm the positions of a select few and have them sign some papers, hence, the party now being thrown was at his home in Wales.

As representatives from organizations with an existing investment in Arthur's company, or the desire to be part of that gang, arrived Vivienne was there to exchange pleasantries with each and every one of them. The aura of charm, wealth, sophistication, grace, and a bit of aristocracy that most of the wealthy families from ages past had lost were still evident in Mrs. Gwynedd. This is why when those arriving commented on the scenery: "It is so classic around here." It was hard to tell which landscape they were referring to. It could have been the house itself, the grounds that were home to well-tended gardens, the view of the river, or Vivienne herself.

It was late afternoon as drinks were being served on the veranda when Malcolm made his presence known. Morgan had not met the man, but she could easily describe him from all she had heard, and though not well versed in literature, a particular image did come to mind. He was tall and always clean-shaven, save for the long white mustache, and every time he was in public he was dressed in black, from head to toe, not a speck of color about him anywhere, at least anywhere anyone could see. His face looked strong—in a commanding fashion, with a high bridge on his thin nose and peculiarly arched nostrils. He had a lofty domed forehead with hair growing scantily across the top but profusely elsewhere. His eyebrows were thick and almost met over the bridge of this nose. The mouth, what could be seen of it beneath the mustache, was fixed and rather cruel looking. On occasion he smiled, and when he did, a rather unique set of white teeth were displayed. For the rest, his ears were pale, and the chin was broad but his cheeks thin. Putting it all together, atop the dark clothes, it gave the general effect of extraordinary pallor. Basically, Nosferatu reincarnate.

"Our agent on the inside, that would be the nurse, needs to see that her patient's wife, that would be Jennifer, has friends." Morgan tried, once again, to explain it all to Elaine. This time she was waving her hands and changing the story ever so slightly. She wanted to make it sound exciting, like an adventurous outing, while leaving out as much detail as possible.

"And we are in this together and wish the best for, for…um, for Jennifer's husband, right? And we must do this at night. Because…um, because the nurse works the night shift. I tell you what…"

She paused a moment, trying to remember what she was going to say but this only served to give Elaine a moment to jump in.

"This is a dreadful place and the smell, my gawd! Don't they bathe in here? And what's with all these trucks! Is someone makin' a movie?"

Not exactly, Morgan wanted to tell her, and would have, if her accomplice stopped posing for any nearby camera pointed her way from outside the windows. The circus Morgan saw on the hospice lawn was, without doubt, the vanguard. The productions to come, she feared, would be on the nightly cable news shows for a good, long time. This thought brought a macabre smile. She had never followed the Schiavo situation when it dominated the news cycle for weeks on end, but she did know of it and felt bad for the family. Deep in the recesses of her cranium where, on occasion, private thoughts did percolate, Morgan wondered if Vivienne had gone too far. No one had any real understanding of Arthur's condition, but then again, Vienne did know if a feeding tube debate erupted in Jersey it would ease the way for her husband to make some changes to the company's board of directors.

"Remember"—Morgan felt it necessary to go over the plan once again—"we're nurses, and this is like a hospital, sort of, and nurses belong in hospitals, so act like one."

Inconspicuousness is really a state of mind or, possibly, largely dependent upon the degree of interest expressed by others. As it were, the small trickle of visitors heading out of the hospice as visiting hours wound to a close were not the least bit interested in the two women surreptitiously making their way in. Those leaving were much more concerned with the mass of lights the television crews were setting up for their first reports.

Morgan and Elaine tried nonchalance when they reached the reception desk, but they didn't have to. It was vacant. As with the visitors leaving the building, attention inside was focused elsewhere. Everyone who worked at the hospice was on their phone trying for all they were worth to get ahold of someone who was really in charge. The developing situation was not in the manual.

Chapter 22
Who Watches over Death?

Cleaning up a mess in a hospital, or anywhere for that matter, is usually not on anyone's top ten list of things to do. Listening to Elaine complain about it just added a layer to the problem at hand so the nurse corralled her visitors and pushed them out the door.

"I believe I've signed in all the right places, and it really was a pleasure to meet you, but now I'm afraid I've work to do. And please, in future, be careful. Luckily, that was my dinner that spilled and not his bedpan."

Through empty corridors, Morgan power walked more to remove herself from within earshot of Elaine's incessant complaining than the need to leave the hospice proper. Elaine never faltered, and by the time the last corridor was reached, Morgan wanted to shut Elaine up, permanently. They quickly moved past staff more interested in the cavalcade of news trucks outside than the pretend nurses inside, and when Morgan stopped at the entrance, Elaine slowed her monolog as she bumped into Morgan from behind. Luckily neither fell, and after a quick inspection of their surroundings, they once again covered their faces before hightailing it back to the limo.

Nurse Flo had stood in the hallway watching Morgan and Elaine scurry off, and when she could no longer hear footsteps, she knew she was free, *at least for the night*. She reentered Arthur's room, closed the door, moved to his bedside to tuck in loosened sheets and tried to put the whole interruption out of her mind. Then she picked up the threads of an earlier conversation.

"Now, my dear, where were we before we were so rudely interrupted? You know, I should charge twice for tonight's efforts, I mean really now, you don't know what I went through babysitting those idiots. Especially the one who just wouldn't shut up!" Flo tossed her head to accentuate her point. The fact strands of hair came loose and followed along didn't faze her, she was used to it. "But then again, did you see the pair on that other woman."

She paused to catch her breath before continuing, "Women as rich and attractive as those two, but one couldn't shut up and the other was fixated on…on…well, who knows what she was really thinking about. Maybe you, I guess. Anyway, neither one can be wired quite right, can they? I mean, they want someone like me to spy on you."

Flo caught herself and at once began to apologize, "I guess I shouldn't be talking about that in front of you. I am sorry." Then she lowered her voice as if thinking out loud, "I'm fairly sure your wife just wants me to take care of you and these others are the ones who want more. I'm saying this so you will think well of your wife, the others can go to hell, and I suppose that is where they will end up. Why do I have to spy on you? Where the hell does she think you're going to go? Oh my, how many hells is that? Don't accuse me of plagiarizing Alighieri. My history prof has already done that."

Nurse Flo had planned for a fun evening with her patient but was beginning to feel a state of agitation encompassing her mood. "Okay, this woman named Vivienne is not your wife. Your wife is Jennifer. But

Vivienne is the one who first called, and…none of them really have an idea what it is I do, do they?"

Arthur didn't reply.

"I'm here to assess your situation, to make a judgment call, and if I don't like what I'm seeing, I will help you find your way to whatever comes next. That is why I sign on at these places, to help. But now, oh shit, now everything is different, and I don't know what to do."

It usually took a little longer for the emotional conflict inherent in her line of work to head her down the path of self-analysis and contrition. In this case, it seems the inevitable onset of depression had already begun, triggered by her instantaneous dislike of those who had just left the room. The growing degree of fondness for the man on the bed made things worse.

"Arthur, I feel like I can really talk to you. You are such a good listener. And that is what women really need." The last line she whispered into what remained of his left ear.

"Anyway"—she turned her volume up—"I brought my books tonight, and as promised, I am going to read to you and show you exactly what King Arthur is all about." Flo said this as she pointed and gave a disdainful look at the ratted paperback on the nightstand.

"Why are you even reading that Goodrich book, there's not even an iota of romance in it. I cannot believe you read crap like that. It's so dry." As she compared literary interpretations Flo leaned over Arthur's face with her arm stretched out in the general direction of his book. "That woman taught comparative literature and philology, not history. I mean, how can someone like that know anything about Arthur?"

Then, moving off her patient she reached into her duffle bag and pulled out a copy of Malorie's *Le Morte d'Arthur*. "I brought Malorie. I think we should read it first, though, of course, I will leave it up to you. At home, I have most of the French efforts, I'm sure if you're reading that fatuous Goodrich you've heard of the great Romancers like Chretien or Marie de France and von Eschenbach."

Here, she paused for a second, trying to get her story straight. "Well, I don't have to tell you Eschenbach isn't French, but his *Parzival* is my all-time favorite. However, as I said, we will start with Malorie. Now for the *pièce de resistance*, do you know about Project Gutenberg, that's an internet-based thing where you can download any of these without cost, and…oh now, where was I?" Flo, like many who multi-task, had gotten caught up in the moment completely losing track of what she wanted to say.

An adage, my kingdom for an adage, is what the micron thin stretch of nervous tissue relayed from one side of Arthur's brain deep into the central cortex, and when the traffic had passed through, a return message was routed. *When in doubt, it is best to just start at the beginning.* It was the best he could come up with given the reconstruction underway in his neural network. Any connection at this time, even if not broadband, was a definite improvement and this network improvement allowed for better processing, which, in turn, brought semi-cognitive real-time thought, to a degree.

"Oh yes, I know." Flo allowed a noxious degree of enthusiasm to creep into her voice. "Before I start with Malorie, I need to explain some things," and explain she did, leaving the prior delivery pattern attributed to Elaine in the dust.

"Most people don't know Malorie's book is a set of eight 'romances' and only the last book, according to the author himself was titled *The Death of Arthur*. I think it was his printer, or was it his publisher…" Flo stopped for a moment and scrunched up her eyes trying to get it straight in her own head but after a few seconds she gave up and charged on. "Whatever. Anyway, Malorie's original title was *The Book of King Arthur and his Knights of the Round Table*, so you see, this was one of the first books printed in England and already artistic freedom was being usurped by the marketing department."

Was that all one sentence?

"Why am I telling you all this I can't really say? Let's just read. Now, should we start with Tristan de Lyones, or the book of Sir Lancelot and Queen Guinevere?"

I wish my Guinevere were here with me, she would keep me warm.

The nurse paused for a moment reflecting quietly before sharing her next thought. "You know, before we start with Malorie, or for that matter, any of the Romances, we really should, like I said before, start at the beginning, before Malorie. We need to ask ourselves the main question, where did the story come from?"

When one is in the moment, they are susceptible to the whims of those around them therefore Arthur was not happy. *Oh no, not Gildas, please not Gildas, he's so self-righteous. He was the televangelist of his day. It cannot get any worse than that old monk.*

"Geoffrey."

I stand corrected.

"Geoffrey," she repeated, "Geoffrey of Monmouth, yes, sir, that's the ticket. Now, I know what you're thinking, how does a nurse know so much about King Arthur? Well, I must confess. I wasn't always in this line of work. Back in the day, and I hate to say, back a few too many days for my liking, I studied medieval literature. I have a BA in it. Of course, you will want to know how someone with a BA in literature is working the night shift at the hospice and I suppose it is about time I come clean with you.

No, thank you, I don't need to be cleaned right now, I'll let you know.

"It's a long story and to do it justice we really should, once again, start at the beginning."

Could you make it quick, I think I have another appointment. Try as he would, his inability to move or relay thoughts audibly made it impossible to stay his nurse from her self-appointed rounds.

"It started in college but my change in direction came about in graduate school really. I had moved on. I was at Princeton studying for my masters. Have you ever been to Princeton, nice place, I can tell you all about the old town."

Oh please, yes, do tell me about the town.

"I was having an affair with my mentor." Obviously, the story Flo really wished to tell had nothing to do with the history of King Arthur or, specifically, Romance literature. Instead, it had a whole lot to do with her own history in the realm of romance. She needed to tell, was dying to tell, and since Arthur was in the room putting up no discernible objections, and most importantly, could keep a secret, he fit the bill on all counts.

"That was romance, I kid you not."

Unfortunately for Arthur, he didn't have many options. He could stay where he was and listen to something from a social critique point of view, which was promising to be very painful, or he could drift away. Arthur chose the latter and wandered off along the only storyline available to him. It is not that he didn't care for the nurse's story. It was Flo, after all, who literally held his life in her hands, so listening might have helped him stay on her good side. More to the point, he just wasn't interested in romance lit. Men and women are different in this regard but to make matters worse, Geoffrey's version of *The History of the Kings of Britain* was not a book he wanted to discuss with anyone, or at least anyone not in his clan. But Geoffrey was the last to stream into his head before the *History of Nurse Flo* took over, making it the only train available.

His first recollection of Geoffrey's work was *Shit!* His second thought on that same topic was *Farce!* To get beyond these monikers Arthur needed to explain and to do this properly the storage vaults of his memory had to be tapped. Arthur was not a history major. He wasn't even a history minor, but he did know a great deal about Geoffrey of Monmouth. It was what he called a familial hobby. The story, as Arthur told it, came bubbling upward like an artesian spring. Signal to noise, it's all about signal to noise. And about the time Flo was walking her patient through her sophomore year at Kenyon College, Arthur was experiencing events far away and a long, long time ago.

Chapter 23
Revisionist Theory

Men and women are not exactly from different planets but the degree of difference within the species is quite remarkable. Without doubt, this difference begins during conception when the twenty third chromosome segregation takes place. Over time, physical distinctions do become obvious. However, much less obvious is the way male and female brains mature, assimilate information, processes it and eventually form conclusive endpoints. This was clear as Nurse Flo warmed up for what appeared to be an entire symposium on her life to date. Whether anyone would really care to listen to this run-on soap opera is hard to say but offering solutions to her problems is not what Flo really wanted anyway. She just needed her audience to listen (and not interrupt). Staying quiet was, at that moment in time, what Arthur was prone to do, listening was not so much in the cards. The masculine derivation of his internal linkage system began to reengage itself, allowing him to move his thoughts away from the influence of the woman's autobiography and off in a direction of his choosing.

I have written farce, and it has been received with open arms as truth, so now I present the truth and hope to God it will be received as fiction.

Deep within his memory, there was a story where a small fly settles on a curtain in the private office of an aged Bishop. The old man is bent low over his writing desk, quill in hand, scribbling furiously. From time to time, he looks up quickly from his task to gaze furtively over his shoulder, then slowly turns back and refocuses on his writing. He pays no attention to the fly even when it occasionally buzzed in a high arc over his head.

The history herein is purported to be, in all, the truth of events, which, for too long, have been difficult to ascertain, as this period in the story of our great country, that is, between the time of the withdrawal of the Roman legions and the advance of the Latin church, has been exceedingly dark. Yet if this rendition of events is to be believed, then I fear dear reader that this truth was not meant for your eyes. Therefore, I risk all to bring it to your attention, though I must ask your allowance, and forgiveness, for in my old age I have undertaken, misguided surely, a nefarious mission as an attempt at redemption. With this confession articulated, despondency sets itself about my person as the horns of that most proverbial dilemma arises. That is, by seeking redemption, I may sink deeper into the abyss from which there will be no salvation. While those who commissioned this work of me have exhibited the subtle hand of the demon, my hope is, by the surreptitious completion of this sister volume, the meek and righteous and most deserving of His holy

presence will be forewarned as I pay for my sins in the flames of eternal damnation.

The truth now, always the truth, we must trust in it, and above all, we must strive to act with the clarity of purpose that is embodied within this most holy of virtues. And so to persuade you of my honest intent, my sin must be revealed in advance of this history, for the parchment, and ink, and even the time for this humble transcriber were in fact paid in full, in advance, for one volume to be copied, and so you see the circumstances of my dilemma. To warn the faithful, and to save my soul, I have committed a grave sin. Read on, I implore you, for in the end you may of your own free will judge the subject to be truth or not, but at least I will have done my part in the telling and you, yours in the judging.

Now I must race against the inevitable products of time, which slow my hand and cramp my legs. If time inexorable grants a reprieve I shall finish this task, both the bidden and the hidden, and then what, I ask? The answer to such a query is difficult to articulate, for I fear distribution of this document, as its owner surely surmises, would cast our world into utter darkness for centuries on end, but to keep this hidden away may cast us into darkness forever.

With his qualifying confession set down on parchment, the writer pauses, tamps off the excess ink, and shoos away the fly before gently laying his quill down. He dries the damp ink on his perpetually blackened fingers by blowing on them, then, in perfect harmony with the habit he had set in stone, he wipes them on a well-used rag. This was a routine performed by rote after having copied thousands of pages in his prime. Now, though, the routine hurt. Those well-practiced hands were arthritic. To make matters worse, he was fighting a pitched battle with his inner demons, and confession or not, he was losing.

He shut his eyes tight, rubbed them with the palms of his hands carefully to not get ink on his face, and let a moment pass, then two, before he brought them down. His head still ached, and his stomach still turned. He opened his eyes and stared at his fingers just inches from his face. It was the only distance at which he could, at his age, still see clearly.

His deteriorating vision made it extremely difficult to write by the light of a few small tapers. Yet his commission had forced him to work at night to avoid prying eyes. The weather didn't help. Outside a cold wind picked up and wound its way through closed shutters and past drawn curtains causing candles to flicker and spray wax, which landed dangerously close to his recent efforts. This drew him out of his reverie and into action. Worn bindings and all, near to one candle sat a very, very, important manuscript.

"This will not do," he whispered and quickly moved the tome. "Just in case." The book was much too precious to be lost this way, not to mention what would happen to him if harm accidental, or otherwise, should happen to it.

When the delegation first arrived, he wasn't really sure if a commission was being offered because they didn't give him an opportunity to decline. When some members of this mission stayed in the vicinity, ostensibly to pray in the venerable cathedral, Geoffrey began to understand, they were there to keep an eye on him and their book.

Those who stayed were not the same individuals who had come to see him many years earlier. Those would be his age, or older, but the young man standing guard outside his door, and his compatriots, represented the same concern. The whole elaborate plan that was years in the making came into focus in one sudden, daytime epiphany leaving only a single question unanswered.

"Why me, Lord? Why am I being tested this way?"

The anger swelled up inside the old man who ended his search, as often happened, in an oath. "I'll make them pay. I swear I'll make them pay." Though exactly who was to be billed and how he would make anyone pay for anything was yet to be determined. And so, while Geoffrey's inner battle was being chronicled through the multi-faceted eyes of the fly, metaphoric miles away Nurse Flo was just getting warmed up.

"The troubles began when I was in graduate school. Princeton, did I tell you that already? I think I did. Anyway, I had what I thought was a charming mentor. Trevor, his name was Trevor Caldwell, but in the end, what a bastard he turned out to be. That poetry reading centaur never loved me, he just wanted my ass. Anyway, I swore after that I'd never date a tenured professor again. You know he gave me a C in his class and made me do some hard work to get even that."

Arthur didn't respond to this, so she clarified, "On my back." Again, Arthur could offer no comment on her revelation. "I dropped out soon after," she continued. "Historians are so misnamed. They should be called novelists, novelists who cannot write their own material."

"On my back, I wish I was on my back…sleeping. I'm an old man, what am I doing? I should be in bed. *Matins* comes earlier with each passing year. Those bastards won't give me a minute to myself."

Though he was the only one in the room the old monk spoke in hushed tones. One of his guests, he knew, was just outside the door of this study. In fact, if he listened carefully, he could hear the man breathing with that distinct rhythmic cadence, which signifies a body at rest.

Rest or no rest, snoring or no snoring, Geoffrey returned to work. A cleft on the left-hand side of the desk held a stack of unused vellum with the margins already outlined. These were, without doubt, the finest quality parchment money could buy. No expense had been spared by his guests. Geoffrey never really knew who they were or what exactly they represented, but they paid him money and had found a way to get his earlier work published. Now they wanted a favor in return. How they had in their possession a book first written shortly after the legions left the Island he did not know. The hundreds of years since that time was dark, there was no history in written form beyond snippets found in the Welsh lit or Saxon chronicles. Yet the tome he now copied was just such a book.

Geoffrey moved the sheet with his confession on it a bit to his right leaving the space in front of him clear, and thus, in a way, he finalized a transaction. An exchange had been made. Before committing words to paper his head had been full of his thoughts and the parchment empty. Now, the thoughts were on parchment and only guilt remained inside his head.

"I don't know what else to say," the historian lamented.

When he had nothing else to tidy up, he slid down from the stool and began to pace the room weaving in and out of the grayish demarcation zone set along the periphery of the candlelight.

"Why me, Lord? I didn't ask for this. Why me?" The man alternated between stammering questions and begging forgiveness, both directed to the ethereal space above his head. "I didn't ask for this," he repeated, and then an idea struck. "Is it all because I've been blessed with superior penmanship!"

He stopped in his tracks, and quickly made the sign of the cross. "Dear Lord, I blame you not! You have granted me this one humble gift to make my way in the world. It is my own avarice that has landed me on the edge of the great precipice." He paused as another idea stuck home, "I must send for Walter, he will know what to do." But Walter was in Llandaff, and Llandaff was not close enough. It took the old writer a minute to remember that. Then he continued his pacing.

"First, they ask me to fabricate a history, a farce, by your leave. They tell me it will make me famous, as a writer, and nothing would have swayed me to this task more than an appeal to my ego. I will surely burn for this."

He crossed himself again, begged forgiveness, and continued, "It will give the Britons something to believe in, true or not," they said, "at the expense of the Scots and the Anglos and of course those awful Normans." They also said it will make the idiot Stephen, oh the poor, poor man, it will make him smile and then stick it to his wife, that miserable Scotti. So copy, they say, what we give you, it will make a grand farce. And I did. I was even surprised they had Trojans landing on our sacred Prydein. Who would believe that? The grandest farce it was, so I wrote, sorry copied, and it was read by many, and hailed by all as a great work of...HISTORY! The greatest, I was told. But what did I care if the fools took it as fact? I had my reward. I had my fame. I was now an historian. And what did that fame do for me? Well, a lot actually. I did manage to land my own Bishopric."

"I am the bishop of St. Asaph." He paused before admitting that while he was appointed bishop, the joke was on him since he dared not step foot in his own precinct.

"They'd kill me if I did. Yet I am wondering to this day how these events are related. St. Asaph," he repeated in a tone conveying both pride of place and guilt of method, "built by St. Kentigern himself in the year of our Lord 560, and then handed over to its namesake when the great man returned to Strathclyde, to *Gododdin*."

The bishop had been set up. He had been manipulated, he had been compromised, and in all respects, he had done well and was, of course, amply rewarded, except for the fact he couldn't set foot in his own diocese. But now, when the old man wanted nothing else but to be left in peace, the bill collector came, all because, as Geoffrey admitted to himself, he had wonderful penmanship.

Both the bishop and the man trying not to listen to his nurse, grappled for a while longer with the turn of events, which had landed them both in their current predicaments. "If there ever was a fabrication, this book is it," Geoffrey assured himself, and then changed tact, "but if it is not, then this most definitely tests one's faith. Lord Have Mercy on me for believing for a moment." Geoffrey paused, wondered if what he was now writing was true, shook for a moment from nervous stimulation, and then surrendered. "Lord above, all I want at this time is to live out the remaining days you grant me in peace."

The days remaining to the old bishop were unknown, but he had a sinking feeling that peace, at least internal, would be a difficult commodity from here on in. The original document, or rather the originals that led to the group of related documents bound together and now sitting on the bishop's desk, were very old. "Once every hundred years, give or take," the bishop had been told, "when we can find someone with your skill, it is then we have a new copy transcribed. Yours will be the sixth."

Geoffrey wanted to ask a hundred questions but the look upon his visitors' faces had told him no answers would be forthcoming.

And so, while Flo rambled on, Arthur assembled blocks of information to embellish upon the story he was going to put down on paper. The story included a search, a search for illuminators, rubricators, and copyists. Apparently, a document needed restoration in the only fashion available in the day, it needed to be copied. This undertaking needed to be kept secret, and so those searching needed people they could convince, bribe, or intimidate properly. If found, the product would last another one hundred years (give or take) and the secret would be kept safe.

The committee seeing to the restoration efforts had groomed their man for this special task for over a quarter century. They did not care if he was troubled by the content, they believed they had him properly under control. The condition of the book was not yet in total disrepair, but due to Geoffrey's age, they needed to cash in quick or find a younger man and begin the process all over again. However, you cannot back a human being into a corner and assume you know what he will do, guards or no guards. They thought they had Geoffrey over a barrel, but he remained a writer at heart, a very curious writer to be sure, and so, after a few more dramatic moments of self-recrimination and qualifying appeasement to the Maker of all things, he pulled two blank sheets off the pile, set them side-by-each on the writing surface and then climbed back up onto his stool. With the clean fingers of his left hand, he gently opened the book to the passage he was most interested in and meticulously adjusted the ribbons to secure open the page from which he would copy. When that was set, he picked up his quill, dipped it, and began copying the story exactly as was laid out in the worn pages, line-by-line on one sheet, and then, when the page was full, he set it to one side and pulled the second sheet into place.

As laborious as it was for any transcriber to write one page, let alone a transcriber with this bishop's advanced age, he copied the exact same lines once again on the second sheet. Only on this page he rubricated. *If it is true*, the old bishop thought, *an insurance policy will be prudent.*

BRANCH I.
INCIPIT.

Hear ye now the history of the downfall of the High King of the Britons. The story told herein was transcribed ver batim from an ancient source, written in this same and most exact of languages, Latin. This important commission was entrusted to me, your humble copyist, at this late hour of my life under the same direction as was placed before five of my antecedents, each engaged on the 100th anniversary of the compilation of the original. "Copy the tome with a steadiness of hand. Think not of what lies within, but rather focus always on the preservation of the whole," is the task set before me as had been set before my predecessors.

Being a bona fide historian, he felt it his duty to point out potential source issues.

> *In the year of our Lord 542, or possibly 539, give or take, dependent upon the calendar in use or the ability of the chronicler of the day, of which I hear there were few, an event occurred that, in all respects, led to the diminishing of His light upon this most humble multitude of sinners, who live upon the three islands collectively known as Prydein. With the wave of human presumption, and arrogance, through force of arms, or might falsehood be more the way of the evil that has infested our simple world, has come the need for those who seek truth and to bask in His holy presence, the need for preserving the truth in secret or risk the eternal extinction of His most holy word. The preservation of this history has been passed down from one generation to the next until at last it falls upon my most unworthy hands, however illicitly, and now I must take this holy rood upon my back and, being blessed only with the gift of penmanship, and timing, transfer the contents of the sacred keepings onto fresh parchment to so perpetuate ideals held herein, until such time as this fellowship of the table round feels the strength needed to complete its ministry.*

The hour had already grown late when Geoffrey began in earnest. It wasn't long thereafter before his hand ached too much, and he had to finish for the night.

"Time was when I could reel off five, maybe six pages a day, now look at me, I've barely done two." He shook his head at the inequity of it all before dismounting. There wasn't anything for it but to quit for the night, writing, that is. But there was simply no way, tired or not, that he could sleep, not until he had read more. "If this is true, then…" he kept repeating this line as he picked up the book and a candle before he left his study. He was heading for a special place, a room most conducive to both catharsis and reading. With book in hand, he treads softly so as to not wake the man sleeping outside his door and gradually wound his way through the corridors of the cloister while swatting at a fly, which had been following him since he had left his office.

At this time of night, he was sure to have the sanctuary to himself and he found it relaxing to inhale the aroma of so many different herbs tied in bundles drying in the rafters. He set the candle on the edge of the overhang, pulled up his robe and positioned himself over one of the openings. The fly found a nice vantage point in amongst a family of relatives keeping well clear of large webs strung across the upper corners of the room. The room itself was off the main hall leading to the bishop's bedchambers on the third floor, and so, being three stories up there was bound to be a little updraft in the chute and this tickled his underside. Suppressing a giggle, he found the chapter he had been copying and began to read.

"The Death of Arthur, *Dux Bellorama*, the *Imperatore*."

The old monk just couldn't put the book down, not willingly anyway. Of course, it was quite heavy so he could only keep it propped up on his knees for a defined period of time before his legs would go numb, and coincident with that timing he was startled by a hard rap upon the door.

"Just a minute," he begged and admonished himself for monopolizing the indoor outhouse.

The man on the other side of the door returned his plea with a menacing query.

"Oh, it's you. Yes, I still have the book, it is safe in here with me. There is no need to worry or"—*or what, threaten me in my own house*—"become alarmed. I've taken good care of it while you slept. I'm sure your master will be very interested to know how vigilantly you and the others go about your assigned duties."

The door was open now, and the old man looked toward the younger, bigger man as he handed over the tome. Being old and wizened gave one the right to act childish at times or so the bishop thought. "Tomorrow, same time?" he teased.

The guard said nothing as he took the book and held it close to his chest. Then he turned and sulked down the hall, heading for the rooms assigned to his delegation. Geoffrey watched, feeling guilty. In his mind, he had just sinned again. It is one thing to be envious of the man for his youth, which, of course he was, and it is quite another to despise him for his possession, the book, which he did. But still worse, the old bishop hated him for his free time in which he could absorb himself in the written word at his leisure.

When the representative of the commission turned a corner and was out of sight, the full weight of the hour slammed itself against the tired old man's frame. He turned and with a brief vision of his inviting bed to guide him he began the short walk to his room. "At least," he gloated, "I have a bed with a stuffed mattress to comfort my old bones, while we've accommodated our visitors with rough…"

Unfortunately for the envious, mischievous, and sometimes spiteful priest, before he could take another step, he heard the soft chiming of bells as the acolytes moved from room to room calling out the arrival of Matins.

"Merde," he whispered in surrender.

Like Geoffrey, Arthur, too, heard the calling of Matins.

"Shit," Nurse Flo spat out. "I've been talking to you all night. It's time for me to call it a day, or is that 'a night'? Don't worry, I'll be back tonight, or is that today? Oh whatever, either way we will pick up where I left off, okay?"

Chapter 24
The Miller's Tale

The international crime solving duo were peering over a photocopy of the note Mrs. McAiden passed to them the moment before she wilted in a meltdown of historic proportions. The original document was now locked away at the FBIs New York office for safekeeping.

> Le sujet est arrivé T.Boro 0100 heures as informed.
> Follow 45 min to domicile of Ellyn Caldwell. Address
> to follow, instructeur histoire Princeton, picture to
> follow avec rapport complet, check mail.
>
> —A. S.

It was their tenth attempt to make sense of the document. At this point, they agreed 100 percent on only one thing: The message could have been more informative. They were also fairly certain, agreeing at about a 95 percent confidence limit, the message had been written by

Samir; the initials matched his cover name, and the handwriting was a dead-on match with a sample received from Christian's home office.

Morgan, identified as a friend of Mrs. McAiden, had been interviewed. The interview itself had been interesting for the two male interrogators given Morgan's style of delivery, but at the end of the day, all she could really do was supply a description of the man she hired and pull his face out of a photo array. The pictures, like the handwriting samples, had been curtesy of *la Sûreté*. All in all, they had believed Samir played a role in the stream of events under investigation, confirming this was not the problem foremost on their agenda. That which was causing consternation, and the scratching of heads was the order from those in charge at the New York field office. "Find the teacher named Ellyn Caldwell."

Tracking down Arthur's mistress wasn't quite as straightforward as either one imagined. First, her name was spelled with a *yn* not an *en*. Next, their first pass on the FBI database of high school teachers in the Princeton area came up empty.

"Maybe I should broaden the search to schools outside Princeton borough or perhaps she is a middle school teacher."

"C'est une possibilité," Inspector Gervais answered absentmindedly.

MacLean looked up and watched his partner smooth the photocopied wrinkles out of the note. "What are you doing?"

Christian shooed the man away as he tried to take a first derivate of the available data all in the hope of calculating new meaning from the words on the page. "Attendre, une minute." He looked up and added, "S'il vous plait."

MacLean waited and watched and waited a little longer before the Canadian finally spoke again, "Régard."

"What am I..." MacLean caught himself before slipping his derivation of the French language into his response. He began again, "What am I supposed to be looking at?"

"I believe your office has translated incorrectly," Inspector Gervais said before holding up one finger. "Un, Ellyn is not a 'teacher' mais peut-être est-elle 'professeur,' et deux, if it says Princeton, perhaps she is a professor at l'université de Princeton, non?"

MacLean shrugged his shoulders while staring at the writing on the table.

Christian continued, "Only your comrades in New York said 'teacher,' and we have blindly followed along, oui? Our target wrote the word instructeur."

It made so much sense when Christian explained it thus. "Et trios." now Gervais expounded his theory on penmanship and font spacing. "I have old documents with Samir's handwriting, he is very well trained in the art of penmanship. We can see that in this note. Everything is neat and, um…well-spaced except just before the name 'Ellyn.' Perhaps Ellyn is missing a few letters.

"Well, that's interesting and might explain why the FBI list wasn't getting a hit, but what do you suggest we do?"

"Je ne sais pas." That was a fact. While the theory was interesting, Christian didn't know what to do with it. "Perhaps we should check the university for a Professor Caldwell and just leave out the first name."

Perhaps that asshole terrorist could have just written down the address on the note is what MacLean wanted to say, but didn't; instead, he took out his trusty computer and did a search for Caldwell, History and Princeton University.

"Glen Ellyn, Caldwell Community College, teaches history. I don't think this is what we are looking for." He tried several variations on the search query but those, too, turned up no useful leads. Next, he tried searching the Princeton University website, but when that didn't work, he went old fashion and was soon put on hold awaiting a qualified representative in the provost's office. Putting his hand over the phone he whispered, "They don't like to talk to the FBI over there," meaning the Ivy League school.

When he finally did get to speak with a human being, it wasn't the provost, it was the next in line. Immediately, MacLean registered the left leaning political persuasion of the woman he was speaking with and so, learning from his Canadian partner, he tried blending in.

"We are just trying to follow a lead, and no one is being implicated in a crime, any crime, and did you get a chance to watch that wonderful speech last night?"

The answer he pulled out of the vice provost wasn't what he was expecting, but he and Christian didn't have anything better to go on, so the two men once again boarded the company car to visit one Trevor Caldwell. Not quite the right name, not quite the right age, probably not the right sex, but the occupation fit, and the address put him remarkably close to the scene of the accident. Therefore, he merited a visit.

The professor's house was set back from the road on a tree lined cul-de-sac. The detectives parked on the street and walked up a well-trimmed path passing what could only be considered a quaint vine covered mailbox with more than a hint of clematis buds portending the display to come. The front door of the faux Tudor faced east so they stood in the morning sun staring into the shadows of the doorway patiently waiting for someone to answer the bell.

The day was already warm, and the thermometer was only going up yet the man standing behind the crack in the door wore a brown cardigan, worn at the elbows, and his hair, what was left of it, was completely disheveled like the blue, button-down shirt he wore half in and half out of his pants. With his toes ensconced in slippers and an unlit pipe dangling from his mouth, a book in his left hand, and a fountain pen laced between the fingers of his right he moved back an inch to open the door a bit wider. Both investigators took in the view and tried to catalogue what was before their eyes, neither sure if the man was an antiquated professor or a professor of antiques.

All three stood for a moment, each giving the unknown party(s) a once over before MacLean opened the questioning.

"Do you know an Ellyn Caldwell?"

In response, the old man removed the unlit pipe from his mouth and placed the fountain pen in his shirt pocket where it immediately began to leak.

"No."

"Then I don't suppose you know this man," Inspecteur Gervais cut in, showing Professor Caldwell a picture of Arthur McAiden.

"Terrible business that," he said, indicating the picture positioned in front of his face.

"So you know what happened to him?" The FBI man asked then kicked himself for the obviousness of the question.

Trevor Caldwell, Professor Emeritus, Princeton University, returned the unlit pipe to his mouth, smiled at the investigators, and said "Gentlemen, where are my manners? Please come in." He turned, motioning the two men to follow, and shuffled off down the dark entrance hallway mumbling apologies as he went along. The investigators followed, sidestepping a large urn holding several walking sticks of various makes and sizes and an umbrella. Perched on the top of one of the sticks was a plaid fedora.

Professor Caldwell talked at them all the way back to his study, and like Dr. Connell at the Biodefense Center, he had to move several stacks of papers and books from two chairs to make them accessible. Then he motioned his guests to sit. "I'll be right back, just need to put the kettle on…ah, anything to eat?"

The professor didn't receive visitors often and he told them so. "Not anymore, not for a long while that is, except Arthur, of course." This he relayed as he poured tea and from the tone of his voice the inspectors understood they were about to be held hostage by a man who, in his working life, was used to having an audience or at least the give and take of intellectual stimuli. It wasn't a difficult capitulation given the amicable nature of their host and the fact they just didn't have any other pressing appointments. So they made themselves comfortable on studded leather chairs amongst books and papers and works of medieval art adorning the walls. The aroma of cigars smoked in days past added to the ambiance as they sat quietly for a moment sipping their Earl Grey.

Two sips passed before the professor asked to see the picture again. After a short period of introspection, he looked up and spoke. "He was such a good man. You should have seen all the people visiting him at the hospice. Many of them I knew. Arthur had introduced me to some, others I knew from the literature or conferences I've attended."

These short sentences were all the professor could manage. He stopped talking, which was a mistake because without the effort of placing words in a sentence it gave time for tears to well up. Once that happened, there was only one place for them to go.

Agent MacLean was a fast learner. His father used to tell him, "Always use the right tool for the job." He did. He turned to Inspector Gervais and nodded. The American figuratively moved aside yielding the floor to his counterpart. Christian leaned forward in his chair and began to ease the professor out of his emotional state. The questions he asked were simple, needing only short thoughtless answers. When the man was again fully engaged in the moment, Christian gradually extended the depth of his queries.

A few minutes later, one of Professor Caldwell's domestic helpers arrived. She peeked her head into the study to get a head count and then left to prepare lunch.

"She usually gets here a little later, but I think we could manage more than a pot of tea if either of you are interested that is. I hope you are. I hate to eat alone. I don't drink much anymore, the hard stuff, not during the day, except now, of course…if you want some. At night, though, I do like my medicinal shot of brandy."

He paused in his narrative. "So did Arthur." The sad reminisce brought a quiet over the room until the old man rallied. "My cook," indicating the woman now in the kitchen, "comes every other day, the maid only once a week, and as you can tell, she didn't come today…or yesterday."

"She," the old man whispered, again, meaning the cook, "is my lover. Not the first and hopefully not the last." The younger men came close to laughing and this bit of encouragement opened the door for some of the most incongruous entertainment imaginable as the professor began to regale them with a story that appeared to have no end, moved in and out of cadence, and understanding, since it was delivered in what they imagined to be a jabberwocky-like verbiage.

> *That he ne visited with his solas,*
> *Ther any gaylard tappestere wus.*
> *But sooth to seyn, he was somdeel squaymous*
> *Of fartyng, and of speche daungerous.*

In amongst the rhymes the professor's purported lover poked her head back into the room calling them to supper. This disruption didn't really slow the pace of the story; it only made the old man work a little harder to keep his elocution steady with a mouth full of food. The spittle aside, and with the help of some transliterations, the detectives got the gist of what he was about, right up to the part where the hot poker came into play:

> *This Nicholas anon leet fle a fart*
> *As greet as it had been a thonder-dent,*
> *with the strook he was almoost yblent;*
> *And he was redy with his iren hoot,*
> *And Nicholas amydde the ers he smoot.*

At this point, the professor stopped, noted the look of surprise on his two guests, and asked in a circuitous fashion, "Am I correct if I say you both know the story?"

Shy embarrassment graced the faces of his guests—each waiting for the other to speak.

"Miller's tale?" the professor prompted.

"Well, yes…of c-c-course," MacLean stammered while Christian nodded along the way people do when they haven't a clue.

"Chaucer," he continued, eliciting more rote nods. "*The Canterbury Tales*, for Christ's sake!"

Chapter 25
Arthur's Tale

With lunch finished, Professor Caldwell led the men back to his study, passed cigars all around and managed to find brandy snifters that, in the dim light, hinted at being clean enough to use. Though a little hesitant to light cigars amongst the stacks of old papers and books cluttering every available space, the investigators took their lead from the older man and soon the room was filling up with a pungent aroma and a lot of smoke. Then the professor pulled a dusty old bottle from some deep recess behind his desk.

Glasses of cognac were handed out, and with all ensconced in a chair of their choice enjoying the fullness of the moment, it appeared a short nap would have been in order for all concerned. Until, that is, Christian, fighting hard against this most hedonistic desire, pulled himself upright (more or less) while asking "Do you have the whole book memorized?"

"Oh, dear no, just the one tale, and I'm afraid I butchered that. I've been off my game for a while now. If you had asked for any other, I would have had to read it. You see, in my day, I was somewhat of an expert on the Miller's tale."

In one deft play, Inspector Gervais returned the conversation to where it had started, "And Arthur, did he enjoy Chaucer?"

Appearing to be at a loss the older man turned and looked directly at his guests. After a long, thoughtful pause, he started to speak in a soft, sorrowful voice. "I don't really know how to begin. Such a tragedy—I feel so guilty."

"Guilty?" The agents were caught off guard.

"Lucan has been a dear, he's come by twice now. He literally held my hand when I felt most low." At this point, the professor almost had his tear ducts overflowing again but managed to hold fast. "The fact of the matter is, if Arthur wasn't here that night..." The professor took a long, deep drag on his cigar.

When the exhaled effluent had cleared his nostrils, he continued, "I know it's irrational. I understand probability theory, but I also understand cause and effect." He lowered his voice to a harsh whisper. "There was no cause for him to stop by so late. But he did. Right from the airport he came to see me."

At this juncture, the obvious question to ask was, why? Indeed, it was not only an obvious question, but it was *the question*. What had started as a routine tying up of loose ends for the agents, to establish the identity of Arthur's paramour and his whereabouts just prior to his accident, had just changed. In fact, the professor's disclosure cast the identity of the mistress and indeed her very existence into jeopardy.

"He was very agitated that night. I'd never seen him in that state before. He threw the Goodrich book right down on my desk and began pacing."

How anyone could pace in the confines of the professor's study was hard for either of the investigators to imagine but it didn't stop them from trying.

"He wanted to know..."

"Professor, Professor, s'il vous plaît," Christian tried to cut in, silently agreeing with the man when he said he didn't know where to begin. "You make the cut-short, non? Perhaps you should tell first of your experience with M. McAiden?"

"What? My experience with…oh, yes, I see what you're about, quite right, quite right, at the beginning so to speak."

"Oui, c'est ça." The adage, be careful what you wish for, came to mind no sooner than the words had left his mouth. Give an academic the floor and you never knew when he would be finished with it. MacLean agreed with what his partner was thinking as he passed his glass across the desk for a refill.

"I first met Arthur at Cardiff."

Both men had brought along mini recording devices which, without the professor's knowledge, were now engaged. Then, easing back into their chairs, they made themselves comfortable. Later is when they tried to distill the essence of what was heard into workable bullet points. It took a while. The professor spoke with sweeping, panoramic depictions of places both natural and within historical context along with mini dissertations on first one, then another romance author all of which needed a good deal of background checks to format.

They were told the professor had spent a year abroad on sabbatical, teaching a course on, what else, Chaucer. He also spent some time researching his second favorite author, Geoffrey of Monmouth. Caldwell told his guests about a time he clearly remembered. He was in discussion with some of the faculty as they were walking amidst a cloister of old buildings.

"If we could only find a copy of Walter's book it would validate the whole thing. This is how I began. I remember it like it was yesterday." Never, before, or since, he told them, had he been laughed at so, not to his face anyway.

"This is when I first met Arthur. He was the young man trailing behind the group. He looked the other way when they laughed. When I peeled off, giving a lame excuse which, I have to say, didn't allow me any saving of face, Arthur followed. I managed to put some distance between myself and my detractors when he made his presence known by queuing up alongside.

"I've always been amazed by his eyes. They were so, I don't know… happy. Perhaps full of excitement is a better descriptor and my, oh my, he did have a full head of hair. The color changed a bit over time, but at least he still has it." Here, Professor Caldwell ran his hand over the remaining wispy strands occupying his pate. "Oh well, what can one do."

"Of course, I thought he just wanted to continue the conversation, and I suppose, in a way, he did.

"You're right, you know." These were the first words the young man said. I guess it was his way of introducing himself. His gaze was locked onto me, but at first, all I did was glance his way wondering why this audacious local would find pleasure in a continued torture of the visiting American.

"When I didn't answer, he just kept walking beside me and talking. He had a friendly, confident way about him, and it didn't take long before I was answering his questions and getting up the nerve to ask him what was bothering me. 'Why did you say I was right?' It was like Dickens wrote, 'It was the best of times and the worst.' Only I had the worst at the beginning, and now here was an interested student, what more could a teacher want?"

The professor had emptied his glass, and so he stopped for a moment to pour another. When he began again, the entire room drifted along with him as he delved deep into his memory to pull out an old conversation.

"I'm Arthur, Arthur McAiden. I must say you do Chaucer justice. Chaucer must be delivered with the right cadence, or it falls apart. His words came alive in your hands."

"Really, well now, I must say thank you, but again, why do you think I was right with respect to Geoffrey?"

Arthur hesitated. "Because it's obvious," he responded. "If anyone could find the original manuscript Mapes provided, well then, there you have it."

"Have what?"

"Walter Mapes was the Archdeacon of Oxford, and an acquaintance of Geoffrey's. And having it, the book that is, is exactly as you said. It is needed to validate one of the most important works ever written as a work of history, QED. Otherwise, the fiction-nonfiction debate will continue, *ad nauseam*."

"So why did they laugh at me?"

Arthur tried one more time to explain: "Because Professor Caldwell, having Walter's book to justify Geoffrey's work is the obvious solution. That is how history, real history is confirmed. You need multiple points of view, corroborating sets of data so to speak."

I didn't quite know how to respond. "You're in my class" was all I could manage.

"Well, I must admit I'm not officially. I'm in another department. I drop in on some of the lectures over here from time to time. Just for fun."

"Just for fun?" I repeated, savoring Arthur's answer. "Anyway, that was how we met."

Caldwell had come out of his trance, but he did not stop his recital. "You see, to really study the Romance texts you need more than a working knowledge of French. It helps a great deal to know a bit of old French, old English, Latin of course, P and Q Celtic, some German. Let me see, did I miss any?"

This query he asked the room in general as he counted on his fingers. Getting no responses in the negative he continued, "Arthur knew them all. He is one of the most well-read laymen I've ever met. I use the term layman for lack of a proper descriptor. I truly believe he was better versed in the topics that interested him than most faculty are, whether it was here at Princeton or any of the elite schools in Jolly ol'. He had... he had, no, excuse me, he's not dead yet, so I should say 'he has,' right?"

One of the two sitting across from him nodded. The other just remained silent, eyes closed, carefully balancing the half full glass of cognac on the gentle curve of his stomach as it moved up and down in perfect harmony with each successive breath.

"He has." Professor Caldwell repeated, "A knack for seeing through the allegory, the flowery metaphor, and sometimes just the plain ol' bull. He can translate original works within a context that becomes correct, both historically and anthropologically. It's almost like he, too, has a little cheat book akin to Geoffrey's use of Walter's work."

"Pardonnez Monsieur, je ne comprends pas."

"Oh, please forgive me, some of the ideas he came up with, well it just seemed like one would have had to have been there, so to speak, to have such a complete understanding. Do you see what I mean?" Neither in the audience looked as if they did so he tried to explain, "Geoffrey, son of Arthur, or ap Arthur, later known as Geoffrey of Monmouth, completed his most famous work *Historia Regum Brittaniae* in the year of our Lord 1136."

The professor took a breath and then barreled forward. "According to what we have in terms of written evidence, Geoffrey claims Walter asked him to translate this document into Latin, hence, pre-Romance. Now, we believe the *History of the Kings of Britain* was dedicated to Robert, Earl of Gloucester, and Waleran, Count of Mellent. What we do not know for sure is whether this was a straight translation of Walter's 'ancient book' or if it contained considerable embellishments, possibly from Geoffrey himself. At the time, the work was taken at face value and accepted by most as a true history of the Welsh nation from around a thousand or so years before Christ to AD 700, give or take. And when I say Welsh nation, I do not mean the small bit of territory we call Wales today. Merlin appears in this book and is later expanded upon in Geoffrey's other work *Vita Merlini…*"

At this point, Christian interjected. "Was Dr. McAiden interested in Merlin?"

The old man smiled warmly, happy he had an audience, before politely answering without the least trace of condescension.

"Oh no, no, no. Arthur was interested in Arthur. The *History* is most noted for its extensive chapters covering King Arthur. Before this book, there were only sporadic lines of reference to an 'Arthur' or 'Artur' found in various places like the Welsh triads, Gildas, Nennius, the Mabinogon, the Saxon Chronicles, et cetera. But none of these references proclaimed him King. The lack of volume on this subject before Monmouth's work makes it hard to get a handle on just who this man was. At best, we have a man who could have been a battle leader of some sort. Old Roman terms such as *Imperateur* or *Dux Belloram* keep coming up as possible titles, but not King. Then along comes Geoffrey and suddenly, we have a pedigree, a royal court, everything."

"So wherein is the problem?"

"Ah, now you've hit the nail square. As I've said, History needs cross referencing for validation. This allows for corroboration and the establishment of an understanding of what terms really meant at the time of their use. Best of all is when similar histories are written from opposing political camps, this helps sort out truth from the victor's version of the truth.

"There are no other works covering this period from which we can corroborate Geoffrey's work. This is what the young Mr. McAiden was telling me the day we met. The time of Arthur was the beginning of the dark ages, and there was a reason for calling it thus. The Romans had left the Isle maybe seventy-five or so years before the story of Arthur takes the stage. The *civitas* structure was in decline. In fact, many believe a good part of the struggle of the day was between those factions wishing to keep a semblance of centralized authority based upon the Roman system and those who wanted to carve out their own fiefdoms in the vacuum left by the departing legions. If people were writing things down during this time period, their efforts didn't survive."

Professor Caldwell paused for a moment giving one of the two investigators time to digest this bit of his lecture before continuing. The other man he let sleep.

"As I said, when first published Geoffrey's work was taken at face value and accepted by most as fact, a true history if you will. It was a best seller in its day. However, since the seventeenth century the poor man has been almost vilified, and his work pretty much taken to be farce. But no one could give a rational explanation as to why he would do such a thing.

"At the time, the book was written there was nothing like what we might call 'pulp fiction' today. An accomplished clergyman was not expected to be churning out works of this sort if they were not true. That came much later, say in the time of Chaucer. So the question of questions to those trying to understand was, once again, this: If it were fiction, why would he do such a thing?

The professor paused for a moment, mulling a few ideas around before continuing. "Today we tend to be a little more forgiving of ol' Geoffrey. The Britons were being completely overrun by Germanic influences, which had started way back when the Legions were leaving the island. Eventually the invaders gained the upper hand but then, just when a status quo was developing, along come the Normans and subjugate both the Anglo-Saxon contingent and those we have come to call Welsh. Geoffrey may very well have been attempting to provide a framework of mythology for the Britons to hang their hat on, as a way of saying, hang in there, you were once great, and greatness may come again. But he wrote in such a fashion, call it fiction or mythology or whatever, so as to not tread on the toes of his Norman masters."

The professor again worked through some thoughts before continuing. "Others believe that the Arthurian sections of the book were true but written in a metaphoric or possibly, allegorical style. Quite difficult to translate today."

"How is any of this then proven?"

"By finding a corroborating text."

"Such as Walter's book."

The older man had come a long way since he had his feathers ruffled in the old cloister at Cardiff. Today, he just nodded his head, smiled, and eventually broke into a hearty laugh. "Exactly."

This woke the sleeping FBI agent who looked around to regain his bearings. "Did I miss anything?"

Christian ignored his partner to clarify one last point. "So Arthur, our Arthur, was interested in finding Walter's book?"

The question genuinely seemed to stump the professor. He moved his jaw to one side and then slowly back. He chewed on the back of his right forefinger and then repeated the question slowly being sure to enunciate each word. Then he paused and looked at the ceiling before answering. "No."

"No?" Christian wasn't taken aback by the answer, just its length.

"No." Professor Caldwell repeated, "As I said before, Arthur was interested in Arthur, so he didn't appear to be looking for Walter's book per se. More often he was just interested in what others thought of Geoffrey and the whole King Arthur legend. For example, on the night of his accident he insisted on coming here straight away because he wanted to discuss this Goodrich woman's book. He was quite agitated by this. It had set him off on his other pet peeve."

"Which was?"

"The only topic that ever pushed his emotional hot button was what Arthur referred to as the *terrorist issue*."

Both men sat up straighter and began to inch their way toward the edge of their seats. It was now MacLean's turn to chime in. "Terrorist here in…"

"Oh no, no, not these ridiculous idiots who want everyone to live in the eighth century. Of course, ideologically they are the subject, but not directly. Fanatics today are like amateur children compared to those whom Arthur directed his most vehement condemnation. The ultimate terrorists he despised were of the fourth- and fifth-century variety."

The agents looked at their host without comprehending.

"Surely, gentlemen, you cannot think of one organization that emerged as a power in Western Europe as the Roman Empire fell apart? An organization so fanatical if you didn't believe their interpretation of scripture you were cast as a heretic. If you were not with them, you were against them, so to speak." Professor Caldwell didn't wait for a confirmation of understanding; he just began to move to other topics. But those other topics would have to wait. The investigators had begun to disentangle from their chairs.

The professor stopped midsentence, noting his time at the podium was finished, politely thanked the two men for supplying him with much needed company and then led them out the door and down the walkway on the pretext of checking his mail. "I'm waiting for my publisher's clearinghouse notification. I'm feeling lucky today."

As lucky as the professor felt, it was the FBI agent who fortune rewarded. As they approached the roadway something caught MacLean's eye. The side of the mailbox heading away from the house was not entirely covered in clematis streamers. A small clearing was there upon which fading letters were visible. On one line the letters on the box spelled 'ellyn.' This inscription sat atop, though not properly centered over 'Caldwell.' The FBI agent inched close enough to touch the box and gently moved aside parts of the growing plant. As he lifted the vines, he saw the name 'Trevor' appearing above 'ellyn.' He turned to the professor and asked. "What is your middle name?"

"Llewellyn. Why do you ask?"

"Professor," Christian spoke up, "have you ever met Arthur's wife?"

Chapter 26
Vertigo

Inner-ear disequilibrium, otherwise known as seasickness, can force the heartiest to their knees. For some, deep ocean swells bring on fits of retching. For others, the rhythmic movements of two interlocked bodies in the heat of passion will do the trick. For those with vision problems, standing near the ledge overlooking an expanse of gently rolling fields will force them to sit, hold onto the ground beneath and pray. Kudos could be heaped upon Nurse Flo for what was happening to her patient. If she hadn't been trying to use Arthur's accoutrements to satisfy her own urges it would have been a bit longer before anyone noticed, Arthur was back on the same side of the fence.

Before vertigo set in, it had been a normal day for the patient. He was still tied down until Flo loosened the restraints a bit. It made it easier for her to mount, and mount she did. When finished, she climbed down and was beginning to tidy up when she had to call for help. At the time, Arthur didn't know the cause, he just felt the symptoms. Nurse Flo, on the other hand, may have known the cause but had no idea of the symptoms playing out between her patient's ears. At first, Flo did not notice any movement, but apparently, he did move quite a bit. Given the chance he had grabbed and pulled at everything in his reach. This included all the wires and tubes attached to his personage. The only good news emanating from all of this was that he became classified as "out of coma." The bad news being, no one at the hospice bothered to call his wife or any of the news organizations who had set up shop on the hospice grounds. As the right to die circus continued playing out his wife also continued to struggle with the decision those camped upon the grounds were waiting for her to make.

Trazodone along with a few other pharmaceuticals had been part of Arthur's regimen since his arrival at the hospice. It was labeled as effective for insomnia and impulsiveness. Those tending to the patient cared little about his insomnia but did worry about any rapid physical activity like what had just occurred. No one commented on the relaxed restraints on the bed when they placed a few calls and waited for the okay. When that was given, they upped dosage.

"We cannot have him moving around"—they all agreed—"until we have a better handle on the situation."

The physical outburst had, to tell the truth, surprised them all. They simply had not expected his awakening.

"Maybe he should have stayed in the ICU a bit longer," a few on staff mumbled. Others took note to ask Guinevere about returning him to the hospital. Who was Guinevere? No one knew but this was who he asked for as they reattached the breathing tubes.

When the hospital staff finished cleaning up and upping his meds, and all was finally back to hospice normal, Flo did, as promised, pull a copy of *Idylls of the King* out of her tote bag, wiggled the only chair in the room up beside his bed, caught her breath and began reading. Tennyson's word usage did the rest.

It seems the dialectic once again channeled Arthur back in time. The events he chronicled now had transpired on a boat ergo, his seasickness continued. Arthur told of how he and his legions had spent the season fighting alongside Clovis. They did not know they were helping the

Merovingian change Gaul into *Frience*. They only sailed across the channel to help those keeping the Visigoths at bay. The fighting at Vouillé had pretty much handled the situation, and so when the call for help came from home, Arthur and members of his war party were quick to board ship and leave Breton behind.

Caerleon, the fortress evolving into a city on the western tip of Hadrian's Wall, was their destination. Messages sent to Arthur told of unrest in the north. By dispatch, he had called for a mustering. Everything was being put in order for a swift move on those massing against his northern holdings. The only problem for Arthur, both Arthurs, was the boat. Neither traveled well on boats. Horses, not a problem, boats, vertigo.

Thank God that's over, ancient Arthur thought. Feeling there was nothing left inside needing to come out he pulled himself back up over the side, rolled off the gunwale and sprawled out on the deck proper. In the shade of the large, square sail and with eyes closed he felt and heard the world around him, counted the seconds needed to reach the top of each swell and held his breath on the downturns. He listened to those watching him and the sound of the swaddled legs inching closer. He didn't need to look to know who it was. He could feel the humiliation to come.

When he did open his eyes, he had trouble focusing. A tangle of red hair was corrupting his entire field of vision. He closed them tight once more, and as the ship took a small dip, he willed his internal organs to stay put. When he felt stable enough, he peeked out again only to find the mass of hair, like a red tinted verge, continuing its obstructionist policy. Arthur moved his head gently to one side in a halfhearted attempt to expand his world view but couldn't manage the distance needed. So thinking it better to just leave them closed he did just that and tried to push the obstruction away.

With his extended arms, he found the head behind the massive red curtain and pushed gently but firmly trying to create space. His effort met with firm resistance. Then, feeling along the crevices and odd protuberances hidden behind the beard his prying fingers happened upon the firmly clenched jaw, which led inexorably to the orifice of Angus. When the tight seal loosened, and the lips began to part Arthur withdrew his fingers a safe distance less they became trapped within the expanding maw.

"Arthur," an unforgiving voice whispered, "you canno' lie abou' on deck where every bloody fool on this stinkin' excuse of a seafaring vessel can see ya'. It's jus' na' rye. You're the *Dux*."

In response, Arthur groaned low and slow. The man to his fore pulled aside the tussle of hair from the edges of his chapped lips and tried a few alternate rhetorical devices to help his friend in his time of need, including logic, concern, pleading and eventually bribery. This was Anguselus, Arthur's war general, always trying to help. "The sea is not so bloody roiled today so can' ya jus' stan' up an' look bloody commandin'…" Lowering his voice a bit he began to beg, "For me? Besides, if this isna' the grandest spot in all creation, then tell me wher' is? You can see *Yr Wyddfa* from here, if you stan' tha is."

At that exact moment, neither of the Arthurs could stand. One was captive to the rolling boat listening to his war chief recount events that had played out upon fields of battle. The other was firmly tied down again and, as such, forced to listen to his nurse tell, basically, the same thing:

> And still from time to time the heathen host
> Swarmed overseas, and harried what was left.
> And so there grew great tracts of wilderness,
> Wherein the beast was ever more and more,
> But man was less and less, till Arthur came.

Even if his eyes were open, with his back planted firmly on the deck, Arthur would have had trouble seeing much more than the sail over his head and the cloudless blue sky beyond. But he didn't need to see; he knew the point well, and in his head, he could see it and what it represented. *Yr Wyddfa*, the tallest peak in all Norgalles is the mass of land that is no longer just a mountain. *Yr Wyddfa* named for the giant slain by Arthur, the Pen dragon. *Only it wasn't me who killed Urien that day. Hell, he wasn't even slain at all, but captured. We had to thank Ambrosius for that. I hate the bards; they never get it right.* Given that the large man blocking his view could see the great mountain at all told Arthur they were coming on to *Ynys Enlli*, the holy island. *With good wind, half a day's sail would get us to…*

> For first Aurelius lived and fought and died,
> And after him King Uther fought and died,
> But either failed to make the kingdom one.
> And after these King Arthur for a space,
> And through the puissance of his Table Round,
> Drew all their petty princedoms under him.

"We'll sigh' *Caer Gybi bey* 'fore long an' from Holyhead, if the day stays clear. My liege if you sit up now, the reward is great. A view of all your fair penns. Whithorn is there and of course *Ynys Mon*. If you squint and look west we can see *Afallach*. Can you tell me where the apples grow sweeter?" Arthur's companion savored the landmarks on his tongue as one might the taste of a fine wine. "*Afallach*," he repeated, taking a second taste and then returned to *Ynys Mon*, "Upon *Ynys Mon* is found the site of your great achievement, Carmelide. It is jus' ahead." That phrase tempted his stricken commander to remember better times.

Carmelide, Arthur knew where he was being led. How many years ago they had put an end to the succession matter on the high plateau of Anglesey. *This was the home of clan Leodegan, this was Guinevere's home.*

> Leodogran, the King of Cameliard,
> Had one fair daughter, and none other child;

And she was the fairest of all flesh on earth,
Guinevere, and in her his one delight.

Flo was turning a page and so had reached a pause in her delivery. She smiled. "I'm glad you like this tale. I have to say, I am a big fan too. You know, the only problem with the whole Guinevere story line, no matter which version you read is this, they had no children. Arthur and Gwen, that is. Without kids, how can you carry on the family name? Some stories tell of one child, Loholt, but no one really knows where that child came from. Some say he was Guinevere's, but Arthur may not have been the father. Others say he was Arthur's son but not with Guinevere. Either way, he didn't survive too long and"—Flo scrunched up her eyes and thought for a moment—"he had no offspring now, did he?"

Finished with her soliloquy, the nurse returned to her reading and, basically, ignored her charge for the next twenty minutes, and so with the nurse emitting nothing but white noise, both Arthurs had the freedom to search for their son. It didn't take long for the man riding the waves to come back into focus.

It seems that the ship's crew and all those others standing on deck had grown tired of watching him lie about. They also tired of listening to Angus recite history just because he could. Finding other amusement wasn't hard. An enormous school of sea trout beckoned. The fish surrounded the vessel for a good half-mile in every direction. With game aplenty nearby, ropes were tied to their short spears and the hunt was on. But as toss after toss brought another prized catch up on deck, the entertainment value waned.

A short time later, instead of fish rising up out of the water they were flying about the deck. Woe was the man who missed what was thrown his way for a miss was as good as taking one upside the head. Of course, catching the spiked fins wrong was not pleasant either. Now this was sport and to add to the degree of difficulty, a cask of the prized wine from estates in Breton was opened. Soon the deck was awash with the rich red hues of spilt wine, gutted fish, and bleeding hands.

"Fish!" Arthur spit out. Given the situation on deck, only those nearby could hear.

"He looks green," a small voice called back.

Those gathered amongst the dead carcasses cleared a path.

"The Greek doctors believe this type of illness, this sickness brought about by ocean travel, to be caused by disequilibrium."

It was Lohot who, for reasons of his own, missed the camaraderie of the situation and came to the defense of his father in the only way he knew how. Only he used a style and language far beyond the comprehension of those around him.

Lohot the strange. Touch him and he screamed, cross him and he beat his head into a wall until you were forced to tie him to his bed. Raise a fist against him and bear the wrath of the Pen Dragon, the bear, for all eternity.

Arthur smiled; his son had come to his defense.

Chapter 27
When Worlds Collide, a Retreat Is Ordered

Lute was visiting his father, and like on the boat, Arthur's son stood behind the crowd patiently waiting until Angus and Wayne moved aside. When space was available, he stepped up to the bed and bent over to update his assessment of the damaged body.

"He's green today, a shade of olive I think and…" Here, Lute paused, looked around the room with his nose held high, sniffed twice, and continued, "I smell something, something most incongruous."

Everyone else in the room, except his father that is, looked his way wondering if Lute was speaking to them or just thinking out loud. Everyone in their own way sniffed the air, but while they savored multiple aromas, most of which were not readily identifiable, no one commented.

"We're in a hospital," Angus eventually gambled a reply, "a sort of hospital anyway. There are a lot of different smells in here, smells you may not be familiar with."

Lute paid him no mind or at least it seemed that way as he continued his discourse. "It smells of polyamines."

"Polyamines, Lute? I know you got your math down and now I'll give you a little leeway with the medical terms, but chemistry too?" That was Wayne.

Rounding out the crew standing nearby was Lucan, the butler, and both monsieur Cai and monsieur de Veer. De Veer being the international legal counsel for the company. Though Dutch by birth, he was Breton on his mother's side, and like Wayne, he shared a bloodline with Arthur, though a cousin or two further down the line. He was not tall, had sunken cheeks, a yellow complexion, and a straight back which, all together, produced the look of an ascetic monk. These three stood back a bit and, for a moment, quietly monitoring the developing situation.

"Lute, tell me, what does a polyamine smell like?" As Wayne queried, he made ready to finger poke mid chest. Wayne had obviously forgotten rule number 1 for interacting with Lute, no touch.

Though cautious, de Veer was well trained, and when called to action, he responded. On this occasion, he moved to a position between Lute and Wayne, and as Wayne's digit approached Arthur's son, it was de Veer who deftly intercepted the advancing weapon. He then repositioned it back out of harm's way. With a not-too-subtle roll of the eye, he silently reminded M. Loathe of the rules of engagement.

Lute looked at Wayne for the first time since he entered the room, which itself was a rare occasion. He shuffled his feet, rubbed his hands together, and made to speak. At the last second, though, he stayed mum.

"You don't know, do you?" Wayne goaded.

Angus sucked in a breath and began to back away, inching for the door, fearing what might happen next. Instead of an outburst, Lute answered the query in the same analytical voice he might use to describe differential equations.

"Spermine and spermidine are polyamines involved in cellular metabolism. They are found in eukaryotic cells in a wide variety of organisms and tissues. They are essential growth factors in some bacteria."

Everyone in the room stared at him, again, except Arthur who seemed to be asleep. Lute continued in a steady monotone, eyes staring straight ahead, "Spermine is associated with nucleic acids at physiologic pH and is thought to stabilize helical structure, particularly in viruses."

Wayne followed Angus's lead and began to retreat, ending with his back against the window.

"The biosynthesis of spermidine and spermine has been extensively studied in plants. Spermidine is made from the condensation of decarboxylated S'adenosyl methionine, known as SAM…"

M. de Veer joined Wayne at the window.

"And putrescine, which is catalyzed by spermidine synthase, also called putrescine aminopropyltransferase."

Cai held out as long as he could, not wanting to leave Arthur's side, but when Lute moved to elaborate on the condensation reaction, he also backed away trying to interest himself in the bedpans piled up near the bathroom sink.

"Further condensation of spermidine with decarboxylated SAM, catalyzed by spermine synthase, produces the tetramine, that is, spermine."

"How does he know all this?" Wayne asked the wall.

For all of his gifts on one end of the intelligence spectrum, Lute, like most suffering in the realm of autism, lacked aptitude in others. He didn't have the ability to register sarcasm. He acknowledged the question without turning or taking a breath, "The group led by Dr. Flores published an article in 'Plant Nitrogen Metabolism' entitled 'Primary and…"

"Sorry I asked." Wayne mumbled and turned his gaze outside until Lute seemed to run out of steam. Thinking the coast was clear he moved back to the bed and again took up space a bit too close to Arthur's son.

Lute raised an eyebrow. Immediately, both de Veer and Angus moved to prevent any possible physical contact. Angus got there first, keeping his voice as monotone as possible. "Lute, dear boy, there are flower arrangements all over the room."

With this said, he spread his arms about in a large panoramic sweep, but Lute was not watching. He tried again, "Is it the plants you are smelling?"

Lute didn't answer but did turn to stare at what the others thought to be the largest of the room's floral arrays. But Lute was not looking at the flowers. It was the well-worn book face down on a small table that had caught his eye. The fact the book was face down is not what drew Lute's attention, the book hanging just a bit too far off the edge did. Obsessive compulsives don't like that. As Lute moved to fix the situation, Cai, Angus, and de Veer exhaled, thinking the biochemistry lesson was over and Lute, having moved away from Wayne, was out of harm's way.

"Now," Angus continued, "can we get back to—"

Before Angus could finish his thought Wayne, not able to leave well enough alone, cut him off. "He doesn't know what he's talking about. Sometimes I think he just does it to annoy me."

Lute flipped the book over, Goodrich's *King Arthur*, set it a safe distance from the edge of the table then flipped his internal rolodex back to the sentence at which he had left off, and with a discernible agitation, continued, "Crystals of spermine phosphate were first described in 1678, in human semen, by Anton van Leeuwenhoek."

"Semen?" Angus asked, seeking clarification.

The room went silent, and everyone except Arthur turned to stare at Lute. He now had their full attention.

"Semen, you say?" Cai sounded as incredulous as he looked.

Lute clarified, "Sex, it smells like sex."

Wayne almost fell over laughing but caught himself in the nick of time, then he composed himself and quietly sniffed about. His face changed; once someone gives the answer, all the clues become so obvious. "You know, Lute, you may be right. But what a disgusting thought."

"That's preposterous!" was de Veer's take, but Cai gave him the benefit of the doubt.

"I do smell something."

Attempting to show solidarity with all in the room, Arthur threw up. It might have had something to do with the greening of his skin brought about by a renewed sense of vertigo.

Angus was no longer standing over Arthur; he was now wrestling the man down a short ladder with the help of 'Ector and Bedivere. They eased him aft along a narrow passage until gently placing him onto a hammock in what was called the captain's cabin, whenever no one with superior rank was aboard. Now it was Arthur's cabin, and as cramped as it was, this is where he now lay awaiting the others.

"We could have taken a seafaring vessel instead of this rotting trough," Angus mumbled to himself as the war counsel, many covered with the residual of the fish toss, squeezed into the room.

Arthur responded, "And lose the element of surprise, besides, this was Malcolm's idea, and for once, I think he advised well. We need to return quickly but without drawing attention."

They had moved fast but in so doing, only an advance guard was with them, the bulk of the fighting force had been left stationed in Breton. "Only Malcolm knows this, and he will have prepared all for our march to the staging area. There we will meet up with other contingents and form tactical groups. Now, the Picts are massing in Caledonia, what we don't know is if they will be heading toward Dumbarton or Sterling."

As the aroma of dead fish filled the room, the council discussed troop dispositions, movement options and supply needs until the other problem, the problem they were sailing away from, came back into play, the Freincs.

"If the Freincs are now *de facto* rulers of Gaul there is a new world out there. We must adapt. The terrorists have aligned themselves with the winning party. As Ambrosius said before we left. If the Freincs win, we'll be given only two options."

Arthur didn't finish, it was too melodramatic for this seasoned group standing before him; they might just laugh. But where was Ambrosius when he needed him? The threat to the kingdom came in many guises. While the present company was well equipped for encroachments of a physical nature, the greater danger was much harder to defend against. One synod after another tightened the noose. The bloodshed in Constantinople, the restrictions in education, the arrest, torture, and execution of Pelagius, all heralded the ultimate conflict to come, and when needed most, bishop Ambrosius Dubricius had wandered off as was his habit lately.

When will it end? When can we stop fighting?

The bleak response came too fast. *Never!* Fighting over control of lands hadn't really stopped since the last *Imperatore* left the island. *How many years ago? Now,* Arthur thought, *I am the Pen Dragon, but encroachments continue. We have only tamped them down. What will happen after I'm gone?*

The despondency of the situation coupled with the sickness brought on by the rolling boat once again played havoc with Arthur's senses. Whatever residual was left in his stomach made its way out in synchrony with a deep roll of the boat. But when all those needed had squeezed into the cabin, and the throw-up wiped away, Arthur dug deep. In a trance-like state, a bad habit he picked up from Ambrosius, he began his motivational speech.

"We all know Cai and Bedivere are not at their best in the field, but they are the men needed in any council be it war or governance." He then moved down the list heaping praise on every member of the council. "Each of you would shine bright in any army in the world. But you are here, and I am honored, for together we have built a *gosgordd* the *Saexon* and all *Alamanni* tribes shake in fear of. Hell, we could march on Rome itself and impose peace. *Restitutor Orbis* is what they will say. The Britons, the restorers of the *Pax Romana*. March on Rome." He almost sang this line as the emotion carried him to a new high.

The others in the room remained quiet, waiting for the introduction to finish. It took a few more rhetorical aggrandizements before he slowed and began to segue onto the message he needed to convey. "Perhaps Maximus was right, but really, once in Rome what would we do? Place our own Emperor on the throne. I think not, for from there he no longer has reach to the Island of the Mighty. But"—he paused—"we could chase the Bishopric out from Rome, oh what a dream that is, but even our own bishop has counseled against such an act.

"You cannot change ideology by force of arms, Dubricius has told us many times, only by passive resistance and a liberal dose of education… or was that 'a dose of liberal education,' I don't remember, but I'm afraid we are in for rough weather and the best we can hope for is to ride out the storm." Arthur then told them again of the long-range plans, hoped they bought into it and then he just ran out of words.

"Today the only question is this: Are they marching on Dumbarton or Sterling?" This was Lucan bringing the conversation back to the here and now.

As Arthur and his men contemplated an impending threat from the growing influence of the Roman Bishopric, and that of the Picts coming down from the north, both threats from without, no one considered the obvious and old-fashioned angle, the threat from within.

"Does it matter? We'll position our mobile force to intercept, but we must get off this ship and up to muster point before they know we've landed…" Angus had joined in.

"If we could just eke out a bit more speed," Gawaine spat, not knowing where the enemy stood but dying to get at them.

"We'll have to pray the wind holds up," Arthur finished and then closed his eyes.

"What's this?" Anna had entered the room. She surveyed the situation and formed her battle plan before the men around her could react.

"He threw up." Angus mumbled, as if he might get blamed for something.

"I can see that now, can't I? Did you call the nurse?"

"He only just did it," Angus began to explain until she parroted the line back at him.

"Well, were you all going to stand here all day and admire Arthur's product?" She swept her way to the top of the bed and hit the call button. Without breaking stride, she went in the bathroom and, seconds later, was out again holding a few towels. She threw them at her son staring him down until he got the message. Then, noting Lute was nervously backing his way out of the room, she at once softened her tone of voice. "It's getting late, it is almost visiting time and Lute, your mother will be arriving soon so please stay nearby." She continued politely berating all the men in the room, "We don't want any visitors to pay their respects to Arthur while he's covered in his morning breakfast, do we?" While speaking, Anna's gaze caught something of interest. She paused for a moment to reflect then asked, "Where's his feeding tube? Why is it not connected?"

No one said a word, and all were relieved, Wayne most of all, when a woman dressed in hospice scrubs arrived and took over the cleanup duties. Anna used the opportunity to vent her frustration, as civilly as possible, by berating the hospice staff in general (and the new arrival in particular) for what appeared to be negligence on the part of the house staff, "No one reconnected the feeding tube!"

When the cleanup was finished, the nurse hurried out the door. Then, promising to have the manager visit, she turned and high-tailed it down the hall. Anna watched, bit her lip, and silently cursed twice before she made an all-clear sign, and when she did, everyone in the room got down to business.

"Howl is already in London," Angus began. He spoke as if Lute wasn't in the room listening, they didn't have time for niceties. "He'll take charge of Lute when Wayne and I drop him off. We will take everything out of the London office before the eighth. Cai will help with transportation. If the vote goes against us, they'll get access to the vault, and then it will only be a matter of time before Malcolm's people figure this all out. Wayne's brothers are doing the same at the Edinburgh and Glasgow offices. Howl has informed the Cardiff crew."

"What about our Gwynedd site?" de Veer asked.

Angus shook his head in the negative. "We just don't have anyone reliable in place there. We might be able to get a team up to Bangor before the text is deciphered. But to send them up into Malcolm's neck of the woods with so many still straddling the fence would, without doubt, be sounding the alarm bell."

Before he could continue, members of the hospice staff entered with the on-call physician trailing behind.

"Last night, he," the physician began, "awoke from his coma."

On cue, Anna fainted.

Chapter 28
Foreboding

"I'm not feeling well, how 'bout you?"

Arthur didn't respond. It might have been the sedatives holding him back.

"I'm very sad," Flo continued, "This, this is making me feel, well… it's making me feel shitty."

To this, he did respond; only, it was internal. *Feeling well? That's good. Feeing well, shitty? That I don't understand. Therefore, I feel, well, confused!*

"You see, Dr. McAiden…"

For a moment, she really had Arthur's attention. *Dr. McAiden, oh no, this can't be good.*

"I got the word, and the word isn't good for you my dear."

The nurse delivered her lines with solemnity apropos for the nature of the message. Flo was also covering multiple topics simultaneously, running them together without a syllabus, which is the bane of men everywhere. Men have trouble following a woman's train of thought as is, when she ramps up delivery speed and topic dispersion it's impossible.

Arthur, in his current state of mind, was basically shit out of luck in this regard.

"Poor me, I've come to like our time together."

Words have never been good to me.

The rewiring process within his internal recesses were not quite up to speed. This left his comprehension more than a bit challenged especially when an allegory or metaphor was in play.

"Apparently, there is going to be some big vote. After that, you're history, love."

I love history too.

"But," she added, tapping her right index finger to the side of her nose, "on the bright side, the real reason I came to your rescue isn't going to pan out. I've helped others move on what, five, six times now, and I'm usually cool, cool as a cucumber. But look at me. You're on the mend, and I'm shaking like a leaf."

After hearing "leaf," something registered in Arthur's direct line of vision, a bracelet. Flo's nervous energy was transmitting down her arms making a series of small figurines on her bracelet move like mini wind chimes.

I never liked cucumber sandwiches, but a trip to Paris would be nice.

Lack of sleep for the man may have contributed to his limited processing ability. This happens to us all. He was worn out, and if measured, he would have displayed classic symptoms of sleep deprivation. The constant bustle of activity into and out of his room during the day was partly to blame. The medications administered were also to blame. They didn't really knock him out. They just dropped him into a lethargic state, which was good for listening but not conducive for responding, or sleep. Nurse Flo reading to him or just riding him for long periods of time each night probably didn't help either.

"Any day now, my love, any day and we will have to say goodbye," the nurse whispered this between sniffles. Then, after wiping a few nascent tears from the corners of her eyes, her mood changed.

"They're idiots! They're idiots out there," she repeated, adding a dramatic wave of her arm as she pointed to the window.

"Have you seen all those people milling around…" Flo paused and stared at her charge. "I'm sorry, of course you haven't. Let me tell you. It's like a big campsite, two really. All those routing for you to pull through on one side of the pond and the others, those with some perverse sense of…"

Nurse Flo caught herself then continued "Hey, that sounds a little like, like, well, like me, doesn't it? You know I've never thought of it that way before. They could almost be my fan club." She tried to laugh at her own cleverness but what emanated from her throat sounded more like a belch.

I wish I had a clue was Arthur's only take on the situation.

"Once the hospice mentions anything about your change in status the news crews will surely leave, no real ratings if you're talking about a man on the mend now is there? I wonder how many of the others out there will stay once the reporters leave. And don't worry, sir, you are on the mend. Soon you'll be getting up out of the bed, movin' about and talkin' and when you do, I doubt you will want to listen to me anymore."

The nurse inhaled, long and slow, "You're such a good listener."

She took one more deep breath as she patted Arthur's leg then she rubbed her eyes to brush away some watery build up. "I haven't been able to get my meds balanced since I met you. I was told you were vegetative. That is why I took this assignment, to help you move on. But you weren't, and this made me question everything."

Having her confessional aired and feeling much better for doing so, she returned to her established routine. She ran through her list of things to do, checked them off as she finished, bathed her charge, and then settled in for a little more conversation.

"I wish I had a cigarette," she began before launching into a blow-by-blow recap of her very busy day. She culminated with a complete itemization of her dinner platter from the local eatery. "You know they have the green and yellow wax beans."

Arthur could only think of one thing: the milky soy extract being poured into his stomach, before the feeding tube had been removed that is.

"I have a surprise for you."

Really?

"I've decided to skip the rest of Malorie…"

Halleluiah!

For the second time since starting her shift, she had his full attention. Like before, it lasted only a few seconds as her utterly exhausted patient blurred the lines between external stimuli and subconscious impressionism. As Flo continued laying out the rest of the evening's agenda, he once again wandered further afield. When Flo mentioned pageantry, nobility, and coronations in the same sentence Arthur envisioned arranged marriages and nefarious power struggles. When she spoke of Arthur's round table with Percival searching for the grail, he remembered family gatherings and haggis. Both nurse and patient penned noble women into each adventure, all sequestered in castles or chapels praying hard to save their Knights-errant. Arthur described text enlightened with embellishments of letters used to mark important passages and entire pages illuminated with bright colors translating words into pictorials. And as Flo hung onto the romance of the Romance Literature Arthur worked through the nuances embedded within the intricate nature of love before turning the page and embracing the overwhelming nature of duty and its hold on a person. Flo was not deterred by his views of the subjects, she couldn't be, Arthur only spoke to Arthur, but she did get distracted.

"Oh my, now what do we have here?"

Colored lights on the ceiling had caught her attention and drew a response from her patient as well. Red lights were playing across the ceiling, spliced with blues and greens and coalescing with bright white. The aurora borealis came to Arthur's mind as Flo left his side and strode to the window.

Standing between the slit in the almost drawn curtains she had no problem zeroing in on the action. Several people off to the side of the building were handling high intensity television lights, which mixed with flashing, colored shafts coming from nearby police vehicles. All sources pierced the shadows attracting the curious and apathetic alike.

"Wha' the heck is going on out there?"

Can't we just watch the display without talking?

Eventually Flo put down the papers she held in her hand, opened a slightly wider slit in the curtains, and inched closer to the glass for a better view. Then she cracked the widow open, and after a short pause to assimilate information, she slipped into a running commentary which would have made a sports play-by-play man envious, "You won't believe this…" she began.

Try me.

"Oh, what a circus!" Flo laughed. "I'm glad no one reported your condition to them, this is macabre theater at its best."

With elephants?

The scene the nurse described was indeed a circus. The opposing factions in the Arthur McAiden vigil had been stoked up. With the window open, Flo could hear them yelling invectives at each other in morbid rhymes. A string of police cruisers had been driven up onto the lawn between the feuding groups. It was their strobe lights that helped produce psychedelic impressions on Arthur's ceiling. Occasionally, an object with ballistic trajectory was lobbed from one camp to the next. The splashing water released upon impact brought a smirk to Flo's lips. Off to the side a bank of klieg lights was being used by television crews as at least a half-dozen independent interviews were being conducted with the water balloon fights serving as dramatic backdrop.

It had become most common in the age of instantaneous coverage. The news media promoted the event to a point where the coverage itself became the news, a stage on which all could seek publicity. Now their cameras zoomed in on the platforms set up on both sides of the field. On these, speakers (and supporters) defiantly declared opposing points of view using placards (held for easy camera access) to accentuate their punditry. It was a perfect storm of prime-time cable news fodder. Closer to the walls of the hospice, red and white emergency lights of a parked ambulance added another staccato splash of color to the mix and around the corner of the building, just visible from Flo's enfiladed position, a troop of uniformed officers with riot gear were mustering.

"I think they are going to use force."

If the carnival atmosphere was distracting, the potential of physical confrontation was downright captivating. Flo was now riveted, and for once, she appeared more interested in what was going on outside than in.

"And think, in my own small way, I can put an end to all of this. If your family or the flippin' hospice doesn't let the word out soon, I will." Flo seemed very pleased, but as her crowing moved her in the direction of self-gratification, her charge was rapidly losing his grip on the present. Somehow, Arthur transformed the lighting extravaganza from a physical display into an intricate stream of consciousness. And as the nurse stood behind curtains staring at the field below, in his mind, a man stood in a different concealed vantage point. Wisps of his long, white beard were the only parts of the man visible to the throng gathering below.

"It looks as if your plan is reaching fruition," Arthur whispered into the man's ear nearly causing the recipient to fall over the balustrade.

"Lord, have mercy!" The older man exhaled as he grabbed his chest and backed further into the shadows. "Arthur! What are you doing here?" His croak was barely audible. "The hour is late. You must prepare."

Arthur turned and looked directly at his oldest and most trusted mentor, "I know the time, but it doesn't mean I'm any more inclined…"

"We've had this discussion before," Ambrosius spat back. Then he softened. "We've worked the rhetoric to death, so many times. So please, not again, not now. Really my lord, this is the only way. Look down there," he added, not needing to point. "This is the largest gathering of the dragons seen on the Isle of the Mighty since the Imperial Legions boarded ship for Gaul."

"Freince."

"What?"

"It's Freince now."

With a breeze channeling into the upper reaches of the hall, the only movement made as the two men stared each other down was the billow of the old man's white hair.

"What?" Ambrosius repeated, buying time, trying to figure out where the dialog was heading.

Arthur continued, leading the conversation away from where he knew his mentor wanted to take it. "The past season we fought side by side with the Roman bishopric's latest conquest, Clovis himself, to push out the Goth. Mark my words, the next time the pride of men at arms sets sail for the continent, it might be to defend our holdings in Breton from the Freincs."

The older man didn't reply, so Arthur figured he had been successfully sidetracked. He had, but only for a moment. When Ambrosius spoke again, he was able to tie two thoughts into one cogent argument. "Precisely my Lord, precisely. If we do not get our house here in order, we will never be able to defend our borders from external threats again. If we do not set in place our system of government, if we continue this fractured existence, we will fall prey to whoever wields the Roman stratagem: divide and conquer. If we do not move our ideology in a new direction, the Bishopric of Rome will cast us aside. Now let me assure you the men in Rome are not born as evil incarnate. It is just the everlasting problem of multiple interpretations. Anything written can be translated by men of differing ideologies to their advantage. Therein our problem lies."

Arthur was young, he tried but didn't quite understand. His advisor did not mean the secular body of powerless individuals who kept meaningless titles in the ancient Latin city. Rather, he meant the insipid creep of the dogmatic fanatics who brokered no ideology but their own.

Satisfied with his dialectic, Ambrosius turned his attention to more mundane fare, "But when the Legions left *Prydein* it was Gaul across the channel, so technically I'm correct."

Arthur, in his turn, put his hands up to his ears in a vain attempt to shut out the older man. He couldn't. Ambrosius gave Arthur a few more words of encouragement trying to sooth the young man's nerves and then returned his attention to the activities getting underway in the main hall.

When Guinevere's contingent entered, the pageantry moved away from the miscellaneous to the correct order of events. Arthur's mentor added more encouragement to his old student, explaining the time each event would take, and when Arthur himself would need to traverse the throng, taking his place in the proper chair.

"Look, son, you can envision the woman as your beautiful wife, and no one can argue that, or thank her and her father for their gifts, she is endowed in this regard as well, but with her comes the final stages of the unification process."

Seeing the old man's attention was locked on the proceedings below, Arthur didn't answer; instead, he took the opportunity presented and began to back away, a few short steps at a time. Slinking away may have been a more apt descriptor, putting distance between him and what he dreaded with his whole heart and soul, hoping to gain enough separation to allow for a clean break. "Just another step," he whispered through clenched teeth. *And then what? Turn and run? Perhaps, I will if I can just round this corner.*

"Arthur, for God's sake, it really is almost time. You must be dressed and in position." Ambrosius was no longer Ambrosius the friendly priest, he was now Dubricius, the bishop. He moved lively for an old man and in two quick steps was at Arthur's side with one hand clasped tightly on his shoulder. Then, he bent close and took a good whiff. "Damn barbarian. Would a bath have been too much to ask, maybe one, just this week?"

Even with the older man's hand guiding him along Arthur's feet felt like lead.

"Arthur please, you must go through with this. This act of sacrifice that you are about to undertake was set in motion by your grandfather, Constantine. It will be the culmination of over three decades of work." What Dubricius didn't say, but Arthur had begun to realize, was three decades of Dubricius's own work. Constantine had left the crumbling western provinces taking up shop on the more stable ground in the east. Yes, it was his family who remained to pick up the pieces strewn about as the western empire crumbled but Constantine was not there to help.

"I swear, Arthur, you weren't half this frightened the last time we rode down…"

"Half the people in that room want to see me dead."

"And the other half will stand firm behind you. After the marriage, all others will fall in line." Dubricius paused, loosened his grip on Arthur's shoulder, took a deep breath and continuing, "Listen, my son, today we twist their arms, tomorrow the hard work begins, but God willing, we will reestablish a civilization here that even the Romans would envy. It starts right here, right now. Without a strong, united front we won't have a season of peace. All this is for the greater…"

"Good," Arthur finished.

"Arthur, you've been our *Imperatore*. More than that, as you are aware—even if you weren't holding the rank the clans would have rallied around you. But being our *Dux*, our war leader doesn't complete the circle. Your marriage to Guinevere puts you in position to claim the administrative throne. And once you hold both positions, then we can begin the hard work.

"My Lord," the older man continued, "we need a quiet period, we need peace. If we can obtain this seemingly trivial condition, we can buy the time we need to return our country to a status like we had when the legions were here, only better."

Dubricius tended to enter a mystic sort of temperament from time to time, usually when he needed his audience to buy into his arguments. So when Arthur turned away, as if on cue the old man noted his internal struggles, grabbed his arm and then proceeded to fall into a trance.

"I, Merlin, saith that in Britain the Great Wolf shall come from the White Launde. Twelve sharp teeth shall he have, six below and six above. He shall have so fierce a look that he shall chase the Leopard forth of the

White Launde. So much force shall he have and great virtue. Now the wolf," Dubricius stopped to explain, "that is you, you know.

"We now know the Merlin"—he stopped again—"of course that's me," and continued, "says this for each to know, to understand with certitude in the time of the King who we shall call…" Dubricius continued his incantation recalling the background to their quest and adventures undertaken, most importantly, the grail itself, "That which might have to be hidden away." Only unfortunately for the Merlin, time was running late. The present ceremony was almost due to begin, so he abbreviated the telling as he mumbled along in hurried cadence.

Finally, he gave up, squeezed the younger man on the shoulders, and told him to go get dressed. Then, not relying totally on psychological persuasion, he pushed Arthur in the direction of the back staircase and followed him down. He had to; time was running out. Below, in the court, the princes from the nearby lands as well as Breton and Freince and all adjacent islands were assembling. Cai was reading their introductions as they passed through to court.

"Auguselus the mighty, king of Albania; Urian, king of Mureif; Cadwallo Lewirh, king of Venedotians, men of North Wales; Sater, king of Demetians, South Wales; Cador, king of Cornwall; archbishops of three Episcopal sees." Cai described the first two, the bishops of London and York, in very polite terms before turning his attention to the third, "And Ambrosius Dubricius of course, from *Carleon*, the City of Legions, Carlisle. This prelate who is prime bishop of Britain, legate of the apostolical see, is so eminent for his piety, that he can cure any sick person by his prayers alone…"

The man following Arthur stopped. "Shit, that's me."

As Arthur relived a decision made centuries before by a man bearing his name, the nurse closed the curtains and returned to his side. What was bothering her when she first entered the room was still poking its head into her emotional stability. "I told you, as far as your future is concerned, the word is good. What you do with your life from here on out I do not know. All I do know is this. I will not be part of it. Our time together has been so, so…it has given me time to think of the directions I've taken, and I don't like what I have become. I do think it will be only a matter of days before I get up the nerve and leave for good."

The tears flowed. Then she stopped dead in her tracks.

"Arthur…you're crying!"

Chapter 29
Holding Vigil

It was obvious Nurse Flo was not happy. It wasn't so much the unexpected visitors at what was, basically, the middle of the night. It wasn't even the fact they were assuming control of Arthur's room. Without saying, she was a little unnerved the hospice allowed them in, but her current temperament had more to do with the person on the other end of the telephone. She huffed and puffed at the two incoming ladies, just to let them know she wasn't really interested in speaking with them. Then she picked up her bag and headed toward the door. As she stepped through the portal, the phone never lost contact with her left ear. Her ranting picked up in volume as she headed down the hall. The steam coming out her ears may have just been a trick of the light.

"You cannot pay me enough. I am not going to do it. I've changed my mind. Why? I'll tell you why. It's because he's not vegetative, never was and he is no longer comatose." The door slammed shut, and when it did, the two entering the room were left hanging because, as Flo physically left the room, she also exited Arthur McAiden's story line.

"Was she talking to Jennifer?" A new character, Dindrane, was now speaking to Arthur's sister. "Her voice was so, so I don't know how one might describe it."

"Vehement, perhaps?"

"I wonder what she was refusing?"

Dindrane was no taller than her aunt but other than height the two had nothing else in common. Both were wearing loose fitting summer wear, which, on Anna, hid aspects of her plump figure but on Dindrane did nothing to conceal the streaming layers of muscle on her compact form. Black curls reached to her shoulders, her eyebrows were two dark lines dabbed horizontally across a wide brow and her nose was thin and sharp, all of which served to intensify her gaze. Her mouth was wide and could be expressive depending on the curl of the lip. Unfortunately, she rarely smiled. She was often too deep in thought to bother.

"Probably was Jennifer," Anna mumbled as she rolled her eyes heavenward in search of a miracle.

Dindrane followed her aunt further into the room as she thought out loud, "Things are so different on this side of the Atlantic." Midstep, though, she stopped, glanced quickly at the body on the bed, and as she did, for a half second, she lamented not coming sooner. Then her brain went blank as tears welled up and began to slowly roll down her cheeks. Then, a weakness hit her knees and her heartbeat came near to pinning the tachometer, but before she fell, Anna came to the rescue.

"Breathe," Anna whispered while holding Dindrane in the upright position. Dindrane heard but it was still a long, slow moment before she finally acquiesced. Then she wiped the emotional discharge off her face using the corner of a very soft handkerchief, which had miraculously appeared in her hand. To avoid a repeat performance, she moved her eyes off her uncle allowing information retrieval synapses to engage. Then she handed the handkerchief back to Anna before finishing her inventory of the room.

The smell emanating from a fresh cluster of flowers registered first. It wasn't hard to find them. There was only one vase still in the room sitting upon a small table near the window. *Curtains*, she registered, *windows, air*. The inspection of the rest of the room kept her busy for just a moment before she zeroed in on one item. A worn looking book sharing the table with the flower vase. Sprinkled about the book like a halo were fallen petals.

Dindrane moved closer to the table and picked it up. "Did he ever show you this?"

"Show me what?" Anna had begun tidying up anything she could get her hands on and so wasn't sure where the topic of conversation had moved.

Dindrane lifted the book up to nose level and took a sniff. "This book, this book about…well, about Arthur."

Anna finally registered the context of the question but was not quite sure of the direction within. "He was always digging into genealogy, his specifically, so he says, and whenever a book on this topic showed up… well, he would grab a copy."

"Yes." Dindrane hummed to herself. "Did he ever find a DNA source he didn't try to run diagnostics on?"

Anna tried not to laugh, "He had the book with him. That is obvious. My hat is off to those who pulled him out of the water and somehow, for some reason, kept it with him when he was flown to the ICU, most everything else was left behind." As she spoke, she gently placed her hands on either side of her brother's face. Then, with eyes misting she leaned over and planted a kiss on his forehead.

"But what about this book? Has he ever discussed this book with you?"

Anna was taken by surprise by this continuing line of query. She wanted to move their discussion onto his physical state and how best, if allowed, to transport Arthur, so she tried to hurry things along.

"Well, now, as I've said, he reads all the books on the subject, but he's been so busy for the last…I don't know, twenty years or so, I haven't had time to discuss it with him, and—" Anna cut her retort short. It had taken weeks to track down the family physician and get her where Anna needed her. There was much to talk about. Arthur's research efforts, apparently wasn't on her list, "Let's talk about our current needs first, if you please."

Dindrane indeed had been hard to find. She had taken a holiday, of sorts, just prior to the day Arthur was airlifted to the trauma center.

"This happens every once in a while," Anna had been told. "She likes to go off on her own. We all do sometimes, right?" Flying solo, it seemed, was a habit many of her fellow nuns held dear. When one spent their life immersed in charitable endeavors amongst the poor, the sick, the elderly, and those with a political rather than spiritual focus, often it was best to disengage from time to time and recharge the batteries. This recharging was especially useful for Dindrane who had experienced both stress and sadness in her old line of work, the kind of experiences that leave many military personnel with PTSD.

The list of places Dindrane may have gone was long, but Anna persisted and eventually by something often attributed to divine intervention, just dumb luck, or a bit of whispering down the lane, someone had answered her call and passed the message along. Why Dindrane had chosen a home for the downtrodden in a very needy section of Edinburgh was a mystery to Anna.

Anna passed her find along to Lucan and both had to admire the woman and admit to themselves she was on a plane of selfless existence far above their own. "Sometimes the need for self-healing takes a back seat to the incessant desire to help those who are…how does one say *more in need*."

Dindrane had taken up the spiritual call to arms, but everyone wondered why anyone with so much medical training wouldn't at least combine careers. But then again, no one was with her and the *Medicines sans Frontier* when the genocide began. This had been her turning point. She returned home with visions of the Rwandan holocaust troubling her sleep. Shortly thereafter, she handed in the stethoscope and ran to a convent, a convent run by one of Professor Dubric's charitable organizations.

Before Arthur surprised all by waking, Anna wanted badly to move him back to England with or without Jennifer's consent. She truly believed if she could convince all to get Arthur back onto his home turf the right to life debate would have swung in, what she believed to be, her brother's favor. Now that Arthur had awakened, the needs changed. The best location for a recovering TBI survivor might be debated but getting all family members to safety was of paramount importance. War with Malcolm's clan might erupt at any time. This is why Dindrane was still in demand; Anna needed an opinion, an objective, expert medical opinion to the question; in his condition, can Arthur be moved? An opinion she believed Dr. li Gros could supply.

Dindrane had replaced the Goodrich book on the table and moved over to the window. She slowly adjusted the curtains into a half-drawn state, and for a moment, her thoughts returned to the night nurse. "I wonder if she is paid by the hour?"

This was a momentary diversion, like a quiet spell. She needed time to mix the information at her disposal in various configurations and test each one before extrapolating the best possible outcome. Apparently, with whatever she saw inside herself nothing was registering in the positive, so she turned outward by spreading the curtains just a bit wider allowing a panoramic view of the two camps to seep into her thoughts.

"It's like a display of toy soldiers," Anna whispered to herself as she, too, moved toward the window. Two factions looking so much alike, so similar and yet differing continually over the eons were arrayed before those watching from above. Now a warm breeze, laced with a hint of humidity carried faint refrains of song into the room. The toy soldier reference, the view and inflow of warm air all returned Dindrane to the camps she had left behind. Camps where every night bodies had been carried out of the hospital tents and tossed into trenches. New trenches were dug each morning.

From her current position, she towered over the field below. *A spectacle*, she thought, passing her gaze from one side to the other with only the pond and the line of security personnel closer to the building, separating the two. "Those on the left look in the mirror and see those on the right." The clear lack of physical divergence between the separated camps made it difficult to understand differing interests. Even so, with contradictory physical attributes lacking, but the acute differences in psychological ideology explained to her on the ride to the hospice, she understood the meaning as shouts fired across the picket line.

Was it two days ago, Anna thought as she, too, gazed out the window, *when their differences of opinion were put aside for an evening?*

That had been July Fourth. Dindrane had caught a glimpse of the celebration as she stood waiting for her boarding call. On the national holiday, the hospice always allowed a small display hoping it would somehow cheer up the remaining days of their patrons. This year, the administration also hoped the placement of something up in the air, something that both sides could enjoy, would lead to a more peaceful coexistence, or at least a reprieve until the man known as Arthur passed away or was passed along to another institution. The latter they had been trying to do since he first arrived.

Unfortunately, the media had, as usual, tried to build up one side over the other, depending upon which channel they broadcast from. Now, two days later, firework displays endorsing a common state of being had been replaced with emotional implorations arguing differing points of view. Dindrane blinked twice and the sporadic shouting matches receded, replaced by uplifting voices of those within tents using song to validate their position. *So many people living within the same realm*, she noted, *having so much in common yet a* difference of opinion was all it took and with that idea floating gently on top she remembered the Tutsi and Hutu, one clan killing, the other running. Slight differences of opinion, after all those years living within the same geographic locale. *Not like it hadn't happened before,* was her obvious and oft repeated evaluation, and as usual, it brought out a sad laugh.

As Dindrane's reflected on a medical team hopping from one disaster to another Arthur, too, was hopping along, analyzing developments that caused Celtic clans to flee or, as the Merlin had formulated so long ago, change their outward appearance. Dindrane envisioned bloodshed in Rwanda. Arthur saw bloodshed everywhere as the empire in the west was changing, being overrun by those believing in different forms of destiny and, more importantly, different religious ideologies. He watched the Christian bishops disputing the nature of Jesus. Bishops in the west came to odds with those in the more stable eastern regions over exact definitions to be used. Each with their own interpretation and clarifications formulated with bloodshed.

The question of Jesus's nature might have been a front for the rivalries over prestige and power as the bishops of Rome, Alexandria, Antioch, Constantinople, and so many other regions vied for control of the movement. Nestorius of Constantinople was the one who tried to moderate the debate. Those living in the geographic fringes, like the Welsh clans, prayed for a negotiated rather than a unilateral settlement. They wanted to base their ideological church on the teachings first brought to them by the man from Arimathea.

Arthur cried as the bishop of Rome moved the differences of opinion from spiritual discourse to a geopolitical sermon: Rome was where Peter had worshiped and died. His group didn't mention the land mass where Jesus was born and raised. The bishop in Alexandria had a different agenda. He began to demonize Nestorius, attacking him for his extended hospitality to the Pelagians and the Arians. Right-wingers were quick to support this position.

As two in the room cried in one form or another Anna watched Dindrane and waited, knowing the worst was passing. For Arthur, she never knew he had left in the first place and so had no idea where he was. She did not know how inside his head there was the sound of clashing swords, from stories told in years gone by, merging with the conflagration of opposing points of view now outside his window. Soon, the Holy Rood placed in the center of the hospice pond turned into an edifice erected alongside the ancient chapel in which he now found himself. For what was a place of worship without a symbol? *Holy Rood, the cross on which our lord was crucified.*

As the crowd quieted, Dindrane blinked once and her vision changed to that of an extensive necropolis. The tents became mounds with stakes placed on each, the swords honoring their dead owners. *Falkirk is near* Arthur wanted to tell her, *near the chapel, near the cemetery. It was the ironworks that, for so many years, was held by the confederated clans. Percy's sword was forged there, and the Imperial army was stationed at Camelon. Sad,* he thought, *the fort with ramparts vast and directly connected to Antonine's Wall has been in decay since the legions departed.*

Just like that, the two had drifted back along the trails to the same historical junction but only Dindrane vocalized the findings. "Years go by, and we forget. As each generation passes, the survivors rebuild and start anew. I can see it, just a short ride from the Waste Chapel where I stood, and the cemetery wherein lay so many of our departed warriors. Our dead leaders will have to be removed as the lands are ceded. But moved to where? To our protected lands? How long will those regions stand, and where will we take Arthur until he returns to us?"

Anna patiently listened but did not respond, she only watched the night darken as the moon passed out of sight. The lights below were fading too, and now only a few thin shafts rose upward. The wind tried to follow suit but periodically it regained its strength and pushed itself beyond the curtains. Once in the room, the stream had nowhere to go but to the back wall where it was turned. The space above the bed then became the convergence of both the incoming light and the billowing sheets. The vortex thus formed gently raised the sheets on Arthur's bed. Anna, who had spent her time listening, grabbed the rising covers trying to hold them down.

With Anna now occupied, Dindrane finally turned back to face her, "You want to move him, don't you?"

Poor Anna. With Dindrane finally discussing what was needed, the wind was forcing the top sheet to rise farther than she would have wished, drawing attention away from far off places and back toward Arthur's lower half. It took a good minute before she managed to tuck the sheet under the mattress. When it was finally squared away, she turned to face her niece.

"Well, yes, dear. That we do," Anna answered in as quiet a voice as she could while holding onto the edge of the bed. "We also hope you can help us find your brother. If he doesn't show soon, I think the company may be lost."

Chapter 30
Scotland

Discombobulated was about the only way Samir, or his alter ego Hicham, could classify their present condition. Before stepping off the train in Québec, he had never met those who were to harbor him in his old stomping grounds, but it didn't take long to catch their drift. After polite greetings were passed around, they let it be known the longer he stayed with them the less they wanted him. Their delivery wasn't quite as straight forward as that of the Sheik in Manhattan, but again, he did catch the drift. And now, as the string of unfortunate events piled on north of the border his stomach became a fermenter giving his agitated state the perfect place in which to brew.

"It is like this," he was lectured by the team leader in Québec. "We are very busy on a rather big...um, effort. And...um, if you have been followed and we have to go into hiding it will...um. Oh hell, we'll be screwed. Know what I mean?"

The man's tone did convey the meaning, and so when Samir was given the okay to travel, "Your handlers in Europe are ready for you." He inhaled, smiled, and said thank-you. Two seconds after those delivering the news left the room he belched once, sat down, and cried. Then he got down to work, or tried to, but with airport security being so tight he just couldn't figure out how best to bring along a package of frozen biologicals and a high-tch recording device, on which he may have captured information pertinent enough to give him some bargaining room.

Samir had never liked to play by rules contrived by others. But by playing by his own, points he had managed to rack up in the game of life were all in the negative. He had a bad feeling he wouldn't last too much longer. With options running out, convincing those he was going to see in Europe depended very much on his plan, a plan that wasn't yet totally mapped out. The plan to date he had whittled down from the grand design he had hoped for when he first started trailing McAiden. Now he only wanted it to make enough of them happy so he could continue living. All these thoughts had been simmering away inside his head well before he boarded the intercontinental. Now, as his plane flew east and July 6 was breaking over the horizon his anxiety began to overwhelm reality. To make matters worse, a way to send the biologic samples had been found. The problem being this; it wasn't his idea. He had to be told how to get his package across the ocean.

"Hicham, send it to us using an overnight courier system." The voice passing those instructions along had caused his brain to spin and a bit of the stew in his stomach to bubble up and out. It had taken less than a second to associate a name with the voice. It was Ali, someone he hadn't spoken with since leaving for Canada oh so many years ago. Yet it was Ali who answered the phone. Ali told him how to send the package and gave him the name of a charitable organization, a group house of sorts, and the address. "Mail it to them, and don't worry, Hicham, our people work there. They will pick up the package and bring it to us. When you arrive, go to that same address. We'll be waiting for you across the street."

To us, to us, to us? Samir thought, *does that mean Ali is in Edinburgh too? And how did he know I've changed my name? Does he work for my handler?* All these questions added to the angst of the man who sat quivering in his seat on the international flight to Edinburgh.

The plane was scheduled to arrive very early in the morning. Early arrivals brought along a problem routinely suffered by those traveling east, sleep deprivation. Back in the time zone from whence he started it was 'round midnight. To make matters worse, on the flight over, each time he began to nod off. Someone nearby would nudge him enough to elicit a mumble of resentment and cause the sleep cycling process to begin anew. Now he had no time to restart. In fact, he had to wash the craving out of his system because sleep was no longer on the agenda. He needed all pistons firing, the meeting he had crossed the Atlantic to attend was without doubt at the life-or-death level of importance.

Hicham's arrival was the first flight of the morning to touch down, and with few passengers debarking, it only took a few minutes to pass through the customs queue. All the time he had spent rehearsing his story wasn't needed, they didn't ask a single question except how long he would stay, and so, as he waited outside for a taxi his focus returned to the man he believed he would be meeting at the address given.

Inside the taxi, all was quiet, except for the occasional belch. If the driver heard these, he didn't respond. Twenty or so minutes later, the car stopped in the middle of a narrow lane in Old Town Edinburgh and the next phase of Hicham's adventure was about to begin. Row homes of various sizes lined both sides of the road, and when the driver pointed to one portico with a small, wooden door three steps up, his passenger paid the fare, extricated himself, and his luggage, and turned to face his destination. Positioned to the left of the door was a sign, a dead giveaway he had reached the right place. It was a small placard embedded in the brickwork. It described more than named the institution.

Starting with the words "Help for those in need," the notice added both the staff and benefactors before smaller cased letters asked for deliveries to be brought to the rear. Below this was placed the name of the proprietor, Dr. Dubric. Beneath the name, qualifications were listed but these were in such small font it could not be read from the bottom of the steps. The exact wording wasn't important at the time, Samir was just happy the street number was correct. Of course, it also added to his continual build-up of stomach acid. *I am close* was a thought finding its way out along with another belch.

As the traveling man swallowed hard to help prevent anything in his stomach from following along, he quickly turned his attention to the ornamental relief gracing the wall to the right of the door. It had the look of a bird of prey. It could have been made of wood now turned black from lack of care or possibly some sort of metallic surface—he wasn't sure. He deduced it was a raptor by the shape of the talons and beak, but from there, it became a bit harder to categorize. It might have been an eagle or something a bit smaller, perhaps a hawk. If he had read the small print at the bottom of the relief, he would have known. The bird was of the genus *falco* and the species *columburius*. In medieval days, falconers called it a "lady hawk." In North America, the small birds of prey were referred to as pigeon hawks, but the sign below the bird gave its more official title. It was a Merlin.

Samir didn't bother reading this. He didn't care. He only stood transfixed on the artwork for a moment as he waited for the taxi to vanish. Then he turned and marched to the door directly across from Dubric's charity. This door was without ornamentation or descriptive announcements of any sort. It only had a number positioned above the frame, a number he had never written down, just memorized. He knocked once and in seconds a woman in a blue burka opened the door. She let him know he had been expected, reached for his suitcase, and led him to the rear of the building.

When they reached a small room at the back of the hall, Samir was passed off to a young, bearded man wearing what appeared to be a worn *pakol*. At once, this man moved to Samir's side and patted him down without even an introduction. A moment later, he took hold of the visitor's forearm and led the way down a staircase. Wherever his suitcase went Samir didn't care because in his mind a well-known allegorical image, having to do with steps leading to hell had come front and center into view.

Samir had never been to Scotland, and so he wondered if it was normal to wear wool in the summer months. Every member of every clan he was familiar with who lived on or near high ground wore woolen hats. The pattern on the hat of his new guide didn't come from west of the Nile. Heck, probably not even west of the Tigris. The man now in front of him could have been from Iran, but more likely from a place farther east, such as Afghanistan or possibly one of the tribal regions of Pakistan. He pondered this for a few seconds, but as the stairway narrowed, the stench increased, and the air became cool and damp—an explanation for the hat was no longer necessary. In fact, it became so cool he began to shiver before they reached the bottom of the stairs.

The room he now entered was only a point of departure for the next leg of the journey. On the far side was a narrow, arched opening leading to another passageway, which was gated. This tunnel was smaller and chips in many of the stones above its entrance marked the passage of time. To the right of the opening was a façade used to cover the gate when not in use. But the age of the building or the façade are not what had caught Samir's full attention. The gate did. It was sculpted iron. It had severed heads capping off curling metal vines, stretching upward toward the chipped stones in the arch above. All of this brought, like Rodin's "Gates of Hell," a prophetic destination to mind. Samir didn't need confirmation but with nothing else to do he asked anyway.

"Where are we going?"

There was no reply. The young guide just picked up a lamp from a shelf along the wall and then connected it to a small chain, which he placed around his neck. Then he pulled the gate open and motioned for Samir to follow. Follow Samir did as his shivers turned from temperature induced to those borne of fear. After descending just a few more steps, the stairway narrowed further, and the odor seeped its way into his conscience. He tried to cover his nose, but it didn't really help. The dampness carried the odor, and the dampness was now all around. This was not to Samir's liking, but the young man in front didn't seem to mind. In fact, the deeper they descended the livelier he became. This is when, without turning around, he finally responded to Samir's question. It was Samir's turn to stay quiet and yield the floor.

"You do not know? The whole city is like this, at least the old part. We are in the old town, you know this, yes?" Samir didn't know. He also didn't answer. "Below us it is over a thousand years old. The people in this city just keep building. The new is built on top of the old."

"Wow" was all Samir could add to the conversation and this led the younger man to flap his wings a bit, figuratively, of course.

"Many cities are like this, right?" To drive his point home, the guide moved to more familiar ground. "You do know in Palestine the deeper the archaeologists dig, the older Jerusalem becomes. There are findings that tell us the city is at least six thousand years old, like Damascus."

"And?"

"And you…" The guide didn't say *idiot*; instead, he reached the bottom of the next level and began walking through a long tunnel bent over double. "If the Jews think they should get the land back because they were kicked off two thousand years ago, then we can claim the land from them by saying they kicked us Muslims off three thousand years ago. See?" As he said this, they entered an intersection. The guide kept to the right and Samir followed. Soon they were descending once again.

"Three thousand years ago," Samir finally whispered back while trying to do the math in his head but never having read the Old Testament, he had to fudge the numbers a bit. What bothered him more was how a man from Afghanistan, or possibly Pakistan, living a thousand miles away from Jerusalem even cared. Being from Morocco himself, Samir had a hard time developing an interest in geopolitics for a section of land that wasn't even on his own continent.

The younger man spat another invective back in Samir's direction. "The followers of the Koran should raise this issue at the UN."

Now Samir was really surprised as he tried to follow along. "There was no Koran four thousand years ago…was there?" With this question lingering he tried to scratch his head but bumped his uplifted hand on the low ceiling. This brought his response reflexes into play forcing him to crouch lower down, which, in turn, caused him to miss the next step. Fortunately, the next step was the last. The man in front had stood tall and was stretching his stiff back so the tumbling Moroccan had ample cushion to help break his fall. When he picked himself up, he stood beside the angry tour guide who dusted himself off and then waddled to the far wall and flicked a switch.

A dirty light bulb hanging from the ceiling now illuminated the room. It took a moment for Samir's eyes to adjust but when they did, he took a quick look around making sure he kept some space between himself and his escort. The room he had landed in resembled a small shed. It had a shelf, or possibly it was a low bench built along the slow curve of the walls. A few old wooden chairs were present, which appeared to be nothing other than ancient. A miniature of the bird of prey he saw on the building outside was engraved across the back rest of each of these chairs. On the far side of the room a closed passageway extended off a nook in the wall. Samir also saw large canvas sacs wrapped in plastic piled about. The labels described various types of rice and other dried foods. His guide, he noted, now stood near a small worktable.

"This place belongs to Dubric's group." At the mention of the name, Samir turned to look at his guide intently. "They only come down here once in a while, usually when some of their younger men are around to haul the stuff."

As he explained, he pointed to the sacs and then to the gate, which shut off the continuation of the tunnel. "Of course," he added with a smirk. "The rice they store here is Basmati, and so some of that usually finds its way up to our house. The people they feed here," he continued, pointing upward as he spoke, "are the poor people, they don't come down. If you need to um, do things…there is this bucket." With the last remark, he showed Samir what could only be described as an empty and thankfully clean bedpan.

"No cell phone signal, and as you can see, no landline, only the light. This isn't our house, so we couldn't wire it as we like, but where you stand now will keep you hidden until we can figure out what to do with you. And if the package you sent ever arrives"—here, he looked upward again to indicate its postal destination—"we'll collect it and bring it down to you."

The young man then took off his hat and handed it to Samir. "I think you will need this." Samir didn't move; he only stood and watched the small battery-powered light drift back up the stony incline from whence it came.

Chapter 31
Tragedy Strikes Twice

A quantum entanglement of sorts, two objects at a distance both entwined around a third, was coming undone. Any sound emanating from the breakup of said linkage is itself hard to measure, though Vivienne had a go at it as she screamed a parting shot into the already disconnected linkage, "I hope you drown in a cesspool of your own making." Then she officially hung up and strutted into the dinette. There she found Malcolm with, as usual, eyes fixed on the morning paper. When she gave a menacing snort, he looked over the top, assessed the situation, and then asked, "Are you joining me?"

"Of course. I haven't eaten a thing all day!"

It wasn't a normal morning for either Gwynedd. They had no visitors boarding and so had no one to entertain but themselves, unless the young woman with the kitchen staff, who had just followed Vivienne into the room, was included, which Malcolm did. To his approval, she bent over to set a place for the lady of the house, scurried out, again to his approving eyes and, a minute later, returned with hot tea and cool juice for both. When she left again, Malcolm was ready for his debriefing.

"Well?"

"She quit."

"Why?"

"She thinks he is getting better."

"So she won't..." Malcolm left that question hanging, looked his wife in the eye, raised one very think eyebrow and changed the topic. What may have been mistaken for a worry line on others now stretched across his pale forehead, "Does this mean he will attend the meeting?"

Trying to cover her losses, Vivienne continued, "Oh, do not worry. The board meeting will be *fait accompli* well before he is healthy enough to tie his shoes but"—she paused—"but he may be out of the hospital soon."

Malcolm was again distracted as the young woman brought in their food. It wasn't until she left the room, skirts and all, before he could refocus his attention, "Do you have any useful information?"

Vivienne held her steaming cup close to her lips, "Of course I do. They still haven't found Percy."

In the room where Vivienne's linkage had recently untangled itself Arthur's sister stood, shaking her head, "I need to know if we can move him, in his condition that is." The family itself had only learned of Arthur's improvement recently. Had they not been visiting the day before who knew when the hospice staff would have clued them in. Nurse Flo was a bit more up to date; but she, too, had not bothered to pass the info along before she physically skedaddled out of this storyline. One more thing the night nurse had forgotten, Arthur's evening meds.

Dindrane did not respond; instead, she placed herself next to Arthur's head and began to lovingly caress it, but just for a moment. Then her fingers started to probe. She gently examined the scar running across the shaved side of his head and the reattached ear. Then her fingers moved to the other side and gently pushed the long strands of uncut hair out of the way. She worked her way down his body, removing each of the constraining straps as she progressed. After her direct physical assessment was complete, she moved to the top of the bed and inspected the readouts on the few instruments still rolling out information. There were no longer any tubes directly inserted into Arthur's body. This she noted to herself as odd. But Arthur did seem to be breathing without the aid of an oxygen tube. When it had been removed, she didn't know. She also couldn't measure the degree of tightness in his jawline, though it still appeared to be problematic. On the positive side, the crushed lung was expanding back into a functional unit.

When finished, she paused, walked back to the window, and stared out into the hazy light of false dawn. Then she swallowed and spoke, "Which outlook do you prefer Anna? Move him by boat and the effect on his stomach may make it hard to feed him, move him by plane and the pressure differential that comes with may play havoc with his recovering nodes. Keep him here and he stays alive, but our family is subjected to the media pandering to the whims of the crowd." Dindrane paused, and when she resumed, the existence of tears was most obvious, "How long they will encamp?"

She dried her eyes before continuing, "I am not sure of this, but I think the odds of his full return, physically, are increasing, and like you, I would prefer if he was home. There is no defined mechanism for transporting someone in his condition, but this discussion is moot if Jennifer says no. So how can we get her signature on the proper forms?"

Progress, thought Anna, then she checked the time before answering, "I do hope we will have that answer very soon, now our next problem is your brother. Have you had any contact with him?"

"No, I'm sorry, I don't. When he's on a walkabout, he is usually of the grid, it may take a month or more before anyone hears from him. Like the time he was camping in the Serengeti with the Dalai Lama. Not sure what that one was about. Anyway, if he's traveling now, Arthur wasn't hurt when he left so he wouldn't be in any hurry to return."

"No one knows what the future will bring," Anna spoke this more to herself, and for a few minutes, she went quiet and prayed for Lucan to hurry along. She didn't have to wait long. A gentle knock was soon heard followed by the door opening. Lucan could now be seen stepping aside to make room for Jennifer to enter.

The butler followed and placed himself between any potential lines of fire. Both he and Jennifer were obviously nervous. Lucan showed his condition by fidgeting with his mobile, placing it into and then removing it from various pockets while Jennifer held her purse so tight it made her fingers turn white. Given the current situation, everyone in the room, the man on the bed not included, may easily have taken part in a firework display of the familial, who's in charge, variety. But if enough of a drizzle dampens the ground *a priori*, then, many times an event proceeds with a more measured interaction.

Trying to start with an amicable tone, Anna asked, "Why did the nurse leave when you called?"

Lucan was Arthur's man…to the bone. Anna and Dindrane also knew he would not lie to them, and so when he explained the hours spent sitting next to Jennifer in the hospice chapel, with her phone safely stationed in his pocket, they took it on faith; the nurse had obviously been speaking with someone else.

Now, with knees shaking, the wife bent over her husband and kissed him gently on the forehead. Then she began to murmur, and when she did, everyone, Arthur included, tilted their heads to listen in. She tried to explain, to tell her side of the story, though, given her state of mind, logical interpretation was difficult. After a few feeble attempts, she stopped and moved to the major aim of her visit, to ask forgiveness.

"He was always good to me. I am, I am…I'm sorry." Jennifer stepped back just far enough so she could still hold Arthur's hand, but her tears prevented further explanation. This is when Lucan stepped in again.

"I knew of Arthur's visits with the professor. I did not know he was going there on that…" Here, Lucan paused, bit his lip, took a deep breath, and continued, "Caldwell and Arthur shared similar interests. Arthur used the older gentleman as a sounding board of sorts. He needed to better understand historical events that led to…"

Lucan paused again, looked each of the women in the eye, motioned them all farther away from the door and lowered his voice. "Led to the denomination to which we adhere. I thought she"—indicating Jennifer with a nod—"knew of this. She didn't. Instead, she believed Arthur had a mistress." A small, sad smile graced his face, then he continued, "That being *a* professor. So she hired the detective. This I didn't know of until the FBI paid us a visit."

Anna could do nothing but wonder, "Does everyone know what Arthur was up to on this side of the Pond but me? We are who we are, we accept who we are, we do not need to confirm how we got here."

Jennifer stopped crying and searched for clues among the faces before her. Obviously, like Anna, she, too, was out of the loop. "He," she began, trying to better understand what she got wrong, "wasn't seeing a…a woman?"

"Madame," Lucan tried again, "please. He was only engaged in historical research with the professor. In fact, you almost met the man. The professor told me he came to visit Arthur the first day. He even tried to speak with you, but you walked right past him in the hallway."

"If my husband was not visiting a lover, why did the detective approach me?"

Lucan couldn't really answer; though, he did postulate, "He was living in Jersey for a while, maybe he became Americanized."

"Side hustle," Anna added as the obviousness hit her.

"The gig economy?" Dindrane asked.

Jennifer didn't respond to any of these guesses; instead, she turned to look at her husband and this is when she asked the group at large, "Where is he?"

Thankfully, before all were led to believe they had missed seeing Arthur's ascendance to the Promised Land, they heard the flushing of a toilet with an accompanying release of exaltation. The sound of water splashing was also heard and then a face appeared from behind the bathroom door. For a moment, Mary Shelly popped into everyone's thoughts, perhaps Arthur's most of all.

"I look like shit," he whispered as he surveyed the scene around him.

He was right on this count. He was also naked and standing thus displayed an appearance many would relate to Dr. Frankenstein's creation. Until this moment, those in the room had only seen the damaged man lying down. Now erect, the body displayed the totality of the insults done to it. The length of hair on the right side of his head clearly juxtaposed the short sprouts finally beginning to reemerge around the scar tissue on the left. The deep horseshoe scar would have been a magnet, attracting all eyes if not for the left ear protruding out at an odd angle like a bird's broken wing. He was trying to stand erect, though the curvature in his back and contraction of his left shoulder were prohibiting this. Below his neckline, scars crisscrossed both sides of his body, visible as red tufts of skin interwoven with the tracks of dissolving suture lines, when not covered completely with bandages.

He stood, thus, for a full minute continuously drying his hands on his naked chest. He didn't look at anyone, just the room at large, trying to register his current bearing and how to plot the proper course onward. Finding the best route, he shuffled back to his bed and climbed in.

Jennifer was the first to move, she grabbed his hand and this time when she leaned over, she planted her kiss directly onto his lips. Arthur didn't say anything at first, he just stared straight ahead.

"Where am I?" he finally asked as his eyes drifted off to visit the others in the room.

Everyone touched by his gaze exhaled and each tried their hand at an explanation until Lucan let it be known, the floor belonged to Jennifer.

"Everything is all right, my love. You were in an accident. We are here to take care of you and, and—" Before she could say another word Arthur interrupted.

"Our son?"

"Lute has already come to visit. You've been…you've been asleep. Do not worry, he's in good hands," she added, using the possessive, "and is heading back to school. Some of our dearest friends are with him. He did ask me to tell you…"

"And Guinevere?"

Three times he asked the whereabouts of Lute and Guinevere. Whether those around Arthur understood the concept of short-term memory loss or not, Arthur was obviously living it. These individuals were of paramount importance to Arthur, hence the repetitions. Jennifer was not phased; at each request she would take a deep breath and slowly repeat her response. Before the third round was finished her husband was asleep.

Turning her head to gaze at the others, Jennifer grasped at the one bit of information she sought. "The old man, the professor, was not his lover, right?"

"No, dear," Anna replied. "The old man was more of a study guide."

Lucan now pulled three sheets of paper from within his coat pocket, the ones the hospice had been begging her to sign; the ones the family needed to legally transfer Arthur out of the institution. He placed them on the table next to the flower vase. Jennifer knew what he was asking and obliged. When done, she searched the room for her handbag, found it and quickly removed something from within. Then she moved back to Arthur's side. All eyes zeroed in on what was now in her hands.

"If we are going to move him, I think we need to clean him up a bit." With that said, she began to snip.

From somewhere within Anna's storage compartment known as a purse, she produced a comb and moved alongside Jennifer. "Here, let me help you, dear."

As the two women worked to make Arthur presentable, Jennifer gave the butler one more task, "I think someone else will need to join us if we go back home." Lucan confirmed the order with a slight nod of his head and mentally adding it to his list of things to do.

Chapter 32
Old Friends

False dawn had moved on and Jennifer's complete understanding marched in step with the advance of day. The sun just below the horizon was brightening the world around the hospice to a point where movement became visible on the field below. It also brought a telephone call.

"Bombs have gone off in London," Lucan relayed. "They hit trains, and…"

Dindrane pieced the possibilities together. "Wayne was in London, wasn't he?"

"Did they hit a bus too," Anna asked.

Lucan answered in the affirmative.

"Was Lute on that bus?" Jennifer pushed out the question before Lucan could finish.

"Not sure which bus was hit."

Every day since Arthur's accident, Jennifer had prayed for his recovery while every night the incoming tide of guilt-ridden anxiety caused a fair degree of tossing and turning. Guilt and the relatedness of events which, like ripples of water, moved outward from the splash she had caused by hiring the private dick. Now, everything touched by the ripple had become connected, forcing her to feel the shame while hoping the reaper had come for someone other than her son. Standing next to her, Anna did likewise. Anna, poor Anna, her brother on the table and now the fear for her son had her standing like a granite statue, mouth locked in the open position. Dindrane, like the other two women, went quiet, seemingly shutting herself off, wondering if Rwanda would ever leave her in peace.

They would have stayed thus for what may have been eternity if it wasn't for Lucan. He moved the women physically, so they all had to regain conscious behavior and then he told them what he needed each to do. In crises, those with tactical expertise are more important than strategists. He focused their efforts on immediate needs and in so doing, within each psyche pain was buried beneath the machinations of the assigned task.

"Mademoiselle li Gros!" He began, looking her straight in the eyes to draw her attention. "You must find all of the medicines we will need to take."

In one swift motion, he let go of her and turned. "Anna, call Teterboro and make sure the plane is ready."

Lucan then turned again, this time slowly. He grabbed Jennifer and, holding her shoulders tight, gave instructions to her as well.

Arthur, too, was busy. The bathroom run had taken too much of his energy supply. He had become very tired and at the same time the quantity of medications in his blood were sinking to levels his body had not known since arriving at the ICU. All this pushed his mind back into the deeper space it had struggled to move out of. His eyes began darting across the blank slate of the ceiling above him while his brain superimposed images of Gawaine and Angusulus jumping over the side as their boat reached shore. From the quay, blue faced highlanders sent arrow after arrow in their direction, and as the action found its way onto the canvas he was painting, his heart rate increased, and his blood pressure rose.

Samir forgot to tell his guide of the need to keep the overnight package frozen. This might have made him angry if it hadn't moved down his priority list to just below "where to find a winter coat." Moving up to the top spot was the chamber pot.

Non, non, non, I cannot do it in that! It's too, too dirty!

Confusion had begun to give way to neurotic psychosis. How many hours before Ali would show up, he couldn't begin to calculate? But with nothing else to do, he tried. The effort wore him out, and when combined with his lack of sleep on the plane, it wasn't long before he drifted into munchkin land. When he woke, a cold trickle was emigrating from his nostrils and several men were emerging from the tunnel, one by one. Ali was last. They greeted each other as two old friends might if they were in front of three other men toting guns, that is, very carefully.

"Hicham," Ali said with a manicured smile as he reached around and gently patted Samir's back. "We brought your package." One of the men held out the overnight delivery. "I hope it's in good shape. Though, I'm afraid we aren't. For a time, we will have to lay low, some of us will, that is."

"Lay low?" was the only response to present itself as Samir, using the back of his sleeve for lack of a better utensil, wiped the dribble from beneath his nose.

Ali's responses were delivered in a mix of hometown Moroccan guttural slang, English, with a Scottish brogue, and French. His French had a distinctly Parisian interpretation and was much more refined than when the two men had lived together. The problem was, in the intervening years Samir's version of the language had transformed itself into the older, Québécois style, which had become his daily ration. All told, understanding, or total interpretation of his old friend's exposé became dependent upon Ali's repetition of events using just one of the three languages at a time.

"We did it this morning, Hicham. It was a success. It will close the infidel's city down for weeks...if not months."

"Qu'avez-vous fait?" Samir's confused response came in the formal, singular, second person pronoun construct.

Ali ignored the formality, "What did we do? What did we do! Oh my, you are behind the times. While you were down here"—Ali clarified by pointing at the floor beneath everyone's feet—"on this very morning, we unleashed the wrath of Allah on the English! We bombed London! The trains, the buses...we destroyed everything!"

Ali's voice rose in pitch as he explained only damping this down when echoes began to reverberate throughout the tunnel system. Everyone else in the room gave a faint cheer and passed around hugs, without kisses. There was nothing for Samir to do but wait for more information to pass his way.

"We killed thousands of them!" Ali continued until one of his compatriots mumbled something about waiting for the exact body count to be broadcast. Ali turned his gaze on the minion who at once got back on board the party platform.

"The heathen will show this on their televisions, helping us spread the word," the compatriot finished, all the while trying to keep Ali's mean stare from burning holes in his torso.

"This is correct," Ali managed as he turned his eyes back to Samir. "We will know how many very soon." Then he took the package Samir had sent and placed it on the small table, "What is this, my friend?"

Samir began to explain the cell stock situation, "used to grow virus" but left out a few key terms such as vaccine and harmless, not realizing his mistake until he noticed how everyone began to inch back toward the tunnel entrance, even Ali.

"Is this infectious?" came his way from Ali who was now the last man backing out.

Samir had to explain and plead at the same time. "They are used to grow infectious virus yes, dangerous no, it's a laboratory preparation of a vaccine strain, it needs to be frozen, or it will be useless."

"This is what you brought? For this you wanted to see…" Ali didn't bother reciting their leader's name, he didn't have to, and when everyone had resumed their place in the room, he continued, "You sent this shit here? What are we to do with it? Why didn't you keep it with you over there?"

"Because I had to come over here." Samir left out "you idiot," took a deep breath, tried to stay calm, and continued, "I cannot go back there. That is why I brought it along. This was my mission, right? All those years I was in Canada, all those studies I undertook, all that effort to find something we could use and…and I don't know why but I thought if I brought it back…"

Ali cut him off. "This is something only you can use. Why did you bring it now? We cannot do anything with it." Pointing in the direction of the package he finished his thought, "Who knows how long we will be in hiding."

Samir tried to push his case, hoping they would not quite understand what he had. "It isn't ready for use. There is nothing we can do with it until I have a lab up and running but since I was coming here on other business, I brought this along. I will explain it all to my contact and hopefully he can get me in to see…"

Ali had moved closer and cut him off again. "Why don't you do that."

"Do what?"

"Tell your contact." With this command came an expression Samir had no difficulty in interpreting. It had been Ali on the other end all through the years. "Only we like to use the term controller."

"So you know about the recording."

"What recording?"

If Samir was chilled before the men arrived, he was warming up now. He had to remove the *pakol* as sweat had begun to trickle down the sides of his face and within each armpit a swamp was in its development phase. His voice too, like Ali's, had begun to rise both in pitch and volume until those around him pointed upward, a gesture they hoped he (and Ali) would understand.

A degree of understanding across the board was dawning. Ali said he knew everything about Samir's activities but obviously he didn't know the nature of the recording, ergo the information must have been sent sheik-to-sheik. Taking the initiative, Samir marched over to the package and ripped the box open. He made certain the small set of vials remained inside as he pulled an electronic device out from underneath separating sheets of insulation paper. "I need to show this to him." This statement, without doubt, meant to the man several notches above those in attendance.

"What? You want to show him this, this..." Ali paused, scrutinized what Samir was holding, gave up and asked, "What is it?"

Samir began again, trying to align word usage with meaning, "I need for him to listen to this."

"Oh" was Ali's formulated response.

"Oh?" Samir tried to interpret in three different languages but unable to translate into any degree of understanding he had to continue forward hoping for the best. "So now you will call him?"

The ball was back in Ali's court. "Well, no. As I've said, everyone is in hiding, you, me, and"—Ali pointed to his group—"them. And he, he is not here."

As Ali was finishing his soliloquy, two more men wound their way into the room reducing the available space to zero. They unloaded what appeared to be a portable cooking stove, several more bedpans and an assortment of other packages.

Whether it was the camping gear in particular, or the room crowding in general, is unclear, either one of those may have been what spurred Samir's pleading. "Can you take me to where he is hiding? He must listen to what I've brought."

Over Samir's request, the last man in began his report. They were all present and accounted for. The opening to the lower level was concealed by the two women staying in the house proper; food was stored along the pathways to the common room. Without completely understanding where, Samir heard there was a place for the pots to be emptied and fresh water retrieved, both of those stations were back the way they came and at least one level down.

With report complete, a few brisk words were passed back and forth between the men leading to smirks. Ali then faced Samir. "Hicham, he doesn't want to see you."

Swallowing hard, Samir understood the situation. He wasn't a top priority.

"In fact," Ali continued, "he asked me to provide you with one of these." "One of these" was a small corset-like contraption Ali pulled out of a sack one of the recent arrivals had brought. Wires hung out from several pockets laced into the corset, each connected to what appeared to be small plastic looking cylindrical sticks. "Do you know what this is?"

"Of course, but why me, why now?"

"Because, Samir, sorry, I mean Hicham, your Sheik in New York thought we would all be better off if you proved your loyalty to the cause in this fashion. Since it is his brother on this side of the ocean who is our Sheik, it was agreed. That is why we are now going to make a video."

"A video? You mean like a movie?"

"Oui, exactement! A testimonial. And you will be dressed in one of these." With a broad Cheshire smile, Ali held up the bomb wielding vest. "To give the world your message before you depart. You do believe …don't you?" Ali didn't wait for a response he just barreled along with a devilish smirk creeping out from beneath his beard, "Oh, you are such a lucky soul, think of the virgins!"

Samir swallowed hard and reached for ideas as his neurotic psychosis gave way to outright fear. "Listen to the tape I brought. I beg you. I know we are separate operations linked only by the philosophy of our benefactors, and I assume those here with you, my old friend, are obviously higher up the holy ladder than I, but if you listen, you will understand. This information is for the Sheik, your Sheik, my Sheik, for all of us. Yes, yes that's right…it's for all of us." Samir tried his hardest to get buy-in. He needed to make directional changes without the real decision makers present. He had to; his life (it appeared) depended on it.

"You know, we probably have a lot of time on our hands, so we may as well listen to what you've brought." Ali grinned. This somehow pushed Samir one rung farther down the pecking order. The other men all gave a short, affirmative laugh.

Samir's recorder was placed in the middle of the table. Within a short period of time and without technical help, Ali did manage to turn it on as Samir explained to the room at large some specifics, like his location, the time of day and who it was he was following. "Dr. McAiden, Dr. Arthur McAiden. This was the night he was in the accident." Being the instigator of the accident was not the issue, so he avoided this altogether.

"This woman's book is right on the mark" were the first words heard.

"That was McAiden," Samir interjected. "He was talking on his cell phone after leaving the house. The house belonged to a professor of history at one of the universities over there." The fact the university was Ivy League didn't come out. No one in the room would have cared.

The audio continued, "If what I've found is right then this Goodrich book may lead others in the same direction. I fear danger if the information comes out too soon. Yes, yes, that's what I think. It might spoil everything. I know, we've been practicing obscuration for quite a long time." The voice paused briefly as McAiden listened. "And yet, there it is, anyone with an ounce of brains can figure it out. All they have to do is read the stupid book!"

Those in the cold, dark room were murmuring as they sought clarification. The diction was understandable from an audio point of view but not understandable with respect to meaning. "I do not know this word" was repeated by several within the audience, each time becoming louder forcing Ali to shut off the device and turn to the only one in the room with a working knowledge of the English language.

Samir gave this a go. "I am not sure perhaps it is a form of obscure, if so, then I think the rest makes sense." The others in the room nodded their heads but still, had no comprehension. Ali hid his own ignorance by turning the machine back on.

"I'm not sure if anyone really believes what she wrote. She's better trained as a philologist than a historian but shit, isn't that me too, and her theories…" McAiden was trying to continue but those listening in wouldn't let him.

"Who is she?"

"What are her theories?"

"What's a, what's a…philologist?" The fact the man asking this got the pronunciation right brought a quick round of applause, then everyone turned their attention to Ali, who had no clue, but thankfully for him, before he had a chance to turn the recorder off again Arthur's voice picked up, both in volume and speed.

"Yeah, yeah, every time someone brings up the Northern Kingdom theory they are shot down. Ignorance is bliss in their world. In ours, how one deals with terrorists and their dogma, is…" McAiden paused again, and the only thing those listening in could hear was a loud, slow exhalation. That was Samir. No one moved, each sat tight with bated breath, but for a few seconds, all they could hear was Arthur nodding his head in agreement. When the voice again became audible, all those who had waited could do was sit like highschoolers in an advanced level college symposium.

"Yes, one begets the other. That is true. But with patience? Are you kidding? We were the ones… Yes, your clan was…but who put in place the strategy…yes, yes, we all did." Arthur paused, laughed a bit and continued, "Your right, none of us is interested in their take on doctrine."

Another pause, and now the audience sat grappling with the implications, just as Samir had so many weeks before. And like Samir, there was no way for those sitting beneath the ancient city of Edinburgh to know, McAiden spoke of events almost fifteen hundred years in the past. The fact the locale of these events was, geographically, pretty much spot on their current location also didn't register but to those listening the words did seem to be aimed at them.

"Forced ideology" found its way out of the speaker, "cannot win in the face of knowledge and anyone reading what this Goodrich woman wrote will pick up on this and…" Another pause and then an explanation: "Oh hell, I hope Jennifer isn't waiting up. Look, Dubric, I've got to go but I'll be home in a few." The voice paused again, and Arthur waited for a chance to jump back in.

"Yes," he finally managed, "the one in Avalon. I will bring Geoffrey's book with me, yes, both books. I told you I found the second one right where I thought it would be, at the *li Gros* estate. Yglais? No, she didn't have a clue. Look, I will explain the whole thing later, but quickly it's like this…" here the message was garbled, and by the time the voice was once again understandable, they had missed the explanation. Ten seconds later, the recording stopped. Everyone turned to stare at Samir.

"Hicham," Ali asked, "do you know who McAiden was speaking with?"

Samir's eyes became extremely wide as revelation encroached in the guise of a two-headed monster. He began to shake as his gaze gradually drifted from floor to ceiling. Every other eye in the room joined Samir's. Minutes passed in the now-quiet chamber until Ali painted the two heads.

"It looks like Dubric's people may be up to more than feeding the poor. They may be on the lookout for people of, um, different persuasions. If we stay here in their lower basement, it cannot be safe for us, but if we leave at this time the police will surely track us down." When he finished speaking, Ali again picked up the vest that was going to be his present to Samir. He gave it a good, hard look before dropping it in one of the chamber pots. Then he wiped his hands on the backside of his pants.

Chapter 33
Multiple Perspectives

The access road to the hospice had turned into a congested parking lot, making it difficult for two cars to negotiate passage. Lucan was driving one of the two. It was early in the morning and no one in his car was in a mood to talk, sleep was out of the question, and it was a bit of a drive to the airport, so they all sat quietly, each in their own fashion trying to sort things out.

Lucan was both introspecting while at the same time being fed minute-by-minute updates through his earphones. He was also keeping an eye on the vehicle now following them, two men, one with camera. This bit of information he decided was best kept to himself. Everyone else in the car had enough to worry about.

Anna, sitting in the back seat, knew her brother's accident had set in motion a disjointed stream of events but was having trouble linking them, on a more macrocosmic level, with the bombings in London. To cloud things a bit further, as the car sped along, references to Arthur and religion began to sink in. "What were you up to?" she whispered in the ear of the incommunicado man sitting next to her.

If Jennifer saw the camera wielding man in the trailing car, she would be hard-pressed to know what his focal point was. But she didn't see this. She was too busy internalizing and, like Anna, trying to link events occurring on both sides of the Atlantic. Both women sat hoping to sort things into a discernible pattern until, that is, Jennifer's phone rang.

"Yes, that's right... Oh really? Well, yes, yes, I am, or I should say, we are... No, no, to the airport. Yes, right now. We are taking him to... Yes, the butler is..."

Before she could finish, Lucan had reached into the back seat, pulled the phone out of her hand, and shut it down. "Everyone who needs to know already knows" is all he said.

Without being asked, Jennifer filled the others in. "It was Vivienne. I don't know how but she knew we had left the hospice, with Arthur." When she spoke his name, Arthur looked around, burped, gave a brief smile, and then went back to staring at the ceiling.

"According to her, everyone seems upset we're bringing him home. How did she know we were taking him out of the hospice let alone..."

Even though busy, Lucan managed to turn inward for a moment. *Sanctimonious bastards, belittle the rank of butler. The name we were honored with is now just the man who opens the damn door. Arthur was different, he knew.* Realizing his mistake with tense, he pulled himself out of his reverie. The planning list he had made many days before needed some updating. This is what butlers do operations; they make certain all the boxes are checked. The books he knew were in the trunk, check. He had reaffirmed this as the ladies and hospice attendants worked Arthur into the back seat. The company jet was almost ready. This he was being told by the voice oozing through the device in his ear, check. The phone itself was recharging its battery via connection with the car's cigarette lighter, check. So far, everything that could be checked was checked, everything else was still in play.

In a sense, to get to the point, those in the car now occupied had depended on probability theory. That probability being Jennifer signing the release forms. Thankfully, the night's efforts had gone well, Lucan had worked hard to make it so. But the morning news reports of trouble overseas had probably thrown the next phase of the operation into question. The ethereal voice streaming information into Lucan's ear was now placing betting odds on its continuation. "Not sure they're going to allow flights into the airspace over there for a while." Lucan had to trust in God, and luck, so he prayed a bit and crossed his fingers, then he continued to move down his list, the plans were in action, there was nothing else he could do.

Officer Kramer was next up. This call was not really needed. The company books and data packages and other items Yglais had insisted they bring along had been retrieved. But being an operations guy, it was always nice to dot some i's and cross a few t's. Officer Kramer had been assigned a task. Lucan had met Kramer when Arthur began his midlife, I'm out of shape, crisis. Kramer taught karate at the local community center. "A little exercise might help" is how Lucan phrased it. He also believed fencing might have been a more proper sport for someone Arthur's age, but Arthur had insisted. "Look," he told Lucan. "How often am I going to carry an epée, or for that matter a fuckin' broadsword into a board meeting? But if I know I can kick each, and everyone's ass, well then, I will feel much more um…confident." Lucan listened, nodding his head, holding his laughter in. Arthur was never in need of physical persuading. No one in their right minds would ever be anything but polite to Arthur when Dagan was nearby, and Dagan was always nearby. As Kramer taught Arthur, and Lucan watched, they all struck up a friendship. The friendship is what put this member of the local police community on Lucan's call list.

The man with the camera following Lucan had no idea the car was headed to Teterboro or had any knowledge of Kramer's enlistment. Apparently, those he reported to didn't know either. The degree of understanding, or lack thereof, didn't stop Officer Kramer from informing Lucan when he and his group were on the job.

"Yes, we're keeping an eye on things."

As with so many other items on his list, Lucan could only drive the car and patiently await further reports.

————◦◖◗◦————

A slight turn of the camera lens being held in the trailing car expanded its view of the front seat. Now both the driver and Dindrane were visible. Like those around her, Dindrane was lost in thought. In her mind, she was searching for her brother, wondering where he was holed-up this time. Then she shifted gears, trying to bring the salient features of the months spent on her neurology rotation into focus.

As the effects of pressure differentials on sensitive cortex function merge with the impressions, minute differences of interpretation of two-thousand-year-old letters on society at large all play against... Try as she would, focusing was hard.

The camera, too, shifted focus. Now its vision encompassed Arthur in the middle of the back seat with his head tilted back, eyes glued to the white surface of the interior roof. He was spending his time wondering why bacon tasted so good in the morning. If it wasn't for the camera angle, it might have been possible for those in the trailing car to spot the drool descending into the recesses beneath his chin.

When he wasn't tasting bacon, Arthur was tracking the point at which the car he was in became nothing more than a statistical compost within the rush hour traffic pattern. When this mote receded, it freed him to pursue other topics, and for a moment, he became busy simultaneously deciphering every aspect of the mysteries of life as he reformed the three-dimensional context of his surroundings. The meds might have been more than a trifle responsible for this uptick in activity. It wasn't so much that he missed his meds; in fact, he had no idea he was taking any, but the change in the level of circulating pharmaceuticals was causing disequilibrium in both the healing and thinking processes. Why the medications were dipping was another one of those unforeseen events. Delegating medical matters to those traumatized by the moment had not been a good idea.

In the trailing car, the man with the camera was spouting an unending monologue to his partner. The man behind the wheel listened without responding as he struggled to keep control on what would have been the wrong side of the road back home in England.

"The sun's up, I canno' use the infra-red anymore, and from this angle nothin' will work. Can' you pass them, jus' once an' le' me get a clear shot?"

The driver, knowing his business a bit better than the man sitting beside him held the car in its current position. He heard the babble with one ear while listening more intently for road sounds with the other. He might have paid a bit more attention to his mate if they had grown up in a similar geographic locale. But being from Liverpool, it was hard understanding what the hell the guy from Glasgow was saying. Hence, he ignored the cameraman and calmly went about his business. In addition, since he had landed in Jersey, he had found the local language completely foreign. This is why he had taken to watching the Spanish language television stations, ones that allowed for English subtitles, just to get the news.

The day's assignment had come in the form of a telephone call. "The butler and the man's wife are heading to the hospice." How the woman on the other end of the phone knew this didn't matter. "Keep an eye on them, especially wherever else they go," she had continued. "Most important," he had been told, "let us know when they leave the hospice and head back to McAiden's house."

His controller had seemed to be prescient when he first began the night's activities, but now, the car he was assigned to follow had left the hospice with three more bodies than when it had entered, and it was heading off in an unexpected direction. All he could do was call it in and listen to the cameraman piss and moan about lighting conditions, camera angles, and how he would get a little less bonus money if the pictures weren't good.

West of the two cars and at an altitude where motor vehicle exhaust fumes were not a problem, a bevy of hot air balloon enthusiasts drifted lazily along. Picture-taking was the purpose of the expedition and take pictures they did, lots of them. Most zeroed in on various subjects below such as the traffic tie-up on the road leading into and out of a rather large complex. In the nearby fields, they also took an interest in those camped besides a small pond. Not knowing what they were looking at they had no understanding of the events playing out beneath them, but from their position, it all made for interesting compositions. The panorama beneath did not visually spread to a home in Tewksbury, though the entire fleet of balloons had moments before passed over Arthur's house.

Later in the day, all photos would be loaded onto the club's computer, then sorted to select the best works for a coming exhibit. As this collating work was underway, a nearby television was broadcasting news of the day. This is how those who had been in the balloons began to piece together activities they had seen from above. The large building with the small pond on its grounds was part of a hospice. The campers seen were not patients, and the long line of cars and trucks trying to get off the premises were the residual effects of an early morning revelation. Arthur McAiden was no longer present.

What the balloonist and others watching the unfolding events on television didn't know was this: Given the hour of revelation, the congregated news teams could not gather a quorum for the high-level, decision-making needed to choose the next best course of action.

"We don't know exactly when he left," one young on-the-scene reporter was mouthing into his phone. "No one did! That's why we didn't follow any cars off the lot you son of a…" The accompanying expletives had the young man looking for a new job the following day.

In another truck, a female rookie reporter was getting her hair sprayed straight for any potential camera coverage on the morning edition. She, too, was having a linked-in conversation. "If we wait a bit more, we can interview the hired help as the shifts change. Right now, the stinkin' security guys won't let us inside even to use the bathrooms."

Then, changing her focus, she let out a squeal with a curse attached "Ouch, fuck!" while grabbing her hairstylist's wrist. "Watch what the hell you're doin'. What day of the week is it? I thought I was wearing red today and now you put…"

In the end, all conversations became pretty much the same regardless of which conglomerated or independent news personnel was holding it. "You know, we've got this stuff breakin' in from England, might be best to switch headlines and cover that for a bit." As each team was reaching the same conclusion, a caravan began to slowly wind its way off the hospice grounds moving as one long articulated insect, each segment following their individual computer-generated instructions, or the van in front of them, all heading home. Arthur McAiden was alive and, as so, no longer newsworthy.

Arthur's house in Tewksbury did show up in some of the early morning photos taken from above. Those in the balloons couldn't resist. The house had police cars stacked up in its driveway and officers moving about in search of, well those high up didn't know, they only watched and took pictures.

On the ground, Officer Kramer knew what was going on and called it in to his superior, "Subjects have been apprehended. Like to thank whoever passed the tip along to us."

Kramer's superior had listened, nodding his head in cadence to the man's pronouncements, wondering how his department would handle the captured individuals. *I bet not a one of them is a legal.* As he finished with Kramer's call, he mulled that thought for a while. *Perhaps we should call in the FBI; something must be going on here. I wonder when the donuts and coffee will arrive. I hate starting work on an empty stomach.* And then, with his mind in full gear, he expanded on his list of important tasks for the day. *I wonder when Guido will be back, I hate it when these bookies go on holidays. I guess he must have taken in a big haul last week.* The captain smiled at his supposed conclusions; *some people are just lucky. If he doesn't come back soon, I might have to drive over to Bayonne and check things out. Gawd, I hate driving in Bayonne.*

After bidding his supervisor adieu, Kramer quickly made another call, this one using his personal phone. "Mr. Lucan," he started, never knowing if Lucan was the man's given or surname, "we got the men… yeah, yeah, just as you thought. They were sifting through the downstairs rooms, the library and office section. They had nothing that looked to be of value, just some technical papers and a few old books. Have a good flight."

The next morning, the headlines would tell how local police captured an international ring, trying to rob a residence in an upscale neighborhood in Tewksbury. At that moment, though, the noise from Lucan's earpiece was too low for the others to hear and the women didn't even bother to ask when they heard him sign off. "Thank you very much." He then spouted a low-volume yet victorious "yes" into his sleeve before he switched back to a conversation on a second line he had placed on hold. It had to do with an oven, "Yes, yes, that o'ven. Listen, we need you to get the packages there on time. Can you do that?"

Chapter 34
Seven Degrees of Separation

Uptake and distribution will differ depending on route of administration and IV to oral had been a very recent changeover. The meds were the same, the route and dosing changed, that's all. Of course, no matter what was different someone did have to administer the stuff, and this might have been the problem. The admin schedule had left the room in Nurse Flo's work bag and the thoughts of those who remained behind were a bit distracted during their exodus from the hospice. Whatever, total reemergence was taking its sweet time. The place Arthur McAiden now occupied may have been amongst the folds in the roof lining inches above his head. Whichever canvas he was using the transference was easy for one to follow.

The full military might his namesake had ever commanded was on the move amongst the undulating hillsides of the North Country. Immediately to his rear bowmen marched alongside those with pikes and behind them came the siege weapons, all parading along *Dere*. On the roadside, he noted each company as their centurion pushed them north through Dunie and on past Falkirk. No longer were they part of the emperor's legions. Now they were his, the Gosgordd of the *dux bellorum*. He was the *Dux,* and the *Dux* was the *Imperator* and the *Imperator* was the dragon, but not just any ol' dragon, Arthur was the *Pen Dragon*.

Arthur's images turned to *Dere* itself, the thoroughfare constructed by his ancestors who had come to the Island as Roman overlords. *Dere* ran along the rolling, fertile countryside stretching south from the northern wall built during Antonine's time. It passed forts, some just shells of their former strength, except *Trimontium* of course. *Trimontium* would last forever. This he never doubted. Today they would pass the rotunda, the o'ven he had heard it called and move south through Lothian, all the way to the wall built by Hadrian. Then, to reach home, the path headed west, to Caerleon, Carlisle, the largest fortress in the realm. How the road was named back then he couldn't remember. These days it was Stanegate.

Both journeys were serving to connect synapses along the routes of joyful recollection. Arthur was going to the airport; he was going home. And home led to images coalescing inside his head. Images of herdsmen taking their cattle to higher ground as the heat of the season began to set in, of flowers too, found in abundance along the riverbanks as his troops marched by.

"I loved to smell the flowers," Arthur remembered. It was the aroma, the smell of nature at its finest, which offset the stench of death that followed his men as they pressed from one engagement to another.

Those who trained his army were now front and center. Men like Kramer, the fellow whose unit he could never quite remember, were always needed. Their special talent, to teach the art of war, is what helped build the Island of *Prydein* and the three adjacent lands into its own nation. It was this group of instructors, more than the *Pen Dragon* himself, who helped put the host of *Cymry* in the annals.

"We would be without hope if not for those capable of working the novice into a competent..." Midsentence he stopped and turned his attention to Dubricius who had, without forethought or warning, appeared by his side. Arthur wondered how he had wormed his way into the generalized recollection while at the same time admitting all tributes needed to be cast in honor of his mentor as well.

"I wouldn't be Pen Dragon if it wasn't for the Merlin."

To the east of the Pen Dragon, a long line of aircraft passed overhead. This close to the Hudson all flights followed a route. Those originating from the north or west looped around Lower Manhattan and followed the FDR drive north and east before veering away and descending into LaGuardia. One flight in this lineup had originated in Montréal. The pilot didn't care one iota about any of the cars nearing Teterboro. He was too high up and too far east. He might have seen the balloons amongst the folding topography of Jersey further west but only if he was using binoculars. Even if he did have the right gear, he wouldn't have been able to look for long, he was too busy. His plane was still west of the city heading south but soon would need to loop around Battery Park.

If the wind is mild today, we'll be okay, he thought just before engaging in a final check on the Teterboro traffic pattern before he dipped and turned over Jersey City (making sure not to sway too far and place his plane in the Newark zone). *Too many airports, too little air space, what the hell were they thinking? So easy on paper. Shit I should have had more coffee, at a time like this, I've got to keep both hands on the wheel.*

If the pilot did have time to gaze about it would more likely be to his left. He lived in the countryside just north of the St. Laurence and got his fill of country living daily. This was why flying around Manhattan was so much more interesting. *No matter how many times I do this... Come to think of it, how many years have I been doing this?*

As big a melting pot of humanity, the city of Montréal was, Manhattan was bigger and the stew created in its pot included bits of everything, though the pilot himself had no way of imagining the building in which, at that very moment, a prayer meeting of sorts was in progress. The pilot didn't know this but somehow the narrator did for this is what he put down on paper. The pilot was now inside the building, but he was not fluent in Arabic and so missed out on the praises the Sheik was singing for those brothers who had, hours earlier, pushed the Jihad along.

Why this pilot from Montréal was in this story must have had something to do with seven degrees of separation. Earlier in the day he had, without knowing, moved up the ladder to what might be called a third or fourth degree. The connection started when he walked past a tall thin man in the airport speaking hurriedly and, obviously, emphatically to a man standing next to him. The man on the receiving end was without doubt higher up the company work pyramid. Details from their heated conversation were vague. The vagueness may have been due to the pilot's need to ingest his morning ration of caffeine. The rapidity of the conversation might have had something to do with this problem too.

The one piece of information he did ingest was the destination of the tall man, Edinburgh. This stuck out because of the bevy of stories on multiple televisions throughout the concourse all related to the tragedy in London. *London is likely heading into lock down mode. Lock down might spread to other airports too. That man*, the pilot thought, *might have a problem.*

The two men moved a short distance away from the pilot, and so, out of sight, out of mind, at least for a while. He did grab his morning ration of coffee, picked up a copy of the *Gazette*, and found a nearby chair. Two sips into his coffee he unfolded the paper and there, staring right off the print in his direction was the face of *la Sûreté*. Putting two and two together he was able to identify one member of the arguing duet. It was Dionne, Gervais Dionne, head of the entire Provincial police organization. Once this was established, the pilot thought it necessary to change his seat. A moment later, he was once again comfortably within earshot of Dionne.

"Christian, the English are all tied up right now, and the FBI only have MacLean available. He is already on his way over." When the man the police chief called Christian didn't answer, Capitaine Dionne continued, "You were assigned to help him in New York, remember?"

"New Jersey," the tall, thin subordinate replied, then he checked his ticket and looked at his wristwatch.

The head of *la Sûreté* waited for more but when none came, he reissued his commands. Then he offered to buy his man something to eat. "Just see what happens for a few days. Look, if the man the FBI is trailing, this um, this Hicham fellow, did work with Samir over here, then our little friend may be joining him over there, oui? If you guys lose him and the British are too tied up to help well hell, then you can come back home. D'accord?"

The conversation was coming to an end as the pilot picked up his belongings and headed off to the commuter entrance. The entire morning encounter he forgot about as he piloted his plane south. But when he turned the craft around Battery Park and hit a turbulent air pocket, it began to come back to him. He wasn't new to the route but still the shaking within the plane touched home as he remembered the morning conversation and then, looking toward the empty space in the Battery Park skyline sad memories of tall buildings and aéroplanes brought him to tears.

As the morning stream of air traffic was rounding Battery Park, security agencies on both sides of the Atlantic were trying to get lucky. Coded discussions between the Sheik in New York City and his relative in England were being dissected by the FBI, CIA, NSA, and the founder of Wikileaks. However, hearing is not the same as understanding. Only two words throughout one five-minute intercept were understood, Samir and Hicham. Neither Sheik cared much for either. This observation came from voice inflection and the fact the name wasn't coded.

Who Hicham was they had no idea, but they put this name up on top of their list. Both he and Samir became the backbone for the FBI's action plan. The only problem now was current events in England. The attacks in London had reduced available personnel, hence the need to ask *la Sûreté*'s head honcho to lend lease their agent again.

"Listen, he knows this Samir guy. Maybe he can find the 'icham fella as well."

The fact Samir was Hicham had not been digested yet in the New York office of the FBI. The report sent by Donna MacLean wasn't clear on this point. In costume, she had sat near Samir and listened in on him several times since the train ride up to Montréal. He was always alone and always mumbling to himself in three different languages, two of which she knew.

"Subject sat alone again but spoke with someone named Hicham… again," she reported in. "I don't think he's on the phone, at least my detection gear doesn't pick up anything. Maybe he's schizophrenic."

On her final report she assessed Samir's actions at the airport in Montréal. "I think when he's talking to 'icham, he's speaking to himself. Anyway, it was Samir who purchased the tickets but the name on them is Hicham."

All of this, including her attempt at spelling Hicham, had been sent along to her husband who was already on his way to Edinburgh. So her report was passed to those up the ladder. Unfortunately, those higher up the food chain had more important things to do than read every word in a report from either MacLean. This is how Hicham boarded the plane for Edinburgh, not Samir, and the paperwork proved this to be true.

It was early in the morning of July 7 when Special Agent MacLean arrived in Scotland. He was ushered into security offices at the airport to await the local agent assigned to help. As he waited, they told him, "Only one arrived, visa says Hicham, no sign of the other guy."

MacLean took a quick look at the photo provided and, never having met Samir face-to-face still had to scratch his head at the features he shared with Hicham. With nothing to do but wait for his driver, he used his time wisely; he multitasked. With a stack of reports in hand, he sat down and went to sleep. While MacLean napped in Great Britain, and those back in the States tried to convince Jennifer to bring Arthur home, the day crept inexorably forward. Soon all parties would be affected by the bombings to come.

In Scotland, events on the ground began to change rapidly leaving the locals with little to no manpower available to lend. The bombings were soon international news and the British Intelligent services; both national and international branches alike, along with Scotland Yard, and the local constabularies were all needed to plug into the country's well-rehearsed biosafety and hazmat-defense programs. As the manpower evaporated into prearranged operations so, too, did MacLean's help on the ground.

"And oh, by the way," MacLean was told by his connection in the New York Office, "Inspector Gervais will be rejoining your team. Take good care of him. And don't let those two Moroccans out of your site."

Unbeknownst to MacLean was the conversation going on back in the home office. Apparently, there had been no one else his superiors could find to send over in his stead.

"Is anyone back from vacation? We need to send some real agents over there, not the old guy and definitely not the Canadian."

Chapter 35
Loose Ends

Things had changed in the brief time Special Agent MacLean had slept. But despite all the bombing-related activities going on throughout the United Kingdom, he had a job to do, and for that, he needed a car. After downing a cup of ersatz coffee and getting help from the overworked security team at the airport, he was presented with something that, on paper, was listed as a car. When the mini-coop finally arrived, he quickly ran an eyeball-based calculation in his head wondering how his frame could fit inside it. Then, assuming the impossible could happen, he performed a quick memory test just to see if he could, when pressed, drive on the right side of the car on the left side of the road. Then he took a deep breath, sucked in his midsection and with a bit of discomfort squeezed himself in. That was the easy part. It took a protracted battle amidst foreign traffic patterns and inverted imagery before he brought the mini coop to a stop on the street where, earlier in the day, one of the two Moroccans he was looking for had been dropped off.

Situated, thus, the only immediate problem he now faced was figuring out what to do next. When nothing came to mind, he sat and counted those entering what appeared to be a homeless shelter. Small clusters of hungry individuals going in seemed to be in equilibria with the well-fed groups who left. On each person, the clothes bedecking them looked as if time had taken its toll.

After an hour of this, he was bored, plain and simple, so he looked around for a distraction. Finding nothing of real interest nearby he took out one of the information pamphlets lying about the floor of the rental. By the time the next hour passed he had flipped through all the pamphlets, twice, and portions of a phone book that had also been left in the car, only occasionally giving the street a quick once over.

Both these activities, reading and watching, were mixed in with a waiting game he was playing. That game involved his telephone. He was waiting for his mobile device to make a connection, any connection, with either his home office or his home-home. Throughout the morning wireless communications had become sporadic, and as the day wore on, they almost ground to a halt. When he finally did reach a voice, it was the New York office and the information passed along was repetitive "the Canadian is on his way," which he already knew. They also warned, "Don't lose those two guys."

MacLean could do nothing, he had no local support, he didn't know much about the locale, had only a general description of the Moroccan's drop off point, was hungry and tired, and he had to pee. As to the whereabouts of the two he was trailing, unless there was a digital trace, all he could do was sit and hope for some activity, any activity, which would let him know his quarry was anywhere nearby.

As MacLean sat stuck behind the steering wheel of a very small car, high-ranking members of the FBI stationed in New York City argued over agent placement. "We need to interpret events going on in and around this case ASAP!"

"At the moment, all we can count on is MacLean. He's like our 'Lone Ranger.'"

"Should we give the Canadian a code name when he gets there?"

Just like that "Tonto" was put onto the paperwork, and since their own cavalry reinforcements were several days away from dropping current assignments, returning to work from planned vacations or just getting brought up to speed, the rest of the meeting focused on operational control issues. This was done via a teleconference between the FBI team in New York, the head of the NSA, ranking members of the CIA, the DIA and their own boss, all of whom were situated in various silos within DC proper. All had teams following various terrorist links, and so, all taking part in the meeting were busy wiping egg off their faces. The bombing in London had taken everyone by surprise. But like organizational sycophants from the beginning of time, those in on the videoconference began the meeting by engaging in a turf war.

The CIA team argued against the FBI treading on their offshore operational territory. The DIA chimed in as well, but when the national security advisor, who was extremely pressed for time, asked CIA and DIA both who they had in place to pick up the trail of the Moroccans it was decided the Lone Ranger and Tonto would stay in play.

"And we'll link the NSA's overhead with priority-one on this. Communication intercepts, the whole kit and caboodle will be fed to the FBI. For a short while anyway, until the CIA gets some of their guys back over from South Asia or the Middle East or wherever you're flying drones today. And," he added, moving his gaze away from the CIA director and across his video monitor to the head of the FBI, "make sure the Yard is up to date with all your activities."

Just like that, the gang in New York had access to satellites with pinpoint optical scanning instruments, the type of info commercial internet-based data tracking companies only dreamed about. Of course, they didn't bother to let their lone agent on the ground know any of this.

Along with the visuals, the FBI also had, without stepping over any vagaries in the law, telephone intercepts too. In other words, with this extremely expensive, high-end equipment at their beck and call the FBI team could instantly triangulate in on anyone, local or overseas, who made cellular contact with their New York suspect. If the caller happened to be inside a moving vehicle hell, no problem, they could follow the car in real time. This is how their first lead of the day played out. The Sheik in England had called his brother in New York. By the time the two men disconnected, those listening in had no idea what they really said but the satellite connection did help. They were not yet exactly sure where the telephone in England was, but they had it narrowed down. According to their satellite's meta-linkage capability the phone was in a car traveling south from Edinburgh along route A68 as it paralleled the old Roman road known as *Dere* Street.

As hard as it was for the FBI team in New York to understand what was being said, it was just as difficult for the passengers in the car. Luckily, all they really needed to know was where they were headed and how they would get there.

"Why do we go south here?" A youngish passenger in the back seat said this as more an argument than question, but the driver wanted to avoid the former and so answered as if it was the latter.

"Because, it says south," he muttered while pointing at a fast-approaching sign.

"Yes, we've been over this, but why not go west?" The talkative man in the back fidgeted as he queried. Every few seconds he turned and scanned the scenery trying to pick out telltale signs of trouble. "No one will suspect us if we go west."

"We can take the smaller roads west when we cross the old wall," the driver responded. The older man, the Sheik, also sitting in the back, rolled his eyes. The bodyguard sitting in the passenger seat tried to ignore them all.

"What wall are you talking about?" A continued questioning came from the young accomplice as he tried to show off his talent for dissecting informational sources. At the same time, he reached over to take the cell phone away from his superior and begin the process of removing the now traceable chip and inserting a new one.

Multitasking will advance my career, without a doubt, he mused, not knowing the Sheik had planned out the future of the man sitting next to him before he was done speaking with his brother.

The driver had no idea his future too was pretty much decided, he was too busy at the moment playing the one-up-man-ship game to care, "Oh, I'm sorry, one of us studied a little history while at university...in this country."

"Just answer the damn question!" the Sheik barked using, without realization, a curse word. At the sound of his voice, all others in the car shut up. The driver knowing the light was on him swallowed hard before he continued.

"Just past Hadrian's wall we can take route A69. That's near Corbridge. It is a smaller road. It parallels Stanegate. We don't have to take that road but there will be a bit of traffic on it, which we can use for camouflage. There are also a few local passageways we can try, if you would like, which are even smaller. For example—" He had to stop for a moment and reread a map resting on his lap before passing the information along to the Sheik. Then the driver exhaled and went quiet.

After what was almost a minute break, the argumentative man sitting in the back sallied forth. "No, we should not do this. If we need to make haste these back roads will slow us down." And so the argument continued.

What those in the car didn't realize, and those listening in to the brief phone conversation could never glean from the limited discussion they overheard, was the tactical aspects to a plan placed deep within a secretive compartment in the Sheik's brain. Once the bombs went off in London, the Sheik knew he would have to hide. Like his brother, he had been under suspicion since entering the county. All along the plan had been for him to go into hiding. The brothers had worked it all out more than a year earlier. It was the last time they met face-to-face and were able to speak without fear of being overheard.

"I need to stay in-country to manage the operation. Being up north will give me some time but eventually they will figure it out. Then I will take on my second identity, drive south to the safe house in Corbridge and leave most of my team there. If the police are following, they will catch them in that area. This is good, they will not know my new identity or destination. The women stationed in that house will drive with me to the ferry. I will shave, and they will be dressed in a local fashion."

The New Yorker added a few caveats. "Kill the idiots just in case they do have an idea where you are headed. And once you arrive at your final stop, see if there is some way to sell the women."

When the terrorists were planning both the bombings and the escape route, Samir was not even a figment in either's imagination. This is why the brothers had to do a bit of contingency planning when the diminutive Moroccan became a security risk no matter which side of the Atlantic he was on. Confounding their problems with Samir was this; they did have to answer to higher authorities other than those of the spiritual demeanor. Whatever information Samir would share with them had to be booted upstairs making the event's schedule in England difficult. Timing is everything, and so they adapted, or tried to.

While high-tech spy agencies were focusing their efforts on a small car traveling south along route A68, on the other side of the country Vivienne sat looking over the web-like pattern of walkways in her lavish garden listening to the parish bells ring. It was a sad day in England for sure. On occasion, she would look up and watch the sunlight reflections off Mt. Snowden while cursing into her phone with the talent of an experienced city-based Madam. When she was finished with the accusatory lambasting of her underling, she continued, with effort, to make sense of the situation. But like all those others stationed within defined geographical locations on either side of the Atlantic, the summation of events hadn't led to clarification.

"The nurse left, and we have no idea where the hell Arthur and that bitch wife of his are and now there are bombs going off in London as we speak. Shit." The curse she whispered as she began walking around her bedroom. "And those idiots couldn't find the books! Without the books we may not figure out what the hell they have been hiding from the rest of us for who the hell knows how long!" This she did not whisper. Then she hung up.

Morgan, listening in from a distance, was completely lost. It took her a full minute before she got the courage to yell back into the disconnected receiver, "I quit!" Then she drank half a glass of gin before asking herself, "Hiding what, the Holy flippin' Grail?" She no longer cared what happened to Arthur's company, in fact, she had never cared at all. She did feel sad for Jennifer, knowing her life would be tied to the injured man, but the company no, she didn't really care for the company. What had drawn her in initially was money. Maybe things would have been different if she had the slightest inkling of what the company did in the realm of medical research or what Arthur's clan held close with respect to religious dogma. She would never know how close her double entendre was for it was time for Morgan to exit stage left.

Chapter 36
The Oven

London was in lockdown, Edinburgh, like the rest of Great Britain, was both in mourning and a state of alarm. Bells atop nearby churches served as a reminder of the horrific events that had taken place in London. The bells also served to periodically pull MacLean out from his slumber. Each time he awoke, he would glance at his watch, note the advancing hour, and hurriedly recheck airline arrival times. He also noted how the street was now filled with people, a whole line of them, all waiting to enter Dubric's. It didn't take a person with observational training at an FBI Academy to notice how this was not the high-end shopping mall crowd. None of those now standing beside his car would be seen at those food courts. That food was not free. The line extended from Dubric's entrance to a spot a good twenty meters beyond MacLean's coop. Many of those nearby passed the time by bending low and peering in at the large man stuck behind the steering wheel. This alone may have been the reason MacLean decided it was time to go fetch the Canadian.

The drive back to the airport was neither fun nor comfortable, but fortunately for both he and Christian, he made it. In fact, Inspector

Gervais had just appeared from beneath the overhanging portico when MacLean drove up. He parked along the entranceway and wiggled over from one side of the front seat to the other yielding the steering wheel to the inspector. After both were seated as comfortably as possible, they exchanged pleasantries, including the pros and cons of using noncommercial means to fly over the Atlantic, before delving deeper into their assigned action plan. The plan neither of them had the slightest hope of completing.

"He was dropped off on a street here," MacLean began, pointing to a section on the small map he was holding. "But it was at least an hour before I got over there. Since then, I've been on surveillance, till I came back here to get you that is. I didn't see him or any other related character. In fact, the only people I did see were those lining up for food."

The two men sat quietly staring straight ahead. Each tried his hardest to formulate a more achievable plan of action. Unfortunately, no tangible idea found the light of day. Christian began by listing possibilities, "I suppose we can go back to, to, where did you say, Dubric's," only to have his thought process cut off as a large Rolls-Royce pulled up alongside the curb in front of them. This action coincided with the appearance of a group who had, seconds before, exited the building.

Three women and a man were pushing Arthur McAiden in a wheelchair. From their only visit to Arthur's home, the investigators had no trouble naming Lucan and, of course, Arthur's wife. The identity of the other two women waxed in and out of familiar memory recall. They watched open mouthed as Arthur was gently shepherded into the back seat of the Rolls by two men who had gotten out of the car. These men neither inspector knew but both concurred, they would look downright menacing at night in an alleyway.

"Now what?" was whispered in unison. Both knowing what they wanted to do was not exactly what they had been ordered to do. And again, in unison, the next question was articulated, "What is he doing here?" This bounced around the inside of their car as the obviousness of right and wrong played out in escalating clefs between their ears.

"We have to find Samir's accomplice." Christian finally stated as they sat watching the car in front of them get loaded up with luggage and passengers. Lucan had assumed a position behind the steering wheel of the Rolls while one of the men who had brought the vehicle remained behind keeping his eyes patrolling in all directions while speaking on his phone. The other man who had arrived with the car, the man the investigators later would learn was Dagan, reassumed his protective position in the front passenger seat and closed the door.

"Yes, we have our orders," the FBI man echoed.

Miracles do come in all sizes and shapes and, usually, when least expected. This miracle arrived riding shotgun in a car slowly driving past. It was a small car, not much different from the one the two agents occupied, and inside the vehicle, an argument was in progress. Ali had slowed down to comply with driving restrictions in the drop-off zone so those nearby didn't miss a beat of the yelling match. Basically, anyone within earshot could hear the clever word play and, if they understood a dialect spoken in a particular region of Morocco, laced with French profanities, they would be able to pick up on the less than subtle nuances.

"This is not the main terminal, you idiot," Ali mouthed loud enough to cause heads to turn in both Lucan's Rolls and the small car behind it.

"But there was a blockade there, you saw it," Samir yelled back for the tenth time. "They wouldn't let us through, especially me, not dressed like this." He pointed to the protruding devices underneath the thobe he wore, both of which were on loan from Ali. "These clothes won't go over too well today, not after London! Get my drift?"

Ali began to load up for his twin barrel response when Samir reached over and grabbed his arm. "Look!" He whispered. Samir had seen what he hoped to be his salvation. "It's her. The one from America." Samir continued, this time in a barely audible tone, "Her husband was the man on the recording."

Ali listened in, but like all those who stress out trying to make quota, he wasn't really paying attention. If Samir didn't get out of the car and blow himself up the yearly bonus might not be as large as in previous years. And one of the problems running a business like the one Ali was immersed in was this, unless Samir pulled the cord himself there would be no glory for the cause and, no bonus for his bank account. This was why shooting his old friend, who was now a royal pain in the ass, was only a last resort.

The Moroccans continued arguing back and forth as Lucan pulled the Rolls out into the traffic pattern. The butler noted right away the two not-quite-Scottish-looking men in the small car slowly moving closer. He continued to watch as their car stayed in line behind his and then another car, this one holding two occupants he did recognize, joined in to form a short conga line with all three now weaving around the few slow-moving vehicles on their way out of the airport. Lucan rolled his eyes; it was all he could do as he pondered life's complexities.

Samir, on the other hand, breathed a sigh of relief. Christian, the man who, at one point in his life, had been an acquaintance at work, had just pulled up in the car behind. Of course, Samir wasn't sure if Christian was trailing him or the Rolls, but for the moment, as his life was tied to the armaments around his waist, none of that mattered. He just needed to find a way to disrobe and leave the lethal accoutrements in someone else's domain. If the man now trailing his car offered a chance in hell, he would take it. If Allah gave him the blessing of life, if he was to survive (and not be thrown in jail), he promised himself he would return to Morocco and perhaps, like his father, settle down and grow olives.

"Maybe," Samir whispered after Ali had moved up behind the Rolls, "it would help if I removed this, this thing?" When Ali didn't answer, Samir tried to continue, offering an explanation. "If the car is stopped and I'm wearing it, well we might get into real trouble then, eh?"

As the parade began to pick up speed, both Lucan and Dagan watched those in the car behind theirs. The larger man drove with pursed lips and the smaller one incessantly squirmed about in the passenger seat. The trailing car was too far back for either man to get a good read on its occupants. Lucan hadn't counted on, and didn't need, two new, unexpected items to add onto his list. But like all good operations men, he had contingency plans. On leaving the airport, he placed an old-fashioned radio call to a special detail. This group was stationed nearby but it still took almost ten kilometers before two dark sedans joined the growing convoy. With the reinforcements in play, Lucan managed to make the occupants of the trailing cars strain much harder to get a clear look at the Rolls.

This unforeseen activity had put smudge marks on his to-do list. Juggling the new variables became all-consuming, which led to him losing track of the one item most important on that list, Arthur. Lucan wasn't the only one with too much on their minds. Neither Arthur's sister, his niece, or his wife were watching him. They all missed out on his hand, which began to move in a slight rhythm, slowly pressing and squeezing the thigh on which it rested. They also missed the movement in his eyes. Those were busy searching for information, trying to pull in data from various external sources and in this way help to create a more current reality. Unable to find what he needed, his reconstructed nodal information retrieval system produced an analogy, a formation of horsemen forming a protective tier around their *Dux*. The *Gosgordd* was on the move. He could sense it. A quick glance along the shoreline confirmed their location, which allowed him to guess the destination. "The rotunda," he mouthed while no one watched. This thought transformed the usual placidity of his face into that of a man whose joy in being had become resuscitated. Now, Arthur began to focus on the host itself, wondering where they were and why he could not see them. *If we head to the Table Round, we must be prepared.* His lips moved but again, no one saw this, and a few seconds later, he drifted off into a dream sleep. His hand stopped moving, and his eyes closed, leaving no tell-tale signs of his presence in the time zone occupied by others in the car.

The inspectors, only two cars behind at this point, saw how the new arrivals were acknowledged before moving into assigned positions. These actions increased the caution level in the car, but it also helped to relax some of their fears.

"Those guys will never get close to the Rolls now." MacLean passed this thought along as they tried to calculate the possibility of how, without the slightest sense of why, Samir and the other man would try to hurt anyone in the lead car. As the caravan left the airport, both investigators had tried to keep count of an ever-increasing number of vehicles in their procession. They stopped counting after five minutes or so.

Their destination sat north of the old mining regions of Falkirk and just beyond the river Carron. A placard near the entrance told the two where they were. Below the property name, a few paragraphs of historical documentation were placed. Luckily, there was a slowdown as all cars had to get in line to enter. Those who could read fast did so.

> During the early eighteenth century, the O'on was tragically destroyed; precise dating of demolition is uncertain, both 1742 and 1743 are given. Contemporary notice of the monument's destruction is found in correspondence between some of the period's antiquaries. Most concur the O'on was demolished on the orders of the local property owner, Sir Michael Bruce of Stenhouse. According to accounts, the demolition was so complete that even "the very foundation-stones were taken away."

When they followed the lead into a public-access section of the property, they found the parking lot almost full and all they could do now was concentrate on hand signals coming their way from a few men standing nearby. Their car was directed over to a spot a safe distance away from where the Rolls was being unloaded. The hand signals continued, making it clear they were to stay in the car, even if they needed to visit the loo.

Seconds later, two more cars pulled into the open spaces next to the agents. One of them held the Moroccans. The other car was loaded with some very well armed security men. Samir and his companion were not being given hand signals; instead, loud voices were being used to convey instructions. The occupants were told in no uncertain terms, regardless of language used, to stay put. When the volume of these warnings settled down, many people began to climb out of other nearby cars and move off down a trail, all heading for the O'on.

A quick count here suggested fifty or more heads were on the move. A further look around the lot told the investigators many more had most likely already assembled farther along. The nearby security men didn't move.

With nowhere to go, they sat as far back as they could in their undersized seats. Seconds later, they heard a sound Michael had been waiting for since he landed in Edinburgh, his phone. He let out a triumphant giggle, "I've got her!" He finally had a secure connection with his wife. "We're following that McAiden fellow," he began. "Ya, ya, he's the guy from Tewkesbury who was in the hospital!" He almost shouted this to make sure Donna could hear him.

Immediately, Christian cut in "Is she near a computer? When a positive response was received, he began reciting words to be relayed along. In just a few minutes, they found where they were parked—though an answer as to why it was this location could only be speculative.

"She says it's Arthur's Oven," the FBI agent passed along as his wife continued laying out specifics causing him to pause for a moment before literally, spelling it out. "She says it's either *O* apostrophe, followed by an *O* then an *N* or an *E, N*, which many archeologists, historians and," he leaned over to be closer to Christian before whispering, "she said philologists, too, have studied this stuff. I think she's just reading it *verbatim*. I haven't a clue what a philologist is, do you?"

After posing the question to Inspector Gervais, he returned to paraphrasing the influx of information from his wife. "The memorable and celebrated small rotunda was considered a well-preserved Roman antiquity. One of the best, or the best, in Scotland anyway. In the 1700s, it was pulled down by orders of the property owner." MacLean stopped for a moment and looked around. "This is a big plot of land."

"Why is McLain here?" The two men were back to simultaneous recital as they watched for signs of what was happening down the trail. Seeing nothing, and not getting a good look inside Samir's car, they focused on the security detail standing close by. If they had seen Samir's face, they would have seen him trying to make eye-contact with anyone who looked his way.

Samir had realized he would never ascend to the management ranks in his current situation, and the only division of the company he would be allowed to work in was the one that had a specific dress code, the one he was now in, the one in which he would have to wear a vest. Basically, no matter what else happened on this day, if he stayed with his old friend his awake time on the planet would soon be over.

"What are you doing?" Ali whispered at him as he noted incessant twitching.

"Nothing" was the only answer offered.

Now, Ali may have been a bit slower on the uptake than most people characterized as average, but the long minutes alone in the car with this albatross known as Samir had allowed him to formulate a new plan. "Is the vest on tight?"

"What!" This came out of Samir's mouth as a short yet perfunctory scream.

"I want you to follow the group to wherever it is they have gone and do your duty."

"What?" Samir repeated, just as loud as the first.

"Oh, don't worry, my friend. I'll drive the car outside this parking lot and wait for you there, so run now as quick as you can, okay?"

At that exact moment, the total lack of intellectual cohesion in the instructions never even set upon poor Samir. As Ali whispered his orders, he also pulled out a gun. Holding it out of sight of the tall men near the car, he pointed it at Samir. Without doubt, the weapon was noticed as quick calculations were running through Samir's head, the foremost having to do with the distance needed to make the explosives no longer in reach of the backup detonator. Samir knew some of those tasked with wearing the vest lost nerve from time to time, and so there was always a backup available to help the man find his way to the virgin horde.

Unable to theorize the distance needed, he began to shake. Switching gears for a moment, he wondered if creating distance or quickly removing the vest on the run would work best. He also wondered if Ali would really shoot him if he refused, which led to tears as he prayed for divine intervention in three different languages. A moment later, the car door opened, and he stepped out.

Before he moved a half step, he heard Ali start the car's engine. Now he had no options, he took a deep breath and in less than a full second removed the throbe, the vest and what was beneath it. Ali stepped on the gas just as Samir's scantily clad body made its appearance, and as he drove off in one direction Samir began to run in the other. Samir's exposure to western culture had not been sparse but Tennyson was never on his reading list. Hence, he could not knowingly connect lines quoted from *The Charge of the Light Brigade* with its author. But he had read Alighieri and that was all that mattered. Several times in his life visions of the world around him had given way, replaced by one thing, the pathway to the inferno. It was happening again just as he began his charge into the valley of death. In his quest for life, he didn't look back.

Once he reached the path, he had to pause, catch his breath, and steady his nerves. No longer running he slowly continued with eyes focused ahead. When he rounded a curve, he completely missed the man standing behind a large oak tree. This sentry looked him over and passed a signal to those further along. Oblivious to this and everything else, including the time of day, the Moroccan continued his descent with the *Inferno* imagery, now in repeat mode, taking a toll on his nervous condition. The more he shook, the more he remembered relevant passages, and by the time he reached the ancient ruins, Samir had ample metaphors of eternal damnation from which to draw.

Then he stopped. The revelations now were, in a way, calming. What had begun as a phantasmagorical extrapolation of known literature had inadvertently transformed into a more observational comparative analysis. He was a few yards shy of an open space within which stood those he needed. What he saw before him was the opposite of any imaginary view of damnation, real, or possibly, an illusion based upon an extreme release of endorphins. He had, after all, awoken to the realization he was alive.

Just a few feet below, on open ground a group of eighty or so men and women were holding hands melding into one large circle. The sun, slowly sinking in the west on this midsummer eve created elongated impressions of those now swaying from side to side. And a slight breeze Samir could feel on his back was adding to the trance-like motions of those below. In the center, within the outlined remains of a building, stood a few others, some of whom he had seen before.

Completely absorbed in the presentation, Samir tried to dig through his memory, hoping to clarify the portfolio now before him. This is when he noticed the two men who had moved silently taken up positions beside him. Instead of looking at them, he continued gazing intently at the man standing in the middle of the assembled group. It was the butler. This he was sure of. The fact Lucan was also the butler only those he was now speaking to knew. Samir watched Lucan turn slowly in a circle to address each, and every participant using a language he could hear, but not even partially understand. All he could do was scratch his head and wonder. When Lucan moved forward, a shape he recognized was sitting in a wheelchair. It was Arthur. A woman he didn't know was slowly rocking the wheelchair like those swaying with the breeze, all following the cadence the butler's voice conveyed. Arthur's wife was there too. She stood off to one side. Others of this inner group stood near Lucan, with heads bowed, each only looking up to stare into Arthur's face every time the wheelchair was turned their way. Samir noticed one other thing; a woman within the circle was crying, without ceasing.

A low, whistling birdcall grabbed his attention for a moment, and looking around, he noted the two men standing nearby move aside as new arrivals, led by an aged individual, walked by. All noise from those assembled stopped. People allowed a passageway to form. A delivery was placed in the center of the ring. Those who carried the package joined the reforming outer circle while the older man took up a position near the butler.

Lucan was no longer multitasking. He was completely focused, drawing off energy from the collective around him. When he did speak again, the swaying resumed. This time he did not have to turn in circles, his voice carried flawlessly. Everyone heard, and to Samir's relief, this time he spoke in a language he understood.

"The sadness of the day is overwhelming, yet we will honor those who have gone before and move on." More than one participant cried now, and Lucan gave them a moment before continuing. "Angus and Wayne, names we have carried for those in their line for eons now we honor. Auguselus from Albania, we could throw a stone and hit his ancestral house in Sterling from this spot. And Gawaine from Lothian. These men have both performed their given tasks. They have put personal agendas aside."

Lucan looked at Arthur, wishing it was he who was speaking because his superior was so natural in these situations, a real leader. For the first time that day, the next words he had to share caused his throat to tremble. "They took time out from our needs to help one person, Lute. This they did for the love of Arthur, yes, but also for the love of all living things. If we learn from their sacrifice, we can fit more appropriately into the grand scheme we call life."

Samir watched, not fully understanding but without a doubt he knew the men named were not amongst those standing before him. As grief set into his own chest, he watched the woman holding Arthur's chair move to the front, kneel and lay her sobbing head in his lap. Everyone in the assembled crowd stopped moving when Arthur's hand rose slightly and came to rest upon the back of his sister's head. Those inside the ancient circle of stone fell to their knees as did the two men standing next to Samir. A lifetime, or perhaps just a few milliseconds passed before Arthur moved his hand back onto his own lap.

Lucan moved over to bury the crying face of Anna within his warm embrace then backed them both up a step or two, took a deep breath, and continued, "They are all damaged, but all three will survive. We will pray for them and…" He paused again to collect himself before continuing, "We are not alone. Within this rotunda still stands Eric, from Edinburgh, and de Gourd, and lest we forget the bearer of swords, the noble bard, the Piper, his servant, the Porter and Equerry, Cai our Marshall"—Cai's small round head bowed low, and he spread out short, compact arms that seemed to engulf the entire proceedings—"and Bedivere, the Seneschal."

When de Veer's name was called, he stepped out from behind a few taller men in the middle of the assembly and turned the light on Lucan. "We will not forget the butler at this most difficult of times." Lucan took his bow, waited as a brief murmur of appreciation died out, and then he spoke on.

"Before Angus and Wayne were hurt. They had retrieved this." He pointed to the delivered goods. "And sent it to us here at the Rotunda. Other packages, all holding items that defines our reason for being, are on their way to Avalon." These words left Samir shaking his head as he tried to follow along. "The days ahead may appear dark. If Malcolm and his clan win, they will allow the Germans to buy in, to use them to fight his battles, to wear us out, and possibly take complete control." Lucan converted back into Celtic, and all Samir could do was watch and be thankful for the time he had been allowed to listen. The inferno had somehow been quenched, replaced by what could only be described as a vision of two roads diverging in a yellow wood.

Two men stuck sitting in their car saw none of this. They had, however, watched Samir strip off his vest, and almost everything else before he took off like a bat out of hell. They also watched several of the security guards stop a car trying to flee the scene. Multiple guns were soon pointing at the driver. By the time Samir was down the path, a good ten meters or so, a gun had been removed from Ali's clenched fist. The investigators also watched a member of the security detail pick up Samir's vest, walk over to the driver's side of Ali's car and, with Ali watching, gently remove the detonator caps. Another member of the team showed Ali a device used to intercept and block electronic signals. These men, like good Boy Scouts the world over, had come prepared and in so doing saved Samir that day. The detonator control switch was taken from Ali too, and then he was asked to leave the premises, which he did without any further discussion, only slowing once to throw a sack with Samir's belongings in it out the window. The security guards knew the police would pick him up soon but by that time the group assembled at the O'von would be far away.

The security team began drifting back toward invisible observation posts, but one came close to the investigators car to relay a message. "The butler would like to have a word with you both before we clear out of here."

Chapter 37
Lothian

It was dark when the two investigators were finally motioned out of their car. Slowly they complied and, when standing erect, began to stretch stone-cold muscles. With hands on hips and necks, arching as far back as possible, they viewed streams of moonlight cutting through fast moving clouds. Then, with chins straining to reach their chests they watched reflections form amongst undulating puddles on the ground. All of this created an ill-lit stage for a long line of bodies slowly materializing, each taking a bow before dispersing into the night. When Lucan appeared, he didn't bow; instead, he stopped right in front of them bearing the look of a man who was more than a bit tired. Behind Lucan, two men of rather large build were ushering Samir out of the trailhead. When Samir caught up everyone exchanged nods and then Lucan spoke, "Malcolm will know you two have followed us from the airport." Without stopping to clarify, he continued, "Those of our clan have been able to keep members of his group away from the site during our, our um, meeting, but undoubtedly, he knows where we are. We"—Lucan paused for a moment as he tried to fine tune the coming request—"think it would be safest for Arthur, and well, I must say, for everyone, yourselves included, if you stay with us for a while."

He paused again, trying hard to fold his request for compliance into one language. "Until we clear the area and get our company documents off the radar screen so to speak. A few other items need to be kept out of prying eyes too, but you don't need to worry about that."

Both the FBI agent and his Canadian partner stood still, mouths slightly open, trying to understand exactly what they had just stumbled into. Both had questions to ask, lots of them, but at that very moment, they couldn't. The man with the tired eyes was in charge and all they could do was listen.

"And could you two be so kind and take this man along with you?" He pointed at Samir. "We had a feeling about what he might have tried when he and his companion latched onto us up at the airport. But our…" He took a moment before finally finding the right word, "Impression, now is simply this. He may have been forced to make a go of it." Here, he showed the source of his information by tapping the device inserted into his ear. "I'm sure Arthur would like it if he was just taken away from the Island."

A group of familiar looking women surrounding a wheelchair were next on stage. Soon this assembly moved close enough to have their conversation overheard. "You saw him move again." It was Dindrane. "He hasn't moved since we saw his little excursion to the bathroom the other night. But seeing him now, well, I don't think the flight damaged his recovery, maybe slowed it a bit but still the cortex must be reengaging." She continued speaking and adjusting the position of her stethoscope on Arthur's back until this group was out of earshot.

Lucan understood the need for information and its dissemination, along with the importance of detailed planning for which Gantt charts and timelines came in handy. "There is so much I wish I could tell you." But he also knew the importance of time, so he gave a teaser, hoping it would move them forward. "There are many more, um, items, yes items, this group must collect before we head west. It will be safer to have these with us as we await the directors meeting." Here, he paused and watched, along with his audience, the loading of a heavy package into the Rolls. "As you can see, Arthur will pull through. But we don't really know when, or"—another pause—"to what degree." There was one more line in Lucan's delivery before he left. "And now we pray Percy arrives in time. Then the balance shifts back in our favor." On this topic, the two investigators could only scratch their heads.

The escorts helped position Samir in the tiny back seat along with his bag, the one Ali had thrown from his car. Then one explained the intricacies of the drive ahead and where their car would be placed within the convoy to maximize its protection.

"One more thing, please hand over your cell phones." He only explained why to give himself something to do. "Even if we block your connections, they will be able to triangulate into your calling position. Figure out our whereabouts, so to speak." He finished talking, held out his hand, and when he did, both men surrendered their mobile communication devices.

Two more Rolls-Royces appeared before any of the cars moved out. Each looked like mirror images of the one Christian had followed from the airport. If one took a close look, it would become clear all three had identical license plates too. The waiting cars were then divided up. Each was ushered into a place behind one of the three seemingly identical leads. When this was done, security teams were placed ahead or behind. For this entire leg of the trip, no one in the car Inspector Gervais was driving had any idea who was in the car they were now following.

Arthur watched everything from within his head and smiled. His *Gosgordd* was on the move heading south around the western outskirts of Edinburgh. Once beyond the city proper, the cars angled east and south along roads on which, even in the daylight, one would have seen very little mechanized traffic. Small signs came into view from time to time. These were all the foreigners had to help mark locations, only most of the information posted was more confusing than helpful, and when a sign labeled with the word "Lothian" was passed, they had no idea if they were at a spot to the south of Edinburgh or a place found only in Middle Earth.

The trail reached Roslin, and as the caravan passed through, both investigators wondered if they were in a place they should know. The cars did slow as they wound through the village, and it was at this point Samir held his head up as high as he could in the cramped back seat. The only thing he saw was Rosslyn Chapel, and so he lowered himself back down, wondering if he was still in a post bomb-laden dream world.

The column continued south, winding along narrow roads that hugged the hillsides before suddenly plunging down into ravines. Some roads curved around stone walls or manicured hedges of beech, or both, which had been placed many, many years earlier and, while aesthetically pleasing, even in blazing sunlight it would have been difficult to see oncoming traffic or upcoming dips in the road. In the dark, it was almost impossible. Luckily, the caravan was moving slow when a marker pointing toward the Gladstone Reservoir was reached. The driver of the lead car was placed there for a reason, and soon everyone was turning into a drive leading to a very old and very well-kept country estate. Once through the entrance gate, large stones became visible. They carried the look of use in ages past, and it didn't take long for those unfamiliar with the estate to pick up on it.

"They've rebuilt on the same spot, it appears." This was MacLean mumbling his findings.

"More than once," the Canadian whispered in reply.

All cars stopped near a series of outbuildings. After a quick count, it became clear there had been a decrease in the number of accompanying vehicles. When the command to dismount was given, Lucan and Dagan emerged from the lead Rolls, Lucan looking as if he could barely keep his head held high or, for that matter, his eyes open. Dagan, well Dagan appeared to have just finished a light morning workout and was ready for more. Jennifer and Dindrane slid out of the backseat, and after two men rushed up to help, Arthur was eased out and placed in a wheelchair. Arthur's sister was nowhere to be seen.

Each car, void of occupants, was placed in neutral and then pushed into one of the nearby buildings. From the outside the structures resembled small barns, but it was clear they weren't, at least not by agricultural definitions. There were no smells of animals, save the ubiquitous cat, and no lofts full of hay or other grains. The smell of oil, lots of that and the presence of hydraulic lifts were both noted. The barns were built for cars and those watching could do nothing at this point but stand aside as all the arriving vehicles were placed inside and, in return, a matching number of different, sportier models were being eased out.

"We will return the car you rented," one of those with engine grease up to his elbows told MacLean. "But for the rest of the trip you will be using a different vehicle, everyone will. This is just in case, if you know what I mean." The foreign investigators said nothing, they didn't know how to respond so they just kept quiet as they watched the proceedings. Samir stood nearby too. His eyes were open, but he did not seem to be looking outward, rather their glazed over appearance was more of an inward, spiritual vision, which may have been due to a lack of sleep or possibly a continued channeling of whatever had taken place at the O'von.

The next activity capturing attention was the transfer of all nonhuman items brought onto the premises over to the new fleet of vehicles. It quickly became clear to all watching one calculation used in the planning had been off, way off. The pack animals that carried the loads onto the estate were much bigger than those selected to continue the journey. Everyone stood by and waited, as those blessed with three-dimensional load assessment figured it out. Then, those assigned the actual physical machinations needed to move inanimate objects tried to make sense out of their instructions.

Everyone continued to watch until an activity in front of the main building grabbed their attention. All eyes now gazed in this direction, and one of those standing near the investigators began to speak to them, though neither was sure if his intention was to pass information along or if he just had nothing else to do. Either way, he had a lot to say.

"Too bad you cannot see the lake from this side of the estate."

As he spoke, Dindrane appeared pushing an older woman who, like Arthur, was wheelchair bound. Several wrapped packages were being carried along behind them.

"That's her mother, Yglais li Gros. We call her the widowed lady. Her husband was Alain. He passed many years back and now Steinert's has gotten ahold of her. She was mid-fifties when it first made its presence known." He paused for a few seconds giving a few tears time to reach his jaw line, then he carried on, "Now, she is just wastin' away. I am told she only eats oysters and grapes, washing 'em down with a bit oh' champagne." As they watched the anorexic woman light a cigarette the two tongue-tied foreigners nodded their heads pretending to know what was going on.

"She's Arthur's half-sister, nonblood so, you see, Dindrane and Arthur are related, in a legal fashion." The group forming around the man speaking alternated their gaze between him and Dindrane. "She's Percy's mum too, if ya' didna' know. Now, all we need do is find Perce and we can keep control. If Malcolm's group wins, they will sell this property." He stomped his foot on the ground to confirm the exact locale. "Probably to some sort of German consortium. You see, Yglais had insisted on adding her contribution to the start-up. We didn't know she had to take a loan out on the estate to do so. Now, like everythin' else, it's in play. Malcolm has no idea why we've held the property for"—the tour guide wanna-be finally noticed the blank looks directed his way—"such a long time. It has nothing to do with Arthur's company. But it is best if we move some things from here, just in case."

Christian tried asking what it was they needed to move, fearing the answer would never come. He was right.

"Well," the tour guide began with a wry smile as he pointed at Madame li Gros. "Her, for starters. She is the most important person to the whole clan. We need to take her with us."

As the man continued to speak, a movement in a nearby field caught everyone's attention. It had first appeared to be just a tree stump, sitting incongruously amid an open field. But then it moved. Sometimes it is difficult to interpret observed events. The investigators had had their fill of this the entire day. Now they, like Samir, had to move away from pragmatic rationality and into a more otherworldly interpretation as they stood watching the moving figure go about his business with the occasional wave of what appeared to be a large battle ax.

When the man stopped moving and once again resembled a tree stump, the investigators turned their attention to different groups standing nearby. All had also been watching the performance. One group was obviously the mounted arm of the organization. It is hard not to note military training, especially if you had yourself, like the FBI agent, been there and done that. Others standing nearby were trained to keep the mounts running properly. They were easily identified as such by the dark stains under all their fingernails. A smattering of older men and women had formed another clique. These now coalesced around the foreign contingent. The investigators cataloged this group as university grade, with the moniker, "Faculty" thrown in.

"Qui est l'homme?" Christian managed, his gaze returning to the tree stump in the field.

The response came back in French from one of the militaries off to the side. "Your mate there"—he started pointing at MacLean—"sat in a car in front of his place of business all day. We thought one of you must know M. Dubric, or at least his charity." The man delivered the message with a smirk.

One of the older men standing closer in offered apologies. "Please forgive him, it has been a long day, and as you might say on your side of the pond, we've miles to go before we sleep."

"It is happening again, is it not?" Someone nearest to the man apologizing joined in.

"Just like it was when Hengist landed on the south shore of the Firth of Forth," another added, "not far from where we now stand."

A third voice, a voice that quite obviously commanded respect from the group delved into events along a more historical perspective, "If we all remember correctly, this," he said; and like the tour guide had done a moment earlier, he, too, indicated the very ground upon which they stood using a quick stamp of the foot, "is where he sent the delegation, the peace overtures to the clan chiefs headed by Gwrtheyrn."

"The Vortigern" came from one part of the circle, which had grown and was now surrounding Samir and the police investigators. Then, at a pace beginning to equal the speed of sound, academic minded sound that is, others picked up where whomever was speaking had left off. And as the voices changed rapidly, it became even less likely the foreigners would understand an iota of what the discussion was covering.

"Yes, yes, of course, it was the Vortigen, the man who brought the chiefs here to slaughter."

"But we still don't know if he was the intended victim or the one who planned the demise of those not willing to bring him fully to the throne."

As everyone watched, the man in the field began to move again and the discussion progressed from mere presentation to outright debate with the voices now dissecting the Vortigen's history, or possibly, the history of his relatives.

"Look at him leading the way, just as the leader of the Brychan clan always has. We remember now, it was the Merlin back then who set the path upon which we trod."

"As a child…"

"Who helped shift the tide against old Vortigen's ambitions."

At this misinterpretation of data, the type of faux pas a younger member of a faculty often does, one of the more classic components of the staff turned and chastised the man. "How many times do we have to remind you, it is not the 'old Vortigen,' but 'the Vortigen'? Vortigen is not a name, it is a title. Must we have a grammar lesson every time?"

Most of the others had heard the reprimand in one form or another before, and so collectively, they wished to press ahead.

"And he recited the prophecy, the death knell, for the Vortigen…"

"Dubricius began his rise as a Brychan prophet by moving to depose Gwrtheyrn. After all, it is well known the Vortigen had Constantine and his eldest son slain."

"All of this was before the Brychan moved to transform us. It was, as one might say, dog eat dog at the time. The legions had left, who was to say which clan would rule?"

"True you are, and the massacre of all by Hengist wasn't novel, remember. Theodoric massacred Odoacer and his officers at a banquet…"

"Yes, of course." The circle chimed in and then began reciting a litany of sorts. "But in the Ravenna, it was a few years later, so perhaps it was Hengist who set a trend in motion."

"Or was it the fault of the Vortigen? It could have been his doing to rid himself of those opposed to his plan."

To whom they needed to acknowledge as the key upon which events were pinned didn't really matter fifteen hundred years later. Everyone laughed before moving through the history lesson in a much more rapid pace to finish up. The order to remount was nearing.

"But the point is we have to move again!"

"Yes, yes, and that is why our honored M. Dubric is reciting the words, which…"

"Which we are too far away to hear."

"Difficult times call for improvisations, no?"

"Look at Dubricius's descendent today, still working the magic." For added attention, the speaker raised his arm and pointed at the man in the field.

"You are correct. Once again, we are heading for those same hills."

"Proverbial hills."

"What?"

"The proverbial hills, we are headed for the proverbial…"

"Yes, yes, I stand corrected."

The discussion began to split into a multitude of opinions each trying to outcompete the other for content of topic and word usage. After a short while, with nothing else to keep them busy, the discourse turned to argumentation. The North Americans, as was becoming habit, wished a recording device was being used, because neither of them could follow what was going on around them. Their Moroccan companion didn't care, he was still off in his own space.

"For almost two thousand years," someone began, "we've met this, and still the best and the brightest attend university, non? We learn to channel desire, to…"

"Yes, we know the local pub you teach at, but we also know of the gradual creep of dogmatic thought designed to instill one particular doctrine, against which we have all had to put up resistance."

"One can judge the quality of the best schools founded by the Brychan and his descendants by reading what their students write." Upon hearing this name again, the foreigners struggled to piece together what was being said until that is, the topic of conversation became focused on the two agents themselves, apparently without needing to engage either one.

"I do think our new friend here must have been a Breton, I mean look at him. I could name you at least three clans with his build."

"Agreed, to a degree, but it is more likely that his clan began a bit further east, perhaps Normandy. They intermingled with the Freincs early on. With his tall, thin stature he may even have some of the Merovingian blood in him, and then of course the Norsemen who…"

Those around the detectives were making the rounds and eyes soon shifted from the Canadian to the American. "Perhaps, but his companion, is he Q or P?"

"Hard to say, no one has supplied evidence of the spelling of his name. He could of course be from the Scotti clans."

"True, true, he does have a bit of that Dal Riata look to him, but without more evidence it would be hard to put him in Airgailla or hell, Argyll, for that matter."

At this, MacLean became red in the face and closed his hands tight. It was the least he could do given the lack of sleep and uncertainty of his present situation. The fists then came up to the level of his stomach, which caused the ongoing genealogic debate to pause.

"Sir, look down," one of them said in a placating tone as he pointed to a spot just above the man's shoes.

"At what!" was all MacLean could manage? Inspector Gervais, three of the scholarly gentlemen and even Samir looked him first in the face and then down toward his feet.

"Your stockings," a second man added, "look at your stockings."

"What about my socks?" MacLean whispered out from his tight set jaw while his fists began to slowly flex and release.

This confrontation was brought about by a misunderstanding. So the man who had commanded all their attention just a few moments earlier quickly moved in front of the FBI agent. In this way, he blocked direct eye contact between the two parties having trouble conducting a civil debate.

"Sir," he said, "it is the pattern of your stockings. They are argyle."

MacLean had little understanding of what "argyle" was referring to. "And?" he queried with just a hint of steam following the words out of his mouth.

"Argyle is the kilt of the clan Argyll." When still no understanding was evident, the man continued, "These men have just been discussing whether you are Scottish or Irish. Of course, the discussion can be moot if you were a descendant of the Dal Riata. This group came from Ireland and settled in, well, they settled in what we now call Scotland.

"Why?" This was the only response MacLean could muster. At the same time, his fists began to unclench, and his arms lowered back down.

The older man smiled. "I'm not sure why but I am sure one of those around us"—here, he turned and stared down his subordinate—"can be a great pain in the arse, can't cha?" This he spat out before moving back to his own discussion with the slightly older, and perhaps wiser group of learned men.

"Yes, of course." He began as he moved away. "That is what Pelagius taught. And that is why we keep hidden as we have. Our derivation of the original teachings, the teachings brought to the Island by Joseph are different. It ran against those hard liners in the south and…"

"One could say it has fractionated, successfully to be sure, and these fractions prevent a unilateral dogma from gaining control."

While the information continued to splatter the night air Samir picked up on the concept of unilateral dogma and the problems of such an approach. It had, after all, affected him. The American was busy too, he was putting a reminder note onto his schedule planner. *Throw away argyle socks.*

"St. Samson," the discussion continued.

"Galahad," came from a man with red hair across the circle, "How many thousands of manuscripts have been written to date and still, no one can figure out what Geoffrey really placed in his book a thousand years ago."

"Closer to nine hundred if I do the math right."

"It was Galahad." The red-haired man continued, ignoring the interruption. "Before him it was that saint who exhorted Arthur's *Gorsgordd* at the Battle at Badon, the same man who later crowned Arthur. St. Dubricius."

At this time, an idea crept into MacLean's head and pointing to the man out in the field he asked a question, "Is that M. Dubricius?"

When no one answered, Inspector Gervais modified the question. "Is M. Dubric related to St. Dubricius?"

No one answered this query either. They were too busy changing formations to get better views of the action around them. The man in the field was now walking toward whatever lay on the far side of the estate, and as he slowly disappeared, a different movement had caught everyone's attention.

"He's moving again!" Samir squeaked. The others turned in time to see the Widow-Lady take Arthur's hand off her own arm, kiss the open palm and place it back on his lap.

Ten seconds later, everyone was moving.

The cars now at their disposal were of a type found on roads throughout the country. "We will blend right in, oui? No one will know who is in which car." This was Samir talking. No one bothered to answer. They were too busy, trying to find the right car to climb into.

Chapter 38
A Bend in the River

Having the last vestige of one's independence taken away usually would draw some resistance from both the American and the Canadian, possibly even the Moroccan if his hadn't already been taken away years before. But watching Lucan crawl into the passenger seat and fall asleep before the cars had even left the compound brought specifics of their own physical state front and center. All three were tired. All three were confused. All three were fast asleep within minutes and had no idea the caravan merged onto a near empty highway heading south.

The distance traveled on A68 wasn't far, about a hundred kilometers or so, and by the time the sun was peeking up over the horizon, Arthur's troop had turned west. Now, whether they knew it or not, the cars were moving along the southern edge of Northumberland Park. For a while, the sleeping passengers continued as such, completely missing signs pointing out the remains of the old Roman wall to their north. They were also oblivious to the outline of a road running parallel just to their south. Stanegate, the road was called. It was another structure built in the time of the legions. Those sleeping missed these informative postings acknowledging the Roman contributions, like Hadrian's causeway and the forts built nearby, *Brocolitin* near mile 31, followed by *Vercovicium* and *Vindolanda*. The snippets of information came and went as did the dreams of those awaiting the return of the king. Arthur did not miss the markings. In fact, they helped keep him where he felt most comfortable.

Most of those taking part in this expedition had been along this route often, so there was no need to read signs filled with historical content. Everyone had, basically, memorized them all. And as with the drive down from Falkirk hours earlier, those driving the cars didn't have time to read the postings, they were all 100 percent engaged in the business at hand, keeping everyone safe.

Dagon might not have been good with Gantt charts, like the butler, but for matters relating to operational security, he ranked very high. Lucan felt safe passing control over to this man, and as those watching, it had allowed him to succumb to his need for sleep. It was Dagon who had placed other members of the team in strategic, well-hidden spots along the drive. These would call in when Dagan passed giving an assessment of the road ahead and the spacing of the trailing members of his caravan. When all cars were checked off, those hidden observers fell in line and brought up the rear.

Not all passengers were sleeping. Dindrane was too busy relaying medical assessments to her mother. "It is possible, if the blood was drained thoroughly from the contusions in the head, drained in time that is, that he might regain most of his abilities."

Her mother didn't complain; she, too, was awake. Within her diurnal rhythm, the post-midnight hours were the most productive. "Of which abilities are you referring, dear?"

"Mother, all his mental functioning can come back. The problem for us...well, for him, becomes, at which level. His physical recovery, well, there are parts of his body that will never be the same."

Yglais had, over time, whittled away to ninety pounds, give or take, but this didn't dull her mental acuity one bit. She was staying engaged, though at that precise moment, she was in need of a cigarette or, perhaps, an amphetamine to keep her addiction soothed, but still, what she wanted to know was not exactly what her daughter was delivering. "What level do you think?"

Dindrane swallowed hard, trying to complete her train of thought. "It is quite possible, at this stage, Arthur understands some what we are saying—in six months or so he might be back to 90 percent if we are fortunate. But he may not even reach that level."

"Oh." Her mother responded and with this said she dropped all pretense of abiding by the rules. She pulled a cigarette from somewhere within her billowing sleeves and tried to light it.

Dindrane grabbed ahold and shook her head, "Not in the car." Then she returned to the topic first and foremost in her head, "As I said, he might not recover at all. At his current level, short-term memory is most likely minimally existent. The recovery process takes time, but no one is ever sure how much of the inner workings comes back. If it holds up as is, he might recognize Percy, but it would be unlikely if he understood why an immediate changing of the guard was necessary."

In a different car, Arthur, too, was awake. He sat behind his butler who was snoring and beside his wife who too, was snoring. Anyone who might catch a glimpse of the man would see a body seat-belted in and leaning over with his head just touching the window. The only observable motions were his eyes. They were busy taking in all that was going on outside the car while inside his head, a place inaccessible to those around him, there was a raging maelstrom on the order of manic-depressive, without the "depressive" part, underway. And since his cognitive functions were not tethered to the earthly space around him, mania in two realities was becoming the norm for him.

About the time of day, anyone awake might begin to crave breakfast, the caravan arrived at an intersection which, once crossed, passed them a short distance north of the old wall they had been paralleling. A few kilometers further along the cars headed back south onto a track known simply as Hadrian's Wall. It was on this road they passed the sign that pushed Arthur into high gear. The sign said Castlesteads, *and that,* he thought, *is probably for the best. It puts a damper on those trying to translate the tale.* With that rambling around in a reengaging cortex, his right hand reached into his coat pocket and touched Goodrich's book. *Changes are slowly making their way through anthropologic communities as academics begin to really understand what happened to my home after the legions left.*

Just a bit south of Castlesteads was the river Irthing where the curvature of its banks had given the fort its original Latin name, *Camboglanna.* This was the largest stronghold on the wall, until one reached *Carleon. Carleon* is now Carlisle and only a few know those who write of *Camlann* tell of the sad day on the banks of the Irthing. Arthur knew this and he also knew of the three hills, the seats, where the man sharing his name often visited when the troops were marshalled: the staging grounds for many a campaign.

This was the route of the funeral procession for those who had fallen. *Only that troop was traveling northeast, bringing the bodies of our heroes to their home provinces for burial, Angusulus to Sterling and Gawaine* . *to Lothian. We didn't know of the treachery to come, only the action at the port that had left them dead.* These sad thoughts coalesced into a treatise covering these events. He wanted to tell the tale. No one in the car was awake enough to listen. It didn't stop him.

Arthur's internal delivery bore the markings of an ancient bard or possibly a modern televangelist. *The tragic effect of the calamities could have been enough to bring the stoutest to their knees. Not us. We came from strong stock. Though we had been suffering incessantly from the encroachment, from our losses, from those trying to bend us to their interpretation of what we held so dear, we would not succumb. I did not have my learned advisor. When advice was desperately needed, the Merlin was missing.*

Angus and Wayne, Arthur told himself as the movement between historical reenactment and the present conundrum continued to switch positions, *were hurt by terrorists for the sin of having the will to help those in need. This one special effort they undertook for me, to help one who had special needs.*

One tribulation compounded upon the other. *For the sin of riding the bus on the wrong day, at the wrong time, for the sin of being simple people going about their daily lives, for the sin of helping my son. And now this,* he continued with the compounding interest bringing the total misery into a higher yielding return. By "this," he could have simply meant his company's fight for independence or, the need to send his clan into hiding, once again. Either way, the problem was related to the chain of events that had started with a multicar pileup in New Jersey.

Anna had wept off and on since leaving the gathering near Sterling. The group she was now ensconced in, like Author's caravan, had stopped to change cars and collect specific items before heading west toward a safer locale. Her troop moved across Caledonia through the area controlled by their friends in clan Argyll, and then onto the Rinns. She wept in fear at times for her sons, not just her son who was lying in hospital, but for his younger brothers too. All were being ushered along to the same location as she.

Periodically, her tears would slow, and when they did, she managed to get immediate tasks set within her mind. But that didn't last. Thoughts always drifted back to her boys. She also wept for her brother-in-law and prayed for his recovery, but more intensely for Wayne. He had always been out front leading the charge. This is how he had made a lot of enemies and enemies would always seek retribution. But never had she thought he would be physically damaged, not if he worked alongside Arthur.

"The unthinkable had happened" was a reflection in Arthur's head as he and his sister, in separate cars traveling in different regions of the country, trod upon similar ground. "*The invincible has been brought low the stories told, struck down by Pagan highlanders. As always, Gawain had raced to be the first to close upon the enemy. He and his men jumped off the ship before the anchor was dropped. We had made port before at Caerleon, the city of the legions, and this was why the surprise had been complete. How had the pagans come within our defenses?"*

"For glory!" Angus had yelled as he made ready to jump.

"Glory," the men called back.

"For Arthur!" Gawain sang aloud as he crawled over the edge and tried to stand erect in the water. As always, Gawain was the first in. This time he was the first to die. Both he and his uncle would now have eternal glory; the bards and scribes saw to that.

As his force formed ranks in the water Arthur eyed those on shore. For as long as anyone in Britain could remember, this is what the highlanders did. They created havoc... *"even when the Romans were still here. But how had they made their way onto the Perth near Carleon?"* This he did not know, and at that moment, he didn't have time to ponder. He was jumping into the water himself, he had to pull Gawain out. Anger then clouded his judgment when he found the arrows buried deep. As ill as he had been on the boat, he immediately regained his land legs, and that day Arthur gave no quarter. The painted highlanders met the bear, and none lived to tell the tale.

It took a day for the Pen Dragon to calm and several more before the bodies were prepared for transport. During this time, his head cleared, which allowed for analysis to begin. Each possibility pointed a finger in one direction and that direction was Malcolm of Gwynedd and his politically adept supporter Mordred. Casting blame became easy as only one name showed up, his own. The Pen Dragon had assembled troops to defend their holdings in far off regions many times. This time the *Gosgordd* was in Breton, and Arthur had appointed Malcolm to command in his absence. The message to return had come from Malcolm, through Mordred. It warned of an incursion from the north and for Arthur to make haste.

Arthur's message in reply told Malcom he would call for a marshalling, and exactly when he would return, including who would sail with him and where they would land. It was Malcolm who had set the wheels in motion and Arthur who had taken the bait. The reason he had placed the pagan in charge on his departure now haunted him.

"*No matter how often I beat my head against the wall, politics always seems to get the better of me.*"

The Merlin did not trust Malcolm. Dubricius had told him this many, many times but that was long ago and now his most senior advisor was only a memory. But for some reason, Arthur had hoped, nay prayed, he had made the right choice. He had envisioned a real strengthening of the realm. Malcolm had converted; he had joined the faith, the faith embraced by the Brychan. This, Malcolm had sworn. Now, with the same strength the traitor had used, Arthur, too, swore; he swore to avenge. But the lack of resources hollowed the threat, and this fueled his current predicament. "*I need to get to where my troops are mustering. Then we will hunt down that traitor and, and…*"

The staging area was not far from *Carleon*, and this was now where Arthur and his contingent were headed. The bodies would travel with this group as a first stop on the way to their final resting places. Along the road to the staging area, Arthur walked in the fore leading his horse and the column behind him all the while thinking of his family, how each would be weeping in their own way for loved ones, and the dream each carried. This was what Arthur sought as he tried to pull himself back from the wreckage the car had caused. The dreams carved out in the vacuum created by the departing legions, a land that existed in the hearts and minds of his people. But now, the country the Pen Dragon held by the strength of arms was crumbling before their eyes as those with differing ideologies strove for control.

Dindrane and Anna had both witnessed horrors. They had often walked among the dead and wounded tending to men with broken bones or stanching the flow of blood from severed limbs. This is what the entire convent of devotees had learned from the teachings of Dubricius. They had practiced the healing arts on men with infected wounds and grieved with mothers, and widows, countless times. Anna had even visited the battlefield at Badon shortly before dark and tread upon the corpses of

Saxon soldiers who came to kill Britons without mercy and, without mercy, were ridden down and slaughtered in turn.

The warriors had laughed in the great hall in the city of the legion as they feasted the victory. "*Such a victory at barely a cost, for us,*" they shouted, but Anna had also seen with her own eyes the cost, the real cost, the cost calculated by the numbers of slaughtered humans. She had spoken out at the time wondering if the inebriated victors would have reveled in the annihilation if these beings had been Christian.

"What would Pelagius have said?" she screamed.

But then again, what had the bishops in Rome said of the Brychan spokesman? What was right? What was not? Pelagius had died because he took a different view.

"As far as my eyes could see," Anna told the scribes, "there were young Saxon men impaled from behind or split like venison for the rotisserie."

That had been after the fact, after the shouting and striking had ended and the only sounds about her were the rustling of leaves and the crying of men as they awaited death. She had known the horror of battles' aftermath but not the fear of battle itself.

This is why all her prior exposure did not prepare her for what she experienced on the morning of Camlann. Anna had never witnessed firsthand the unfurled brutality of men of war practicing their craft. She had run for her life that day with the other mourners, and when cornered, they had turned and drew their knives, prepared to take their own lives, if necessary, but it wasn't. Their guards had fought to the last to protect the women before Bedivère arrived.

The Seneschal, the man Arthur counted on when sitting at table plotting political strategy or completing harvesting ledgers, was riding with the small group of knights who constituted the Pen Dragon's bodyguard. Bedivere was not the man for this job, but he was the only man available. Those marching who were not part of the burial procession were on their way to the mustering, and so Arthur thought it safe to allow

Bedivere to ride thus for a while since those usually in charge, Angusulus or Gawain, were the bodies being transported.

The cavalry usually opted for the higher ground when traveling along the Irthing. The Roman Road itself was well constructed but in places it tended to follow too close to the water and the soil on either side could be soft. This is why Bedivere's troop was a respectable distance off road when the pagans charged. Just one more turn in the river, that ever twisting river, and they would have been within sight of their destination.

From their vantage point on the slope, the horsemen spied this first ambush. The painted men were heading straight for the wagons, the wagons carrying the dead.

"How can we be brought to death so close to the largest fort along the wall?" This the women near the wagons cried as they backed away and drew their weapons.

Bedivere quickly organized his charges into battle array and began to move them down slope in support only to spy a second group of warriors. These had emerged from a wood further along the riverbank. This armed collection was moving in behind Arthur, obviously planning to attack his leader from behind. Glancing along their line of advance he noted Arthur was unaware for he marched forward, leading his horse as he strode amongst the advanced company.

A decision needed to be made. The group of blue painted men heading straight for the women and ancillaries tending the bodies were the closest. Those advancing on Arthur's group needed to make up distance. In addition, they did not appear to be painted men of the highlander variety. In fact, they were clothed with colors of one of the local clans. Unfortunately, time was making it difficult for someone with Bedivere's military abilities to prioritize. The cry from the women is what helped him choose.

His cavalry advanced swiftly and being forced to make the decision at all brought great anger and with this came the desire to inflict pain. If Bedivere hesitated in making his decision no one would have known.

Despite his age he rode to the front and wheeled his men with a precision not even the Romans could have managed. Then they charged.

The speed of the gallop took the troop under the hail of arrows without breaking stride, or line, and so they thundered forward intimidating everything in their path. And if that was not enough, when they were within spitting distance of the few Picts fool enough not to run, they did something unexpected, they lowered their flag tipped *assagai* at the last second and slammed their solid wall of horse and spear tip into the enemy line smashing through instantly and moving on to chase down those who were running hell bent for the cover of the wood. In an instant, dozens of broken bodies lay twisted amongst the wagons and Bedivere was faced with his second task, to stay and fight a rearguard action as he removed noncombatants to safer ground, for those in the trees would surely return the moment his troop left or, bring his men about and satisfy his first inclination, ride to Arthur's aid.

Bedivere did not hesitate, and given the conditions, few men would have managed better, but Bedivere was not Arthur, nor was he Angus who the Freincs called *L'ancelo*, nor was he the competent, battle tested Gawain. He was none of these men; he was Arthur's advisor for all things but those military. The decision he made in the heat of battle was a classic mistake. He split his force in the presence of the enemy. Half stayed with the noncombatants with orders to evacuate them and the rest, the rest rode with Bedivere to relieve Arthur's column. This mistake would have been written in any battle manual for those in future to learn from if that is, the day's activities had ever been saved in written format.

Neither section of the battle was saved until the trailing infantry column managed to arrive at about the same time a group of auxiliaries from the staging area fought their way through from the front. Sometimes, it is better to be late than to never arrive at all. Malcolm's men were forced to flee. But so too were Arthur and his family and without them in place Malcolm's vision began to take hold as he politically tore the unified lands apart.

Arthur had killed his man on this day, but this man had wounded Arthur, which sank him to a new low. Revenge was sweet he told himself and all others who stood nearby as he lifted Mordred off the ground.

"Do you know who this is?" He screamed at those who could hear. "This is the Vortigern come back to life."

Not exactly, he had to admit to himself, but let the others call a magus or two if they need it sorted out. He was not Vortigern, or Vortiger'n or Fortiger or Gwrtheyrn or Guothigirn, or even the stupid Brythoic variant Guorthigern, no matter how you spelled it, the boy wasn't him, but he was married to the old pervert's granddaughter and "she is related all around, even to me."

It was her voice that sang that day as she tended to Mordred's body, "And now we will rise to power again as the Constantine family falls."

Arthur knew all along how danger wore many hats, and though it hid deep after his victory at Badon Hill, it had never disappeared. He began to understand what Dubricius had prophesized. Now he had to agree with his mentor. In the long run, it would be better to educate than annihilate, but the problem was this—one needed both sides to agree to such an arrangement. And therein lay the rub. How do you get both sides to agree to a proper course of action? Back then, the best they could hope for was survival, and even now on the eighth of July, as he rode toward Carlisle, Arthur repeated a lament those before him had often sung, "*The problems have not gone away.*" Most of those traveling in the caravans that day knew their history, and like Arthur, they feared the same.

The caravan of cars was well past Castlesteads before Arthur began to relax and concentrate on things more personal, his son. Tears flowed with only Dagon being aware and Dagan, being more skilled in the art of military preparedness than therapies related to consoling those injured, thought it best to keep the observation to himself.

Chapter 39
A Ferry Tale

The Island of the Apples would be there forever, but Dagan was on a schedule, Lucan's schedule. Lucan had no idea what might happen along the way to Mann; how could he? The bombing in London surprised everyone. Now, keeping a low profile and moving fast were the orders given. All Dagan knew from his instructions was this; there was an early morning ferry to catch. To stay on schedule, he moved the caravan past Carlisle without stopping and directed the troupe southbound along the M6 heading for Heysham.

Everyone was awake when the caravan reached its destination, though a mist covering the shoreline helped create a dreamlike impression of what happened next. Cars would not be driven aboard the waiting ferry, so everyone dismounted and were directed to queue up along the pier. As they shuffled into line and waited to board several unknown women tried to move to the front. They couldn't help but attract attention being dressed in whatever young ladies wore when out and about in London on a Saturday night. They were accompanied by a middle-aged man whose face seemed to have passed through a grist mill.

He, too, attracted attention. Every grown man watching empathized. Shaving was never fun.

"I cut myself like that, but my face doesn't get all puffy," this MacLean whispered more to himself than his companion.

"If one doesn't shave often the skin can become sensitive." Inspector Gervais gave his take on the situation while stroking his chin with thumb and forefinger. Thirty seconds later, the two men stopped analyzing shaving habits; the man with the puffed out face and his entourage were now racing back down the dock. Because of the fog no one could see what had happened near the boarding ramp, but the two investigators were trained and one brief shout from whoever was chasing was all it took.

Inspector Gervais stepped out in front of those about to run past and calmly held up his hand. It seemed to work. They slowed to a halt not three feet in front of him.

While watching his old boss at work, Samir slid in the opposite direction trying to meld in amongst those standing in line. As he tried to disappear his eyes kept scanning the facial features of the man with dried blood on his face. He wasn't looking at the butchered chin, but rather at the man's eyes. He had seen those before, though he couldn't remember if they were on the face of the devil himself or the man's brother in New York. With knees shaking, he took one more step back and prayed for the gift of invisibility.

The man who had come to a complete stop sized up Inspector Gervais standing tall in front of him. Then he looked back at the form of Dagan beginning to come into view from behind. He turned his head forward once again this time catching a glimpse of Samir and became locked in a stare down with him.

"Hicham," he spat and then began to pull a gun out from beneath his jacket.

Seeing this, Christian spoke to the man in a monotone to draw his attention as he moved a few steps away from the waiting line. There was nothing else he could do to minimize risk. Shifting position did draw the gunman's attention. This allowed his partner a chance to jump in. Within seconds, the former marine had broken several of the man's bones including a rib, the bridge to his nose and the wrist in which the gun was held. When Dagan arrived, he pulled MacLean off the fallen body, picked up the gun and then tried his best to get the over-dressed women to stop screaming. It took a few minutes before members of the local constabulary arrived, and just a second later, the Metropolitan police were on the scene as well. It was the crew from the Yard who whisked the battered man and his entourage away.

As those remaining waited for the dock to clear, Dagan gave his thanks to the two investigators in simple, short sentences. Those who risk their lives in the line of duty know what to be thankful for and how to convey their gratitude. Then Dagan moved off and conversations along the quay returned to normal, in a sense.

"Middle Eastern, without doubt."

"I guess that was the first time he'd shaven in quite a while."

"Those women obviously don't go western often."

The bottom line was in and, given what had happened in London the day before. "Odds are, he's connected."

The fact the man with sensitive skin was also connected with Samir registered with the Investigators too but not having all the information they needed they were forced into speculation. "Do you think..."

A short distance away, Lucan was debriefing Marlow, the captain of the boat. "I had no idea. Your team was forming up with each arrival, so I thought they were with you. Hell, what can I say? They could have just been tourists, right? Sometimes weekenders don't have a clue what the schedules are. People just show up and expect us to..." Captain Marlow gave up on that line and humbly finished. "They could have just been out for a day trip."

"We chartered this run. That is not the current issue. How you identified them is."

"I told you, I had no idea," Marlow repeated and sometimes events run their course like that. You plan and plan and plan some more, but in the end you either get beset by unforeseen setbacks or, on occasion, a stroke of luck accidentally finds its way to you.

"As we were preparing to board passengers the port authority was on the radio with me. The Yard was looking for a cast of characters, London you know, and as they started spewing out descriptions, look who tries to board my boat. Now, this guy didn't look anything like the photos coming over our line and we didn't suspect him of anything. Again, we thought they were part of your gang but when he was asked if he wanted something for the cuts on his face well, you saw, he started to run."

Scotland Yard had been following the Sheik since he left Edinburgh, but those riding the Ferry that day would never know this. The fact there were a few dead bodies in Corbridge they would read the next day in the newspapers. Snippets of information did leak out but before MacLean became privy to any of this he had returned home and gotten the low down from his wife.

"Every once in a while," Donna relayed to her husband splayed out on the couch in front of her, "we do cooperate with those on the other side of the Atlantic."

The immediate transfer of information from overhead satellites to the FBI to the NSA to MI6 to MI5 and on to Scotland Yard is how the Metropolitan police were only minutes behind the Sheik as he tried to board the ferry. It is also why the head of the NSA began planning for some reassignments in the NYC office of the FBI. This he shared with only one person, the director of the Federal Bureau of Investigation.

No one, not the Investigators, not Lucan nor anyone in the procession waiting to board knew any of this and really didn't care. They were preparing for the next leg of their own journey and were happy just to have the hindrances removed. In fact, Lucan whistled and sent his eyes heavenward in thanks as shafts of light began dissipating the fog just as the local and national police were leaving the scene. But it was still a good thirty minutes after the ferry left Heysham before everyone relaxed and began to enjoy the ride.

Everyone except Inspector Gervais that is. He was leaning over the rail watching the disappearing shoreline and trying to keep rhythm with each bounce of the vessel. This activity was not fun. To take his mind off his stomach, he tried counting waves but watching them didn't release the tightness in his gut. Trying a different approach, he stood as still as possible and gritted his teeth wishing he was somewhere else. No matter what technique he tried he still had trouble keeping whatever was broiling in his stomach below deck.

"Nice day for a boat ride, don't cha think?"

Watching the Canadian suffer was entertaining for the man from Jersey. He needed the diversion. MacLean had been trying to make some sense of what they had been witnesses to since arriving in country, all to no avail. The big question seemed to be why the group being herded along by Lucan had again asked them, in no uncertain terms, to board the ferry. They didn't complain. Things had become interesting, or difficult, depending on how one defined the situation, and by staying, both inspectors hoped to better understand Arthur's contribution to the events they had witnessed.

"Pardonnez-moi, je n'aime pas les vagues."

The waves didn't bother MacLean and he was ready to pass a few lines of humor at Christian's expense, but this idea quickly took a back seat. Samir, he noted, was bending over his carryall sack. The Canadian watched too. They both saw him remove a pouch, stand back up and slowly inch his way along the rail putting a good ten meters between them.

Without saying a word, MacLean tapped the arm of Inspector Gervais to make certain they were on the same page. The two men were, and together both snapped into action by nonchalantly watching the boatload of passengers walking about, bending their knees in unison each time the boat swayed and trying hard to stay away from any sea spray coming aboard. They also noticed the trailing gulls swooping in from time to time hoping to get a crust or two thrown up their way, but first and foremost, they watched the Moroccan. They noted when he slowly settled along a section of the rail and turned his back to the deck with eyes seemingly focused on the water in front of him.

The detectives separated to approach their target from either side, each, in their own way, cursing themselves. Given the nature of his appearance when transferred into their custody at the O'von they had not searched his bag. Now they saw the little vials he was holding in his hand and visions of their interview with the head of the biodefense laboratory came back to haunt them. They moved into striking position without the slightest idea if Samir held their death in his hands. But before either could pounce in what might have been the last heroic moment in lives dedicated in a true sense, to serve and protect, Samir turned around and spoke directly to them.

"No need."

Both men stopped, frozen pre-swoop.

"Two days ago, I mailed this over. It was frozen then. When Ali's men put it in my bag, it was only a matter of time before"—here, he digressed for a moment—"what do you call this bag? It is not a suitcase for I have no suits to put in it. Travel bag is that a good word?" He paused shrugged his shoulders and continued, "I suppose that will suffice. When they put it in my travel bag without dry ice, it thawed, and my future froze. So now I pour that future into the ocean."

He emptied the vials into the water below and then sucked in his breath while trying to hold back tears. "My own future was sunk the minute I landed in Edinburgh, am I not correct?"

The agents exhaled, believing they were back on solid ground. Everyone who had been standing nearby quietly moved away except Dagan. He had suddenly appeared leaning against the railing next to Samir. Lucan was not far behind. It didn't take much encouragement for Samir to pour out every bit of what he had pent up inside. "I just wanted to be famous," he stated and then had to explain he didn't mean what they thought. "I wanted to build, to discover, to push back the frontiers."

"Frontiers?" was queried by all those still within earshot.

"Mon dieu, of science! The frontiers of science." Here, he stopped, thought for a moment and then added, "What I had in my mind, what I really wanted, I think, was to be the one who…" The difficulty iterating his most deeply hidden desire into a language that wasn't his was proving hard. "I wanted to, to reestablish, I think that is the right word. To rebuild the center of science back to where it started or perhaps, I should say, where it thrived, at a time when a country like this"—he pointed back to the coastline to embellish his point—"had nothing."

The geographic locations of centers of learning had never been front and center with either investigator but Lucan knew and with a nod of his head he admitted the man was right. "At one time, there were more scholars between the Tigris and Euphrates than exist today between London and Glasgow."

"I was sent to Canada to learn, to become better educated, to put myself in positions with access, but I also was to melt into the background. Me, they wanted me to be nobody until that is, I was needed to do their work."

As he spoke, Samir's voice gradually inched into a higher pitch. "I didn't want to be a nobody. I wanted to be, to be…"

Samir paused until the FBI man prodded. "Be what?"

"To be me! But famous and rich. Save the world, who knows what else? I had an idea, but to pull it off I needed to discover something which would become marketable or"—he paused and turned red—"or acquire someone else's IP and make that marketable."

"Acquire?" MacLean prodded, not really following the Moroccan's word usage.

"I needed to meet Dr. Connell." He said this looking Agent MacLean in the face. "She sets the trend these days. Her group is reproducing the deadliest of viruses, recreating an evil so powerful."

"Is this why you visited her lab?"

"That is not what I wanted." He quickly added, "I didn't go in looking for this evil. Just the opposite."

Questioning looks came his way, so he moved to explain, "I wanted something else. I wanted what McAiden brought to her lab. This, this here…" He slowed, fought back a sob and waited for the deck to straighten up before pointing to the now empty vials before continuing, "Is what I needed. I didn't mean to run into his car."

At this point, he changed tact. "His company was on to something I needed, no, something I wanted. They had solved the vaccine production problem." With this out of the way, he switched back, "It was an accident!"

He apologized for the accident several more times and then the rest of his story easily flowed out to the listening audience. No one knew Samir's father, so they couldn't trace his business acumen to a familial inheritance. None of this mattered. It was obvious. Samir was a businessman in training. Since arriving in Montréal years before he had dreamed of starting his own company. He wanted to make money. The rest is like "boy meets girl," very simple, but not very straightforward. Being forced to flee Montréal and laying low in New Jersey was not good. A dead-end career move, literally. Then Labib called and the fires were rekindled. Divine intervention was Samir's take on McAiden's techno advances. Labib told him where he could find such samples. Next, he did what every aspiring businessman who began their career in science would do. He "borrowed" a sample of the material McAiden was sharing with the Connell laboratory. All of that was easy to understand, but why had he still been following Arthur? Easy, he needed short-term financing. He was, after all, living a Bohemian existence in New Jersey.

"I needed money. When I lived in Québec and worked for *la Sûreté*, I had engaged in what one might call 'private' detection." Here, he looked at Christian who nodded his head. "In Jersey, I did some odd jobs with Second Storey. When I started following that poor man"—with a nod of his head in the direction he believed Arthur to be sitting—"hoping to find a way to borrow his written protocols, the 'how to' so to speak, I found he was visiting un professeure at night. On my own, I approached his wife, or who I thought was his wife, and told her of his nocturnal engagements. I left out a few physical descriptors of course and this is how I was hired. I set a high price and it worked, or it would have if I didn't run the man down. I told you that was an accident, didn't I?" Samir stopped talking and those around him, thinking he was through, began to move away. Except for Lucan and the two Investigators. When only these three were close, he continued, "Something else happened. I recorded him speaking on the phone with a man whose name was Dubric and everything…well, everything fell apart." Now Samir had finished talking and began to place the empty tubes back into the shipping container.

When he finally moved out of earshot, Lucan spoke. "I am sorry. I was told when he dropped the vest all danger was cleared."

The two investigators nodded their heads but were more interested in something else at that moment.

"Did he say he recorded Dr. McAiden speaking with Dubric?"

Lucan had a brief response, "First I heard of this."

The three men stood speechless for a while staring out over the ocean until, by chance, their attention was drawn inside. The main cabin stretched a good way along the deck and through its exterior windows they saw a man standing on either side of Arthur as he slowly walked a path along its interior. It only took a moment of this before Arthur began to look green in his face. All those watching smiled. Some even passed along what everyone else thought, "Seasick. Just like ol' times. He must be getting better."

With a show to watch, the rest of the trip didn't take long. The morning dampness evaporated away, and the bright sunlight on the cloudless blue canvas allowed a view of the Isle of Mann ahead and the shoreline left behind. As the boat progressed westward to the south, the island of Anglesey came into focus and those with sharp eyes might have been able to see the Rhinns to the north.

Chapter 40
Pools of Sorrow

The ferry pulled into Douglas with what seemed to be a haul of happy tourists or, perhaps, tired tourists happy to be home. In fact, like soldiers returning from war, "We're home" was a phrase the American and Canadian heard more than once. The welcoming groups of friends and relatives sure acted that way as outstretched arms greeted each debarking passenger. Those waiting and those returning instantly melded into small, cheerful groups like, well, like one would expect to see when welcoming loved one's home. At this stop, there were no caravans waiting to whisk the troop on to another secretive rendezvous, just open arms, and joyous praise.

"We're safe" was another phrase uttered often. Even Lucan was heard expressing this when he shook hands with a thin man the investigators had seen before. His name was de Veer, Messier B. de Veer. De Veer was in the background for most of the ride over, but as the seas calmed and the docks came closer, everyone had moved up toward the bow for a better view. He was also one of the first off.

"Wasn't he that guy walking past our car yesterday?" When no answer was given, MacLean kept trying. "You remember, we were over near Sterling, in the parking lot and..."

"Oui," Inspector Gervais finally responded.

As the two investigators stood watching events unfold, Samir sidled up next to his old *Sureté* comrade and pointed at de Veer. "Do you know what a Seneschal is? Je ne comprends pas cette mot."

When Christian attempted a definition, "Seneschal is...I think it is a...I am sorry. I, too, do not know." Common ground was reached, which pushed Samir to reestablish connections with the Inspector, "Do you remember when..."

Now all three foreigners stood upon the Island of Apples watching the passage of information between the man they knew to be Arthur's butler and the man they had learned was called the Seneschal. Lucan was smiling like a winner and his deep-set eyes were hard to miss as they engaged those around him. There had never been anything too theatrical in his look but now, as a great weight had been lifted, the joy he felt did produce an infectious aura.

"The board meeting is over. Percy showed up at the last minute, as we all hoped, and prayed, he would and..."

Before Lucan could finish the Seneschal delivered the punch line, "As the rules had been written he voted Arthur's shares." A cheer went up all around and in response the speakers smiled and waved. Those debarking were happy to learn their tactical retreat had turned into just a short get-away from their daily routines. It was now a vacation, with a chance to embrace the wonders of the isle.

Even so, there was still work to be done. The meeting may have ended in success for Arthur's current venture in the world of medical research. The efforts to take the company public had not come to fruition, but mistakes had been made. The need to keep the founding principles secret was better understood and efforts to do such were underway as had been done so many years before.

In a fainter voice rising from his sunken cheeks, de Veer continued, "Until Arthur is fully recovered, or the mantel is passed to Percival, we must continue with the plan."

The butler looking down at the small puddles around his feet concurred, "You are right, my dear friend."

The emanation around Lucan's head quickly dissipated and he returned to his workday countenance. He and de Veer spoke to several of those nearby giving instructions, and then they approached the two inspectors.

"We will return items to their original locations but not until, until…" Midsentence Lucan stopped and changed direction. "We have come far. Everything is in motion. The meaning behind these objects may never in our lifetimes matter again but we will keep them hid a while longer. I believe this is the right thing to do."

De Veer agreed with the butler. "Until Arthur returns to us, this is what we must do."

The Seneschal then stepped back as Lucan tried to quickly sum things up. To do this he held up his right hand and counted off as he extended each finger. "One, a ferry will arrive in a few minutes. Arthur's sister and her sons will be aboard. When it returns to Dublin, you can get on it if you like. Two, you can catch a flight home from Dublin. All avenues are open to you now. Three, as you've both heard, our holdings are safe. Four, the other…" Here, he held his breath for a moment, trying to distill the proper terminology for their adversary. "The other clan is now keeping a low profile. They probably know where we are and being here"—he pointed down at the ground—"means everyone is safe, and five," before he reached his final summation the Canadian interrupted (though, the American was about to also).

"May we stay a short while longer?"

Lucan smiled. "Interesting set of events, is it not? Can you figure us out now?"

Christian answered using a humbled voice designed to help push his agenda to those seemingly in command. "I must say, that is very unlikely, not without access to all the books you are keeping hidden. But it is not the history, per se, that is of most interest."

"Not the history," Lucan shot back as one immersed in issues written on a straightforward list of daily activities might, "Then please, you must tell me what is."

Here, the American added his take, "It is the people. It seems that you are all dedicated to, to, hell I don't know what, something, some cause. Whatever it is, it is bigger than one man, but at the same time, you all seem to really care for this McAiden fellow."

"Two men," the Canadian merged himself into the American's response. "You have been looking for M. li Gros, this Percival of yours, ever since Arthur was first hit by the car, non? To do what? Save the day? *Et voilà*, he appears, and so he does. I must read your local newspapers to see exactly what he saved, for it might be more than the control of one business enterprise."

"I am sorry. I do not believe the meeting yesterday will find its way to the newspapers, especially not at a time like this. I am also sorry both of you have been caught up in this mess, but we all thank you for your help with, with him." He pointed at Samir who stood just a few feet away. "I will tell you one thing. Arthur's company is not the most important item at the moment." He paused, scratched his chin, and continued, "You are correct. Both Arthur and Percival are very important to our cause as are so many others." Lucan paused again, thought for a moment, stared at the two in front of him and then reached a decision. "M. de Veer can take you along to the gathering tonight, but then I'm afraid if you stay longer on the Island, it will be on your own. I will be traveling back to London later today. The crisis, our little crisis, is over but I will be needed there to help make other arrangements. It's all in a day's work, right?" Lucan checked his watch and then held out his hand, "Everything here on the Island is in motion and now I must bid you both *adieux*."

As Lucan moved off, Arthur walked past. As before, he was being escorted by two men who only stepped in if his gait looked suspect. This time, as instructed, those along the quay pretended to ignore the man unless he stopped nearby and spoke in their general direction. This he did not five feet from where Lucan had been standing.

"At this time, there was shown to a certain hermit in Britain, through the agency of an angel, a marvelous vision concerning St. Joseph, the man from Arimathea, the Decurion who took our Lord's body down from the cross…"

"He is reciting," de Veer whispered to the investigators. When they nodded in agreement, he continued, "From Helinand de Froidmont, something written a long time ago."

"How long?" was the question both men asked.

"Oh, I would say, though I don't remember exactly, in the early eighth century, perhaps around 715 *anno domini,* give or take."

Dindrane then passed walking alongside her mother's wheelchair. She, like Arthur, was mid-presentation. Hers was a running commentary of Arthur's movement and speech, only she spoke into the ethereal void of her telephone. "What is he reciting? Everything he's ever read. No, no, you know what I mean! It is lines. He's reciting lines from books. Is it random? Well maybe random passages, but the people here are telling me everything that does come out is in some sort of chronologic order.

"Yes, I know we should expect this sort of thing?" Dindrane responded to an incoming opinion. "But he isn't really conversing, just reciting. Oh my, well that is good news. Now get me connected with the rehab center on the other side of the Isle." She moved the phone from her ear, turned a smiling face to her mother and whoever else was nearby and let out a joyous, but guarded, pronouncement. "He is getting better, this is just the beginning, but he is getting better."

"And concerning this bowl, or dish, in which our Lord supped with his Apostles, the history called 'of the Grail' was written down."

At this point, Arthur went silent and a wry smile covered his face. Those standing nearby seemed to acknowledge his reference and they raised their arms in salute. Then, just like that, the narrating man moved along and, looking from side to side, continued his recitations. As he passed one, then another group, those listening formed into parties, each betting against the others as they tried to place the origin of the lines heard.

"Nineas! That had to be Nineas?"

"That was Gildas, you babbling idiot. Only Gildas wrote with such venom, though he was right to do so, and you do remember the lashing he gave that bastard Gwynedd, the one who lived back then of course. Man, we could use Gildas now, 'ai?"

The dock led directly up to the street where a waiting car opened its door for the approaching orator. Here, Arthur stopped and slowly turned to face once again those he had passed. Then, with a voice traveling over the background of the boats passing, the squeaking seagulls seemingly stationary above and the incessant traffic moving about the nearby streets, he cried out, "The precepts of Christ came to our Island in AD 37, the last year of Tiberius Caesar. Within six years of the death and resurrection, the church was setting up shop in Britain. For this, we thank members of the Davidic lineage, Joseph of Arimethea and his son Josephus. Now, you must ask, who said the first church was in Glastonbury, Maelgwyn of Llandaff that's who. He lied about this. We let it ride because it helped us stay beneath the radar when the bishopric of Rome came calling. Now that Goodrich woman will shed a light on everything, everything we've kept hidden for the last…" His voice trailed off as a group of men quickly helped him lower his head and sink into the waiting car.

"Well now, that was a close one, wasn't it?" escaped from de Veer's mouth. Then, noting the two men next to him were showing interest he ushered them along to their waiting vehicle. "Your friend from Morocco will ride with a different group but will return to your care soon, someone wants to have a word with him."

The American of Scottish (or possibly Irish) descent and the Canadian whose genealogy might place his forefathers in Breton (or possibly Normandy) were assigned a car with de Veer and a driver whose name they learned was Howl, though they were uncertain, like with Lucan, whether it was given or sur. Howl was more elderly than de Veer and, like Lucan, was neatly dressed. He had high shoulders and a short neck that gave way to what might have been described as an egg-shaped head. They would find that he was engaging but also had, what the two investigators agreed upon when they discussed him later, a pleasant vagueness of manners.

When the car escaped the confines of Douglas proper, the Seneschal passed around plates and what appeared to be crystal. "Water?" he asked and prepared to pour from a large bottle, which had materialized alongside a basket of food. Then he dug through the basket and pulled various items up onto his lap. With quick work, he sliced off sections of each hidden treasure and disseminated slices onto waiting plates muttering all the while his appreciation of Lucan, "It is good to have an experienced man around when there is knife work to be done."

Each offering from de Veer helped complete a decorative display and pinpointed various gastronomical hot spots. The distribution of food went well for everyone but the driver. For him, items were placed onto his left hand in small increments, which were then quickly shoved into his mouth. With each allotment placed, thus Howl's hand would move back to the steering wheel for all of ten seconds before it returned to the receiving line.

Before the mobile banquet began, the two in the back had hoped to talk about Samir or, more directly, who he was riding with, and why. But as they moved beyond the port a green countryside appeared and their thoughts drifted onto other topics. The verdant field after rolling pasture after well-trimmed apple orchard (the island had to get its name from somewhere) became a scrolling canvas of soothing visual cues. Everyone in the car unwound and, while looking at their drinking glasses, wondered if anything besides water had been added. Tranquility set in, hitting all like a soft pillow and the tension built up since arriving in Edinburgh drained away from the two investigators.

"Did you ever read Tolkien?" de Veer asked while in between bites. Without waiting for a response, he continued, "It is told to us, us being those who spend a good deal of time on this island, the idea for the tree herders, the Ents, came to him when he visited Mann."

"For the women," Howl butted in while trying to quickly finish chewing. "The idea for the males was Caledonia. You know that."

"Of course, but I'm not sure if they do," de Veer responded while motioning at the occupants in the back seat. Then he smiled, leaned farther back into his seat, closed his eyes and continued, "Tolkien and I had good times when we hiked the woods in the fall, we stole a few apples then too."

Howl chimed in again. "Well said, but you must tell them it is just a figment of your imagination."

"Oh, please, let me have some fun. My father did know the man and he did come to our country home on occasion. When he was with us, the conversations would quickly move away from whatever was trending and onto better topics, like his writing."

"Tolkien was an academic, so of course, he would discuss his work. I do hope your father did not engage him in religious discussions too.

"It was hard not to. Tolkien came from Anglo-Saxon stock, a staunch Roman Catholic. You know, with just a wee bit more information passed his way, he may have been swayed in our direction."

"More information, did he need more? He had almost figured it all out. He read Taliesin you know. That's the Welsh bard." Howl clarified for the men in the backseat to help them follow along not realizing those in the back had been lost since landing in Scotland.

"Tolkien understood," de Veer cut in, "it was Owain who killed the Anglican king of Bernicia. My word, this is written in the Anglo-Saxon Chronicles. Tolkien knew Owain's father continued the fight against the Saxons, and it was King Redderch." Here, he stared directly at the driver. "It was Hael, the king of Redderch, who solidified Strathclyde at Arthur's Head."

"Yes, yes, the battle that allowed argyle socks to gain market superiority for the next 1,500 years." The attempt to change the subject didn't work, de Veer would not be steered off course.

"Please, Howl, what do you think can happen now? These men"—he took a quick look at the two in the back seat—"are not going to write a book on the subject. Are you?"

Inspector Gervais kept his face straight, answered honestly and in the only fashion he felt would keep the man talking. "I have no clue what you and M. Hael are talking about or what any of you have been talking about the last twenty-four hours."

For a brief moment, de Veer was caught up in the same misunderstanding infecting his passengers, so he tried to clear things up from his end. "That's Howl," he said, pointing at the driver. "Hael, was his namesake from a few years back, and yes"—he turned to address those in the back—"this Howl and that Hael share the same tree."

As Mike and Christian tried to sound out the differences between Howl and Hael, the Seneschal turned back to the driver and continued.

"Mungo wrote it all out: In the beginning of sixth-century Scotland, south of the Clyde and Forth, was still inhabited by the ancient Britons, who were bound together in a loose confederation known as the kingdom of Strathclyde. Their Guledig, Arthur, in a series of battles between the two Roman walls of Tyne and Forth had temporarily crippled the power of the invading Saxons."

"Can we get back to Tolkien please?"

"What do you think I'm doin'? You brought up the religious…"

"It is just too nice a day for a history lesson. I would rather hear the stories Tolkien wrote of Edith and Evenstar."

Each added reference drove the back-seat duo deeper into the abyss of incomprehension. "The Roman walls of Tyne and Forth?" MacLean asked before Gervais could add, "Evenstar?"

Howl tried hard to multitask. "Tyne is Hadrian's Wall, and Forth is the smaller structure built between Glasgow and Edinburgh." But he picked up speed and shut out all other routes when he began to focus on what he wanted to talk about, "Evenstar, yes Evenstar, now you're talkin'! If you know anything about Tolkien's writing you know of his fictional characters *Lúthien Tinúviel* and *Arwen Evenstar*. Who do you think was his inspiration for her?"

Those in the back remained silent.

"Edith was his muse."

"Edith?"

"His wife! It was his wife, oh my, I thought we had an educated assembly here." Now in his element, he chuckled, "Don't you guys do any research? Tolkien's wife was the source of *Lúthien*. Her story became the chief part of the *Silmarillion*. Edith was Luthien. Now, I'm sure you don't know this so, I am going to tell you…" Tell he did. Howl spoke of the love affair of John Ronald Reuel Tolkien and Edith Bratt, of how they strolled the woodland near the town of Roos where Edith began to dance for him in a clearing among a sea of white flowering hemlock. "When she passed, Tolkien was very sad. He wrote a letter to his son, though most believe it was really memoirs to himself centering on the love of his life, 'how her hair was raven, her skin clear, her eyes brighter than you have seen them, and she could sing—and *dance.*' Do you see? Edith in the hemlock was the meeting of *Beren and Lúthien.* Tolkien often called Edith his *Lúthien.*"

"Who was *Luthien* in the story?"

"*Lúthien* was an elf.

"And *Evenstar?*"

It was de Veer's turn. "You may be familiar with *Aragon* and *Arwen Evenstar* from his better known work. In her time, *Arwen* was called the fairest like *Lúthien* was in the First Age. She rejected her Elven immortality to marry Aragorn and die with him.

Love touches people in so many ways and the story of ultimate love tends to lay it on thick. It's effect on the two men in the front seat was obvious, both were pretty much balling now, so it took a minute before either could continue.

"Like *Beren* and *Aragorn*, Arthur loves his elven queen, his Guinevere."

"Guinevere?"

"Guinevere is Jennifer."

"How can Jennifer be Guinevere?"

"Jennifer is a modernization of the Celtic name where *Gwen* means 'fair or white' and *Hwyfar* is 'smooth.'" In Celtic, Guinevere can be spelled ten different ways, but spelling isn't really the issue here."

"No? What is?"

"Phonetics."

"Oh."

"Bottom line is this: Arthur loves his wife."

"He loves the name too. I mean he named his dog Guinevere."

"Whatever, but, Howl, look, when he finds out it was Jennifer who hired that guy to spy on him, what do you think will happen?"

"Well, they will have some catching up to do, won't they?"

The tears began to flow again. This time, it didn't stop, and so the two in the back had nothing to do but internalize their thoughts and quietly watch the countryside move past.

Chapter 41
The Fisher King

Many cars were heading west that morning. The car Howl was driving was taking the scenic tour. Others were on a more direct route or were just moving faster. The car in which Arthur sat was leading this charge, and for the first time since being airlifted to the ICU so many weeks ago, no trained medical personnel were nearby. This didn't register with the man, or those who were escorting him. They were all too busy, Arthur with an incessant delivery of his take on the meaning of life while those sharing the car were trying to throw a few tidbits back his way (whenever he slowed down for a moment that is). How the man could even talk through his clenched jaw was a miracle itself, but how he, a trained biologist could describe the relatedness of Einstein's "spooky action at a distance" and "the wormhole connection" was a step beyond. And to add icing to the cake, his delivery was in French.

"Didn't know he was fluent in French."

"He isn't."

"Then how is he…"

"Don't have a clue."

"You must understand"—Arthur had switched to English—"what I am saying is, well, open to interpretation, and it gets difficult for any of us to really follow.

"You all have heard talk of the boson, the force that binds, and by this I don't mean gravity, and of course, Higgs will undoubtedly win the Nobel for his efforts because his boson will have a role to play in the grand scheme. We all must agree with this theorem." Arthur's voice somehow rose in intensity as he switched back to French. "If we are connected it is not at the molecular level, or the atomic for that matter. It is from a place far deeper where all…"

The others in the car listened in, each in their own way wishing for comprehension, or if food was packed somewhere in the car, it would soon be found.

"You are right in saying it is subatomic. However, even today with what we are learning with the giant colliders we are no closer to really understanding, and…"

Usually, questions are saved until the end of the presentation, but the driver was looking for a way to take his mind off food. "Understanding what?"

"The ultimate being, that which has created the universe is not, perhaps I should say, cannot, be found in a particle as a singularity but in fact is at least three parts. But this is the argument that caused so much bloodshed in the beginning, is God a Triune, and if so, how do we best describe this in terms that make sense in our world? Now, let us not say we need to worship multiple god entities but rather there is a distribution of the composition of the ultimate intelligence into intellect, empathy, and the third part that we can only say is the force that holds all together. This force is not devoid of the first two; it just occupies a different place and is composed essentially of love. Now, when I say "composed" of love I mean "is" love.

Both men in the front seat smiled and slowly drifted their eyes heavenward.

"The *dux Belloram* felt this. Everyone prayed for him, and you do know love, from within, can emanate. Love can affect outcomes. Love intertwined from so many was the force that pulled me back. It had to be." Arthur paused, looked up for a moment and then continued, "Perhaps we should ask one who studies philosophy what their take is." This was delivered in the form of a question directed at the man sitting next to him.

Dubric bowed his head in the speaker's direction. "I am not an existentialist! I just study the topic" was all he said.

Arthur continued as if no response was given, "Okay, now it gets complicated."

Everyone else in the car tried not to laugh, including Samir whose knowledge of French had him following along.

"If the composition, or should I say, definition, of our Ultimate Being is intellect, empathy, and love then the existential existence is based in the following, the esthetic, the ethical and the religious. Given that, we can construct a logical system to describe the esthetic, what we see around us, and the ethical, how we feel, but a system to describe existence, the why we are here question, this we cannot do. Therefore, the love of... of our Ultimate Being and the religious context of the existentialist may both be unfathomable. Does this mean they are the same, and if so, is proper religious dogma based on love?"

Arthur began speaking as if he was once again looking at the body below from a higher perch. "I admit there is no way for us to really measure the 'love effect,' and as we all know, I am not fully recovered. My existence within our three-dimensional space is still reforming. Sadly, in an intellectual format, once my mental processes become repaired that is, what I have seen and heard from beyond the confines of our physical existence I may no longer remember. I mean what is quantum entanglement if it cannot connect elements across all spheres of existence?

"Perhaps one can reach an external understanding of this if we use a refinement in our measurements of the space between particles and waves, Schrodinger gave us a clue. And Heisenberg too, but can we get on to the real fundamentals here? How can any of this have been borne from the first naked singularity, there could be no event horizon if there was no universe, and you all know as well as I we are far from understanding this. Are we going to accept the big bang or not? If we do, then according to general relativity, the initial state of the universe, at the beginning, and by beginning, I cannot say whether this is right before, or actually during, a big bang, was a singularity. But we cannot use either general relativity or quantum mechanics to describe this. They both break down if we go this route and in general, quantum mechanics does not allow particles to inhabit a space smaller than their wavelengths."

In the car shared by the police investigators, the discussion had moved off romance lit and onto more of a basic history format.

"But what do these books you are carting around have to do with your beliefs?"

"You mean, our religion?" Howl tried to define the query before answering while de Veer tried to change the topic.

"Nothing…"

"And everything." With this said, Howl put on the proverbial brakes and, like de Veer, decided to change tack for a while. They became tour guides giving informative descriptions of every region of the island, whether on the travel itinerary or not.

"Have you read the *Prose Lancelot*? From the island one can see five lands if you count the island itself as one that is."

"On the island, we have tropical lowlands to the north while in the south…"

Somewhere along with the information dump, Howl began to reveal their destination, "We're headed for Peel, where, if the weather holds up, we will get a wonderful view of the home of the Fisher King."

Howl paused for dramatic effect until de Veer beat him to the punch line in a low, guttural delivery "The Peel Castle."

"The Peel Castle?"

"Some of the references cite it as such, do they not?" Howl threw out this line.

"When it was built," de Veer cut in, using a more business-like demeanor, "they didn't build stone castles. When we say 'peel,' what we are referring to is what the Romans would build when making a military base. A stockade of sorts would be erected around the encampment. The bark on the tips of the wood would be 'peeled' back and then they were sharpened. Didn't really matter here, though, the buildings were up on the rocks, so no one could assault the place successfully."

"Very well said, but you forgot to give the other name, didn't you," Howl added to his partner's treatise, thereby reminding de Veer of something important.

"Well, of course not, I thought we would keep at least one secret."

"We could try to keep a secret, but as our man Arthur has been worried for quite some time, it will not be long before everyone figures it out."

"Figures what out?" MacLean's voice trickled into the conversation.

"The Peel Castle is the Grail Castle." The driver hurried through, not allowing de Veer to get in his way.

"Was the Grail Castle," de Veer corrected. "The Grail Castle was the Peel Castle was Carbonek, but whatever name you give it, it doesn't exist today. What we see on the rocks today is the remains Vikings built when they assumed control hundreds of years later. They arrived in the eleventh century and slowly expanded on what was already there. The stone structures still standing were added on sometime in the thirteen hundreds."

Howl's response moved in de Veer's direction, albeit slowly. "Well, the buildings don't exist but the theme we put in place is still here, right?"

The theme touched upon was left covered for the rest of the ride, but whatever that theme was, it kept the investigators wondering.

Chapter 42
St. Patrick's Island

Howl had the car in the home stretch paralleling the river Neb. Soon the well-tended acres of green gave way to rock strewn fields and the river itself began to disappear down crevices that channeled it to the sea below. The outlying fields would have disappeared too, becoming the tops of cliffs overlooking ocean if the car had continued along with the river but Howl had pointed the vehicle north, and as the river behind sank away, the excitement in the front seat rose. Peel was close.

Downtown Peel was just coming into view when Howl turned onto Mill Road, and a minute later, the car passed over a small bridge at the narrow southern end of the harbor. On the far side, he turned onto W. Quay and headed north again driving past numerous boats all preparing to head out to open waters for a night of work. It didn't take long to get to the end of the wharf itself, and just a few hundred feet farther on was a large rock outcropping sticking up out of the water. Here, Howl pulled the car into a small parking lot. The four men now sat and watched the sun beginning its descent, painting the clouds amassing overhead in various shades of orange and yellow.

The causeway, MacLean noted, did continue. It connected St. Patrick's, the rock outcropping, with Man. At that point, the road became a single lane as it hugged the northern flank of the isle before disappearing around its western edge or branching out into a second causeway, which helped define the protected harbor of Peel.

"The Fisher King would be very proud," Howl whispered to himself as he watched boats on the far side of the causeway. "They're all heading for the best grounds known to man."

"St. Patrick laid the foundations for a monastery here." M. de Veer said, pointing at the rocky prominence. "Geographically speaking it was once more like *Ynys Trebes*, the island capital of what we might call the Benoic region, and like there, at high tide, the water would cover the space between the rocks and the shoreline." He didn't have to point to the ground below, but he did anyway as he noted the confused looks upon the faces in the back seat.

"You can see with the rocks built up around the causeway, well the 'island' is more of a peninsula of sorts now, isn't it?"

"I am sorry, but what is *Ynys*?" was all MacLean could manage before his mouth went dry and it was the Canadian who finished the query. "Where is *Ynys Trebes*?"

"*Ynys Trebes*? What is *Ynys Trebes*?" de Veer took a deep breath in anticipation of his next delivery, but before he could begin Howl tried to simplify matters. "I think it would be better to just place it, like M. Gervais asked."

"Oh, well, yes, I see your point, thank you." De Veer nodded his head and then turned once more to those in the back seat. "One would call it Mont St. Michel today, right?"

"Mont St. Michel," Christian managed to know something for once that day, so he interjected himself into the sightseeing tour. "I've seen pictures of Mont St. Michel. It is off the coast of…where now? I cannot remember, Normandy or perhaps it is Brittany.

"Exactly right, it is a small island that would, today, be right between Brittany and Normandy. As mentioned, it was the capital of the Benoic region of Armorica, until the clans were pushed back by the Franks."

"I've seen pictures of the island. It does look to be a beautiful place. There is an abbey on the island as well, isn't there?"

"Yes," Howl responded, now not caring for decorum or stealth. "The Benedictines built an abbey there. But did you know that by building the abbey they tore down the ancient library. Excuse me, I digress. Their construction started many years after Patrick began the cloister over here." At this, he pointed to the small piece of rock, and with that said, the vision of the two men in the back seat focused on both the island and a small display map set just a few feet to the side of their car. This is how the excavations came into view.

"St. Patrick started building here sometime around AD 440. Durbricius was the bishop toward the end of that century, and this is when the work was extended to become more like a place of learning, a school. Mont St. Michel wasn't finished until the early seven hundreds, and again, there was so much lost on *Ynys Trebes*."

MacLean tried a tongue in cheek honorarium. "Does this mean you guys won?" It didn't work so he moved on, "But what was done here, and what are you doing here now?" As the question implied, visions had appeared of people moving about on the top of the rock outcropping. Unfortunately, from the angle held by those near the causeway a view of the archeological undertakings on top of the island was impossible to see, and with the sun beginning to set, those in the car could only squint in that general direction.

Just moments after MacLean uttered these questions, another vision stole his attention. Out of nowhere, two men materialized beside the car. One of them opened the trunk and began removing packages transported from various stops along the journey. The other moved to the driver's side where he thanked Howl with a nod of his head and spoke in through the window. "He's here," he said, pointing with his chin. By "here," the man meant the ancient remains atop the rocks. All eyes followed catching a glimpse of a man being held upright by two others.

The packages were quickly removed and then both men wished Howl and de Veer luck before moving down a heretofore unseen path. A small boat on the seaward side of the causeway awaited the packages they carried. Within seconds, two other cars pulled up and parked beside Howl's. Those, too, were unloaded by the same men who had rapidly returned from the water's edge. When the boat was loaded, it took off into the reflecting glare of the descending sun. The cars emptied thus began to head back the way they had come.

De Veer spoke softly as Howl began backing the car out. "This was a place for those wishing to come and study. Dubricius picked up on the idea from Patrick, and so, to make a long story short, we are where we are today." The two inspectors sat up straight with heads turning from side to side straining to see everything or anything that might help them understand.

"The whole island was alive back then." Howl picked up as de Veer slowed, "So many came here to learn. We had an important center for education and for religion too, right here." By "right here," the two men in the back seat understood that the driver meant both Peel, their current location, and the Island of Man itself. "Until the Roman church sent that *Germanus* fellow to stamp out the movement."

"To stamp out any who didn't buy their version of things, right or wrong, like they did to Pelagius."

"Why was Pelagius vilified?"

"His ideas. He believed promoting good was more important than promoting that which we cannot understand. Salvation can be achieved if you work or, should I say, live without…"

De Veer was moving to drive home his point when Howl cut in. "What we had here didn't fit in with those setting the agenda in Rome. They wanted full artistic control, just ask the Arians that."

Howl and de Veer seemed to have worked themselves up into a frenzy, but no longer being young, battle-hardened warriors, they had to pause for a moment and catch their breath. When they resumed, de Veer had ratcheted down the pace and tone of his delivery.

"Early on, both the religious, and how do I describe this? Academics? Yes, that works. Both the religious and academic groups that coalesced here were under the protection of the Fisher King, and as we know, even back then, on any given day one could count the fishing vessels into the hundreds."

As they made their way out of town, those in the front tired completely and those in the back had nothing left to ask. Total quiet settled in until they turned onto a street named Patrick Lane. The quiet within remained but the focus of each reflection changed as the internal peace was punctured by tires finding every existing pothole along the wagon trail called a street by whomever drew the maps.

The sky was dark when the road wound between a church and adjacent cemetery. Here, they pulled off to the side and shut down amidst a bevy of other vehicles. They had reached what may have been an abbey. A cloister running along the flank of the church suggested as much. But whether it was a convent or monastery, neither investigator could tell. The evening helped cause this problem. A thick mist was crawling along the ground, engulfing every object it met. With no street lighting to pierce the night's darkness, or encroaching mist, images entering one's view were tamped down. Those bodies they did see moving about closer to the buildings became surreal apparitions slowly floating along. They were, after all, on Mann, the Necromancer's Island, upon which the veil of concealment was cast. This they didn't learn from their tour guides. They felt it when standing near the headstones as the fog thickened.

Chapter 43
A Changing of the Guard

Staying close together, everyone followed Howl up the long stone path. As quiet as the last of the car ride had been, it was quieter now. Each body seemed to be drifting along in the mist until they reached the end of the trail. Now they squeezed together in front of an old wooden door. No knock was needed. The door had already begun to open giving the light within a chance to pour forth and melt the ghostly imagery into nothingness.

Howl stepped inside followed at once by the investigators with de Veer bringing up the rear. Now they stood in a neatly kept antechamber. Those who had entered before were wiping shoes and removing outerwear before bowing their heads in silent prayer and passing through archways into the main room. It was the refectory, it had to be. It was quite large and had several different versions of the Celtic cross adorning the walls. Many people already inside were mingling about in conversation or calling dibs on chairs placed around large wooden tables.

Pitchers of drink were being brought into the room by young men dressed in simple tunics tied at the waist with cloth belts. Each of the servers were also adorned with crucifixes, and of course, work aprons that reached down below the knees on the younger novices. To which denomination the monastery belonged was not obvious, but both investigators did note the simplicity of the clothes worn by those who were obviously in training.

Music with cultural stylings of the island wafted through the hall, infecting many who, without thinking, were quietly humming along. Smiling was also infectiously spread around the gathered mass, along with hand holding. Some were also swaying back and forth in their chairs or standing in an almost trance like state, like that which Samir had seen at the O'von.

Arthur was seated at the far side of the room. How he could have traveled from Peel to this room before them they would never learn. But there he was, sitting upright in his chair with arms resting on the table in front of him. He was still and seemed to be tired. His wife was next to him with her head on his shoulder and both arms tightly wrapped around his chest. Her eyes were only half open and it was clear liquid had recently spilled forth.

Dindrane sat at a table near Arthur's. She was busy writing on notepaper, and they were to learn, wishing her mobile phone could make a better connection. The Widow-Lady sat beside her and around this table Anna sat, too, with two young men on either side of her, each holding a hand or touching one of their mother's shoulders.

Samir was also in the room. He sat a few tables down the line from Arthur's. He was speaking with a man wearing a strange, furry-looking coat that had long dangling threads. "Is that hair?" MacLean whispered.

"Camel hair perhaps?" was Inspector Gervais's response.

What type of hair remained undetermined, but it was definitely a leather belt around his waist keeping the coat nestled in tight. His own hair was white, hung loosely about and dangled well below his collar. Some strands even found their way to his chest ensconced in the top pockets of the coat. The man looked familiar. When he nudged Samir with the edge of what appeared to be a heavy cane, the two inspectors registered their findings. This was the man they had seen out in the field in Lothian.

"That is Dubric," Howl whispered as he motioned them to a table.

"Of course," came as a rote response from both.

"A direct descendent of Saint…" De Veer, too, was whispering.

Howl ignored de Veer, "He is the Merlin and"—both investigators choked as they watched Dubric look in their direction and wink—"he will be visiting with you both soon."

The Merlin turned back toward Samir, smiling as he spoke, and a moment later, he put his arm out, grasped the Moroccan's shoulder, and whispered into the diminutive one's ear. This brought a promising nod of the head. Then he stood up and moved away. As soon as he did several others standing nearby moved in to join Samir, or at least to fill their cups from the pitcher in front of him.

The room continued to fill, and the escalating noise dampened down the background music. This was why Dubric walked over to the dais just beyond Arthur's table. Here, behind a small podium, he found the volume control but just before he cranked it up, he heard a round of applause. Uncertain if it was for something he did, or was about to do, he stood up straight and looked out across the room. He smiled for a moment and prepared to acknowledge their attention when he noted the applause was not for him. A young man had just entered the hall walking alongside Dagon and several other escorts.

"Percy is here," Howl stated the obvious as he began pouring large mugs of beer for himself and anyone nearby. Everyone in the room had turned their attention toward the new entrants and watched as Percy moved from table to table shaking hands, smiling, kissing some, patting others on their backs. All those holding hands let go for a moment to touch the young man as he passed.

Beside Percy strode the most beautiful of creatures and mid step she stopped, tilted her head to one side, looked Arthur's way and at once broke stride and raced over to him. Upon reaching his table the female with lustrous yellow-gold fur licked her best friend more than once on his bent over face. Then, like a mother protecting her sick child, she sat beside him without moving, as a sentry might, carefully watching those who came too close.

She is, Howl told them, Arthur's Guinevere. It was obvious to anyone who looked, Arthur was happy. Jennifer, too, smiled and gave a quick giggle as she petted the Lab.

"We are home," she whispered to her husband.

Percy moved closer to his mother's table, and everyone watched the older woman push her wheelchair out from the table to give her son room to enter her embrace. They held each other tight for a long count, and when Percy finally straightened up again, Yglais could be heard telling him "Do it, do it once, we'll all join you."

Others nearby concurred and Dubric moved to set in motion what was requested by all. A moment later, music could be heard gently infiltrating every corner of the room.

"It's the Beatles," Howl said after quaffing down a generous helping of ale. Then he poured himself some more. "They're a big hit around here you know." A quirky smile went with the understatement.

The music was emanating from speakers hidden somewhere high up among the supports, and attempting to find the source, the investigators noted the presence of solid hand-crafted workmanship all around. They had no idea what they were seeing was built many years before that Italian guy first sailed west from Spain. Returning their gaze to the dais they also noted the young man positioning himself there was born long after the Beatles had dissolved their partnership. Everyone in the hall went quiet when he raised his arms and at just the right moment, he began to sing. Even on the Isle of Mann karaoke had found a home.

"Words are flowing out like
endless rain into a paper cup…"

All eyes were on their knight in shining armor as he worked his way through the first verse. The scene now playing out could have been taking place at a pub anywhere in the world with some silently mouthing along or busy finishing their drink while awaiting their cue. The chorus came as Percy's last line wafted up to the heavens with Dubric using his arms to draw the chorus forth.

When everyone began singing, Percy slowly moved over to Arthur and gently stroked his uncle's forehead. Then he bent low and whispered something.

Arthur's eyes opened wide and just like when Guinevere licked his face, he smiled. Then he rose from his chair, held tightly onto Percy's arm and together they moved out to the center of the room. Guinevere followed close behind.

"Nothing's gonna change my world."

faded out from the choral accompaniment and Arthur obviously knew it was his turn. Everyone was now on their feet inching closer.

"Thoughts meander like a
restless wind inside a letter box…"

Now, there was no way to adjust the volume for everyone sang forth with every ounce of desire ever felt within a human being. If there was a dry eye in the house before this verse it ceased to be. Sometimes spiritual journeys require a special guide to be present but mostly just a like-minded audience, each dreaming the same dream. This is all that was needed. Emotions can be infectious, and infection can lead to group response, and so it was as everyone continued to move forward, each soul melding with the group. Soon everyone was standing in a semicircle around the podium, holding hands, swaying, and singing as the chorus returned with regularity.

Everyone, that is, except Arthur, after his solo he and the dog returned to their seats. Now he watched and smiled, and as the chorus became a whisper, glasses were raised.

"To Wayne," Percy sang out raising his glass, and those in the room turned to Anna who was crying while she mouthed the words.

"Nothing's gonna change my world."

"To Angus," a whole group along the back wall wailed as they pounded their chests.

"Jai Guru Dé-va Om."

"To Lute," the voice of Jennifer sang as her knees shook and tears flowed.

"Nothing's gonna change my world."

Arthur, too, cried; and like those all around, his tears mixed with the beer sloshed about upon the tables. He cried as a human would, pouring forth his hopes and dreams and this brought joy to those in the hall for they could feel he was alive and back in the proper time zone.

Tears slowed as the karaoke ended and this is when the man with threads of white hair, now mangled with the damp sweat from his forehead, moved close to where the inspectors sat. Howl offered Dubric his seat. Everyone else excused themselves, and so within the blink of an eye Christian, Mike and the man they only knew as Dubric were the only ones seated.-

"I am Dubric, Dubricius if you want the whole thing, and yes, I am a Brython. Once a Brython, always a Brython. But please don't think it is unnatural for passing the priesthood along from within one clan"—here, he smiled as he got ready for his punch line—"after all, you've read the

Old Testament, am I right?" If they had or had not Dubric didn't really care, he had to finish his introduction, "Only one clan held sway over this part of their community. Yea, of course I'm right."

The smile on Dubric's face shrank, "We are all moving across the Universe now, aren't we? It just takes an open mind to find the best path."

Before either man could respond, he continued, "Your man over there"—here, he pointed with his chin at Samir—"he'll be okay. I think it might be best to keep him in your country, though." This he said staring at Inspector Gervais. "There might be some opportunities for a man like him in Québec."

When neither man answered, Dubric explained.

"We just needed to give him another point of view. People tend to interpret life, the meaning of life I should say, in different ways. It all depends on which side of the street so to speak. If people would just, umm, just try to understand what is on the other side, then and only then do I believe the world would be a much better place.

"Arthur liked to delve into things. Still does, it seems," This he added remembering the car ride earlier in the day. "Once he told me how he envisioned humans as a giant organism or, perhaps, an amalgamation of components, yes, an amalgam, and parts of this amalgam becomes a stronger force that influences all the others, to herd the others, if you will. This is not a good thing. To escape this kind of pressure each individual part needs to understand they are blessed with an ability to, umm, an ability to think on their own. If they do, voilà, you get change. The difference between prodding and conspicuous herding had to do with delineating an organism's ability to evolve. Sometimes that can be a very fine line."

Food was brought into the refectory, so Dubric tapered off his delivery and the feast began. It just so happened that most in attendance that evening had visited before and takin' a liking to, basically, the local cuisines, home cooking so to speak. Every member of the order, abbot included, was now waiting tables and those receiving were smiling as plate after plate was placed within striking distance of forks. The tapas came out steaming and then an assortment of cheeses made an appearance alongside tubs of fresh butter and breads that were still warm from the oven. It wasn't breakfast but no meal on Mann is complete without kippers, sweet queen scallops sautéed to perfection came along too as well as a few other dishes, courtesy of the fishing fleet at Peel, all served just to balance out the unique flavors of the lamb, Loghton lamb. As people ate conversations decreased, but in direct proportion, the laughter increased.

Having helped himself to generous portions of just about everything brought into the hall Dubric found a way to wipe his chin and then got up. "Now you will have to excuse me. I have one more thing to do tonight. Please don't save my spot. I'm not sure if I'll be back this way."

Just as he rose, the room became quiet. Both Professor Dubric and the graduate student Percival Li Gros approached the center of the dais. A man who seemed to have a senior post in the monastery, possibly the abbot himself, helped position the two men and then de Veer joined in holding what looked to be an axe, the handle of which the two investigators had seen earlier prodding the Moroccan.

Having no working knowledge of the language in play, neither the investigators nor Samir could understand exactly what was said but everyone else in the room seemed to get the gist of it. After a few words were passed back and forth, Percy announced whatever it was he needed to say and then the axe was handed from the old Merlin to the acolyte.

It was now Percival's turn to talk and talk he did. Those visiting Mann for the first time had no measure of the line between fact and what was going on inside this storyteller's head but listen they did and just as Scheherazade bewitched her audience with songs of jeweled keys, Percival, too, regaled the crowd.

"Let me take you back in time," he began.

Tales of Britain before the Roman conquest were his starting point, extracted from oral traditions carried down the line long before written words were in play. He spoke of the derivation and melding of Celtic myth into Christian symbolism. He followed this with stories of the resistance to the Roman invasion and the systematic subjugation of one section of the island after another. Then assimilation and continued resistance were woven into the story.

What came next surprised those new to the island and seemed at first to be just a passing footnote. It was the story of a wandering merchant who came to the islands from *H'arimathea*. Those around the room listened to each nuanced line, hearing as only they could, the story within the story. The merchant, it seemed, came to the isles to trade in tin and left the Holy Grail in his wake.

The merchant was of high standing and very good at both accounting and taking notes. He practiced what we might call a dying art form today, stenography. He wrote everything down—everything he saw and heard in and around Jerusalem, and he carried his journal with him wherever he went.

Percival came to the end of his tale and Dubric rose from the chair he had sunk into halfway through the dissertation, "There, he knows all he needs to know. I am no longer needed. Percy will take over." Dubric said this as he wiped the remainder of his dinner off his shirt.

The ceremony was finished, and so on cue, scones and tea were brought out. The feast was nearing an end, and when nothing else edible was to be found, it became an unwritten signal. The party was over, and so everyone began to move quietly into the night.

Chapter 44
Progress Is Subjective

Emily Selwood's Journal
Greystone Park Psychiatric Hospital

The feast in the refectory was the last piece of Arthur McAiden's writing assignment he passed along to me. A week later, he was to be released and we had no time to spend discussing his literary meanderings. That statement is only partly tongue-in-cheek. When McAiden first became a patient of mine, I thought the writing exercises would help with his cognitive and neurolinguistic deficits and, possibly, give me an inner glimpse of how he was feeling. At first, I was amazed. He said he had no recollection of his accident, most TBI-ers don't, and yet what he wrote seemed to me to be an extremely detailed account. Don't get me wrong, the writing was good considering how retarded his speech was at the time, but I began questioning his, let us say, accuracy. When he told of his admittance to the "Lady of the Lake" hospice, a place he never visited, at least not in this world, I surmised he was creating his own fictional biosphere. Toward the end, he delved into bosons and other subatomic particles, and triunes all the way up to the intersectional crossroads in our search for the ultimate intelligence. This train of thought could have been due to his head trauma, what is known as acquired savant syndrome, or he may have just been leading me on.

My doctorate is along the lines of neuropsychology, so I had no way of grasping any semblance of the higher math he spewed out. It didn't matter at the time if I understood or not because it was helping him advance toward our finish line, his release from the rehab institute. Whatever he wrote, it didn't hurt. It drew him out and this is what I had wanted. But as he neared his graduation from the rehab program, we didn't have time for that any longer. I had to run him through his paces. Basically, I had evals to conduct and this meant my patient had to put his creative pencil down and subjugate himself to the process.

Several times during his visits to Kessler McAiden told me he had difficulty in complex conversations, especially when there were multiple people speaking at the same time. Basically, quick changes in topic were tough for him, but his writing told me something was going on upstairs, and like all TBI survivors, his scores varied. Results on all the standardized test questions let me place him, with a degree of accuracy, into the proper level with respect to his age and prior educational history. In all cases, he scored higher than the psych discharge scores from when he left his inpatient stay at the Johnson Rehab Institute (JRI). For example, when he first arrived at Kessler, he was suffering from perseveration disinhibition, repetition of a particular response regardless of the cessation of a stimulus. This condition is no longer evident. The cognitive and psychological tests I administered included a bunch of the standards like the Wechslers, the Reys, and the Becks. Basically, I ran him through his paces, and like I mentioned, he did well on some, not so well on others, but all were better than when he first came to us.

Overall, McAiden demonstrated Superior verbal abilities and high-average performance abilities, again consistent with estimates of premorbid functioning. With that said, he performed in the average range on a measure of complex problem solving, which is an improvement from the earlier

JRI evaluation but continues to be below expectations. Dr. McAiden also experienced mild word finding difficulties on a confrontation naming task, but these difficulties were not apparent in conversation. Phonemics and semantic fluency were within the low average to average range, which again is below expectations given the written works he passed to me, his background and occupational history. Of course, there was significant improvement on these language tasks as compared to his evaluation prior to his time with us at Kessler. Audio-verbal memory improved to the average range, which is still below expectation considering his level of education. Nonverbal memory is within expected limits in the very Superior range. Recognition for verbal memory reflected a significant number of false positive errors, but recognition for nonverbal material was intact. Basically, his general intellectual abilities were largely within premorbid estimates. Mild cognitive deficits continue to be seen in the areas of confrontation naming, verbal fluency, learning, and memory.

That was my summary. Above average to superior in many areas but after reading what he wrote I was surprised how low he scored on measures of verbal fluency and learning. I sat in on the final meeting discussing his discharge and gave my report. The on-site physician, the head of the cog-rehab group, the head of the occupational therapy section, Dr. Smart from Johnson Rehab, my patient, and his wife, were all present. The meeting went well. We all agreed if McAiden felt strong enough to move on he would be released from our care. With that said, we believed everything would continue from this point to his official graduation from Kessler but then we hit a snafu of sorts.

In New Jersey, he would be allowed a retest for his driver's license after we signed the paperwork releasing him from our care. Smart asked him how he felt about getting behind the wheel again. He gave an unexpected answer. He said he would not be comfortable getting behind the wheel of a car ever again. This threw us all for a loop. I dug through all my notes to see if I missed anything. If he would never again get behind the wheel of a car, then perhaps we did not read his condition properly. After a few minutes of back and forth, he clarified. Yes, he would get behind the wheel of a car if he needed to rush a friend to hospital. In fact, he said he would drive with the pedal glued to the floor if time was of the essence, but that didn't mean he would be comfortable. We gave him a pass. A few minutes later, tearful goodbyes were said by all. That afternoon I filed my evals and turned my attention to the other eight patients I had been assigned to follow that quarter. I thought it was the end of my involvement with this patient. It wasn't.

One month later, to the day, I received a call from my boss who is also the regional Institute director asking me to set up a time to meet with her and a representative of the police department. Nothing urgent and nothing confidential, so she said. It seems the policeman wanted to close the book on an old case with a statement or two of the patient's current psych condition, and for this, he specifically asked to speak with me. Why me? I like to think of myself as an expert on this topic, but I have never been asked to give my professional opinion outside of scientific conferences. My ego took a bit of a hit when I found out it was one of my old patients the policeman was interested in. I was not told who the patient was except I had tended to the individual within the last year.

I sent some dates and times I could work around my schedule over to her. Nothing urgent my ass. She set up the meeting, in her office, the next day, rain or shine at three in the afternoon. Fine, except for the fact I worked at the Chester facility and her office was over in West Orange, it was now the heat of summer, and they didn't tell me which patient the police were interested in which meant I had to bring along my laptop and a ton of paper files not yet entered onto the database. It gets worse. My car's air conditioner had ceased working weeks before, so driving at three in the afternoon was torture. I made it to the West Orange office almost on time, jumped out of the car with my computer, and files in hand and looking like the sweatiest mess ever, I ran to the building and up the steps. Huffing and puffing I entered her office, and this is where my real problems began. An FBI agent was waiting to greet me, not a policeman. When he stood up and introduced himself, I shit my pants. Figuratively, of course.

This was the first time I met a character from Arthur McAiden's storyline. He looked basically as Arthur had described. A two hundred and twenty pound, much of which used to be muscle, West Point grad with some aging going on around the edges. The only part that wasn't clear from what I had read about the man had to do with the lost look in his eyes.

The *tête-a-tête* with Special Agent MacLean didn't last long. There wasn't much I could tell him beyond what I had written in my e-val. But he didn't really need me to tell him this. He already had this info. Whatever happened to doctor patient confidentiality? I wanted nothing else than to scream bloody murder. I didn't scream; that is, I held my breath, counted to three and then as politely as possible asked the FBI agent how he had managed to get his hands on my report. Neither he nor my director answered this; instead, he told me he wanted me to clarify some of my assessments.

Trying to refrain from blowing up, I kept my answers simple and short. The questioning didn't take long to finish, but as I was getting up to leave, he had one more question. It took a while to get it out but without doubt, this was the reason he had come to see me.

"McAiden told you a good deal of his, um, how should I put this, his um, his adventures. Didn't he?"

"Adventures? That is an interesting way of describing it."

"He said he put it all down on paper." Here, MacLean paused, pinched his chin between thumb and forefinger, looked at my director, looked at his shoes, and then continued, "He said something about 'in the style of Jeffrey.' I asked him what that meant, but I just couldn't quite grasp what he was saying…"

I wasn't quite on my game, and not knowing exactly how to respond, I tried delaying tactics: "Geoffrey with a *G* or Jeffrey with a *J*?"

"How the hell should I know?"

Fearing I had stepped into a conversation I didn't want to be a part of I took a deep breath and tried to ease myself out. "What did he say?"

MacLean paused again, shrugged his shoulders, and continued, "He said something about reading between the lines."

"What?" My response was more a question to myself, though, it did come out of my mouth, and hence, MacLean answered.

"I'm not sure," then he paused and pinched his chin again before he continued, "Shit, I don't know. Probably has to do with politics. You know, half of what he spouts I can't rap my head around. He did speak of certain embellishments he put into the storyline, and when he compared himself to this Jeffrey guy, I asked if I could see it. He said it wasn't possible because"—here, MacLean paused, *I knew what was coming next*—"because he gave it all to you."

"What he wrote for me was at my request. It was part of the therapy session. He wasn't writing any sort of treatise. I was just measuring how his cognitive processes were…"

"That's nice, but I need to get everything he wrote. Did you bring it with you?" Short and to the point, everything became clear.

"No" was the first and only word used to convey a response as I searched my memory for the location of that folder. Was it in my office, had I brought it home or was it a part of the pile I had brought with me? I didn't throw it out, did I? Needing time to perform a mental search I offered up my laptop. "His case report is in here, not the pages he wrote by hand."

"Too bad, I would have like to have read them."

"Sorry," I responded and began inching toward the door. "Now I have to go, I have patients scheduled this afternoon."

When MacLean turned to speak to my superior, I made a beeline for the hallway. I almost reached the stairs, but I was not quite fast enough.

"Wait a sec."

I didn't, but he caught up with me before I reached the ground floor. "Things happened in England," the FBI agent whispered. Things that he just couldn't wrap his head around are what happened, and this made me wonder if there was a fiction/nonfiction dividing line in McAiden's writing. Perhaps there was a bit of reality ingrained within his narrative. The man standing next to me was no longer a bad ass government hitman. He was more a lost soul begging for help. Some of what he saw, he told me, was real. He was there, he touched it, he felt it, he breathed it, but most of it he just couldn't understand.

"In my line of work, I need evidence," he continued. "How can I believe what I saw when, when hell, I have nothing to base it on?"

"Welcome to my world," I wanted to say, but I didn't. Instead, with hands still holding my computer I reached over and pat his forearm, promising the man crumbling before my eyes I would look for any notes my ex-patient may have written. Then, not knowing what else I could say, I mentioned if he wasn't enrolled in the Kessler program, I couldn't really dedicate any of my time. Then I passed along names of those who were not, like me, institute bound that is. "One of these might be able to take on individual patients." After that, I made a run for it. Now I must convey the following: I have had only one other direct interaction with Special Agent MacLean since meeting him in West Orange but recently his wife, Donna, and I have become friends.

Chapter 45
Tewksbury

What was now front, and center had to do with Arthur's writing. What he wrote was interesting and a modicum of this effort may have been based on personal experiences, like the accident, but after reading the first few pages, I had put it into a folder marked "fiction." Don't get me wrong, it was a nice story, though there could have been a bit more character development. But in my mind, it was mostly a figment of his imagination. As far as therapy goes, it pointed me in the right direction. I assigned copious exercises related to speech rehabilitation and memory progression for the Kessler staff to administer. Now, now I had an FBI agent crying on my shoulder telling me my patient's writing might have had more than a dash of truth mixed into it. What had I missed?

Back at my office, I found the folder I needed; it was under one of the many piles of documents in need of archiving. Pretending to have taken ill, I cancelled my afternoon appointments and headed for the nearest office supply store to buy some jump drives and make use of their copy machines. I scanned the hard copy of Arthur's writing, every, last, fuckin', page of it, twice. His manuscript now existed on two different electronic repositories and three bundles of paper. Then I headed to my bank and deposited one of each version in my safety deposit box. After that, it was off to a coffee shop for a caffeine fix, and while sipping and thinking, I flipped through my patient's dossier, zeroed in on his address and phone number, and gave him a quick call.

It took a moment or two for my ex-patient to zero in on who I was and then I had to fumble around with the truth, saying I just wanted to engage with him in an ad-hoc follow-up study. Why I asked if we could meet at his house he didn't question, and for that, I was lucky. If he asked, I had no idea how to reply; it had just come to mind midsentence. The next day, I packed up my computer and a copy of his storybook and headed for Tewksbury. Since this car ride was a product of my own initiative, the hot weather didn't bother me as much.

I had not slept well, how could I. I had no idea what was going on. There was no way I could keep calm when continuously hearing that FBI man crying inside my head. Driving through Tewksbury didn't help my angst either. I had never been in this section of Jersey before, and it became obvious the wealthy souls who live here did not buy McMansions. They live in those old-style manor homes, the ones in no need of the mac-prefix. McAiden's address, Sherwood Lane, placed him in the same zip code as the estates I was passing; however, his home was situated a bit west of the highest-end, high-end district. When I arrived, I noted the house, it was very nice, but nowhere near what he described in his writing. It was more along the lines of a middle-class residence, on the upper end of that scale.

The house was part of a subdivision of sorts, connected to and within walking distance of a nearby town. I parked in what was a multilane driveway, got out, looked around, and took a deep breath. No matter which window of my condo I looked out of, the view was nowhere near as nice as what was now before my eyes. The house looked to be older than others nearby and had a wide wraparound porch. I could see portions of gardens on both sides with varietals in bloom, none of which I could name. It hadn't taken long to find the place, but it did take a while to convince the gatekeeper, his wife, to give me a few minutes with my ex-patient. Jennifer was home from work this day because I was to learn, they were expecting visitors and I was not one of them. To make matters worse, her husband had not mentioned this to me nor had he, in turn, relayed to his wife my planned visit.

I had met and interacted with Jennifer several times during patient assessment conferences over at the Institute. These were always on professional, friendly terms, but now, the look in her eye told me today might be different. Supposing her stress was related to the influx of visitors who she knew of, I tried to exchanged pleasantries and told her there was nothing wrong and how I was working on a paper evaluating treatment paradigms for recovering TBI patients and sorry to come by on such a short notice, but I was in the area etc., etc., you know, the usual crap. She resisted my entreaties until I swore, I only needed a few data points for my research, and it would only be for a few minutes of their time. I wasn't planning on doing any scientific paper so, in a sense, I lied, but then again, I wasn't planning to write a book on my own troubles with this patient, which I am. Looking back, it is hard to say if this little lie covered both angles.

Access was reluctantly granted, and she allowed me to enter. Ten seconds later, I was standing in the foyer noting how high the ceiling was above the deep hallway ahead. A stairway along the wall to its left was made of some type of wood that had been polished many, many times. To the right was what Jennifer called "the reception room." It was almost as big as my entire condo. Many chairs were centered around a stone fireplace, the size of which I could have walked right into. A piano was farther back away from the fireplace and near it sat a card table. To my left was the dining room. This room had sideboards, a dining table that could seat a goodly number of people and chairs to seat them all.

I only had a quick look at these rooms as Jennifer began marching me down the center hall, but I will say this, what caught my eye the most was the use of color throughout, like Matisse after too much coffee. We quickly passed rooms on either side that were hard for me to categorize.

One might have just been a reading room. It had bookshelves aligning its walls, a small couch, and a chair or two in the center with some sort of display case nearby. Another room may have been an office, it had a desk with a computer on top and one more that had what appeared to be a television in it, but that door was only open a bit, so it was hard to tell. Anyway, as we got closer to our destination my eyes were focused in that direction, soon I was standing in the kitchen next to Arthur, Jennifer, and his dog, yes, the dog's name was Guinevere. This room, like in so many homes I have been in, was basically, the command center.

The room was reasonably clean and had a warm, accommodating feel all of which helped in its multiple uses. The table in the eating area seated four without a problem and was placed alongside a window giving one a good view of the back of the property, all the way up to a tree line fifty yards or more to the west. I couldn't see it from where I was now standing but was told a path led through the trees and linked up with a rails-to-trails, which stretched about fifteen miles through this section of the county.

"Nice for bike riding," Arthur told me this as we seated ourselves at the table. All I could think of was an old song telling how "our house is a very, very, very, fine house." Only I didn't see any cats, just the Labrador, and as I sat, I felt a warmth radiating all around me. Jennifer had started a pot of water, and when it was ready, asked if I drank tea. When this word was spoken, Guinevere tilted her head to the side giving Arthur a look. He quickly found her a treat, whether it was advertised for canines or not, I do not know. Jennifer soon brought three cups to the table and sat opposite her husband. My seat was between the two, staring out upon the expanse of grass and trees. The dog, well the dog was somewhere under the table and her tail was in constant joyful motion. Now we all had something in our hands, or paws, as we sat, drank, ate, and talked. Whatever happiness was within the wagging tail beneath the table was transmitted to my ex-patient, his smile now encompassed his face from ear to ear.

Why had I really come to Arthur's house? I really wish I knew Because, if one doesn't know what they are looking for, how do you know when you find it? Maybe it was just to give him the pages he wrote while at Kessler. I suppose I had some ingrained fear of the FBI. If they wanted it, let Arthur give it to them. Another reason was a bit more difficult to explain because again, I wasn't exactly sure myself. Worst of all, the FBI man was in the same quagmire as I. We both had trouble reading between the lines, so to speak. Maybe I was hoping a face-to-face conversation with my ex would help in this regard. I had not counted on his wife being in on the conversation.

Jennifer was the first to speak. From her I corroborated some of what I knew and, in my mind, made changes to sections of her husband's writing. Yes, they were Welsh, husband and wife, moving to the States to oversee company operations. They had one child who was autistic and "gifted," attending university up in the Boston area. All in all, Arthur had described his son correctly, changing only the location of the university. Yes, Arthur was a founder of a start-up biotech venture. The key word here being "was." Since his time in rehab, he had not yet returned to the work force.

"Arthur," Jennifer continued, "spent two weeks in the ICU then two more in JRI, but you know all this."

She was right, I knew of his time in the trauma center and the weeks spent at the Johnson Rehab Institute too, so I wasn't sure what she was getting at. What she said next helped me understand and realize she was close to springing a gasket.

"I enrolled him at Kessler and three times a week I drove him to your outpatient rehab. Only an hour-plus out of my usual commute to work, in each direction." Her delivery was terse and just shy of angry. The slight tremors in her hands led me to believe this diagnosis. Arthur sipped his tea and patiently waited for the venting to finish. Eventually, it did, "Arthur still needs help you know. I think our running out of insurance coverage sped up his release from Kessler. Am I right?"

"It is a long, slow process," I replied, trying to give them both some encouragement while ignoring insurance altogether, "he scored very well on his testing when he finished with us and I'm sure, over time, he will get even better. Now," I was hoping to segue the conversation over to topics I wanted to discuss but while fidgeting in her seat Jennifer beat me to it.

"This is about that FBI man and our trip to England, isn't it?"

She was more than a step ahead. Her question was like a cue ball smashing into the racked set. Chaos ensues as all objects ride the rolls and pitches dictated to them until they come to rest in their ordained space, in this case, Arthur's space.

"I told you I would take care of this, so please," Arthur paused for a moment and smiled at his wife, stretched across the table to take her hand in his and tried to kiss it. Alas, he couldn't stretch that far but something in its meaning was transferred. A glow seemed to envelope husband and wife, or perhaps it was just an aura based on the sunlight reflecting off the window. She calmed down, took a deep breath, smiled sweetly and then reminded her husband visitors would be arriving soon, "The delivery service needs a place to set up and…"

"Got it covered Luv, maybe Gwen should get a walk in before everyone…"

From his position at the table Arthur pointed to a section of the back yard his wife could only see if she turned around. I eased up a bit in my chair and arched my neck so I could look up over her shoulders. Together we counted the tables set up amidst a rather well-tended garden. Satisfied, Jennifer rose, called the dog and within a minute they were out the door.

Arthur and I were now alone in the room, and for a bit, we sat with attention focused on both ladies named Guinevere working their way across the backyard. When Jennifer bent low and unhooked the dog's leash, Arthur tried to get my attention, but I continued to watch those outside disappear into the woods. When I did turn and look directly at my host, the damaged side of his head was dead center in my field of vision. The surgical scar along his left temple was now buried amidst uncombed tuffs of hair and the reattached ear, which protruded a good bit off center seemed to have settled in nicely.

"How are you feeling" was drawn out from my observations. Very pedestrian, I know. I wasn't really expecting a detailed response, but this is what came my way. "When we first met," he began, "I tried to express myself verbally, but word usage was difficult. Longhand slowed me down, gave me more time to search for words I needed to fit the context. Jennifer is clearing the house of paper and pencils. She wants me to articulate."

"Oh" was my response. I didn't have time to say more, Arthur continued as if he had been drinking coffee all day.

He began by covering topics I already knew, "My rotator cuff, left side, pulled loose the day after I finished the Kessler physical rehab program. I declined the suggested operation, no desire to go under the knife again. I still have many residual problems, most physical, some not. The mechanics of process relay are the worst. Thoughts upstairs"—here, he touched his temple—"converted into verbal transmission just isn't working unless I am really, really focused. Even now word usage can be a bitch. Did I say that right?"

He came up for air, looked me in the eye and resumed speaking, "Right now, I am very focused. Did you bring the pages I wrote for you?"

Before I could ask how he knew, he continued and in a few short sentences had pretty much tied all the strings together.

"MacLean went to see you." Not waiting for a response, he went on: "And when he asked about my writing it made you rethink its relevance, beyond my demonstration of legible penmanship." He smiled, I nodded, and he continued; "MacLean worried some of it may have been...I don't know what, he needed closure of some sort. Like most people, he has trouble interpreting everything he reads or, in his case, sees."

Stupid me, my eyes must have grown to the size of grapefruits, and this is what caused my host to giggle.

"This is funny?" was all that came out of my mouth.

Arthur wiped the smile off his face, "He has visited several times since we all returned from England. He and that guy from Canada were following the Moroccan, and yes, the Moroccan is the link. He was following me, the FBI was following him, he didn't induce my wife to hire him, I made that up, but her friend Morgan did, hire him that is, which led to the Gwynedds, and so on and so on. But each time MacLean has swung by, he asks the same questions, none have anything to do with the man the FBI was following, all having to do with what he was exposed to in Lothian and again over on Mann. The last time he was here I told him I don't remember anything anymore, which is, basically, true. Then I made a mistake."

"A mistake?"

"I told him of my writings and where he might find them."

There were a million questions I needed to ask, but I left those aside and stayed with the basic, "Why did you write your wife hired the private eye if she didn't?"

Arthur paused, pulled on his left earlobe as he stared off into the distance. Then continued, "Most of what I wrote is true, I think. Some maybe was written for a future audience, an entertainment factor if you will, was needed. But some was my attempt to explain where I was and what I saw when there. This I needed to get down on paper before my mind reengaged its filter system. Of course, I don't remember all I wrote so…"

Here, he held out his hand and I complied. Without doubt, I had come to give his writing back to him, how he knew this I do not know, just one more thing to wonder about. I dove into my tote, found what he wanted and put the pages up onto the table. Then he softened his tone. "I'm sure you've made e-copies of this, and I don't care. For me, this is my only record of what I wrote. Now, ask away, but make it quick we are having visitors soon."

Have you ever been to a busy ice cream parlor? When you finally reach the counter, you just can't decide and the people standing behind start to fidget. It was like that in Arthur's kitchen. The time factor accentuated the difficulty I had in laying out my set of questions. I wanted to start with the accident and move on to his stay in his make-believe hospice, Nurse Flo and, of course, the private dick. All of this was needed just to set the table for the big question; what the hell was his overseas hiatus all about? With fingers indicating the order, I listed my inquiries, and to myself, I prayed he would give me something tangible to hang my hat on.

With the accident, my question was rather simple, how the hell did he know what was going on, he was found in a ditch and, basically, comatose. He stopped reading the pages I had just handed over, looked me in the eye and said, "I wasn't in the ditch, not exactly, I was, um, sitting elsewhere. I had no idea I was ever in a coma. Incoming information was processed but not really released until that is, I met you. Writing was my first outlet. What did I process? What I saw from the branch I was sitting on, what I watched when tied to the bed in the hospital, the television was never turned off you know and, more importantly, free movement of thoughts within my head. My nodal cortex was disengaged. That was a result of the coma, right? So basically, I could fly wherever I wanted to go or delve deep within unused sections of my own gray matter. You're a neuropsych, do you know how this works?"

I didn't respond, so he just barreled along, "I remember speaking in French, thinking my way through advanced physics, chemistry, philosophy, and a bunch of other crap. As I began to register again in real time, there were memories, memories held inside my head for ages and those that had come about as I struggled to return. I feared I would forget everything. I became obsessed with memory, my memory or, what one might say, what was left of it. Memory is fragile, it changes over time depending upon any, and all, insults to the vault in which it is stored. It can change, or worse, evaporate. Without memory, how can one live?"

He paused, and if he hadn't turned his head, I believe I would have spotted a tear. He did brush something off his face before he returned his gaze and picked up where he left off.

"Perhaps I should say, without memory we cannot live on a plane above the other beasts that inhabit the earth, and I ask, how can we have a soul if we do not know who we are? Even without physical impairments, memory is elusive. It can even be treacherous. I was scared, I needed written proof of something very important to me. So I wrote it all down, in your office."

Arthur took a sip of tea, closed his mouth, and stared out the window. Several times on the pages he had written at Kessler he had described speakers in a trance-like state. Now, when he began again, I was seeing him in just such an altered consciousness. He again described how the television in his room at the rehab hospital was on at all hours. Then he mentioned something that was being broadcast almost 24-7 during his stay in both the ICU and the rehab hospital and all I could do was blame myself for not putting two and two together. I had seen the coverage of the woman who was declared vegetative. Each and every broadcasting station aired this daily. There was a fight going on between factions of her family, some wanting, others resisting, the summonsing of the Angel of Death to the bedside.

"You wanted to know about the nurse? In my mind, Flo was the devil, or perhaps, the angel of mercy. The vegetative state is the kiss of death. As I look over these notes, I can only imagine Flo as the one who, upon command, would pull the plug. Inside my world nurse Flo existed. In the physical world, her namesake did too. Flora Kevorkian."

"Were you dreaming then as you watched this on television?"

"Dreaming? Dreaming? Not sure, but what difference does it make? What is here? What is now? For a while, I had no understanding of either of these states. I have no recollection of my time in the ICU. The recovery hospital maybe. Only, I'm not sure if it is a memory or perhaps, it, too, was just a dream? I did not know where I was. It was late at night. I was in bed. The bed had a mesh fence of sorts all around which ran up, basically, to the ceiling. It seemed to form a cage around me. Dreaming right? I tried to call for help, but my mouth was barely able to open so all I could do was whisper. Nothing seemed to hurt at first. Therefore, I believed I was in a dream, though I questioned myself on that a few times. I had never experienced anything like it before and I was curious. What type of dream was it? I tried to touch the netting. It looked to be soft, like streamers. The problem was my hands were tied down. I couldn't reach out. I tried again to call out but like before, I couldn't manage anything above a whisper. After my second attempt, my jaw started to hurt, and then my neck and shoulder tightened up. Straps ran across my chest so I couldn't look around. All my limbs and torso were tied down. I couldn't see much beyond the netting, but I did note a curtain that appeared to cut the room in half. On the far wall was the television and it was turned on but there was no sound. At least there was no sound I could hear. I don't remember what was being broadcast, I only remember it added a dim light to the room.

"Did I mention the pain? At first, nothing, but as I sat reconnoitering it did make an impression. I cannot even guess how long I lay there, days, weeks, or perhaps just seconds, time itself didn't register. But I do know I had an urge to relieve my bowels, and this caused alarm. I couldn't get up. I couldn't call for help and I couldn't really see beyond the curtain. I tried to free my arms, repeatedly but to no avail and eventually, this I remember very clearly, I couldn't hold the BM any longer. Then, to applaud my own efforts, I sprouted urine too."

Arthur stopped and looked out the window giving me a chance to chime in. "Welcome back," I wanted to say but held my tongue on that and moved on to something I was begging to ask, "Why did you say you were taken to the hospice. I know you didn't go there. Johnson rehab was the first place you went after the ICU."

"Some things get mixed up in the translation, language can do that. I didn't go to 'Our Lady of the Lake,' but I did visit 'The Lady of the Lake,' right?"

"You did?"

He paused, inhaled deeply, and continued, "I really shouldn't tell you this, but Percy's mother, Yglais, is 'The Lady of the Lake,' or perhaps I should say a descendent thereof. The group I was with had stopped at her house on our way to Avalon. At her house were things we needed to bring with us."

This he said without a bat of the eye, and when my incredulity showed, he stopped talking. What could I do? I had come with the hope of getting to the truth. There was so much I wanted to know, but if his version of truth lay buried deep within the reams of romance literature, well, hell, I could read that at home, if I wanted to, which I didn't, so I felt it best to move along and be done with the entire mess. Before I stood up, Arthur changed topics. Perhaps he just wanted to move away from his adventures in *Neverland*, but it only got worse. He was now trying to explain the relationship between quantum entanglements and miracles or, perhaps I should say, the ability to explain either of these miraculous interactions in a physical sense.

Luckily for me, Guinevere appeared from within the woods and began to bark. We both rose and moved closer to the window. Her bark was less an "I'm home" salutation and more an acknowledgment of the deer. Several were present in the yard grazing casually. They all lifted their heads but when they recognized the source, they ignored her and resumed eating.

"In her younger days, Gwen liked to chase 'em." This was Arthur, reaching back, "Never caught one but enjoyed the run. Over time they built a sort of symbiotic relationship. She doesn't chase 'em, and they leave their droppings for her to enjoy at her leisure."

The deer eventually moved beyond the corner of the house while the dog, well, she kept looking around for anything they may have left while avoiding Jennifer's attempts to keep her moving. I watched the *pas de deux* as Arthur quietly spoke of freedom, freedom not as a reward but the struggle itself. The struggle from bondage in all its forms. "We are individuals," he said, "who must fight temptations and learn to transmute matter into other dimensions." Only he didn't say "other dimensions," it was more along the lines of "into the Spirit of matter." Then the central point of his discourse dissolved into nothingness when we heard the back door open.

The patter of feet was heard next and a moment later Guinevere trotted into the kitchen. After petting her twice, Arthur motioned both of us toward the front door. The dog assumed the lead. I followed, not realizing Arthur had stopped to wait for his wife. Assuming Guinevere knew a shortcut when she veered from the hallway, I followed. It was the room I had classified as "the reading room" on my way to the kitchen. Apparently, this room was off limits to both me and the dog. Arthur, watching us from his location back in the kitchen, yelled at the dog to stop but Guinevere was a Labrador retriever, a not-too-well-trained retriever, who didn't like to stop until she retrieved whatever she was looking for. In this case, the couch. Before Arthur threw the same command my way, I had joined her in the room. Trying to catch up, Arthur yelled another command at the dog and, I assumed, at me as well. Guinevere barked back and then jumped down, tail wagging and skedaddled out a side door before her owner arrived. I was caught like a deer in the headlights, I just stood still.

He pointed in the direction he wanted me to go, which was, basically, in the same direction the dog took, and I made to oblige, until my eyes caught a glimpse of what the waist high display case held. It had a very clean and sturdy glass lid. A framed document had been placed over the top covering much of my direct line of sight into the case. Despite my host's plea I moved in this direction, and what I saw in the frame I had read before:

> *Now I must race against the inevitable products of time, which slow my hand and cramp my legs. If time inexorable grants a reprieve I shall finish this task, both the bidden and the hidden, and then what, I ask? The answer to such a query is difficult to articulate, for I fear distribution of this document, as its owner surely surmises, would cast our world into utter darkness for*

centuries on end, but to keep this hidden away may cast us into darkness forever.

Without thinking of the man standing behind me, I tried to open the cabinet. It appeared to be stuck. Knowing I had little time to spare I gave it my all, exhaling along the way. As I did so I heard two voices joining me. One was the hissing of air as Arthur gasped and the other was the cabinet's vacuum being released. Now, with lid in hand but only partially opened I gazed inside and saw two books side-by-each, lying face up on a velvet cloth. One was a worn paperback version of Goodrich's take on King Arthur, the other, a copy of *Historia Regum Britanniae*. For me, that brief glance was all that was needed to once again freeze up. Arthur had to physically move me aside. When I was out of the way, he gently closed the cabinet lid and pressed down to reseal it. When the vacuum engaged, he grabbed hold of my elbow and ushered me along to the front door.

Chapter 46
Now What?

Once outside, we stood for a moment watching Guinevere chase a squirrel. Neither one of us made a sound. I was hoping for some words of forgiveness while fearing those of recrimination for disregarding his request. I should not have opened the box, but the book was there. It was not a story written on parchment. I was aware of its existence, I wanted to touch it to gain a mental association with the object. When I did turn to look, he nodded his head, smiled a bit, and began angling me toward my car.

As we strolled, I was the first to speak. "Is it all about this, this book?"
He smiled.
"What is so special about it?"
He looked away but continued to guide me along.
As we moved closer to my car, I descended into the mode of last resort, I begged, "Tell me…please," and he responded. I was not sure if he was paraphrasing from the book in his study or the pages he had written in my office. Either way, it did not matter, I just prayed it would lead to some closure for me.

"For so long, we have forgotten how to keep our memories alive. Without them, how will we remember who we are? The knowledge we hold within ourselves arrives in various forms, is processed, stored away, but it also needs to be shared. People sit around the fire and tell stories, later, these will be called legends, or possibly, myths, but in the instant when they are first being related and heard both the speaker and those listening believe in them as the holiest of truths, as absolute reality."

He paused for a moment. "Because we are human, it is best to reach back and get the story from its original source otherwise it becomes transmuted by interpretation. Oral tradition worked for a while, but as we sat beside the proverbial fire, we needed to have the stories written down. Geoffrey was the one we hired last in this regard. Our source was, basically, once removed from the original, the original then had vacated the premises so to speak. The story told of a universe being nothing more than the smallest of motes, which expanded into, well, into everything. And he said, without love, it would not be held together. Within each of us is this love, love is what shapes and holds our souls. Love is part of the triumvirate. Love is the Holy Ghost, it is the force that binds, without love, there would be no structure to our universe, there would be no sun, no earth, no place we call home. Within this reality, we could not move into other realms, without love, we could not meld two souls into one."

When we reached my car, he put on his gentleman's hat and opened the door for me. With a smile on his face, he added one more line, "I'm sure our scientists will figure it all out one day." As I climbed in, I heard him giggling. That was all I could get out of him because Jennifer was leaning out the front door yelling something about "they" who would be arriving soon, and how he should freshen up a bit. Once ensconced behind the wheel, I rolled down the window and passed him one of my cards. "Just in case you want to talk some more."

Arthur took my card and smiled. Then he stepped back and told me I had all the information I needed but he'd keep it, "just in case," and as he slowly moved a step back, the dog came and sat by his feet. She barked twice as I backed out of the driveway, her way of saying goodbye

I suppose, and as I drove off, something in the yard caught her attention, and so off she went.

I was almost beyond visual contact when I noticed a car pulling into my vacated spot. I slowed down to watch and eventually stopped on the far side of the road. Three men climbed out of the vehicle. Guinevere, too, noted the new arrivals. She stopped chasing whatever it was she had in her sights and joyfully bounced over to greet the first one out of the car, a large man with a full head of red hair and a disheveled beard to match. The second man out was younger, impeccably dressed but limped a bit as he moved slowly forward to embrace my ex-patient. The driver appeared last planting a ninja warrior image in my brain. In order of appearance, all three I pulled out of Arthur's writing, Angus, Wayne, and Dagan. They exchanged words with Arthur, but I was too far off to hear.

The scene was quickly disrupted by Jennifer's arrival and the next thing I knew she was escorting them all to the backyard. All but Dagan, he stood still with his eyes fixed on me. I have no concept of quantum entanglement or the effect of subatomic particles on others at distance, but I do know this, Dagan's stare made my spine tingle and a bit of sweat appeared on my forehead. I took my foot off the brake and moved along. I thought I was done for the day. I thought I would drive home, take a hot bath, open a bottle of, well of whatever I had left in my apartment and just chill. But life wasn't ready for me to call it a day. Here is what happened next.

As I rounded a curve that put Arthur's house out of my line of sight, I was surprised to see someone I knew, with binoculars in hand, sneaking along the side of a house a few lots down from where I had just been. It was the FBI agent. When the sirens call, what can a lonely sailor do? I drove through one intersection before pulling the car over and then backtracked on foot as inconspicuously as possible hoping most of the homeowners were still at work or carting their kids around from soccer practice to violin lesson. I approached the house where the FBI agent had disappeared and moved along the same line of advance.

MacLean was not in the backyard and the angling of the property lines made it impossible to see Arthur's home from where I now stood. A quick scan of the tree line at the back of this yard suggested a spot he might have gone to get a better angle. Perhaps at night, it would have been hard to find MacLean but in the middle of the day it was easy to just follow his trail, broken branches and deep footprints were a dead giveaway. I'm not even half his size but I know I was making noise as I approached, did he turn? No, but he did start talking as if he had been waiting for me. "'Bout time you got here."

Then he handed me the binoculars. "Have a look."

In the short time, it had taken to catch up with the FBI agent, a large gathering had assembled in Arthur's backyard. As I scanned the crowd MacLean started barking out one name after another, like a drill sergeant. "You saw the first group to arrive, Angus, Wayne and that Dagan fellow. Now they're in the middle of the assembly, to their right I see my old tour guides Howl and de Veer speaking with Dindrane (that's his niece, or something) and Lucan, he's the one wearing the suit. To their left, oh shit now they're forming a circle. Hand back the binoculars."

Even without the optical help I could clearly see those in Arthur's yard as they formed a circle around the owner and the well-dressed man MacLean referred to as Lucan. Everyone in the circle was in physical contact with whomever was to their right or left and all began to sway as if there was music in the air, though from where MacLean and I now stood, we couldn't hear anything. It was mesmerizing, though, and even if I could not hear what was going on a pleasant feeling seemed to drift my way. I forgot everything for a moment and just stood and watched. Unfortunately, the good feeling didn't last.

"Now look who's here. That's Percy and…"

MacLean didn't get a chance to tell me more. Three men were now standing behind us, these neither MacLean nor I had heard approach.

"Not nice spyin' now, is it?" is what made MacLean spin around and assume a defensive posture.

"Who the hell are…"

All three visitors were ready to burst out laughing when the man in the middle said, "Locksley, Robin Locksley, that's who I am and I'm here to escort you back to your car."

"I don't have to…"

"No, you don't have to, but you will."

"What makes you so sure of that?" MacLean's ire was up. He dropped the binoculars and while staring at the men in front of us he reached behind his back. I could only think of one thing, he had a gun, but I'll never know for sure as the next sound heard was that of two other bodies, one on either side of us, step out from behind camouflaged positions. Each held a bow with an arrow already in the locked and loaded position. Both arrows were trained on MacLean.

"What the hell right do you have to…"

"Sherwood is our 'hood,'" both new arrivals sang this out.

Like a flash of light, all words and physical props coalesced, Sherwood Lane, the forest, bows, arrows, Robin, Locksley, and with this, I was left wondering which rabbit hole I had fallen into. The men around us could contain themselves no longer. They all burst into fits of laughter. When that subsided, the one named Locksley spoke again. "It's our job to keep prying eyes off the affair you just happen to be, to be prying on. Now, it would be best if you just let us get you back to your cars and see you off before…" He paused for a moment, stood erect, and seemed to become rigid, as if a chill just seeped through his bones, "Too late."

Locksley moved aside and there standing behind him was the man now known to me as Dagan. The men from the hood nodded in his direction before quietly vanishing.

Dagan now spoke. "I don't think you will need them to help you to your cars."

"No, I guess not," the FBI agent replied.

I just nodded my head and then fainted.

Chapter 47
My New Home

It was the heat of the summer when I enrolled myself at Greystone; it is winter now. It took a little while until the right dosing for my meds was found and that definitely helps. I had spent a few too many nights bouncing off the walls. Now I can focus my thoughts and try to make some sense out of what happened. Unfortunately, it is winter, and I've been assigned a room in which the seasons don't seem to matter. The heater will come on, this I was told. But alas, they did not specify when. So now, when not in session (re: therapy), all I can do is bundle up, sit by my window, and dream of water lapping on a sun-drenched beach as I watch the snow pile up along the walkway, too cold to move and too stupid to fix the heater myself. Maybe when hell thaws, I'll venture outside.

Things could be worse. In the old days, they might have chained me up next to Woody in Kirkbride. Lucky for me, Kirkbride was torn down a few years back. Yet isn't it sad, so many historic monuments are no longer part of our consciousness? Without a place in the historical context of the therapy offered, the new buildings just don't have the ambiance projected out as the Kirkbride had, and whatever improvement they bring to the facility doesn't matter to me. I am not billeted there. I've been assigned to one of the outbuildings. There is a bit more privacy in these, a few degrees of freedom, but that's it, just a few and in the winter—too few degrees of warmth. Note to self; in future, never, ever accept assignment in room forty-two.

Ensconced here, I do have a lot of time on my hands, and when the meds really kick in and tamp down my wanderlust, I've been doing a bit of research. Not spiritual, let's say more along the lines of a physical hands-on approach. For example, I did not know from whence my patient had derived the lines he wrote at my behest. Using internet access in the main building, the ubiquitous search engine helped me figure this out. Apparently, besides paraphrasing *The High History of the Holy Graal*, Arthur relied on many other sources. Thank God the Gutenberg library has free access to so many historic volumes. Being now well read in this topic, perhaps I'll try for a master's degree in romance lit or some other shit like that, if I ever leave Greystone that is.

My patient had obviously studied these works as shown in the pages he wrote for me. But to diagnose if you will, the meaning, I needed to dig deeper. I needed to separate fact from, well, I won't say fiction; I will say, imagination. To do this I needed scalers. Easy, right? Hah. One might say this is a classic critique of all biographies. The author advertises the work as nonfiction, but how can anyone produce dialogue for people they have never interacted with? My task could be called straight forward, but it was not simple. I needed to know who I was dealing with, where he existed in our physical world post-accident, where else he might have visited during the recovery process and finally, who the hell he really is, or was. And this takes me back to the accident.

Accidents have the tendency to entangle many lives, especially the lives of those who had no notion of their spatial or emotional proximity to said event. The effect of outward moving waves caused by such an action cannot always be described in the physical reality of the dimensions we inhabit, but this is what accidents do; an event, one event to be exact, outside the control of those around it can affect so many seemingly unconnected motes. The accident may not have been the beginning of Arthur's current storyline, but the event is what spawned a chain reaction culminating with me now spending my days at Greystone. It was also the easiest of all the little snippets Arthur wrote for which I could get some sort of verification. Yes, there was an accident.

Greystone allows me to place telephone calls, and in this regard, I would surely have maxed out any type of limited call plan. Along the way, I engaged in a few video chats as well and I made a new friend, Donna MacLean. She sought me out. She became extremely helpful as I tried to put Arthur's story into some semblance of order. In return, when she visits me at Greystone, I sit and listen. She, too, has a lot on her mind, all having to do with her husband. She thinks he might need to matriculate at Greystone too. I agreed with her on this point and offered her my opinions *gratis,* though if her husband was one of my patients, I would charge him a bundle because if it wasn't for him coming into my life, I would have put Arthur McAiden's writings away in a box and archive it on a shelf somewhere and basically forgotten all about it. Life got much more complicated after my exposure to the FBI man. I could no longer ignore my own inability to believe in something without physical proof.

In the past, one always needed a bit of Faith, but my professional studies directed me toward truth, the need for a more tangible, measurable entity. Yet my patient tells me it is measurable, or it will be soon, and so there is a linkage in what we believe and our presence here on earth. But my confusion lingers as I slowly freeze to death at Greystone trying to understand the interaction of particle quantum states at distance and how any of that relates to miracles. This saddens me no end, but even worse were his thoughts on love, without which two souls could not meld into one. He had this in spades, I do not. Perhaps love is the force that brought him back. Thinking along these lines, I noted how, over all the years I spent at Kessler, those patients who graduated and moved back into at least some semblance of life beyond the rehab institute had just that, support in one form or another in their lives. Those who had no family or help beyond paid caregivers were discharged from the institute as their medical insurance became depleted but would be right back the following year when the insurance kicked back in. These people could not seem to reach the next level of recovery. I see now how Arthur was on the opposite end of the spectrum. When I put it in this context, I begin to understand the charge I felt in the air whenever he was occupying space near either, or both his Guineveres. Whatever those swaying in Arthur's backyard were doing I do not know but I must say I felt the, the gestalt. Love, kindness, the force that binds, whatever you want to call it, was amplified once they interlocked their hands. I wanted to stay and watch and perhaps learn but I guess I was just not ready. I was sent away. The poor FBI agent was denied twice. This makes me wonder what it is we do not have or, perhaps, will not embrace. Faith? Love? In what? I have no idea, and I suppose this is my problem, and if any of what I have just postulated is true, I am afraid I will be staying at Greystone for a good long time.